"...exas is a huge, complicated state, ...ne for authors to get right. Not s... ... *Friendswood* does a near-perfect job capturing the feel not just of the titular city but of southeast Texas as a whole. . . . One of the most interesting novels to be set in the Lone Star State in quite a while."   —NPR, Great Reads of 2014

"Masterfully observed . . . The characters' attempts to grapple with the legacy of this destruction form the tender and harrowing heart of the story. . . . This is a place you live in as you read."
                              —*O, The Oprah Magazine*

"*Friendswood*, the lyrical new novel by National Book Award Finalist René Steinke, is the kind of 300-plus-page book that devours you in a couple of afternoons. The prose is nimble but sure-footed, the narrative suspenseful, and the characters universally recognizable— regardless of your familiarity with the small-town Texas paradigm of church, high school football, and a stream of background music from such Southern songwriting eminences as Porter Wagoner, George Jones, and Patsy Cline. . . . *Friendswood* is a rare blend of beautiful, suspenseful, and seemingly artless prose—you may stay up past bedtime to find out how everything turns out—but also of optimism: hope minus any form of proselytization. Like the country singers who are quietly woven throughout the narrative, shrugging off suffering through song, *Friendswood* offers an unassuming remedy for the troubles we humans always seem to find ourselves in: love thy neighbor. Simple, right? Doesn't hurt to be reminded of it. And it's also one hell of a read."   —*The Literary Review*

"A compassionate and compelling novel that explores the points of view of multiple people living in a run-over small town where everyone is as bound to the land around them as they are bound to each other, no matter how much they wish otherwise. The past is never quite past, and the mystery of how it all fits together is very seductive. Steinke gives us a rich and poignant story of human loneliness rendered through evocative, poetic and beautiful prose."   —Dana Spiotta, author of *Stone Arabia*

"I loved this book for many reasons, not least its hardscrabble, plaintive tone and atmosphere of looming suspense. All of America is here. This is the one we've been waiting for."

—Wesley Stace, author of *Wonderkid*

"René Steinke's *Friendswood* is as arresting, haunting, and heartbreaking as contemporary narrative comes. With lyrical and emotional depth, with an empathy only the greatest writers possess, Steinke shines a light into the shadows of the American spirit and doesn't for a moment avert her gaze."

—David Grand, author of *Louse* and *Mount Terminus*

ALSO BY RENÉ STEINKE

Holy Skirts

The Fires

FRIENDSWOOD

RENÉ STEINKE

RIVERHEAD BOOKS

New York

RIVERHEAD BOOKS
An imprint of Penguin Random House LLC
375 Hudson Street
New York, New York 10014

The author gratefully acknowledges permission to reprint the excerpt from William Goyen, *The House of Breath*. Copyright © 1949, 1950 by William Goyen. TriQuarterly Books/ Northwestern University Press edition published 1999 by arrangement with the Doris Roberts and the Charles William Goyen Trust. All rights reserved.

The Library of Congress has catalogued the Riverhead hardcover edition as follows:

Steinke, René.
Friendswood : a novel / René Steinke.
p.   cm.
ISBN 978-1-59463-251-8
1. Families—Texas—Fiction.   I. Title.
PS3569.T37926F75   2014   2014012106
813'.54—dc23

First Riverhead hardcover edition: August 2014
Riverhead trade paperback edition: May 2015
Riverhead trade paperback ISBN: 978-1-59463-383-6

Printed in the United States of America
3 5 7 9 10 8 6 4 2

Book design by Gretchen Achilles

This is a work of fiction. Names, characters, places, and incidents either are the product of the author's imagination or are used fictitiously, and any resemblance to actual persons, living or dead, businesses, companies, events, or locales is entirely coincidental.

For my son,
Porter

Something in the world links faces and leaves and rivers and woods and wind together and makes of them a string of medallions with all our faces on them, worn forever round our necks, kin.

—WILLIAM GOYEN, *The House of Breath*

1993

+ +

ROSEMONT

One of those evenings, before they knew, Lee walked past the Clarks' ranch house, as sunlight shattered through the leaves overhead. The fan of a lawn sprinkler bowed down again in the green yard, and a few drops dotted her shoulder. Jess ran in front, dark hair splayed against the narrow back of her shirt, sneakers snapping against the concrete. Lee followed her around the bend, where the Bordens had planted an orange plastic Texas on a wooden stake right there in the garden among the mari-golds. In the flat distance, another crop plane droned low in the sky, a silver spray trailing behind it, though nothing grew out where the refinery used to be.

Jess waited at the stop sign. She was twelve, and her teeth seemed too big for her delicate mouth, her arms extra long, as if they grew ahead of the rest of her skinny body. "It's okay, right?"

"We figured, yes," said Lee. "But, listen, don't show off, just ride the horse like you've practiced."

"I don't know why he worries. I'm a good rider—Dad knows that."

Jess took her hand, and Lee held some lost part of herself just returned. "Yeah," said Lee. "But let's not push it."

They turned the corner, and the sunset spread before them, two sparrows perched on a fence, radio jangling out from someone's window. In one yard, a man stood holding a garden hose that shot at a row of hedges; his white T-shirt glowed phosphorescent in the dimness, as if he were trying hard not to disappear.

"Can we hurry it up?" said Jess. They walked over the footbridge, over the cold, steely noise of crickets. On their street, Jess let go of her hand and ran around to the back of the neighbor's house, where the horse was tied to the gate. Lee called after her, "I'll be out there in a minute."

At home, Lee found Jack in the kitchen, smoking by the open window, squinting, face turned to the bright orange sun. They'd made up in bed that afternoon, but she was afraid, when he saw Jess on that horse, that he might get angry again. "I like that dress," he said, eyeing her.

"It's not a dress, it's a skirt."

"Whatever." He smiled.

She went over and touched his forearm, kissed his sweaty, stubbled cheek. "You smell good."

"It's a wonder what a bath will do." He pulled his shirt away from his chest and fanned himself a little. "Hot though." He sighed, tapped his ashes into the sink. "Let's go on outside then, I guess."

With that limp he wore as a strut, Jack went to set up the lawn chairs in the backyard. She took off her shoes to feel her feet in the grass, and she looked out at Banes Field, scrub weeds and stooped trees. The old, defunct refinery still stood there, as if there might be some reward in the futility of it; the small plane flew low now above the flat warehouse and white cylinder oil tank. From here, she couldn't see the perimeters of Banes Field, only some of the other houses whose backyards ran along this edge. And though the whole block shared a nearness to the field, she could still pretend that she and Jack were the owners of it.

Jack fell into the chair beside hers, handed her a beer. His face was shiny and tired, wet blue ovals in the underarms of his shirt.

He winced, leaned back into the yawn of plastic chair. "I'm nervous."

She tapped her ring against the glass of the bottle. "It'll be fine."

From behind the slope, their daughter emerged on the black horse, loose shirttail blowing, and her silhouette melded to the animal's, a sober, elegant loping against the sky.

She slapped Jack's leg. "Will you look at that?"

He craned his head to see. Jess could ride well now, but she was taking it slow. The neighbor girl Rachel was out there guiding the reins before she stepped away, red hair swept up in the breeze. Jess, her body so small against the vast brown field, took the horse into a canter, circled back, and waved at them.

Lee took Jack's hand, rubbed her thumb over his calloused palm. She'd won him over again, but it was better not to gloat.

"Hey there!" Cal McHugh called over the low hedge that split his yard from theirs.

"Hey yourself!" Jack sat up and tilted his bottle in Cal's direction. Lee could see the citronella candles lit up on tall black stakes over the patio, where Lisa walked out, barefoot in a purple dress, carrying amber highballs.

The unkempt yard on the other side of Lee and Jack's was bound by a short wooden fence with hand-sized holes in it. Rachel's sisters ran out to the edge of the property in their nightgowns, screaming, "Jess!" One of them pulled a pink plastic wagon, jiggling with rocks. Another trailed a doll with electrified hair.

Farther away, two houses beyond, in the yard Lee couldn't quite see, a party started to gather at the Turners', laughing and shouting, dim music cartwheeling over in the dusk. The air was cool now, the sun fallen to that slant that nearly gilded the brown grass in the field. Jess took the horse into a gallop, turned, and disappeared behind the warehouse, then appeared and disappeared behind the tall metal poles that looked like pistons.

Lee glanced at Jack's face, the tense cords in his neck. "She'll be alright."

She could see, next door, the McHughs watching Jess too, but casually. Cal lit a cigarette, opened the lid of the grill, and Lisa stood behind him, chatting at the back of his head.

Out in the field, Jess galloped in a shot from behind the warehouse, her small body leaning over the horse's strained neck. Lee was proud of how she'd learned to handle her stride and the reins. Jess patted the horse's neck, and it slowed down, turning, head gradually more heavy, somber, nodding yes to its pace.

Down the block at the Turners', over the party's murmur, a man started to sing loudly, *"All I'm taking is your time."* Jess rode toward them, smiling. Her dark hair, unwashed and dull, fell awkwardly against her round, flushed face. She looked triumphant and exhausted, her torso slumped toward the huge saddle, the reins held close to her chest. She rode right up to the azaleas and bellflowers in the garden, bowed her head, and the McHughs applauded.

Later, Lee and Jack would wander over to the Turners' party, and Lee, a little drunk, would stroll into the field and look up at the moon's scribbled design. From where she stood in the vast dark, the stars pinning down the night, the long weeds up to her knees, she could hear Jack's balmy laughter.

It was an evening that would melt into the summer, calm, humid, and expansive. The air did not yet smell of dead lemons. The red and blue sores hadn't yet appeared on anyone's neck. The black snakes hadn't wriggled up from the ground. And she had no idea that this world was not without an end.

2007

LEE

IT WAS SUNNY AGAIN for the first time in days, and light mirrored off all the wet surfaces. Post-storm, people drove slowly, though traffic was sparse. Here and there fallen branches and toppled road signs lay on either side of the road, but things were getting back to normal. She drove past the empty elementary school, past the ball fields, where a set of bleachers had collapsed. Up ahead, the Mexican restaurant looked intact, but a telephone pole had blown down in front of it, the wire crossed over the white face of the building. A fire engine sirened at the corner, swerved its long red body to the left, and she turned in its wake down Sunrise Drive, past the car dealer's mansion, and past the high school, where a man stood at the pole, stringing up the flag again. She came to the stoplight, and turned onto the business strip.

At the peaked roof of the Methodist church, the cross tilted like a weather vane. DONATIONS HERE read the hand-lettered sign. She parked in the driveway, took the old quilts and blankets out of her trunk, and walked into the wet grass. A bedraggled man sat at a card table, next to a hodgepodge of furniture and stacks of canned goods. The man's face was jowly and flushed, and though she didn't know his name, she recognized him from Rosemont. He'd been a friend of her old neighbor, Sy Turner.

"Here you go," she said, setting down the blankets.

"I sure do thank you." He was flipping through the pages of a Bible without looking down, a fidgeting gesture like shuffling a deck of cards. "I got a family or two could use those about right now."

"Which neighborhood?"

"Empire Estates." He shook his head. "Right up against the creek. It'll be a long time before some of them get to live over there again."

"Well." She was afraid he might start reciting Scripture. "Glad to help." It had been ten years since they'd had to abandon Rosemont; she wasn't surprised he didn't remember her, but she didn't want to remind him either. "You need any furniture?"

"We got folks that need everything." He opened the Bible, closed his eyes a moment, and pointed at a spot on the page. "Here you go." He read, "'Let every soul be subject to the higher powers. For there is no power but of God.' Romans thirteen. That's yours for the day."

"Hmm," she said.

"Chosen just for you, no extra charge."

She got back in the car and drove to the other side of town, marking the damage, the WELCOME TO FRIENDSWOOD sign blown down, the roof vanished from the German bakery, gray water flooding the low-lying parking lot of the bank. During the two days of storm, her TV still had reception, so she'd been able to follow the news—the hysterical, windy frames of rain and destruction—and when that exhausted her, she read the old paperbacks she'd had on the shelf, a few sayings of Emerson, and then a biography of Loretta Lynn that took all of her concentration as the wind lashed through the trees. She'd stared at the dark glass in the windowpanes, not fearful—because what could touch her now?—but waiting, as the body of the world thrashed around her.

Inside McCall Hardware, it was crowded, and the line at the register was long, people holding boxes of nails, aluminum siding, hammers, and sump pumps. On a low shelf next to a stack of orange gardening gloves, she found a good hand shovel with a pointed tip, and went to pay. In line in front of her, there was Doc, fit and buoyant, his face cheerfully smudged with a day's growth of beard. "Glad to see you all in one piece."

"Told you I was." He'd called her seven times during the storm, worried about her alone in her house.

"Well, now I can believe it," he said. When Jack left her, Doc had offered her the job at the office and became her protector, though he had his own wife and son. "You know a worm is the only animal that can't fall down."

"Okay, okay, I'm not a worm. But I'm alright. I just lost the shed out back."

"Alright then. Us! We've got to pull up carpeting." He held up a flat, razored tool. "When we got up this morning, there were all these dead little frogs in the living room, but that's about it. We're lucky."

The man at the counter started shouting at someone behind them. "You looking for a dehumidifier? We're all out. Try a box fan. Got more of those than you can shake a stick at."

"Listen," Doc said. "Take the week off. We're going to have a heap of cancellations anyway."

She'd actually been looking forward to work, to the escape from the swirl of her own thoughts. "Are you sure?"

Doc's eyes had melancholy circles under them. "Absolutely." He patted her shoulder, went to pay at the counter, and waved good-bye. She was glad he didn't ask about the shovel.

So close to the coast, they were used to hurricanes, but this had been one of the worst. Where Crystal Creek had run over the road, she was afraid the highway might be shut down, but it was open again, at least as far as the exit. She turned onto the dirt road, her car pitching over craters, and saw that the big oak tree had snapped in half, the naked interior of the trunk left jagged and pale, its leafy branches sprawled out along the ground. Before the Rosemont houses had been torn down, there were men monitoring the site all the time, and even for a year or two after that. Now it was just Lee, the unofficial guardian, filling up empty, sterilized jelly jars with dirt.

As she got closer, Tubb Gully was swollen all the way to the road's shoulder, and brown water lapped at the wheels of her car. Farther on, even a half mile from Banes Field, rotting wooden signs with weathered paint were posted along the chain-link fence: CONTAMINANTS DANGER and NO TRESPASSING.

She'd already trespassed a dozen times in broad daylight. The last time she'd been chased off the property by a speeding white truck. Taft Properties—and the city—didn't want her taking soil samples from Banes Field, but Professor Samuels said that after so many days of rain and the rise in the water table, there was a good chance the soil would show a tip in the toxin readings, and that was reason enough to try.

The fifty-eight acres were divided by Tubb Gully, weeds and the old equipment on one side, overgrown woods on the other, where, along with the batting cage and dugouts of a Little League field, there were still a few abandoned homes left standing. Lee

kept to this unwooded side of Tubb Gully, closer to where they'd
buried the chemicals years ago in a number of truck-sized vinyl
containers, no better than giant Tupperware, really.

When she came to the hole in the locked gate, she parked the
car. She grabbed the new shovel, the canvas bag with the camera, glass jars, and a map of Banes Field. She got out of the car
and went to the gate, which was chained, but only loosely. She
squeezed her frame through the opening where the end of the
fence bent back, her breasts and hips just grazing the rusted
metal as she pushed through. Inside, the field was muddy, the
weeds pounded flat. The white tank stood about a half mile away,
surrounded by freestanding pistons and pipes.

That day years ago, when she'd first seen the oily sludge come
up out of the grass, she'd thought it was a snake. She'd rushed
inside the house, found Jess doing homework at the table. "Don't
go outside," she'd said. "Stay here."

Today the ground was so soft that her boots weighed down
with mud, and she had to slow her pace. Clouds rushed overhead. Closer to the warehouse, there was a thin gasoline smell,
and the mud had an oily, purple sheen.

The dull exterior of the warehouse was spray-painted TEX in
orange and JAY LOVES RUBY in black, the walkway along the edge
glittering with broken green glass. Nothing was inside, but they'd
left it standing, some secret business still fuming, and the white
truck that chased her the last time had seemed to come from the
back of the building. She stopped at the tank, a rusted cylinder
thirty yards around, patched in places with green mold. A squirrel ran up the ladder on one side. A few black birds perched at the
curve of the top, looking out.

Somewhere nearby, a dog was barking. She went on, pulling

her feet up high to get through deeper mud, her boots and the hems of her jeans caked in it. Finally, she came to the slope where the weeds grew up to her shoulders. She pressed through the stalks and leaves to another chain-link fence, this one cut open. As she made her way through the loose wire tines, they tore a hole in her shirt. She jumped down the incline.

About a hundred more yards through dandelions and spear weeds, the remnants of old Rosemont splayed across the land and into the trees, all the ruins of her old neighborhood, knitted into the foliage. Bits of cement lay across the weeds and brush beneath orphaned telephone poles and lampposts.

She followed the rain gutter that had once run alongside Crest Street. A dingy fire hydrant squatted in a patch of yellow wildflowers, a streetlight hooked over a wild-haired bush, and farther on, ten yards of old asphalt ran through the weeds. She spotted the shell of an ancient air conditioner with a bird's nest on top of it, and a rusted metal rectangle on the ground that claimed NO PARKING BEYOND THIS POINT. She stepped off the asphalt back into the mud.

A decade ago, just before they'd razed most of the houses—a leftover sign sat in Fred Borden's yard: FOR SALE, 2-2-2, WITH 45 PLUS KNOWN TOXIC CHEMICALS AT NO EXTRA CHARGE. A security guard trolled the empty streets in a golf cart, windows mostly boarded up, doors padlocked shut.

Now, at the edge of the woods where Autumn Street would have been, a square steel frame clung to cement, what was left of someone's house, and an ancient garage freezer tilted against a tree, its door swung open. This used to be her block.

On one of her early visits back here, inside a piece of door and marking the crumbled remains of her own house, she'd found the clover brass knocker. What else was left: a stump of brick chimney attached to a slab of concrete, three small stone steps that had once led to the front door. But nearly each time she came back, she found a different artifact in the ruins—an old beer bottle, a plastic lawn elf, a chair.

She stepped up through the red thorns and down again into the weeds of the entryway, past the living room of grass and cinder block, and then she stood in her kitchen, where yellow weeds with sticky flowers clung to her jeans. She looked out where there used to be a window. The air had a kind of empty commotion. Over where the laundry room had been, she noticed a few birds, grayer than the old pipe where they'd landed, pecking at the cement. She felt the old upstairs ghosted above her, the bed where she'd slept with Jack, and Jess's bedroom, with its window overlooking the street.

In front of her, the oak tree she'd planted for Jess when she was a baby was strangely still alive, perfectly shaped like one you'd see drawn in bright colors in a children's book, its leaves lush and healthy. Jess as a toddler used to walk around its base, saying, "Hear those birds?"

She'd let Jess and her friends run all over that field, even as far as the warehouse when they were older. Cows would sometimes wander over—the grass yellow and dry in summer and winter, only green in the spring—where Jess found odd bits of pipe, fluorescent-colored scraps of rubber, tiny pink pebbles the size of coarsely grained salt, which she brought home with her in her pockets.

Jess would say, "I'm heading out, Mom," and she'd run, barefoot, through the door. That ugly field had seemed benign for so many years, fooling everyone with its open space and common weeds, its sorry-looking stooped trees.

She hadn't eaten since morning and felt weak, but the sun was lowering over the trees now, and there wasn't much time. As she made her way to the other side of Banes Field, the ground slid beneath her steps. The dog was still barking, though it didn't seem to have come any closer. She went through the first gate and down the slope that led to the land Taft Properties had bought.

It was now marked out for construction with small wooden survey stakes topped with orange plastic flags. They stood out against the brown grass like bright artificial goldfish. Unbelievable. He didn't even have a permit yet, and the land had already been surveyed. Taft claimed that this area didn't have the same limitations as the land beneath Rosemont, but even Lee knew that soil fifty feet underground had subterranean movement. The chemicals could still leach to the surface over here.

She pulled out the jars and the shovel from her bag, bent down, cleared a section of weeds away, dug a shallow hole, and filled the jar with soil. Twenty feet in the other direction, she bent down, dug a hole about eight inches deep, and filled another jar. The mud was deeper in parts of this section, and some of the survey stakes had toppled. She went on working, all around her the wet, dead grass, the chaotic bushes, the past pressing down from the sky.

There was a voice she heard in her head, sometimes with Jack's intonations, sometimes with Jess's. "Time to leave." She wanted to get a sample near a bald spot in the middle of the gray weeds. A wasp droned close to her, and she flung her hand to hit it away, but it got close to her face, buzzed against her cheek, then looped and stitched back. Wincing, she flicked her hand again and stumbled. The wasp flew off.

Then she saw the thing about twenty yards away, as big as the bed of a pickup truck. The gray corner angled up from the mud beneath a sick-looking sapling. Was it some lost bit of cement? She went closer, her boots smacking in the muck as the dull shape clarified itself. One flat side of it had wrestled up into the air, the other side still sunk into the ground. A giant, filthy, gray vinyl box. The top of it was charred with a bright pink and brown stain, and a crack jiggered its way down the middle, where a copper liquid leaked out in a thin, jagged stream. Her heart punched in her chest. Back in January, Professor Samuels had said this could happen, though it had seemed so unlikely then. "You get enough rain, it shifts the water table—it can pop a container right up."

And there it was. For years, the container had been safe down there, but now the land had excreted it, the way coffins sometimes came back up in a flood. Her head filled with pressure. In the distance, the pine trees seemed to lean forward. She smelled something acidic and bitter, benzene fumes or worse, and covered her nose and mouth with one hand as she took the camera from her bag with the other. The light was already going, but she'd get the picture somehow. She pressed the button to open the lens.

This was the thing she'd been waiting for, but didn't know how to name, the thing that would redeem her. Over the woods, the sun, a bright orange candy set on fire, dangled. She snapped the photographs. The dog barked again. She took twenty-two pictures of the upturned container. Then she ran.

HAL

HAL DID BETTER with the husbands on closing sales—he tried to catch the eye of Mr. Coller, who kept looking away. "I don't know," said his wiry wife, as they rounded the corner to the kitchen, new, pristine cabinets gleaming like wet Wite-Out over the dingy ones that had been there before. "I'm just not feeling enough space on this side of the house, enough air." She fluttered her hand toward the living room off the kitchen, which Hal admitted was smaller than most, but recently tiled and sunny, a room that carried cleanness and possibility like a new prayer.

That was when Hal officially gave up.

Finally, he'd been able to start showing houses again after the storm, but only those on this side of town, where there hadn't been flooding. For the moment, there were goddamn few houses to list, and now he also had to battle Mrs. Coller's vague feng shui ideas. He could never tell if that nonsense would work for a sale or against it. Another woman had remarked on this very house that the energy was just right, that the doors opened exactly where they were supposed to open, the windows at exactly the right angles to the sun. He smiled at the husband when the wife started talking that nonsense, telegraphed through his shrug, *You don't get it either?*

He was pretty sure Mrs. Coller didn't really want to buy but had some ulterior motive with her husband, some manipulation he wasn't privy to. Women did that sometimes, wanting to see a lot of houses on the outer reaches of their price range. But it was a strange time to try something like that, just after a hurricane.

As they left the living room and walked through the bright entryway, a skylight shining down, Hal tried to remain optimistic because that was how you made sales.

Mr. Coller chuckled at his wife's objections. "But that sure is a nice pool!"

Hal wanted to shake him. *Don't you see what she's doing? I'm not a marriage counselor, buddy.*

Still, Mrs. Coller had the last word. "I'd like to see that one on Lottie Lane."

At first, he'd done pretty well, sold a big house out on Windsong to an executive at a drug firm, and another one just down the street to a surgeon. But now some people just recklessly relied on the Internet rather than, God forbid, pay a live person, and so his luck had turned. He no longer felt like the son who'd got the blessing and more like the one who'd been cast out. He knew if he was to keep making a living at this, then he had to find another strategy, an exclusive, or sell commercial properties, not residential ones.

"Okay, then." Hal led them out the front door. "Let's go take a look."

He believed he needed to pray more. He needed to get rid of bad moods and doubts, especially when he was out on calls. That was the devil trying to get him. And he'd said good riddance to the devil last year when he stopped drinking cold. So, as he opened the door of his SUV for Mrs. Coller, he said a quick prayer to get his head back in the game. Mr. Coller got in the backseat, and they drove off.

"Nice car," said Mr. Coller.

"It does me alright," said Hal. He'd bought it at an auction last year, a great deal, though he could barely afford it. In real estate, your vehicle was the office—you needed a good one. They passed Avery Taft's new subdivision off Blissfield Drive, but he didn't even point to it because it was out of their price range and most of the houses weren't finished yet. They were building at least two more subdivisions too, now that the market was whizzing. One of them, he'd heard, would be out near the old Rosemont site, that blight on the landscape. Taft Properties was his best hope—he wanted an exclusive listing for one entire inventory—and he might have a chance at it too, because Avery and he used to play football together back in school.

"Now this here house," said Mr. Coller. "It's close to the flood zone, isn't it?"

"It's on the higher ground," said Hal. "Hurricanes come with the territory, right? But that last one was just a fluke and a monster and it caught some people. You won't find anything higher in League City or Pearland, I tell you that."

"Oh, we're not looking to move outside city limits," said Mrs. Coller, staring out the window with a pursed smile. Darlene said that only women really lived in houses, and men just ate and slept in them.

Hal glanced in his rearview mirror at Mr. Coller, his head turned to the side, a hand rubbing at his chin. He looked like a guy who'd just remembered he'd forgotten to shave or take out the trash, and Hal got the feeling the guy's whole life was full of jagged moments like that—one mistake after another rising up to laugh at him. Just watching him, Hal knew he was liable not to interest them in the next listing either.

Later, he went to Joe's Barbeque, sat eating a snack at the small rickety table, but the meat tasted metallic and it had a strange hard texture. He could only eat a few bites.

There were photos on the walls of the varsity football teams since 1940. As he looked into the stony faces of the players from 1941, a pride pressed up in his chest: honorable tradition. Pushing through those brick walls. His hand moved into a fist, the muscles in his legs tightening. And there was 1980, he and Avery in the front row. They'd shared a flinty nostalgia for Coach Rowan, who'd made them run so far they vomited; who made them play fully suited up in 110 degrees; who had a habit of saying, "Go down there and hit those monsters hard." Coach liked to use a pointer decorated with Indian feathers when he narrated plays in the field house, and he drank large, powdered protein drinks the color of celery. Hal had been a good player, and missed his lighter, firmer body, those cut muscles and the litheness that came from weights and drills that made him feel like an alley cat. So he made cracks about getting fat, though he wasn't really, just middle-aged soft. But he'd never been as good a player as his son was.

Hal felt closest to his son when he sat in the stands, watching a game. Cully, beneath the gladiator shoulder pads and blue-and-white helmet, could swivel his hips and cut a corner with a grace Hal had never had. He felt this was somehow his son's true self, the way he caught the ball to his heart and ran past the thicket of other players, the green space widening behind him, the way he leaped over the goal line, the applause a huge cosmic radio, just about to announce something big. And here it was, another season, and Cully had already been catching miracle passes during two-a-days.

Driving to his next appointment, late because of construction on 243, he heard a clattering song on the car stereo that made him tighten his fingers around the steering wheel. It was a song that reminded him of last year and the drives on which he'd caught himself singing along to the line about running away. Hal thought of that mobile home in League City he'd gone to each week last winter—painted purple inside, the threadbare couch, the chair sprouting stuffing. The affair only lasted seven weeks, but it had nearly killed him. Dawn had long, too-thin legs, and when he pulled away from kissing her, she had a wry tightness in her mouth that reminded him of what he was doing. Now that he really needed a clean slate, the memories kept crudding it up: Dawn's tan, skinny legs wrapped around his waist, and the tiny shoes she wore, and the way he'd come home and feel sad at the sight of Darlene, her face in a nimbus of blue TV light, her grin set like a tiger's. He had to stop himself, because too much thinking along these lines took him to places that deviled him. To pray was more rational—it put things in their places; it put God back in charge. "Stop me from worrying," he said, and as soon as he said it, he felt a wave of warmth for Darlene again, the feeling he had looking at her in her baggy shirt and jeans, the pretty angles of her eyes. And he saw Cully sitting next to her at the dinner table, their identical noses and triangular chins.

Darlene said if only he could learn how to relax, they would be happier together. "I don't mind picking up after you or the snoring," she said. "Just the bad moods."

"And the drinking."

"Well, yes, but that's all done with, right?"

Sometimes after work she rubbed at the knots in his shoulders, and whenever she did that, he felt held by her in this life, purposeful and safe, the way he'd felt years and years ago in the old house in the country, when his dad still had some kindness in him and before his mother started looking so scared.

Hal forced a smile and walked out to the front of the drive to meet the couple who wanted to see a Tudor monstrosity, all gray turrets and fake-old brick, everything fake English, with a strange topiary of a misshapen horse out back and a bright pink shed, where the owner used to keep rabbits. The husband wanted to see the garage first, of course (they almost always did). It was potentially a weakness in this case, because it was just a two-car, and there was a partition down the front wall (fake English brick with vines) so that if they owned a truck, it wouldn't fit inside.

"What kind of car do you have?" Hal asked casually.

"A BMW is our other one—this is a little small for storage, but not bad," said the husband, jutting out his lower lip.

Not bad. The thick whine in his voice irked Hal, but he tried to get past it. He found that if a client annoyed him he almost never made the sale—people just liked to feel liked.

They went to the front door, and the wife was cooing about the beautiful ivy, and Hal was praying that the key would work because he didn't think he could keep his temper if it didn't, and he was distracted by the wife's large breasts snug in the rainbow that arched over her sweater. He needed to get a sale. He needed to be clean in the mind, to turn this bad luck around.

The key fit in the lock, perfect. He opened the door, saw pricked-up brown ears and bared teeth. Shit. The skinny flank scraped past him, sharp, buzzed fur, and the dog ran into the street. The wife screamed, and Hal ran after the mutt. He chased it past mailboxes, past birdbaths, into a wet grassy yard, the stubbed tail bounding ahead, the little pink asshole teasing him.

The dog ran around the curve in the street, and Hal ran as fast as he could now, his chest heaving, dress shoes slipping and clacking on the pavement, sweat gathering in his armpits, the skirt of his suit jacket flying.

He was out of breath, in terrible shape, his face hot with effort and rage. He raced around the corner and the dog was gone. It would ruin the sale and he'd lose the listing too, plus he'd feel guilty as hell. Why didn't the seller warn you when they had a pet? Common sense. There was a goddamn drought of common sense around there. Too many people just wanted to fail.

He ran around back into a yard where a rusting swing set straddled a sandbox, then back around to the street dappled with tree shade, where a yellow car sped by. His eyes stung, and he felt the wind crushed out of him. Then he saw the dog's stubbed tail sticking out from behind a big oak tree. Hal snuck up behind it, grabbed the mutt's mangy flank just in time to have the dog pee on the leg of his pants.

+

WHEN HE GOT BACK to the office, he went straight to the bathroom, splashed water on a thin brown paper towel, and swiped at the stain near the hem of his trousers, but it still smelled of urine, maybe even worse than before. Coming out of the bathroom, he walked past the cubicles and tried not to look at the other agent, Stan, who seemed intent on finishing up more paperwork. Hal sat down and just breathed for two minutes. He felt the ache in his heart for whiskey, and said a tired prayer. *Help*. He checked his voice mail, and there was a message from Darlene to pick up a carton of eggs at the store; a message from the broker about someone's credit standing; and, then, like an answer to his plea, there was one from Taft Properties: "Hal, old buddy. Any chance you can come by the office on Wednesday?"

The fluorescent overhead lights seemed to stutter and blink, and Stan looked up at him from across their desks, as if he'd heard the message too. Stan, with his round, pie face and grating laugh, would never amount to much as a salesman.

Hal called Avery back, thinking he ought to try to move up the appointment if he could do it casually enough. Avery's assistant answered the phone.

Hal stammered, fumbling for a way to gracefully change the time. "Say, is Avery around tomorrow?"

"Nope," said the assistant—her name was Sahara? Shawna? "Wednesday isn't going to work?"

"No, no, it's fine, it's fine. Tell Avery I'll see him then."

Sahara or Shawna said, "Avery said to bring some business cards with you if you can."

Stan stood up, his pants loose and pouchy on his chubby frame. He gathered some papers, saluted Hal good-bye, and walked out the door.

"Will do." This was it. He felt it. He'd prayed good, and he'd prayed right. Avery might just offer him what he wanted.

Hal hung up the phone, feeling the unnatural stillness of the office. He looked up at the bulletin board above his desk, a lost phone number pinned there that had once meant something, and next to it, the picture of Cully, kneeling reverently on one knee in the bright green turf, his football helmet clutched under his arm, his padded shoulders broad and proud over the number 12, his face so full of hope.

WILLA

THE RAIN CAME DOWN, a tattered curtain closing over the world, or sometimes like a million tiny glass doors. One had opened to Willa just before the storm blew in, and she'd seen behind it, an old man in a black cowboy hat calmly sucking on a cigarette as the wind lashed through the trees, his legs cycling in a haze of silver just before he evaporated. He'd appeared only for a couple of seconds, and as usual, she didn't know what it meant. Sometimes at the edge of her sight line, she saw bright streaks of blood or unscrolling clouds. When she lay in her bed, she'd seen a shotgun hovering near the ceiling darkness, turning and turning again, like a blade in a fan. Outside her window, a sequined dress billowed in the noon sun, then broke apart into rags. Another day, the number 7 pressed up through the mirror, precise and haloed, as if it were cut out of light. She discovered, sitting alone and staring at a pinhead, that she could will a wobbly vision into place, but couldn't predict what it would be. This extra sight was a weird new ability like double-jointedness, come to her late in the summer, but she didn't know if it was real.

She hadn't told anyone, not even Dani. Saturday there was a shed party in the woods, and she might tell her then. Cully would be there with his dogged eyes and secretive mouth, his tallness. That night in the spring, at the stadium near the concession stand, she and Dani had been talking to him, and he jokingly put his arm around Willa, let his hand rest on her shoulder for a few seconds, and when his fingers flicked at the seam of her shirt, it knocked the breath out of her.

Trapped in the house because of the rain, and bored, she stared at the dead plant on the windowsill in her room, until one of the stalks kicked into a leg and started walking out of the pot. The leg grew fur, and then a wing, fleshy at first, and then more transparent, and it flew through the glass of the window. She got up, went to the computer, and looked up *hallucination* online. She tapped her foot on the floor, her forehead hot as she scrolled down the blue screen. First she read about a Korean mushroom that, if swallowed, made a person see fluorescent-colored birds. Then she discovered tangled maze designs that you were supposed to stare at until your eyes blurred, and out of the blur, a picture emerged of a face or the silhouette of a cat. On a mental health site, the words *psychosis* and *schizophrenia* were highlighted red, and her fingers on the keyboard started to tremble. She read the questionnaire: "Do you feel unexplainably sad or afraid? Do people understand you when you speak? Do you ever hear or see things that others can't?" She wondered if other people saw similar flashes of shape or color, as if the air had hidden wrinkles in it that held things, objects that appeared just for a few seconds when the atmosphere unfolded.

In a spiral notebook, she wrote down a list of the visions that had appeared so far. There had been a little girl, reaching up with both arms for Willa to hold her. There had been a naked man with thick thighs and a beard. There had been a plate of sugar-dusted cookies. An old pot filled with pencils. It seemed that if she could find a shape or a pattern, then she might take hold of their meaning, but written down, they were just words, and had none of the shimmering tenuousness of the visions themselves. The list had made them all seem fake, like moving the pointer on a Ouija board or lifting up a girl with your index finger at a slumber party, saying, "Light as a feather, stiff as a board."

Her dad knocked lightly on the door and ducked in his head. "Your mom's got steak going. About finished with that?"

She pulled the notebook to the edge of her desk. "Yeah."

His face looked tired, distant, as if he were still thinking of work. "T-bone and potatoes. Go on and put that book away." He winked and went back down the hall.

What would happen if she showed him the list? Most likely, he'd send her to see Pastor Sparks, who had surprised eyes and a woolly voice. He would say a demon had manifested from the television or the Internet, something she'd been staring at so much, it had found a pathway to her heart.

Just a year ago, she and her dad used to go running on the old golf course in the early morning, light pinking over the brown grass, and only a few people out, maybe an elderly couple drinking coffee on their back patio or a girl practicing herkie jumps in her yard. The sweat would drip off the tip of her dad's nose and chin, and he'd only talk in short bursts between breaths, but he'd ask what she'd been doing in school, and whether she thought she might like to run a marathon someday, and what she thought of the new houses over on Palm Street. And if they'd still had that habit, she might have told him on one of those mornings about the things she'd seen lately. But sometime last year, his schedule at work changed and he didn't have time anymore, and she'd noticed he'd also stopped looking directly at her face, as if it somehow embarrassed him.

She went downstairs for dinner, and her little sister, Jana, was wearing a headband with red felt devil horns glued to it. "Ha!" said Willa. "Finally dressing the part."

Willa's mother shot her a look, then set down the bowl of mashed potatoes.

"I don't like that fooling around with Satan, myself," said her father, and he reached over and lifted the horns off Jana's head.

Jana covered her bare, blond head with her hands. "It's just pretend, Dad."

"Be careful what you joke about," he said.

There seemed to be a lot of reverence for Satan at their new church, where Pastor Sparks gave prophecies of the Apocalypse in a fierce, cheerful voice—because everyone in that room would be saved, he said—and as he read the verses from Revelation, Willa lost his meaning in the surge of images—locusts like horses with human faces, the Wormwood star falling from the sky to the sea, a ten-headed dragon with horns and diadems. Her father seemed particularly alive to these sermons, as if he wanted certainty in the face of coming danger.

After her father said grace, and everyone had cut their steaks, he started talking about Lee Knowles. "I heard she's just gotten stranger about the old Rosemont site. Made a scene last month at the city council meeting. And when did she start wearing men's shirts?"

"Those are Jack's," said her mother. "She started that up years ago, after he left, don't you remember?" Lee Knowles had been her mother's good friend, back when they were still in high school. Willa wanted to know what had caused the falling out. She couldn't imagine not being best friends with Dani, and she guessed that whatever had happened between Lee and her mother must have been catastrophic. Some insult or betrayal the other one couldn't forgive. Her mother started talking about meeting Jana's new third-grade teacher, how they'd all had an unforeseen vacation because of the storm and now it was about time they got back to school. Willa stopped listening and looked out the window at a bee banging itself against the glass, its tiny furred face.

LEE

SHE'D KNOWN SOMETHING WAS WRONG with Banes Field, that spring, 1996, though she couldn't place it. The light hung at strange angles on the round white tank. The windows of the warehouse had been painted black, and she saw a boy wearing a red baseball hat walk in and out of it several different times—he always carried a wide, purple cylinder thing over his shoulder. It looked like a giant, shiny thermos. And there was a fat, brown-skinned man too—who wore a hard hat and overalls and smoked cigars while he walked. He walked around the field at odd hours, or sometimes cut the weeds in a riding lawn mower. Even the weeds had begun to look odd—they were sparser but also more varied in color and type than she remembered. At night, she heard a strange piercing whistle, and in the morning, there was a bitter stink in the air. Jack would stare out the back window in the kitchen and say, shaking his head, "I wonder what Ms. Banes is going to do with all that." They worried that she might sell it to a developer, and they'd end up with a parking lot or a shopping center right in their backyard.

One morning Lee had settled down with her coffee in the sitting room after Jack had left for work and Jess had left for school.

She was rattled, maybe because of Jess's struggle with algebra last night, the way she'd moaned over her homework, all those less-than and greater-than marks, like open mouths, the opaque spells of the equations. Lee had given her a glass of soda and worked through the figures with her as best she could, and she hoped Jess would do okay on the test that day. And she'd comforted Jack at breakfast with pancakes because he had to fire someone at work, and he said, "There's no kind way to do it. There just isn't." She turned the pages of the newspaper, the black print running all over the columns. Watery light came down from the high window, the picture on the wall of the owl: alert, looking for something to eat in the watercolor green, looking not to be eaten, the painted tree branch fading out at the edge of the paper. But Jess had earned As in all her other subjects, and Jack would find a way to not be cruel—he always did. In the news were warnings about computer hackers, warnings about fighting in the Middle East. She read an editorial about why kids should say the Pledge of Allegiance in school, why the flag should stand in all the churches, and she felt the chirpiness and aggression of the man's words right there in the room. She stopped reading, stopped drinking coffee, and studied the shadows on the wall. She wanted to be grateful. After all she'd been through as a kid—her mom's drunken fits and their sporadic, shameful poverty—she had this nice house, a husband who sang to her, who brought home trinkets he thought she'd like and didn't nag her. She had a daughter with sweet, curious eyes who liked to tell jokes and tried so hard to be good. And Jess was good, even as a teenager, despite the hollering over the math. Leaves rustled against the window, and gradually, Lee's nerves had calmed. The room returned to her in its solidity and quaintness, the pale couch, the gold-stemmed lamp, the paisley curtains.

In the afternoon after Jess came home from school, Lee had gone out to check the garden, which was at the edge of Banes Field. The parsley bush was a lush and large bucket, and the azaleas, pink and silly like wadded tutus. Out in the field, there were bare patches of dirt where the weeds had died. A cow wandered over and stood munching grass by the gate. It had brown and white spots, and looked over at her dumbly. She remembered that cow now because it had disappeared when she looked again later, as if it had fled.

About a foot away from the knotted root of a tree, she spotted something black and shiny in the grass that was piled up in a coil, and crosshatched with pink and brown diamonds. She thought it hissed. She moved closer, ready to jump away if it was a copperhead. But when she got near enough, she could see the thing was dead. It was curled there against the first bright spring grass, slick and oily, weird perfect coils. She bent down to look, and then she saw there wasn't a head. It smelled rank and vaguely of petroleum, and when she put her finger against the slime just at the blackest part, her skin came back red and stinging. She crouched there in the grass, looked to the other side of the yard, and saw the sludge had squirmed up in other places too, near the hammock, and out at the edge of their yard, next to a lone dandelion. As the breeze lifted and rocked the bird feeder hanging above, she felt an uncertain dread. In the other direction near the garden hose, there were three blue-black coils lying there in a triangle, as if by design. They seemed to writhe and sputter in the bright sunlight. She kicked at the black coil beneath her, and stomped on it until it was flat and crushed, then she wiped off the sole of her shoe in the grass. As she watched her movements, she began to understand that the sludge had pushed right up out of the ground, some greasy offal that had sprouted everywhere, as if it had been purposefully planted. She went inside, and locked the door, pressed the mat against the seam at the bottom, as if the stuff might be able to slither its way inside under the doorjambs.

She went into the kitchen, where Jess sat at the kitchen table with her books. "There you are," Jess said. "You were gone awhile." The book was opened to diagrams and graphs, and an empty glass sat next to it. Jess bent closer to her work and chewed on her lip, barely looking up from her writing.

"Don't go outside. Stay in here." Lee went to the sink and stood washing her trembling hands. "There's some bad stuff out there."

When Jack spoke to the Turners to see if they'd seen the same sludge in their yard, Sy said, "Yeah, it's some runoff from the oil refinery, but I checked with the city—the EPA says it's such a small concentration of stuff, it can't hurt anything."

Now, years later, almost no one remembered or cared, but the sludge came up out of the ground for months. It appeared under downstairs windows, lay along the seams of sidewalks, and a few of Lee's neighbors mistook it for dog shit. Sometimes it looked like worms or a mass of crushed coffee beans. People who touched it got rashes or sores on their skin. All over Rosemont, the sludge wriggled into rose gardens, around the bases of birdbaths, and lay in piles under hammocks. People worried, but were reassured that the EPA had tested the soil and declared it safe. Then one day, the sludge appeared, thick and oozing and with a streak of fluorescent green, under the swing set of the school playground. A mother found her little boy playing with the black coils, petroleum and dirt in war paint across his face.

+

WHEN LEE LOOKED NOW at the photos she'd taken of the escaped container, she was disappointed. The pictures were dim and indistinct because it had been dusk. You could see the rectangular outline in the mud and the big pink stain—but without anything around it to put to scale, it was hard to see how big the thing was or how clearly it was plastic, not wood or metal. She watched the photos slide out from the printer, each time hoping the next image would be more clear.

Outside the kitchen window, a cat slinked through the white bowl of porch light, and one of her neighbors, a man who seemed to be constantly out in his backyard, laughed loudly and whistled, and then some tinny pop music rose up from the other direction. The phone rang, and when she went to answer it, she spilled her cup of water.

It was Jack. Finally.

"What was the name of that dog?" he said.

"You shouldn't be drinking, you know that?"

"Who said I'm drinking?" But she could hear the growly slur in his words. "I don't think it makes a goddamn good bit of difference what I put in my glass. But I keep thinking about that dog, the patchy one that followed her home that day and we kept for a while until the owner showed up. Real mangy." It had been weeks since he'd called.

"Mabel."

"Mabel, that's right. I get these things lodged in my brain. She cried like hell when we had to give it back."

Lee would not let him pull her into that sad place. "Jack, where's Cindy tonight?"

"I don't want to talk about her. Why won't you let me just talk?"

"I always just let you talk, that's the problem."

"You know the other thing I was thinking about? That hat with the old Astros insignia."

"Yeah," she said. Jess had worn it all the time at the end, even in her bed. They'd all gone to a game that summer, and Jack had bought her everything, the jersey too, the little dog with orange saucer eyes, the small plastic cups with *A*s painted on them.

"She doesn't want you talking to me anymore, does she?"

"Cindy? No, she sure doesn't. That's right."

When he called, Jess felt close and far away at the same time, as if she were hiding somewhere, tiny, in the pulsing phone waves between them. Lee felt the pressure tightening in her chest and shoulders, the slow, sure, squares of grief building, one on top of the other; she wouldn't be able to shake it for a while after this. "So why do you call?"

"I can't not, I guess." She heard a clinking of glass. "She's afraid of the terrorists, did I tell you that? She won't go shopping anymore because she heard somewhere that Dobie Mall was on some watch list."

"Huh." She liked it when he complained about Cindy, made her seem silly and too weak to handle him, though she knew his grousing would never amount to anything. And tonight, even his phone call, that pleasant scratch in his voice, his laugh, even all this couldn't knock down the grief stacking up in her chest, block by block. "Do you want to know what I saw yesterday just outside of Banes Field? I'm pretty sure it was one of those containers of chemicals risen up out of the ground."

"Now, why the hell are you still going over there?" There was a washing sound on the phone.

"I don't need to answer that. Look, if this doesn't stop that construction permit, I don't know what will."

He sighed. "Well, don't expect them to throw you a party."

"You could act more happy for me."

"Let's see what comes of it first. I wish you wouldn't do that stuff anymore. I wish you'd just—"

"You're not in charge anymore, remember?"

"Jesus, Lee. You're right, I'm not." He paused, and she imagined he was taking a long swallow of something—Jack Daniel's or beer. "Can I tell you why I called? I watched this old movie last night—you know, a Western—and the saloon girl reminded me of you. She just showed up for a few minutes, but she had this way of slamming down a drink."

"I don't do that." He was so sentimental sometimes, she wondered if it was calculated. When they were together, he'd had a way of using his sweetness to get her to agree. Or if he was angry, he'd walk fast over his limp, which only exaggerated it.

"You would do that," he said, "given a glass of beer."

They talked awhile longer, reminisced and bantered as they were prone to, and then Jack's voice turned slow and thick, and he said, "I believe I'm going to go lie down for a while and watch the game."

"You do that," she said, but he hung up before she thought he heard her.

She'd expected to get a call from Mayor Wallen by 4:00 at the latest, but she just kept working, thinking he might call before 6:00.

The room felt heavy with light. The bed was Jess's old bed, with the purple-checked bedspread, and her bureau, still scratched up, pale rings from damp glasses on the surface. Whenever Lee met someone new, a friend of a friend or a new person at work, she always told them as soon as she could that she'd had a daughter who'd died of a blood disease, so that Jess's death wouldn't come up again by accident in casual conversation. She needed to control the number of facts she told, or else she might fall apart at some inopportune time.

Against the wall, she kept the boxes, files, and reference books and a small table where she worked, just under the school picture. In the photograph, Jess tilted her head—as if she were suspicious of the photographer—was she laughing at herself or hiding or thinking about how she'd look to some boy? She wore a light blue sweater, which disappeared into the fake sky background. With her daughter's eyes looking out over her work, Lee could sometimes muster the feeling as she gathered figures and shuffled through papers, that she was still taking care of a child.

She turned on the TV and inserted the old video into the VCR that she'd kept just for this purpose. Whenever she found a new shred of evidence, she watched the video, though it pained her, and at this point she'd studied the footage a hundred times. The screen flickered on, and there was Rue Banes—alive again—in her pantsuit and frilly high-necked blouse, sitting straight and bird-like on a hard chair, a paneled wall in the background. Her face was wrinkled and powdered, with a long jaw and a large nose, but her mouth was girlish. She grinned as she neared the ends of her answers. Again and again, Lee needed to study the old woman's expression, to see if there was any trace of guilt there.

"It goes like this. Back in the fifties, I was offered a deal. I had this little company that had been my dad's, and Garbit Company wanted me to take the waste from them and refine it into new products. My company and I were promised technical support. I was promised a profit. I made some money, sure, but after a year or so, I was on my own. I had no idea of what some of those chemicals did, but Garbit knew, sure."

The question she was asked next was muffled on the tape, but she nodded, placed her hand patriotically on the lapel of her red jacket. "No, I did not. I had my man dig a pit, and we poured the waste in there. Every year, the agencies came out and tested the soil, and except for one or two times, the levels came out clean." The tape flickered, and her head came back at a different angle, looking huge and heavy on her thin neck.

She spoke as if her old self belonged to some employee she couldn't take responsibility for. It was hard to believe she hadn't known the chemicals she'd dumped were toxic, or that she'd forgotten what she'd buried when she sold the nearby land. "Once or twice the smell got bad, and when I told Garbit, they sent out a small plane that sprayed a perfuming agent to cover it." Not once did she say "I regret," but there was an occasional flicker in her eyes, or in the awkward angle of her lipsticked mouth, and this made Lee pity her. This was why she watched—how could this woman with small, crinkled eyes and a friendly, straight-talking voice have caused so much suffering?—it wasn't clear whether or not she knew it. "Look, Good Lord, I had no idea. If I'd known, I'd have found something else to do." Lee had heard that her foreman used to hire teenagers after it rained, to dump chemicals into Tubb Gully and Crystal Creek, one to do the dumping and one to watch. Stewart, one of the ones who'd done the dumping years ago, had developed unexplained brain damage. Lee still saw him at the service station where he pumped gas, his shoulders hunched as if they could barely stand the weight of his large hands. "And the truth is, I'm sorry," Rue Banes went on. "But these bureaucrats at the government agencies? They don't understand oil. They don't know the business. They just love their chemistry."

Lee remembered how the McHughs had tried to have a pool installed in their backyard, but they couldn't make the excavation stable because the dirt contained so much oil, which also leaked up through the cracks in the cement of their driveway. When the EPA came out to do tests, though, they took a sample closer to the house, which was *procedure*, and the soil came up nearly clean, so no one knew what to believe.

Back then, Lee had been out walking one day when she met her neighbor Michelle Smalls, crying because there was a woman on Cherry Street who'd just given birth to a stillborn baby, a boy with his heart attached to the outside of his body. "On his back, if you can believe it. That family!"

"Somebody needs to find out what's in that crap they're finding around here," Lee said. She'd had no idea then of the violence already slamming within Jess's blood.

"I know sad things happen like this all the time. They do," said Michelle. "But still."

On the tape, a man sat next to Rue Banes, but Lee could only see his arm and leg, a gray suit. And in the background sound, there was a commotion of more people entering the room of the filming. "Ms. Banes," a man's voice said.

Rue Banes suddenly stopped smiling, looked up imperiously over the camera at something else. "You see, I am not the only one," she said. "I cannot be the only one responsible for this."

The video flickered off.

Just before six o'clock, Lee called Mayor Wallen again, but he'd left for the day. She imagined him calculating how to have the container safely removed, how to excavate the field again, and who would pay for it all. She heard the voices of neighbor children bouncing on the trampoline next door, car doors slamming, the whinny of screen doors. Outside the window, the warm, blue last light of the sun fell upon the grass.

Jess's desk was cluttered with papers—torn-out newspaper articles and reports on benzene in the water table and names and phone numbers of all those bodiless voices she talked to at the agencies, two old snapshots of the sludge coiled up near a tree. In the file cabinet, Professor Samuels's studies were arranged in the top drawer, and in the middle drawer, the cancer count records she'd culled from the local hospitals were arranged by year. In the bottom drawer, a file on each chemical they'd identified in Banes Field: vinyl chloride, benzene, fluorene, copper, toluene, styrene, and forty or so others. The chemicals needed to be evacuated, packaged, and sent out to the desert or else burned up safely in an incinerator (and it had to be an expensive one that wouldn't pollute the air). People's eyes glazed over, reading the data, but when she could get someone's attention at an agency, or on the city council, she felt the ground steady beneath her. At the very least, Avery Taft shouldn't be building near that field. The land should stand empty.

She sat at the desk, making notes on a yellow legal pad. She dropped her pen on the rag rug, and when she reached down to get it, there was a dark hair caught in the red weave. Who knew how long it had been there? She tugged it free. Long and curved. It might have been Jess's—probably was. She laid the hair on one of the papers on the desk, ran her finger down the line of it.

DEX

THEY LIVED IN A TRAILER parked in a field adjacent to the Baptist church. With the old folks' home on the corner, ambulances wailed down their street every other day. They kept the grass neat, and Dex's mother tended a garden; and except for the occasional visit from the elderly preacher, who wanted them to attend a service, the Baptists mostly left them alone.

Dex's mother sat at the card table with a stack of bills, writing checks with one hand, eating potato chips out of a bowl with the other.

"Hey, Mom."

She looked up, her full face sweet and worried. "Want something to eat?"

Dex flopped back on the couch. "No, thanks." He was tired from assisting at practice—he'd had to haul the equipment off the field, dragging several tractor tires and rolling the bulky pass caddies through the grass while the players ran laps around him on the track.

"I'm beat too," she said. "Ms. Redmond had me typing this endless brief. Has all these special formats." Behind her, on the little shelf, there was a hula girl with a red lei whose grass-skirted hips swayed when you lifted up the figurine. Lately, it seemed so pathetic to him. And there was a tiny painted landscape, a waterfall and a pink beach, two people the size of flies making their way into the surf. In block letters, it read HAWAII, 1990. These were souvenirs from the trip his parents had taken just before he was born, and they had always stood on that little shelf.

"I'm thinking of asking your dad to get you a new truck. That old Ford worries me—the door's all rusted out."

"It runs fine."

"Well, today's fine isn't tomorrow's fine. School's about to start, and you'll need something you can depend on." She pushed away the potato chips and fixed him with a serious look, her chin doubling.

His dad never said why he'd left, only told Dex, "She's a good person, and you respect that. Always." When they were still married, as soon as his dad got home from work, he showered and slapped on cologne from the black bottle before he even kissed her, and whenever she was mad, he would follow her around the house calling her "Leah!" or trying to get her to laugh. She hadn't been fat three years ago, when he took off for the oil rig, his face smileless and dim in the cab of his truck, the bed rickety with stacked boxes.

She rubbed the side of her mouth with her finger. "Your dad can afford it. You know that every month when he sends his check, he sends me a little note too." She reminded him of this often, as if it had more meaning than it did. "He's been asking what he can do for you—he's been asking if we need anything more."

His dad was so secretive now. He lived in that house in Port Arthur, with the adobe brick and gray shutters Dex had seen in the photo he'd emailed. There was a swimming pool in the sub-division, and jungle-themed putt-putt golf nearby. He kept tell-ing Dex this detail every time they talked on the phone, laughing about the waterfall at the end of the ninth hole, and how the ball spit up out of the elephant's trunk at the end, even though Dex had outgrown that kind of fun a long time ago. His dad worked down at the coast on the Shell oil rigs—was gone for a month at a time. He worked with a guy named Tipper who sang "like a sick dog." His dad ate barbecue wherever he could find it, would drive for hours through flat fields and tiny towns to some secret smoky pit behind a gas station, where you could walk close to the fire pit, because he just had to see if the meat really was as tender as everyone said it was. Oil work and barbecue. What else did Dex really know about him now? Sometimes he sent chain emails with jokes he thought Dex would like—they were attached to pictures like a dog driving a car or an opened can of beans with a mouth drawn on it, a tongue hanging off the lip.

"Well, if Dad wants to get me a truck, far be it for me to stand in the way." He wouldn't mind a black one, with four doors instead of two.

"Alright then," she said.

She got up and turned on the radio behind her to the country station and sang along to the tune. *"I'm already in love with the tomorrow of you."*

His friends thought his mother was hilarious. When they came over, she'd pass around bowls of pretzels and M&M's. She ran a private joke with each of them, how Weeks needed fancy shoes to go with his hair, how Lawbourne was a salesman but she wasn't buying. But at this point, Dex doubted any man would love his mother again. That would be left to Dex and his sister now.

"You with your gray hair, you with the lines at your eyes." She put the bowl in the sink, her hair dark and glossy under the light, her hips pillowed beneath the loose brown dress.

"Your sister's a great girl," said his mom.

He knew she wanted him to assure her again that, no, they weren't raised in a barn—and so he tried to be funny. "Uh-oh. Where's this going?"

"She's like an Energizer bunny, and she's smart." On the wall behind her, there was a framed picture of his sister, Layla, in a cheerleading uniform, holding up her pom-poms like small heads of blue hair. His mother took a bite of a marshmallow cookie. "I want you to look out for her next year."

"What makes you think she'll let me?"

"Oh, don't give me that. You need to find out who her friends are, and I've told you I think it's a shame that you kids don't date anymore, but whatever, same rules I had—she can't go anywhere where there's boys and no parent. If she doesn't like that, tough."

"Layla, does she even like boys?" If only she would laugh.

His mother puffed out her cheeks and sighed, then took another bite of the cookie.

"Hey, Mom?" he said.

She looked at him, chewing. The doctor had diagnosed her with diabetes last month.

"You shouldn't be eating that."

She swallowed and smiled a closed-mouth smile. "Oh, I know. New diet starts tomorrow." She got up and left the kitchen area, her hair piled up in a nest at the back of her head, her legs moving lazily and unevenly, some slight imbalance in her he hadn't noticed before.

✝

DEX KNEW HE HAD an inside self that was still unfamiliar to him, a shadowy thing he glimpsed while driving straight on the highway. Each time after one of his dad's visits, when his dad got in the car to leave, Dex heard the whisper of it, and kissing Sue Williams, he'd felt it. Dex had taken her to the homecoming dance; bought her a big, fat fake mum corsage that hung off her shoulder like a small, beribboned white cat. He knew the truth, that he was skinny and unsmooth, prone to getting shit from the football players, just as liable to get laughed at as liked. Only a girl like Sue could have changed that, taught him the language he needed to talk to that trapped stranger inside himself.

Then one week after the dance, Dex was walking down the crowded hallway to the cafeteria when he spotted her, laughing and swinging her hair, sitting on the lap of Greg Hycliff. She'd nightmarishly become a different person, one who happened to be covered in Sue's skin and clothes. He began to shake, and a pain pricked at his neck. Before she saw him, he turned around and walked the other way.

It took him a long time to think about a girl again. Willa Lambert sat on his right side in English. Dark hair, pale skin, pink lips—pretty if you studied her long enough, but if you didn't, her face might wash by. She was quiet, tall and narrow-shouldered, and the way she glided when she walked made him notice her breasts, set high and small.

Once they'd been assigned to work together on the imagery

in *The Great Gatsby*. The other students were cutting up, but she flipped through the book studiously and told him to look for mirrors and eyes. From the side, he could see through the gap between buttons on her shirt, the top of her bra and a delicate gold cross on a chain, so thin it seemed at first like a line of light on her skin.

She said, "See, that's the set of eyes on the billboard that looks down on all of them. What do you think it means? Is it supposed to be their conscience?"

"I don't know, God?"

She shook her head, her skin reddening. "God doesn't smirk on a billboard."

She hung around with the other church kids who went on trips together and came back with T-shirts that said JESUS RULES. But she was also friends with Dani Banks, who had black hair, large breasts, and smoked and drank and did not go to church.

"Don't you think Nick is an idiot?"

"No," she said slowly. And she gave him a pitying look. Her eyes were pretty, long-lashed and bright when they settled on him. She had this barking laugh that didn't match her delicate mouth—he liked that too. The next day, she asked to be his partner again, and he felt the envelope opening again to the inside self.

For a few weeks he hovered around her after class, making jokes about their teacher or teasing her about her sparkly shoes. Then one morning he walked past her at her locker and said hello, and she stood there, with her shoulders squared, staring into her locker, not even turning her head, her face shadowed by the blue door. "Hello," he said. "Willa, HEL-LO!" Making an ass of himself so people stared. And still she didn't turn around. He figured she was upset and needed some quiet—his sister Layla got like that sometimes too, but it was still irritating as hell.

"She's weird," his friend Weeks told him. "Like someone possessed by the souls of Siamese kittens." Weeks called her KitKat. "All that makeup like cat's eyes." Once in the sixth grade, Weeks told him, she'd barricaded herself in the bathroom and wouldn't come out. He knew this because it was during homeroom, and he overheard some girls talking about it. "She wouldn't talk, wouldn't come out—they just heard a tiny meowing from her in there."

"Bullshit," said Dex.

"That's the God's truth," said Weeks, who had a small peanut-shaped head and floppy red hair and cheerful pimples like polka dots on his cheeks.

Dex didn't tell Weeks that he kind of liked the makeup (the long-lashed part of her eyes), but he suddenly doubted his perception of Willa. Girls were unreliable, like those shape-shifters in the stories they'd read for English—pretty one day, ugly the next—he could picture half the girls in his school turning into trees or a deer or cows. Part of him was disappointed that the cute girl who maybe liked him had been turned into a weirdo, but the other part of him was still hopeful.

"She seems nice enough to me," said Dex. He thought he'd felt her lean into him from her desk the last time they'd worked together. "Maybe she just didn't feel good."

Weeks raised his eyebrows. "I don't know. Meowing?"

It was true that Dex only saw her at school, not at the house parties or in the laundromat parking lot, where people drank beer and swallowed orange and yellow pills they'd stolen from their parents' medicine cabinets. But that might only mean she

was still undiscovered—not in the right crowd, but not neces-
sarily strange.

Last Tuesday the teacher asked them to exchange their
essays, arguments as to whether or not there should be a military draft—they'd both argued against it. He could tell hers was
well written, and he didn't see any grammatical mistakes, but
his mind wandered as he read, and he knew that if he didn't
make a suggestion, he'd lose her respect, so he wrote, "This is
okay, but it needs more flash." Willa handed his back to him with
a little clucking sound. Her round handwriting said, "Just say
what you think." She'd drawn three stars below the comment.

HAL

ON AN INDEX CARD taped to his dashboard, this Bible verse: "Beloved, I pray that you may prosper in all things and be in health, just as your soul prospers." He moved his lips to the words as he read them now, to put them inside his body. On the way to Avery Taft's office, as he drove past the green fields and the crosses of telephone poles, he felt the prongs of the consonants on his lips and tongue.

On Sunrise Drive, he could see in the distance the attenuated 7s of the football field lights and the bland brick rectangle of the high school, where he hoped Cully was concentrating on what he was supposed to be learning.

He passed the Reese house, which he'd sold just below the asking price back in December. With its austere gray brick and stately pillars near the front door, the gold cupola on the top of the roof, it looked like a trophy. He'd sold it to an insurance man who'd been skeptical of the elaborate game room, but Hal had convinced him that a built-in pool table could be therapeutic, and they'd had a long talk about the game. Hal had been praying. He needed more blessings like the Reese house sale, like the other night with Darlene, when her breasts had looked full and white in the lamplight, and she'd said how much she needed him. He'd been trying like hell to free himself from sin.

When he turned the corner, the sunlight swiped against the windshield, and he parked next to Avery's white Mercedes in the lot. Taft Property's office was a model home near the entrance to one of Avery's subdivisions, a palatial colonial with three stories and two balconies, four large white pilasters from roof to bottom like great, neatly creased scrolls of paper. Not to Hal's taste, though he admired the effort. Hal straightened his tie in the rearview mirror, brushed the lint and Danish crumbs from his blue pants, and got out of the car.

Inside, the receptionist, Sahara or Shawna, a cute blonde wearing a suit that looked too old for her, called Avery on the intercom to announce that Hal had arrived. Avery appeared at the top of the staircase, dressed just like his foremen, only a little more expensively, a little more showily. The boots were blue snakeskin, and the dark jeans looked pressed.

"Howdy, Hal. Come on up," he said. As Hal made his way, he felt overdressed in his suit and tie, weaker because of it. At the landing, Avery slapped him on the back. "How've you been?" His curly dark hair and red lips were deceptively youthful.

"Good. Good."

"So, what are you thinking about this game? Think we can get around that Monster Thompson?"

"Well, I tell you what, Coach says they've been looking alive— looking crisp."

"Glad to hear it. I don't want that thing we got last year. You got to close the deal when you've got them down." When they'd played Brenham last season, they'd let them come back, lost by just one point on a field goal in the last seconds of the game.

"Well," said Hal, "that's for damn sure. Nobody likes to get kicked in the stomach like that." Avery asked about the lineup—who was in, who was hurting—and Hal told him what he could, bullshitted the rest. As Hal sat now in the wood-paneled office, Avery's millions seemed to sing through the oaky, shellacked walls.

The assistant brought them two bottles of water and two glasses, and quietly left.

"So, how are you, old friend?"

"Doing great," said Hal, thinking *gifts of the spirit, gifts of the spirit*.

"How many catches does your boy have this season? Ten? Fifteen? Couple hundred yards maybe?"

"Something like that."

Hal didn't want to have to ask Avery directly—it didn't seem right. Avery would surely offer him something, on the basis of his record, on the grounds of their old friendship, and then maybe Hal would get him around to the idea of Avery using only him to sell the new homes.

"Hal, the reason I asked you over here, is you know that old house I own out on Route 2351?"

"Sure." Hal's stomach buckled. That house was a ranch with ugly green shutters and the Texas Tea and Pawn on one side of it, the Jugglers' Saloon on the other. Was it possible to be destructively hopeful? He'd seen a For Sale sign there for months but hadn't known it still belonged to Avery—it had once been Avery's parents' house. "I've had that O'Bresley working on it, and he's gone nowhere with it. I thought you could give it a try. I'm pulling the listing from them. I'm sentimental about the place, but I don't have any illusions. Someone should tear it down and build another commercial property there."

Avery must have known how difficult the sale would be, but Hal wasn't going to put it in that light. He was trying to get back on his game now, get a chance to prove himself.

"I'll take it on, sure."

"I sure would appreciate you. I've been thinking for a while that we ought to work together."

Now the light seemed to shine brighter in the room, and Hal was thinking of how he might turn this opportunity to just the right angle—it was a thing he used to be able to do in football— take a broken play and turn it into a big gain.

"How's all that business with Banes Field going? You going to start building out there soon?"

"Well, I gotta tell you, we've got the financing all lined up. We've got the architectural plans. We've even got the contractors. And honestly, I'd projected that we'd start sales at the end of next summer. But this thing with the Rosemont–Banes Field site is holding us up. It's a real pain in my ass." Despite all his success, there was a laziness in Avery that Hal couldn't quite put his finger on, a reliance on others' goodwill.

"Didn't I hear something about the EPA clearing it again— for what, five years? Ten?"

"They did clear it. But believe it or not, there's still a tree hugger after some glory where that's concerned." Avery cleared his throat, sat back with his hands clasped behind his head. "Well, glory's one word for it, I guess. Don't get me started. Let the government take over what you eat and what you drive, where you live, where you shit. It's a mess. Do you know what I heard direct from my buddy at NASA? Why the *Columbia* shuttle exploded? They used a new green fixant for the tiles instead of the old one (which worked perfectly fine) because it contained asbestos. Now, I'm asking you, who cares about asbestos in outer space? Who's going to breathe it? E.T.? And, bam, the tiles fall off because of some shitty eco-friendly subpar glue."

"You know," said Hal, grasping the rope of this chance, "I believe we're meant to prosper. If the land's there, we ought to use it." He had a strong feeling Avery had not been saved. On the wall, there was a display of old Texas license plates, dented and rusted, the lost codes of numbers making some kind of art, and next to that, a discreet cabinet of crystal decanters and glasses and bottles of bourbon.

Avery's lip curled up on one side. "Yeah. That's what my grand-dad would say—don't let opportunity go to waste. Do you know, thanks to the eco-nuts, we haven't built a new oil refinery in Texas for decades? Can you imagine those old facilities? Safety, my ass."

"Well, the Rosemont situation has been taken care of—no question about that—after all the settlements." He'd wanted an exclusive to the other neighborhood, Pinelands, but this new neighborhood, after it was built, would be a nice follow-up.

"Look. If you ask me, I don't think there was a single good reason for all those people to lose their houses in the first place. Was there cancer? Yes. But you know something? Did you notice how people used to just die of it? They didn't count it up the way they do now. That's got to make a difference. I'm not convinced there's any more cancer now than there ever was. In the old days you just went when it was your time."

Hal shrugged. "Exactly." He was foggy on the details of what had happened to the Rosemont neighborhood all those years ago, remembered a few people got sick, and they'd buried the toxins instead of the other options they'd had. That, and some people still believed it was all a hoax.

"Can I trust you to keep something under your hat?"

"Absolutely."

Avery looked at him, eyes narrowed, as if he were mentally measuring his face. "You want an exclusive, don't you? It could be effective, I've been thinking."

"I sure would like that."

"The building permit over near Banes Field isn't even the problem anymore. That's practically a done deal. The only issue is, I've got this lady on my ass. She's been on me in fact for a couple of years now. I don't really know what her deal is, but I heard the husband—supposedly a nice guy—left her. Her name's Lee Knowles. You know her?"

Hal felt the stirring again in his chest, that hope he felt sometimes in church. "Well, she's my neighbor. I sure do know her." Darlene had taught her daughter, maybe, or another one of her kids? That wasn't luck—that was a blessing.

"She actually paid a shitload of money for a study of the ground soil. Just to stop me from doing anything out there. What kind of cup of crazy is that? After the EPA said the soil was cleared. I mean, what's her deal? It's a fragile sort of situation right now. We've got time on our side—no one is thinking of Rosemont anymore. But it's the sort of thing where if she makes a big enough stink, well, nutty as she is, it could affect the sales of my homes." He sighed. "I have half a mind to just take the plans, the contractors, the whole shebang, and buy another piece of land somewhere, figure out some way to write off the loss."

"I don't blame you."

"Just write it off. I'd like to do something for this town though. Really. People need to work."

Hal had been staring at the cross in the windowpane, and

now the words came back to him: *Beloved, I pray that you may prosper.* He was beloved. "You know something, Avery, let me see if I can talk to her. I might be able to make some headway there with my neighbor."

Avery raised an eyebrow. "I keep thinking there must be another side to this. Does she own property somewhere?"

Hal didn't remember anything about the lady except he'd noticed she was good-looking for someone pushing fifty. And she'd kept her dogwood tree up in the front. "Let me find out for you."

This was his way in. Hal had prayed about it, and now he could visualize how it would happen. He'd do this favor for Avery, prove himself worthy of opportunity, and then he'd get the exclusive.

Avery stood up and walked over to an easel holding a large tablet of paper, and he picked up a marker. "Let me draw it for you." He scrawled a long black swath across the bottom. "That's Banes Field, okay? The chemicals, covered up, buried, safe." He picked up a red marker and drew a blocky cluster along the black line. "That's where Rosemont was." He drew arrows. "Now, before they buried the chemicals inside the supersonic plastic, you can see why this area was in trouble, but to my mind, now, even this territory right here is safe. It's safe, and it's dirt cheap." He changed his marker to a green one and drew a giant house hovering just above the red area. "But here, here is where I want Pleasant Forest to be—we're about a quarter of a mile from where the edge of Rosemont used to be. It's even safer than that. Hell, that's why they're letting me build there. And to tell you the truth, I've got my eye on the old Rosemont property too." He drew a smaller green house over the red. He stepped back and nodded at his illustration, turned around with a bounce in his step. "I don't know why they didn't think about it before."

"Well, I guess people are scared off by the lawsuit with Tulver Homes and all that."

"They had that lawsuit because they never told the buyers about Banes Field. The beauty of this plan is that I've got two one-thousand-page binders of evidence from federal agencies clearing Banes Field for human health. All I've got to do is show them the binders and have the buyers sign a release."

"Should anything happen."

"I don't think it will. But look, you never know when you're liable to get another eco-nut trying to forge a connection. I'm not even convinced there was a cause and effect back then, when all the chemicals were still wild and free. We live with chemicals, Hal. Our granddads probably took baths in oil."

Hal pictured his own grandfathers, the one a grocer, the other a claw-fingered locksmith, and he figured Avery's had had more luck. "Well, it's true—oil's a natural commodity."

Avery stood up and ambled around his desk to signal the meeting was over, and Hal looked down at the floor—he felt like he'd forgotten something, his wallet, his briefcase, but no, he'd left all that in the car. Avery shook his hand heartily, then patted his shoulder. "Sure is good to see you, Hal. We should grab a beer sometime."

He needed to make some money badly, but he left Avery's office feeling he should have said a prayer before going in there. He needed to think about how much God wanted to give him.

Driving past the flags of city hall and the colorful flowering bushes of Robertson Park, Hal thought about what Pastor Sparks had asked him to do at their last meeting, to write down on a

card what he hoped to be doing five years from now, to write
down how much money he hoped to be making. And they had
sat there in the pastor's office and prayed over it together. God
wanted him to have a more abundant life, that was clear. Jesus
had kept him from drinking this past year, and the rest would
surely follow. He believed that. He really believed in that. "Amen,"
he said, laying out the plans in his head.

What had happened all those years ago at Rosemont? His
memory was vague, but he knew he'd read about it in the papers,
resented it when the media got involved. The *Houston Chronicle*
wrote it all up, and the place got listed as a Superfund site, a way
to cheapen the landscape and a way for the government to shame
all the companies that had inadvertently polluted. He'd still
been working at the engineering firm back then, and the talk
around the office was about how this was going to take down
property values. It was what happened when people let ideas get
the best of them, ideas instead of real flesh-and-blood people
who needed work. All that hysteria about cancer was mostly
misplaced fear about death—and if you came to the Lord, then,
maybe you weren't afraid of it anymore.

He had almost never seen Lee Knowles leave her house, as he
and the family always did, on Sunday morning. In fact, even
before now, she'd been one of the people he sometimes thought
he should witness to. Now he imagined talking to her calmly
about why she should drop the issue with Banes Field, how her
once-pretty face would open up to him, and she'd begin to trust
him, her big blue eyes softening. He'd knock on her door another
day, or she'd come to his, ask him if he could fix a broken lock or
faucet, and when he came to her house, he'd ask her casually if
she knew Jesus, and she'd look shyly down into her coffee cup

and her eyes would well up, and then he'd offer to take her to church. All the goodness wound up in a ball that just kept rolling and rolling in his mind—he'd get the Avery Taft exclusive, and Lee Knowles, in turn, would start witnessing to others instead of protesting the local housing business.

At dinner that night, Darlene would not eat more than a raw cucumber, and Cully kept looking away from the table to the TV in the den, as if wishing it were turned on to a game. Hal told Darlene about his meeting with Avery, but was careful not to get her hopes up. "I'm going to see what I can do to help him with that sticky situation with the permit."

"Oh, hon. Do you know someone who can get it pushed through?"

"It's already practically in the clear, actually," he said. "It's more a matter of getting Lee Knowles to stop making a fuss."

"Oh, our neighbor over here?"

"That's the one."

"Her girl was real smart and cute—her little girl, real sweet— Just talked too much." Darlene blew a tendril of hair from her face in a sigh. "Lee's gotten odd since then. Can't blame her really. If that happened to me." She shook her head and shuddered. "You know, she died."

"What do you mean?"

"I told you. Her daughter, Jess, the one in my class? She died of a blood disease a while back. Right after everyone ran out of Rosemont."

"You did not tell me that."

"I sure did."

"Well, then, I forgot." He tried hard to remember. He honestly wasn't sure if she told him things and they rinsed over him, or if she imagined she'd told him things and forgot she hadn't. He supposed it didn't matter. But it made him feel crazy, as if she owned whole hours of his life that he'd either lost or she'd invented and labeled as true.

"That's why she's doing all this—it's grief." She was clearing the table.

"Rosemont was years ago now."

"Would it matter if it were Cully?"

"Darlene." But if it had been Cully who'd died, Hal would have found a more constructive way to shuck his sadness. He'd volunteer at the soup kitchen or he'd pray for a sign pointing him to the right action. That land had been rescued and healed. He would never get in the way of building something good. He would never get in the way of people who needed work. He stood up to help with the dishes.

Wiping the towel over the serving dish painted with fish, Hal thought about Lee's daughter. Without a face, she was just another one of Darlene's past students, a series of letters in a name. He couldn't summon much feeling for her, unless he thought of losing his own child. And even then, it was God's will, right? There was a purpose there, somewhere. It was what you did with your suffering afterward that really mattered.

"I think I can talk to her."

"Well, you can sure try." She picked up a glass, pushed a scrubber inside it. "Your mom called today."

He didn't look up from his drying the dish, not wanting to see anything in Darlene's eyes that might depress him.

"She sounded real good. She was playing checkers and even going to the dance class. The nurse said she hadn't missed church all month. And, Hal, she was sharp as a tack, I swear, just like her old self. We should go out there and visit soon."

His mother had started to lose her memory and her manners. He prayed for her in a dutiful way, but didn't like to picture her in full anymore, with her palsied arm, her drooping face. "Sure," he said, not meaning it.

"She misses you, Hal."

"I think she misses you more than me, to tell the honest truth. She talks to you more."

"She's afraid she'll say the wrong thing with you, Hal."

"Mom? Nah."

"She is. She just wants someone to chat with. She was real cheerful."

Darlene let the dishwater out of the sink, and turned to him, placed her hands on his sides. His eyes went to the honey-colored cleavage of her tank top. She seemed sexier tonight for some reason. He was feeling God's abundance, he was feeling the beginning of prosperity.

Cully called over from the table, where he was scooping ice cream from a carton. "Dad, you've got to go. What has it been, like six months?"

"You want to come with, then?"

"Sure, I'll go," he said. The last time they'd visited Rockytop Arms, he'd been loud about how much he hated the place, no matter if he loved his grandma, the smell of urine and laundry detergent and old cafeteria food, and especially the old ladies who were strangers and wanted to touch him. Hal was surprised he'd agreed so easily.

"Alright then, let's make a plan."

Darlene flashed her smile. It had been her idea for Hal to wind his way back to sobriety by learning to do something rather than brood, and funnily enough, though he'd have hated most people to know it, she'd taught him embroidery, how not to prick his finger pulling the needle through the cloth—how to do a knot stitch, a simple stitch, the absurd hoop in his big hand. Darlene made him feel sometimes like a jackass who'd lucked out beyond all reason to end up with such a beauty. And he hadn't been drunk since he finished stitching that crude image of an old man's face, crooked through the eyes. Darlene had framed it and hung it on the wall to remind him. "That's you," she said. "If you make it."

WILLA

SOMETIMES, IF SHE DIDN'T FOCUS on the visions, it was
almost like they weren't there. Yesterday, in the tree outside her
window, Willa saw a small, round, gray woman, reaching up her
arms as if to be held or to praise, but Willa refused her any attention, because there was homework to do, and the woman scared
her; and when she looked up from her calculus, the woman was
gone. The poetry she wrote might be tipping her brain to this angle.

Today she'd stayed after school for the Lit Mag meeting, and
she was the first one there. The classroom with large windows
faced the trees, and now and then, in the breeze, leaves would
brush against the glass. It had always been true that certain
things had to be aligned before she could write a poem, a kind of
clearness in her head like a blank sky, and she had ways of creat-
ing that clarity, staring at the grain of paint in the wall, touching
the curve of each fingernail with the pad of her thumb, and she
could acquire this feeling of being a plant slowly stretching out
leaves, or a creature growing wings in a cocoon. But at night now,
she was afraid to write, because she saw too many not-real things
that in the moment were as real as her hands.

She took out the poem she'd written last year during Texas

history class. Ms. Stinehart said after a test one day, "If you don't learn it, it's all going to die. It's dying anyway of course, but if you don't learn it"—she snapped her fingers—"it's gone." Dani was also in the class. They'd read about the Overland Mail stagecoach trail, friendly Chickasaw Indians, the fire-breathing secessionists, the branding symbols of the big cattle ranchers, Jim Bowie, the Grass Fight outside San Antonio. Whenever she could, Stinehart brought the discussion back to the Battle of the Alamo. She stood up straighter, a wire of rancor in her voice when she mentioned the "Texians" holding out for thirteen days, waiting for reinforcements that would never come. Stinehart was a member of the Daughters of the Republic of Texas, and lowered her voice to say that she herself had helped with the preservation and upkeep of the site, keeping the flora historically accurate and monitoring the wear and tear of tourism. Willa got fascinated by one of the handful of survivors of the Alamo, Susanna Dickinson, whom the Mexican general Santa Anna had allowed to escape with her infant daughter, Angelina. He gave them a blanket and two pesos and sent them to Gonzales to warn the others of what would happen if they continued to revolt.

Willa had written a poem about Susanna on that journey, calling up the landscape to help her—the flat, needling horizon, scrubby grass grown brown in the heat, bluebonnets covering a field like a flock of sparrows, and the vast, secretive space of sky with only God behind it.

Bumpton, with his lumpy pimples, came in the room, and a little later Res, who constantly chewed on the inside of her cheek or clicked her tongue piercing against her front teeth. Willa had really only come to see Ms. Marlowe, their advisor, who arrived last, her deep voice encased in a loose silk tunic. "Alright, everyone, let's get going." As Res read aloud her story about a black-haired stranger who slept during the day, vampired by night, Willa started to yawn. She wondered if the visions she'd started to see might make her a better writer—and then whether painters or sculptors saw imaginary things that seemed momentarily material. Bumpton said Willa's poem was weird and that made it good. Ms. Marlowe talked to them about keeping a record, about writing every day. She read aloud two lines from Willa's poem and said, "Well, that just makes you want to stop chewing your gum and swallow hard."

After the meeting ended, they all shut their notebooks and wandered out of the classroom. Willa, walking down the hall, saw the knot of guys hovering near the doors, drinking cans of Coke, some of them in gym clothes because they were going to football practice, or leaving practice, or waiting for more practice. Her crush, Cully, was standing there among them in his regular clothes, shoulders slumped, arms folded. She walked past them, felt their eyes on her. She pulled in her stomach, felt the tight press of her jeans at the tops of her thighs.

"Hey, Lambert," Cully called out to her.

The hairs on her head prickled, and she stopped. He shot out from the group of guys, grinning, and they seemed to watch him as he moved toward her.

"What's up?" he said.

She liked something about his mouth. "Just coming from Lit Mag. It was lame."

"You're a writer or a photographer?" He was only pretending to be impressed, but she liked that he was pretending.

"Writer, I guess."

A few of the guys were still watching them. Did it mean

she was a joke to them, or did it mean Cully had been talking about her?

"What do you write? Mystery stories?"

"No." She smiled. She wouldn't say "poems" because he'd make fun of her. "Just stuff I'm thinking about."

"Me, I hate writing. Those English papers, shit. You should help me sometime." One of the guys behind Cully snickered, but when she looked over there, they all had their backs to her. "Where are you going now?"

Her mom was supposed to pick her up—and was probably waiting in the parking lot, smoking a cigarette with the window rolled down.

"Just home."

"Huh."

She wanted him to kiss her, someplace where no one would see. He would place his hand on her cheek and draw her close, and she would hold the hard muscle at the top of his arm. Her dad might even approve of Cully because he went to their church, and that somehow made Willa more determined that he should fall in love with her.

"Better get going then," he said, and touched her lightly on the shoulder. She felt the wind go out of her. "Want to come with me out to lunch next week?" He could leave campus because he was a senior, though she'd have to find a way to sneak out.

"Yeah."

"Good."

As she turned away from him, the lockers seemed supernaturally blue and precise, the sun crazy-cornered through the glass doors.

＋

IN HER ROOM, she lay on the bed, watching how the light shot through the leaves just outside the window and dribbled delicate shadows on the wall. She lost track of time, as the small dark shapes shimmied above her and she thought about Cully, the dimples in his cheeks and the slight heaviness in his jaw, which seemed to hold so much unspoken feeling. Small rectangles of light from the curtains shifted on the ceiling, and she heard the air conditioner whir on, her sister shouting something downstairs. Cully's dad was a realtor who'd once shown up drunk to a football game. His mom used to teach the second grade. She knew these facts about him, but from other people, not from what he'd told her himself. He didn't know yet that he needed someone like her, someone who knew how to feel sorrow. Sometimes when she passed his house, flat and caramel colored, the front door hidden around a corner of the porch, she so badly wanted to know what went on inside, the dull brick practically glowed with significance.

She called Dani and told her Cully had asked her out to lunch.

"Oh, Willa, not him. He's such a slime bag." It was the kind of thing she liked to say.

"I think he's nicer than that."

"Define nice."

"Look, I can't help it. I'm going to figure out a way to get past Attendance and go out with him. You've done it—was it that hard?"

"As long as you get back for fifth period, you'll be okay."

After she hung up the phone, the air got too cold, and she slipped under the quilt on her bed, heard cars passing on the street outside, and she could smell herself—deodorant mixed with a milky salt. She felt the weave of her jeans under her palms, and watched the light and shadows mixing on the ceiling, pushed her hand just under the waist of her jeans, where her hip bones made a hollow there, let the tips of her fingers graze the damp cotton between her legs. Then, just above her, the shapes of light swept away, and she saw an old-fashioned camera pressing itself through the plaster, the lens extending itself like a blunt nose. The flash popped, and the light fashioned a lion's mane, a sharp-toothed, open mouth. She pulled her hand out of her jeans, sat up, saw the dirty clothes on the dresser, and when she looked up again, the ceiling was flat.

Her mother knocked on the door and walked right in. "I need you and Jana to clean up the kitchen." Willa still felt the camera hovering over her, though she knew it wasn't there. She couldn't speak. "What's with your hair, missy? This thing sticking up over here." Her mother came over to the bed and pulled a lock of hair to the side of Willa's face.

"I don't know. I was resting."

"Your eye makeup is all over the place too."

"Mom."

"I'm just saying." Lately, her mother acted like there was something different, something wrong and out of place in Willa, as if her mouth held some ugly and mean expression that meant no one else would ever love her.

LEE

AT RUSH'S HOUSE, they drank bourbon. Rush's husband, Tom, clownishly scowled in and out of the room the way he always did, the news turned to mute on the large-screen TV over the fireplace. On the other side of the room, there was a lamp whose base was a cowboy boot, and on the wall behind it, a painting of running horses and a collection of embroidered sayings inside picture frames. Lee tended to let her gaze brush over them, but now her concentration landed on that one she disliked—the smug prayer about accepting what you couldn't change and having the courage to change what you could. The needlepoint ended in a flock of birds. As if every anguish was meant to disappear into *wisdom to know*.

Rush pulled her feet up under her on the black leather couch. With her blue minnow-shaped eyes, and her triangular cheekbones, she had a grand beauty and a bawdy, gap-toothed smile. Her breasts were heavy now, in her billowy sheer blouses, her long blond hair always shiny and straight, like her daughters' (there were bottles of shampoo and blow-dryers crowding the shelves of the bathrooms). "You ever see Charlotte anymore? I swear she saw me and walked right past at the school the other day. Her girl Willa waved though."

"Char's eyesight always was bad."

"Or it's her manners."

Lee remembered the last time she'd seen Char's daughter, a sweet-looking, serious girl with big dark eyes. She'd come in for an appointment with Doc, and she'd been carrying one of those god-awful paperbacks with explosions on the cover that try to get people to think the world will be done with by Christmas.

"At least since she got Christian," said Rush. "I mean, we all used to be so close. You know what I call her church, that Victory Temple? The way they go on about things, I call it the Viciousness Temple." She laughed. "You ever talk to her anymore?"

"Not really. I don't think she hates me. She's just waiting for me to be saved."

"Not going to happen." Rush pulled at the jade pendant of her necklace, raced it back and forth on the chain. "Hey, Lee, are you alright? Your mouth is doing that thing."

She wasn't sure how much she wanted to say.

"You've been going out there again, haven't you?" said Rush. "Goddamnit, they buried that poison. And what good does it do you? Probably dangerous even being out there all by yourself." She stood up to turn on the radio on the bureau.

"I saw something different this time."

"I bet you did." Rush flung herself back on the couch, drew her knees up to her chin. "I just feel like I have to trust people in order to live, don't you? I mean, me and Tom aren't moving, and you're not either. I don't want to spend the rest of my life fretting about stuff we can't even see."

Rush's youngest girl ran in and out of the room, asking for

nail polish. Rush addressed her by only slightly moving her head in the girl's direction, and told her not to interrupt adult conversation. She had an imperial way of sitting tall and calm, while the rabble rushed around her.

"Do you want some chips? Or I have some really good Hershey's."

"No." Lee savored the bourbon in her mouth. "I'm just saying, there might be news."

Rush looked away, brought a cigarette to her lips, let it flick upward before she lit it. "Whatever you say."

"Jack called again yesterday."

"Honey." Rush had a way of communicating her disapproval with just a look—as if her thought were too ugly to actually name, and this made it consequential.

"He still likes to talk about her with me. It's his thing. That's why he calls."

"What it is, is he still feels married to you. I don't care if it's been years. Takes a while for that to go away for some people. I don't care if he has a girlfriend."

"But for me, it's all gone. Except when he calls. And then I'm reminded. Actually, I kind of depend on it. I think it keeps me sane."

"Can't be nice for his girlfriend, though."

Just then, Rush's teenage son, lanky, stiff legged, came in the room. "Bryce, say hello." Rush's face changed, her cheeks filled out and lifted, her eyes widened, fixed on him. Lee remembered that feeling of brightening and opening as soon as Jess entered the room, everything flowing in her daughter's direction.

"Going over to the Lawbournes'," he said, fumbling through the things on a table and picking up a set of jangling keys.

"Uh-uh, mister. No, you are not."

Bryce was sixteen, but he looked younger, a smatter of light freckles on his nose, his cheeks smooth. "Are you kidding me, Mom? I can't go out in the middle of the afternoon?"

"That's right. You're grounded. You're not going anywhere."

Bryce sighed, threw the keys down on the floor, and mumbled audibly, ". . real pain in the ass!"

"Excuse me?" Rush started to stand.

"I said *whatever*." Bryce stomped out to the hallway.

Rush flung up her hand and turned back to Lee. "Sorry. Teenagers! They act ugly and then about a minute later, they want something from you. Don't you wish they'd just grow up?" She touched Lee's sleeve. "Sorry. I wasn't thinking."

"No," said Lee. "Don't worry about it. You're right."

Jess had actually been mostly well behaved, except that night during the winter after they moved—just before she started the chemo—when she came home at 3:00 a.m., drunk and stumbling out of a boy's car. Lee watched from the window as Jess wove her way inside, but instead of going to bed, she went straight out back to her tree in the yard and threw her purse over the flowers there. By the time Lee got outside, Jess was practically asleep. Lee rattled Jess's shoulder. "Goddamnit. You're sick. Do you hear me? You can't do this."

In the dark, her daughter's face looked monstrous, fuchsia lipstick smeared, black running beneath her eyes, one cheek strangely twisted up and scraped. "I can do it. That's the point, Mom."

And then Lee said the thing she'd regret. "You selfish little bitch. You're stinking drunk, when I'm breaking my neck trying to take care of you?"

"Then don't." Jess wobbled as she stood up.

"You don't mean that." Lee helped her inside, and Jess fell over her arm and gagged, but nothing came up. She gagged again, and spit fell from her mouth in a long string. Lee settled her on the couch and put a big black pot on the floor near her head. "Goddamnit, your dad and I love you so much." She was trying to soften what she'd said before, to take it back, but Jess was already asleep, her mouth gaped open against the silk-upholstered pillow.

Now loud drums pounded from inside Bryce's room. "Good Lord," Rush said. "He's practicing. Why in the hell we ever said yes to that, I don't know. You wouldn't believe the mouth on that one." Lee remembered how their families used to gather, the adults playing cards, their children outside riding small, motorized cars around and around the house, Bryce chasing the older girls.

Rush rose from the couch, went over to the radio, and turned up the volume for the Hank Williams outlaw song. "Let me get you some more bourbon."

That night, Lee couldn't fall asleep, wrestled with something she couldn't quite remember that Professor Samuels had said about the water table. He'd had a mild stroke a couple of months ago, and she hadn't been able to consult with him for a while, though his wife had written that he was doing okay.

When she finally did fall asleep, she dreamed of Jack and Jess, as she often did. They were floating away in a large boat that was also at times a house, the water turned to land and back to water again. She didn't recognize the house, but it was unremarkable except for the log crashed into its roof, which occasionally caught on fire. She knew how to keep it from igniting, and how to keep the boat from sinking, but the problem was communicating all this to Jack and Jess, who waved to her from the deck or the rooftop, but couldn't hear anything she said. Again and again, she wrote down messages and carefully folded them into paper airplanes that she threw in their direction, but they didn't seem to notice.

†

Doc had offered Lee the job, part-time at his office, years ago. Thinking she was broke but not wanting to embarrass her, he'd said, "I just want to keep an eye on you is all." He let her do her Banes Field "side work" at the office. His sister had lost her home in Rosemont, and Doc believed in her project, but he never would say it publicly.

That afternoon, while Lee was in the back, confirming the appointment schedule, Ash Bernard came to the reception window. He had no hair, but pink scales covered the entire globe of his scalp, with ridges and continents of lighter pink against the oceans of darker red. His ears stuck out from his head, and because they were oddly clear and untouched by the disease, it seemed that he might only have the sense of hearing. Or she wished that, because though his eyes were nearly swollen shut, she was afraid he might see the shock in her face at how bad it had got.

"Hi, there." He nodded.

"Ash, how are you?" He carried a box of cigars and wore a blue tie with yellow sailboats.

"Hey, pretty lady." His voice seemed weirdly upbeat. "I've got an appointment. Should be about three o'clock." His mouth looked like a wound.

"If you could just update these forms for us," she said, handing him a clipboard through the sliding window. Doc was signaling to her from the back, where Ash couldn't see—that he was running late.

"I sure will." Ash reminded Lee of a dapper, friendly snake. "Can you tell me, is it safe to park on the street right there or am I liable to get a ticket?"

"Oh, you'll be fine," said Lee.

Ash went to take a seat in the waiting room. He was one of Doc's regulars, a sad case of acute psoriasis, brought on, she suspected, by women trouble. He didn't always look that bad, though, and if she just focused on his eyes, she could speak to him naturally.

After Ash went in to see Doc, Sandy Clouter called. Though she'd moved away to Memphis, she kept in close contact with her Rosemont friends and often called Lee with updates. Sandy seemed lonely, now that her kids had gone off to college. She clung to the gossip and to the timbre of her own voice a bit too much. "I wanted to let you know—it's real sad," Sandy said. "Nick Busby has kidney failure too. I'm sorry, but that man was juicing carrots and veggies all the time, racing around on his bike. He should be healthy," said Sandy. "Shouldn't he?"

Lee told her she'd add his name to the list. There were so many chemicals in Banes Field, the EPA couldn't even name them all—who really knew what the risks had been?

That day the phone rang surprisingly often—the woman with a sensation that felt like "tiny beads rolling up and down her skin," the man who had a mole as big as a nickel on the top of his head, the woman who wanted to know what Doc could do about the worry wrinkles between her eyes. In the midst of all this, Professor Samuels's wife called. "He wanted me to tell you he can still direct John in the lab and get soil samples read."

"How is he?"

"Oh, he's getting stronger. Stabilized. His talking's still slurred, but I can understand him. He wants to get back to work, soon as he can."

Lee had packed the recent samples in a box and put them in the trunk of her car—eight mismatched jelly jars with cheerful gingham on their metal tops and masking tape labels for their locations. "Tell him to just rest and get better," she said. "And then I've got some photographs to show him."

At the end of the day, Lee went in the back and restocked the cotton swabs and hand sanitizer. She turned off the lights in the waiting room, gathering up the old encyclopedias and *Texas Monthly*'s that had been scattered from the reading table.

She was about to leave when she saw the phone's blinking light in the dark office. It was Mayor Wallen, finally. He said he'd been out to Rosemont, and they'd even sent a few other men out there too—experts—and none of them had found anything.

It was as if he'd reached through the phone and shoved her back in the chair. "Well," she said. "That's impossible."

"Lee, you know what it looks like, don't you?" She thought of his long horse teeth that he'd bare when he laughed, how he'd smelled of sweet tea the last time she'd been in his office. His voice was gentler than usual. "You have to remember there was a lot of cleanup after they demolished the houses, and with the storm, I don't know, it probably got moved around. I'm fairly certain this was just a case of some debris."

So many years ago now, that man in Rosemont, Bob Etson, had stood outside his house with a megaphone yelling, "Stop driving down our property values!" He'd stayed put, right up to the end, not believing the "nonsense about chemicals," and a few years later, he died of liver cancer.

In the beginning, even Lisa McHugh had insisted to Lee that the sludge had been planted by O'Bresley Realtors, who wanted to drive down the value of their homes, so the land could be repurchased and sold for an exorbitant price. "Cal heard it all at work," she said. "He thinks there's a spy or two living on these streets, reporting back." But her voice got flinty and stern as it did when she talked about "the blacks" who'd moved in on Berry Street. "It's a shame. We're not going in for all that hype about it being poison. You can't believe what these folks will say to try to get something from you." The people at the end of Sawyer Street refused to let their homes be razed; they thought they might one day want to come back.

Apparently, property values trumped everything, still. Lee tried to muffle her anger. "Mayor Wallen, it's right where they buried the container, according to the cleanup plan. I looked at the document."

"Huh. But that thing was buried at fifty feet. It wouldn't come up so easily out of the ground."

"The rain did it. It pushed it on up."

"That's what you think, huh? Well." She heard something slam in his vicinity. "Be my guest. Go take a look for yourself. There's nothing out there but empty land waiting to be put to good use."

✝

SHE PARKED THE CAR near the chain-link fence and put the hazard lights on. As she walked out under the sky, the wind whipped at the brush and weeds. Women worried too much about how they might get mirrored back to the world, how they might be judged. Well, her mirror had cracked. Let them arrest her for trespassing. Twenty minutes later, she located the place, the survey stakes constellated around her. She was sure. But now there was nothing to see but dried mud and flecks of weeds.

She dug for an hour or so, until her biceps felt as if they were being stabbed by small knives, and she couldn't lift the shovel anymore. The hole was only about a foot deep. She hadn't hit anything solid yet. The crickets came out and chattered. Her feet felt heavy. Her body ached. And she'd have to excavate the whole field to be sure. Hell, she'd need a bulldozer.

When she looked up, there was the black ring of an old tire, a scatter of stones, patches of brown grass. The air looked dusty now that it was dusk, and it was getting harder to see. Pain revolved around her arms. Her palms were chafed from gripping the wooden handle of the shovel, and there was a cut on her wrist. She stared at the turned dirt, got down on her knees, and reached into the hole, swiping away the dirt at the bottom, feeling around for the flat plane of plastic.

She dug for another hour. She pitched the shovel into the ground, pushed it in deeper with her boot, and lifted up a shovel of dirt, two shovels of dirt, threw it behind her. She didn't even worry anymore about what the toxic shit might do to her. It was too late for that. Either it got her or it didn't. When the hole was the size of a small bathtub, she heard Jess's voice in the sound of the digging, *Mom, Mom, Mom.*

DEX

AT THE GAME, DEX paced the sidelines. It helped to count steps, to push his hands into his jeans pockets beneath his loose jersey, because he didn't like to show his nerves. He felt as if the crowd was looking down at him from the bleachers, staring a hole through him, and he had to remind himself that it wasn't him they were watching, but the green-lit field and Scott Gilt lofting a beautiful pass.

Coach Salem called him over. "Go warm up Teak—I'll send him in next quarter."

Dex signaled to Teak, and Teak came over so Dex could check the tape on his knees, and then Dex started him loosening up. It was the third game of the season, and they'd barely won the first two. He tried to watch the game out of one eye while he helped Teak get ready. Last week, he'd had to go and help Louder off the field twice, and ice down and wrap up a sprained knee on the sideline. He was always at the ready for injuries, and it kept him on edge, a tiny alarm clock in his chest that might at any moment go off. There was a totality to these nights too, the huge black sky, the unblinking white lights, the band's horns and drums, which made the field seem heavy and fraught—the enormity of the past and the infinity of the future about to crash together any moment.

Dex was aware that people thought a student trainer was only the sad shadow of a guy who couldn't play football himself. But he actually liked riding back from games on the bus with the coaches, overhearing their decisions about drop-in-a-bucket plays and power sweeps and the Gilt Special. Coach Salem had invited him to be a trainer because he'd known Dex's dad, and Dex liked the bristled sternness of Salem—even if it was hard to read his face.

The Mustangs handily trounced the other team, and it felt like revenge or praise for the hurricane, the scoreboard flashing into higher and higher numbers under HOME, the band blaring, the crowd's howls and applause almost like a living thing itself, about to take off and stomp down the bleachers and out into the roads.

After the game, it was his job to account for the equipment in the field house, and he needed to tend to Hershel's newly sprained ankle. Hershel said the whole time, "It's okay, I got it," then winced whenever he tried to put weight on it. "Thanks, man," he said, after finally giving in and letting Dex retape it. He was one of the decent ones, not exactly a friend, but someone whose playing Dex could honestly admire, because off the field, he didn't talk shit.

Dex sorted the dirty uniforms and checked the lockers. After he'd changed his clothes, the players were already gone, and Coach Salem was turning out the lights, "Come on, son." He followed Dex out. It was just beginning to get cool at night, but not enough to wear a jacket.

Salem walked Dex to the parking lot, nodded to him before

he hitched himself up into his truck. He wasn't going home to his wife because she was dead. Cancer was the rumor Dex had heard. What did Salem do at night? It was difficult to imagine him watching TV or sleeping. Off the field, he was a mystery.

From habit and because he didn't want to go home yet, Dex drove over to the laundromat in the dark Stones Throw shopping center parking lot, where he knew some players and other guys would be, drinking hidden beers. When he got there he was disappointed not to see Weeks's car, but he pulled his truck up behind the others anyway, and took out one of the beers he'd stashed under his seat.

Cully Holbrook sat alone on the hood of his truck holding his mouth that way—as if he knew some secret you wanted to know. "Hey, Dex." There was a cell phone in his hand.

For some reason Dex had yet to fathom, Cully was always friendly, but that didn't make Dex like him. "Nice win, huh? You'd think we'd have given them at least one, just to keep things interesting. I swear, I just got bored after a while."

"Yeah."

They were quiet for a minute as Dex popped his beer and poured it into an old coffee cup he kept in his truck. The coffee mug read # ONE DAD, and when he found it in the back of the cabinet, he felt he should get rid of it, but instead threw it into the cab of his truck.

"Nice!" said Cully, holding up his beer covered in a brown sack. "Cheers." Cully bragged as if he needed to cover something up. Dex almost wanted to feel sorry for him.

"Well, here's to you," said Cully. "Looks like your truck could use some work." He nodded at the gash in the side of the bed, where Dex had rammed into a light pole in a parking lot.

"Yeah, someday," said Dex, shrugging.

"My cousin's shop does good work. Spiton's in Alvin."

"Have to keep that in mind."

"I could get you a deal."

"Huh."

Cully was probably waiting for a girl to call him back. For some reason, one of those things another guy couldn't see—the females liked him—a possum grin on his face, and he was cocky in that way, tall and rangy, looking as if there were something on his tongue that he might or might not spit out.

Dex nodded good-bye, then walked over to the group of guys leaning against one car or another. Only Trace acknowledged him. "Hey, Dex, my man." A bottle cap pinged on the pavement. Dex leaned against the hood where Trace was. "Hey."

Through the window of the laundromat, in the fluorescent lights, a slumped-over woman was putting coin after coin into a washing machine. The sign on the window said WASH 'N DRY in letters like soapsuds. Underneath his nervousness, he felt a familiar dull rage in his forehead, and savoring a sip of beer, he wondered why he'd even bothered. Weeks was supposed to show up—maybe he'd be there in a minute.

The talk fell to silence, and Scotty, wide and squat, with a big smile of horsey teeth, started singing a George Jones song. His hand strummed just over his huge belt buckle.

"Go, Scotty," said Trace. The other guys sniffed, shuffled their feet, pulled away from the cars, then leaned back again, so they wouldn't have to join in.

Trace kept talking. "So me and Scotty went down to the old golf course right after the hurricane—to that place way out from the houses near where the sixteenth hole used to be—it's all grown over, the sand trap's gone, but the hills are still there, little ones, so you can go up fast and fly." Trace always talked so meticulously about mudding, as if it were his sole occupation, the reason he'd been put on earth. "And, man, it was good. We got just the right lift, right, Scotty?"

"Damn straight."

"Then Angie puked." The guys laughed. "Girls are always asking me, 'Take me mudding, take me four-wheeling.'"

Lawbourne had a toy cap gun, and he was shooting the caps at the ground, the ashy smell snapping up in the air around them.

"You know what?" said Dex. "Once I went over off Veemer Road, where those Rosemont houses used to be. Weeks noticed that the gate wasn't locked, and we drove right in. No hills, but it's a great big stretch of nothing." That night, he and Weeks hadn't even been drinking. They were just on their way home from the movies, and the ground was wet, so they decided to stop and give it a try. Weeks was laughing so hard he was snorting, and Dex's hands burned against the rubber padding on the steering wheel. As they churned through the mud, looking straight out the windshield, the stars and blackness whipped over them like a wild blanket, and they let the back wheels fan out, raising splatters like huge ripped curtains.

"Was that before or after you stole the mailman's clothes?" said Scotty.

Dex looked down at his blue work shirt and pants from the thrift shop. "After." That was always his way with these guys—deadpan.

Lawbourne shot the cap gun into the air, a flash of toy silver. He shot it again, with a determined look—actually aiming for something, and the smoke rose up in the dark.

"No, we went out there too once," said Trace. "A bunch of us, people sliding around in the back. Shit. If you can get through the gate, you can drive all over that place. We followed this one road all the way back into the woods, and then the girls got scared."

Dex felt something in the back of his throat but didn't know how to say it. And didn't want to waste his words with this crowd anyway. He knew from his dad how petroleum could make people sick—he knew all the right precautions to take if you worked with it. Those oil residues in Banes Field had been buried and sealed up, the way they were supposed to be, and now the place was only gnarly land, good for mudding and not much else.

"It was too bad because, you know, we were thinking of taking girls inside one of the ruined houses, nice and empty. There's toilets and staircases—all kinds of shit," said Brad Razer, a pocket of Skoal caught in his cheek. Suddenly Dex could smell the menthol. He'd never been inside one of those abandoned houses, but he'd heard people had left TVs, clothes, chairs, and Weeks claimed he'd found bottles of perfectly good whiskey inside a metal cabinet.

Bishop Geitner, who didn't play but somehow was friends with all of them, came over holding out a bowl full of pills. "The blue ones are Ritalin, the orange are Klonopin, the green Xanax. Take your pick, pricks." He had a face like an angry bird, a sharp small beak of a nose, and small dark eyes, a mouth that disappeared when he wasn't talking. He stood there, stringy and average height, with the football players. Dex wasn't interested in taking whatever someone had stolen out of his mom's medicine cabinet. Beer worked just fine.

He'd heard about what Bishop and Trace had done the other

night when two goats escaped from a farm and somehow ended up on the sidelines of the football field, but he didn't believe, no matter how drunk they were, that they'd really bash in the goats' heads with bats. He believed the part about setting their tails on fire, farting around with cigarette lighters maybe, but he didn't believe Bishop and Trace would actually beat them. There were jokes that they'd fucked the goats first, but he didn't believe that either.

Trace grabbed a pill, and a few of the other guys gathered around Bishop, who held his head back as if he wore a heavy crown.

Cully had a girl with him now in the cab of his truck. In the shadows, Dex could just see that her head looked tiny against the passenger seat, but when Cully opened the door and the light went on, Dex saw her face, mouth open, laughing, sharp, fake-looking eyebrows.

"Fucking Cully. What's he do?" said Lawbourne.

Dex shrugged.

"He's got, like, I don't know." Lawbourne shook his head, sipped his beer, and stumbled a little forward.

"Maybe he's just a good liar."

"Damn. I'd like to learn if that's all it is."

An invisible thing seemed to crowd in the dark around them, as if despite all the space across this sprawl of asphalt there wasn't enough room for all of them to be there. They started to talk about girls then, who'd sent which naked picture, because you couldn't see the girls' faces, only their racks—they were shouting over one another—and Dex started to walk back to his truck because it didn't seem like Weeks was going to show up after all.

Suddenly, guys started making goat sounds and laughing.

Trace was following Dex, so drunk or high that he walked in a very slow, jangly way, careful not to spill out of himself.

"Got a bone to pick with you, Dex."

"What's that, Trace?"

"You told the coach."

"No, I didn't. I don't know what the hell you're talking about. I don't talk to the coach about you."

"No one else would do it." Bishop came over to them, but he could barely keep his balance. "Do you know how much shit we're going to get for this? How many miles my buddy's going to have to run?"

"Hey, I heard the story from someone, but I didn't really believe it. You want to go beat up goats at night, that's your problem."

Cully's truck streaked out of the parking lot then, the red taillights straggling behind it, the motor gunning.

Bishop, Trace, and now Brad and a couple of others stood around Dex.

"Come on, man. Dex wouldn't do that," said Lawbourne. He called over to the other truck, where some guys stood smoking. "Hey, Hershel! Dex is an honest man, right?"

"Damn straight!" Hershel called back, holding up his beer.

"Bullshit," said Bishop. "I'm not even on the goddamn team, and I wouldn't care except you're messing with Trace." He grabbed Dex's arm and squeezed it.

Dex shook him off. "Get the hell away from me. I'm leaving."

Lawbourne said, "Bishop, come on. Don't be an asshole."

Dex walked as slowly as he could over to his truck. There was laughter behind him. He couldn't tell if it was the joke after the tension explodes or if they were laughing at him walking away.

He got in his truck, shaken, and turned on the radio loud. He pulled out of the parking lot methodically, because he didn't want to seem in a hurry. He drove for half an hour through the extra-dark streets, stalling before going home, past the mansions on Sunrise Drive, down Riverback Avenue, where the old trees hung overhead, no one else on the roads. He circled around to the intersection where the gas station was still lit up and turned onto 2351, where he passed an occasional car, and a billboard with a vodka girl, smiling down as if she knew him. He was on his way to Houston and would soon turn around at the San Jacinto exit, so he could go back home. This was the time of night when drunks rammed their cars into telephone poles, when guys ended up thrown out on the side of the road, vomiting, or got lost somewhere out in Pasadena where you could get drugs in baggies at the closed-down and abandoned drive-in, right under the giant plastic man with one hand broken off. But for now, just driving forward made him feel okay again—he'd get his currency back from Bishop and Trace. Headlights mopped the black road ahead of him, and the overpass arched in the distance. Dex tried to think about what his dad would say about all of this, but nothing came to mind

LEE

Lee met Jack in the ninth grade when she'd moved from Beaumont with her mother to a tiny apartment over by the Perry's department store. He felt sorry for her at lunch, sitting all by herself, and brought his sandwich over to say hello, and he was so friendly it took twenty minutes for her to believe in it. Jack knew nearly everyone, his parents having lived in town for decades before he was born, but she didn't have another conversation with Jack for two years, when they found themselves, one day, throwing birdseed from a float in the homecoming parade.

They almost got married right after high school—the spring after she'd found her mother passed out in her car in a parking lot in daylight—but they decided to wait. They both went to the University of Houston, spent weekends at the beach in Galveston, where Jack rented a house on stilts that stood right in the bay. They'd been walking on the shore, water lapping up against the hard sand, sunburned and sweaty, when Lee's mother, in her house twenty miles away, walked up the stairs and died of an aneurysm. On their stroll that morning, Lee found three whole sand dollars, their middles still thick under the stamp of the clover, their thin edges uncrushed, and as her feet skimmed through the beery foam of the water's edge and Jack walked beside her, singing badly, she'd felt a peace that she would only remember long after she heard the news. If it had happened that her mother had died from the drinking, Lee would have blamed herself, but the way it occurred, she didn't blame anyone.

She moved into the house with Jack's family, and two years later, when Jack got a job, they got married. Neither of them had planned on staying in Friendswood, but that was how it had turned out. Jack liked feeling famous, he joked, walking around a town where everyone knew him. Lee liked it less, hating put-on cheerfulness, but she had friends, people like Char and Rush and Maisie Rodgers, whom she'd gone to school with, who'd got married or started businesses nearby.

She certainly never thought of it as an oil town, as a place with tainted air or soil. People rode horses on the shoulder of the road. Kids fished in the creeks. The woods were still uncharted, and unnamed species of trees still grew there. Back then, you had to drive for twenty minutes before you saw the highway.

She and Jack were outdoors a lot in those years because their first place, before the Rosemont house, was so small. They strolled along pastures where the cows watched them steadily as they munched or turned away; they took long walks out along the dirt roads where the horse farms were. Jack had a friend who would let Lee ride his horse out all the way practically to Pearland, while Jack hung back, smoking, by the crude wooden fence. She remembered how she and Jack sat outside at night in those days, drinking beers on the hammock, or wandering the side roads, bottles tucked inside their jackets.

The night Lee guessed that Jess was conceived, she and Jack jumped over the fence to the fig orchard where Jack had worked as a boy, and they lay down under a tree. Her back pressed against soft broken fruit and leaves, and when he looked down at her, his grin seemed to spread against the sky.

Jack, smelling of sweat and beer, pulled off her shirt and reverently laid his whole hand over her breast as if he were swearing an oath. She pushed up her skirt, felt the soft hair on his legs against her smooth thighs. That night she wanted him, but more than that, she wanted to go through him, into the vine unfurling on the barbed-wire fence, into the branches holding green fruits like small charms. "Relax," Jack kept saying. "There's no one else here."

The open mouths of crushed figs pressed against the backs of her thighs, and she wanted to give herself over to the humidity and green. It was an odd lust, spreading into her fingertips, the fig trees in their rows; the moon; the dark, fecund air; the moist dirt; the ocean twenty miles away.

All during her pregnancy, Lee said that must have been the night the baby was conceived, though there was no way of telling for sure.

✝

LEE'S CAR WAS IN THE SHOP, so she had to walk the mile to city hall, but she planned to stop at Maisie Rodgers's house on the way to drop off some samples from Doc. Going along the side of the main road, busy now with four lanes of traffic, she felt exposed in the grass along the curb, but there was no other route. Cars honked at her, and she looked up to see a blurry stranger giving her the finger or a shadowed friend waving hello.

She rehearsed what she'd say at the city council meeting, going over the technical information in her head. Though she had the photographs, evidence was no guarantee they'd listen.

She crossed at the busy intersection of Friendswood Drive and the highway, cars humming all around her as she waited for the light. She crossed, found the sidewalk next to the bakery's parking lot, and kept her eyes trained on the trees, thick trunked and wild leaved above. She walked past the firehouse, saw the remnants of the homecoming float over to the side, blue-and-white crepe paper still stuck in the chicken wire.

Maisie Rodgers lived now on a road that ran alongside Robertson Park, but years ago, she'd lived on Crest Street, the area closest to where Taft wanted to build again. She came to the door in fur slippers and jeans, and said hello with her wide smile and sleepy eyes. "I brought you something," Lee said, handing her the small bag of tubes and bottles.

"Thanks, honey." Maisie hugged her. "I've been using that last thing Doc gave me, and I think it's working." She touched the edge of her chin.

"Well, there's mostly just lotions in there, but there's a fading cream he said you could try." In the living room, the air conditioner droned loudly over the matched white furniture and photographs of Maisie's daughter, Laura, in her dance gear—fringed halters and cowboy hats. Laura had been Jess's best friend, and now she was twenty-six, a professional dancer at the big rodeo shows. Lee had gone with Maisie and Ben once to see her performance with ladders and white flags.

"I ran into Rush at the wine bar. She said she's trying to get you out more." Maisie turned her face under the window light, and Lee saw the scars beneath her makeup, on her chin and cheek. The rash had afflicted her months before they'd proven anything about Rosemont, and the scars, despite all Doc's prescriptions, had never quite gone away.

"I've just been working a lot," said Lee.

Maisie had news about Joe Stacken, who'd gone to a party down in Mexico weeks ago and still wasn't back, and Ruthie Winters, who'd got so angry at her mother, she threw her cell phone into the pool.

When Lee told her about spotting Avery Taft's survey stakes, about the photos of the container, Maisie said, "Are you shitting me?" She shook her head. "Back in the summer, I heard someone from the EPA was coming around to see Rosemont folks again. He went to see the Shipleys, the Browns, and I think even over to Pasadena to see the Juarezes."

"And I can't even get anyone at the EPA to return my calls."

"I thought he was just asking about how they were doing, checking in, but maybe he was looking for something more? I don't know. Maybe he had a line on Taft? I just thought it was, you know, same old, same old. They have to cover themselves, right? I should have told you, but we went right up to Mobile after the hurricane, had to get all new drywall down here, so I haven't been around."

"Do you know the guy's name?"

"No. But I can give you everyone's addresses. That was my street—all those people. Every year, we still send Christmas cards." She was smiling broadly as she rummaged in the drawer to get paper and pen. "I wish we could see them all more often."

When Lee left, Maisie stood at the front door. "Where the hell's your car?"

╈

AT CITY HALL, Lee always tried to sit near the front, so that she'd be noticed. During the tedious talks about zoning and property taxes, she fidgeted on the folding metal chair and watched the faces of those men on the dais—the mayor throat-clearing and slicing the air with a flat palm, the lead councilman surveying them all from above with that thin smile. It was rare that she managed to get her concerns on the agenda anymore, but during the time set aside for other business at the end, she could usually say a few things about her research before adjournment, and maybe two or three out of thirty people would listen.

An older man she didn't know sat next to her—he kept staring at her shirt.

"Call to order." Mayor Wallen sighed behind the podium, but she didn't believe in his feigned exhaustion or in his modest blue jacket and khakis. She believed in the black deadness of his eyes.

Avery Taft sat at the end of her row, his cowboy boots jutted out in front of him on the floor. They'd put him on the agenda to "report on the commercial viability of the former Rosemont site and its area." No one would prosecute, but it might be illegal that he'd already surveyed the land, even though the "debate" had been last month, and the official vote wasn't until November.

There was a report on zoning for a liquor store, a school voucher. The way these meetings worked, you'd think no one ever listened to anything. For years, it had seemed that way, but Lee had made little cracks in the system, little marks they couldn't easily erase. She knew that room better than she'd known any classroom in her school years, the stacked photographs of the earliest football teams—1939, 1940, 1941—those earnest unguarded faces staring out, trying to look tough, their baby faces exposed under shiny, neatly oiled-back hair. The American flag on the stand. The walls that had once been cinder block but were now covered in fake wood paneling with strange patterns like stretched-out faces in the grain.

Councilman Burns, with his large, blunt face like a bull's, introduced a representative from the EPA, a Ms. Dawson, and he leered as she stepped up to the dais in her tight teal suit.

"Good afternoon." With her pert blond pageboy, Ms. Dawson had one of those overly animated faces, the wide eyes with brows that shot up just for hello, the enthusiastic *and*s and *but*s, the excavated smile.

"I'm here at the request of the city council, to address Taft Property's request to build next to the old Rosemont site. As you know, that area, which had been listed as a Superfund site, has been treated with the method of burying the chemicals in approved containers." Lee still hoped that in the end, those photographs meant she'd won something. Ms. Dawson went on with the official line, repeated the version of history Lee had heard a hundred times, her words clipped and chirpy, as if it had all been good news.

"We've done extensive testing, and we've found with our scoring systems for near-term decisions, there's no real risk to human health from these chemicals. We've done a cumulative risk assessment choosing a subset of environmental stressors. And now we can confidently give permission to build on those adjoining acres." She seemed too sunny to be human.

Lee raised her hand. "I have some new evidence that gives a

different picture of things." She grabbed her photos of the container and started walking to the front of the room.

The woman held up her hand to stop her. "Excuse me?"

"I have some photographs here that prove something else might be going on, plus I have evidence from a soil study last year showing that concentrations of benzene have actually only declined five percent since the chemicals were buried. I have charts and data on the cancer rates of residents, most of them living within two miles of Rosemont. They are five times the national average. How the hell can this not be a threat to human health?"

The woman nodded aggressively, her mouth screwed tight. "I have not seen your report. Can you have that sent to me? What we are saying is that we can't determine that the small amount of chemicals still being released from the former Rosemont area have any effect on human health. Cancer rates, as you know, can be deceptive. There are many factors . . . other health stressors such as nutrition, smoking habits, an older population."

Lee held up two photographs, and turned to show them to people in the metal folding chairs, some looking bored, some grimacing in alarm. "Do you know what these are? These are photographs of a rogue container of toxins that came up out of the soil. Pushed right up from the water table. After the hurricane. Right there, next to the building site."

"May I ask how you got those?" said Ms. Dawson, smoothing her sleeve.

"Well, do you really want to know? To hell with it. I broke into Banes Field, and I saw it myself, took the pictures with my camera."

Mayor Wallen stood up from his seat and stomped the dais. "Ms. Knowles." He directed his gaze over the crowd as if looking to signal someone. "Your trespassing aside, would you let Ms. Dawson give her report?"

Lee used to be able to act nice, to command a crowd, but she'd been worn down by so much flatness, so much indifference. "I'll let her do it alright," she said. "I only want to add to it. Look, I'm not a scientist, it's true. But I have data. I've collected it. And, goddamnit, I can look at things with a degree of common sense."

"Alright, there," said Councilman Burns, holding up his hand. "We're very familiar with your work, Ms. Knowles. And we've established that there was no container on the site the day after you supposedly took those photographs." His skin seemed to have a green tone.

"Well, familiar. I'd say so," she said.

Mayor Wallen would not sit down. "I don't guess you heard me."

Lee wished that she had something more. "How many times have I been here saying the same thing? Twenty times? Thirty times? A hundred times? Well, that's right, and I'll say it again. You're looking at me like I'm angry, well, you're goddamn right, I'm angry. Because no one goddamn listens." When she sat down again, the chair scraped the floor.

Ms. Dawson looked back at Burns, and he nodded and winked. She addressed Lee directly. "We have our study. I'd be happy to take a look at your results."

Lee hadn't been able to keep her cursing in check, and now even her reasonable tone made her sound like a nutcase. "I'll be happy to send it to you, Ms. Dawson. Just give me the address, not just the general EPA one, but yours in particular."

Ms. Dawson held her face very still, then calmly blinked her eyes. "I will do that."

When the meeting broke up, she met Avery Taft in the hallway as she came out of the ladies' room. He was tall, getting pudgy around the middle, but his ruddy, sharp face bore a greasy, unlined sheen. "Ms. Knowles, I sure do like your snazzy shirt."

"No, you don't."

"And I sure wish you'd stop hurting my business." The pitch of his voice went higher at the end, a question that wasn't a question. He'd adopted a flourished, slightly feminine way of talking. "People need work. Times are hard. And, damn it, they still need houses. Affordable ones."

"They don't need to get sick ten years down the line because Avery Taft sold them a pretty colonial."

"Weren't you just sitting there in the meeting, or am I mistaken? Did you not hear the report from the lady? You can't get any better than that. What more do you want?"

"More," she said.

"Oh, man." He chuckled, shaking his head. Then he smiled and pointed at her, making a clicking sound with his tongue. "You're good. You better watch yourself."

✝

THAT NIGHT, Lee opened the cabinet under the sink and lay on her back with the flashlight and her tools. The pipe had been leaking onto the kitchen floor, dampening the bottles and scrub brushes she kept down there. With the flashlight, she found the dull green pipes and felt along each for cracks, then with her fingers encircled on each washer, she felt for the loose one. She used the wrench to tighten it. The metal ridges were worn down, it was so old, and soon she'd have to replace it, but for now, it would do. Sliding herself out of the cabinet dark into the light, she felt a small satisfaction. To be able to fix things relieved her, and when she was calm at night, she could feel her body come alive again. In bed later, she might even be able to summon up a version of Jack, his face unshaven and lamplit above her, his body moving ghostlike into hers.

She'd only had sex with one other man since he'd left. Hadan, who installed heating systems and sometimes played cards over at Rush's. It had happened suddenly one night after a dinner party when he drove her home and they stayed up drinking and watching an old movie. She had the feeling, as she sat with him there in her living room, how nice it was not to be alone, even if he had a snort sometimes in his laugh that irritated her, and liked to call her "little lady" as if she were a child. His big stomach pushed against the buttons of his shirt when he sat down next to her on the couch, his thighs wide and meaty, and despite herself, she spread her hand there on his jeans, and they were kissing, and he pulled her shoulder out of her shirt and started rubbing it. She didn't remember much after that, but she was glad when he hoarsely said good-bye in the watery blue dark of the morning. He called her later that day, with little to say, and she was embarrassed. She'd wanted to keep the memory pure with Jack's hands on her, their weight and warmth, and after that time with Hadan, it took a long time for her to get the memory back.

In the middle of the night, she woke up seeing an email line glowing in the dark before her: YOU ARE A LIAR. It was in her dream, a message on the screen from Avery Taft, her computer also oddly an oven where strips of bacon fried in a black pan and a fire burned in the next room. She wrapped her legs in the sheets and tried to settle herself down. She stared into the vague shapes behind the dark.

Rush called in the morning to see what had happened at city council. "I showed them the photographs, I said my piece, and it didn't seem to make a damn bit of difference."

"Well, you tried. How about you come out to New Braunfels with us next weekend?" Rush told her about the country house, the walk along the river, the German beer house where there was dancing.

But to leave now, that would signal a collapse. "Maybe in November?"

As she hung up the phone, her eye caught on the bright green letters of a binding on the bookshelf. Idly, she took down the book. *Ecological Defense Manual.* A guy from Texas Green League had sent it to her in the mail ages ago. She had been speaking with him on the phone about the solvent levels that Professor Samuels had found, and the guy had been apologetic, but said he didn't think they'd have much traction with his boss at the agency. "Look," the note that arrived with the book had said, "here's the real deal. Tells you how to do everything. If you're really angry (ha!) . . ." He'd sent it as a joke, to give her some perspective. Aside from the typography, the cover was the color of a brown paper bag. There was a quote from Thomas Jefferson on the first page: "To lose our country by a scrupulous adherence to written law would be to lose the law itself." She'd heard about these ecos, come across their exploits and missives on the Internet, but until she started reading now, she hadn't understood how practical the strategies were: tree spiking to prevent loggers, plugging the discharge pipes of polluting factories, taking out survey stakes in land marked for development, disabling building equipment. There were photographs and diagrams demonstrating each act, and there were lists of what to wear, what to bring, as careful and efficient as a Boy Scout's guide. The longest chapter was on security. "We may repeat ourselves here. That's purposeful to protect us from the greedheads. Security protocols are crucial. Above all, do not get caught."

The book was ridiculous, with its misspellings, illustrations like panels from a comic book, a cheerful fierce tone like a cruel teenager's. The pot-smoking guy from Texas Green League had wanted her to get ahold of her rage. She had a problem with her anger—she knew that—she and Jack had been over that a hundred times. But what the hell was she supposed to do with it? Tame it and put a bow on it and trot it out like a pet?

DEX

ON THURSDAY Ben Lawbourne invited him to his house for lunch and because he hadn't done his homework for Munson, he decided to skip class and go. His mom had written him a couple of spare notes for times like these, which he kept in his locker—so he could leave school if he needed to. She trusted him that way. He was only supposed to use a note if he was tired or needed to study for a test, but she wouldn't have been too mad to know he was hanging out with Lawbourne and Weeks—she liked those guys. Still, to cover his bases, he decided to tell her he'd left to get her prescription filled at the pharmacy, rather than after school, when he had practice.

He walked into Braun's Pharmacy and handed the slip to Eugene, whom he'd known his whole life.

"Howdy," said Eugene, taking the paper. "It'll just be ten minutes."

"Fine," said Dex. He sat down at the old soda fountain. There were only three stools, but they were all empty. While he waited, he looked at a magazine, read an article about one of the actresses on a TV show he'd never heard of—she only drank a special kind of water blessed by a psychic and said she liked to taste the blood of her lovers.

"Ready," said Eugene from the window. "You say hi to your mom for me, alright? No school today?"

"I'm on my way to an appointment is all," said Dex.

Eugene winked at him.

Dex looked down at the typed sticker on the little bag. "For diabetes only. Take two tablets daily."

First his mom got diabetes, and now the doctor was worried about her heart. She must have gained a hundred pounds since his dad had left. When he was getting ready for school that morning she was eating doughnuts out of a box, her hair lop-sided, her nubby bathrobe awry. He wanted to grab the box away from her, but then he felt sorry for wanting to deny her sweets.

THE LAWBOURNES' HOUSE was a big brick two-story with twelve windows, a three-car garage, and elaborately trimmed bushes, and Mr. and Mrs. Lawbourne were off in the Caribbean. By the time Dex got there, Louder was so drunk he couldn't walk across the living room without stumbling on the fur rug.

"Look, it's Dexterous Dex," he said, his words purring together. "You have any more fly moves for us, Dex?" It was an old joke by now, but Louder wouldn't let go of the night Dex drank six shots of Jim Beam in the bathroom at a school function and got up on a table to dance by himself. Louder started clapping at an uneven beat. "Work it, man!" That same night Louder had put his hand through a window and went traipsing through a party waving his bloody fingers at swooning girls, but no one teased him about that now.

"How much have you had to drink there, Louder?"

"Not as much as Holbrook. He's got a girl up there, in the flesh."

"The shark bites again, huh?" Dex was too used to his bullshit to take this one.

"Dex, Dex, Dex." Louder shook his head, slapped him on the shoulder. No one paid any attention.

Three guys he recognized but didn't know sat at the kitchen table, flipping quarters into a pitcher of beer. Kyle and Trace played pool, Trace screaming, "Damn! Damn! Damn!"

There was definitely a rich lady behind the decorating of this living room—with its cowhide pillows, leather couches, the deer head on the wall, the table that seemed to be made from a tree stump but polished until it looked wet. All of it was rapidly falling into a mess, but it felt like the lady's presence was still there. He wanted to let loose and have fun, but the room got him thinking of his mother again.

Charlie sat on the couch with his feet up, watching the football game. "Hey there, Dex," he said lazily. Dex sat next to him, surprised to see him there, but surprised to see himself there too. Eyes lowered, feet up, Charlie seemed in a game trance, the TV showing replays of a tackle from different angles. Dex opened a bottle of Lone Star and took a sip, but he felt distant from the whole scene, worrying. His mother had been fat for a while, but this morning he noticed her ankles were so swollen, her leg poured directly into her shoe. He couldn't get that image out of his head. She had to stay cheerful, and junk food helped her keep her sense of humor. This morning, she'd said, "I've got my Weight Watchers later." She always acted as if she were dieting, as if she were losing weight rather than gaining it.

Dex wanted to take care of her, but he couldn't force her to eat what the doctor told her to eat. Even if he tried, she would just laugh and wave him away.

Snow came in through the grand entryway, grinning and slouching. He sat next to Dex and Charlie, took a beer from one of the six-packs and opened it in one fluid motion. Behind them on the kitchen island, there were ten or fifteen bottles of liquor. Snow took two brown prescription bottles from his front jeans pocket and set them down on the table. "Have at it—potluck. Valium and Klonopin. Straight from Bishop."

Dex took small sips of beer. He'd gone to practice drunk before, but it was four times as hard, carrying shoulder pads and helmets, having to write down the plays the coach rattled off to him and trying to look at him straight on, hoping his eyes didn't look as raw as they felt. If Coach Salem guessed it or saw it, he'd automatically lose his job. And he needed to deliver the diabetes medicine to his mom.

"Just got a copy of that *Aristo*," said Snow. "Have you played it yet? It's exactly as if you're in the desert shooting Arabs, and it gives you this burning shock if you miss. Sand blows up the screen. Very fucking cool."

"Yeah?" said Charlie. "Do the bodies blow up? You know, they use that game in training camp. It helps your reflexes."

At that moment Dex wanted to drink as many beers as he could hold. He understood why his mom couldn't stop eating, how sometimes you just wanted the thing you wanted until you drowned in it.

Louder and Weeks were playing some game with a frilly pillow, throwing it back and forth. "This is why you can never get laid—you smell like a fart-making machine. And you're telling me you wear cologne? Fuck!"

"Your nose is stuck in your own asshole."

Someone had built a small tower of fancy throw pillows, pony skin and brown velvet, with a lone potato chip on top. There was a gathering of bottles on the table with wads of paper towel stuck into the mouths like crumpled white heads.

Jim and Rick had joined Trace at the pool table, and the room was dark except just the lamp shining down over the table in a little temple of light. When one of them leaned in to shoot, the face looked flattened and white as a paper mask.

Louder came crashing down over the couch, grabbed Charlie in a mock embrace, started singing loudly, *"All my exes live in Texas."* There were five empty bottles of Jim Beam sitting on the mantel, Dex noticed, their black-and-white labels official looking, efficient, and old-fashioned. It was only then that Dex realized all at once that every single guy there, Snow and Charlie included, though he was quiet, was dead drunk. Dex kept his eye on the TV, listening to the cue hitting the balls on the table, a loud Brad Paisley song about alcohol back in the kitchen, Rick singing angrily along. They listened to country music as a gesture to their parents' tastes, fakely sincere, pretending cowboy honor—but inside the joke they could puff out their chests and sing as if it mattered. Dex felt different—those singers so often sounded like his dad, or a version of his dad his mom liked to sing along to.

The sliding glass door opened, and Bishop came inside. He flipped his hand in Dex's direction. "Who invited you?"

Dex didn't answer. If they still thought he'd had something to do with telling Coach about the goats, there wasn't a thing he could do about it.

Brad passed too close to the couch, glared at him. And again, the thought of drowning came to Dex.

He needed to just leave and get back to school, maybe even study for a few minutes before the science quiz he was supposed to take in sixth period, but he felt sluggish amid all the frenetic talk and the guys swaying around him.

Brite came in the glass door, dripping wet, his boxers stuck to him like damp newspaper. "Towel?"

"Try upstairs!" Bishop yelled, and Trace and Rick started cackling from the pool table. "Yeah, upstairs, dude!" There was a round of laughing and a couple of silly hoots.

"We're like the last three cowboys, dudes up against the Indians," said Snow, grinning, a bulge of Skoal in his lower lip, so he had to talk out of the side of his mouth. "They think they're going to kill us with their arrows, but only because they don't know we've got guns."

"You're crazy," said Bishop. "We're not three anything. I'm on my own. I'm going to get a pharmaceutical that makes you feel like you're flying, literally. It turns everything tiny so you feel like a giant. A little of this, a little of that."

Dex felt a nameless rage against all of them, wanted to hit Bishop's smug, rosy face.

"A pharmaceutical, I said. Not a meth drug, not a drug dealer drug. But people will get addicted. That's how I'll make it."

"I highly doubt it," said Charlie, in his mock-professional voice. He had a way of pretending he was an executive at a company.

Dex ate one of the sandwiches sitting on the table, idly watching the highlights of a football game. The players running against the green and then frozen in midthrow, midcatch, or sprawled over the goal line. He would go back to school and take the biology quiz in last period—he didn't feel like making that one up. He'd studied for the test last night, but right now he couldn't remember even the first species. He decided to lay off the beer. Snow went into the kitchen to look for more food.

Snow came back with a plate of sandwiches, laid them down on the tree stump. Dex turned to Charlie. "Tsk-tsk. All these guys drunk off their asses in the middle of the day."

"Livin' large," said Snow.

Dex had a vision of his mother huge, so large she floated up off the ground, her dress splitting at the seams. "Someone better make some coffee pronto, or they'll be puking all over the couch," said Dex.

"Not that I'm partaking—I've got a girlfriend. But you have to be wasted, don't you think, if you're going to put your dick right where another guy's has been?"

Dex looked at Snow for signs that he was lying. "Come on, there's no girl up there." Snow's face seemed stretched out at the sides, eyes jumpy, even as he pretended it was no big deal.

Just then, Dex spotted a flimsy blouse on the floor, all pathetically gathered up beneath a chair leg, He felt the beer come up salty in his throat.

"There is, buddy." Snow's hand shook when he reached for his bottle. "You know Willa Lambert? Seems like she has a few drinks in her, for sure."

The room tilted, and there was a crashing of glass somewhere. Dex thought of Willa's long, pale fingers, the short pink nails, laid flat on his desk on top of his typed paper. Goddamn Cully Holbrook. The football score flashed beneath the players against the green. 21–7, 21–7.

Dex stood up, shook out his legs. Charlie's eyes were closed, and a gurgled buzz came from between his lips. It couldn't be Willa, could it? It was just because she was nobody's sister and had that eye makeup that they talked about her that way. *KitKat*. She wouldn't offer herself to just anyone. But then again, she might be up there with Cully. Cully had a way.

Dex thought he wouldn't say good-bye, just leave. He maneuvered past Weeks, leaning over the pool table for a shot, and walked fast toward the front door.

The entryway was tiled the color of bricks, and the sun caught in the chandelier overhead, sending down sharp white squares as he walked out, past the bright green plant on a stand by the door, a cactus holding up its arms like a prickled angel.

He got in his truck and drove. He had to admit that he didn't know Willa all that well. Still, he thought it showed bad taste that she liked Cully Holbrook. Maybe Snow had got her mixed up with someone else—there were other girls like her, not particularly in any group. He hoped that was it, that he'd hear another girl's name mentioned tomorrow. As he raced past the Walgreens and the stately gray Quaker church, a hard thing lodged in the pit of his stomach.

He passed over Crystal Creek, where back before parties, guys used to construct elaborate ramps out of old plywood and jump their bikes over the water. They had contests to see who could get over the widest part, and he remembered when Weeks had fallen in with his bike, hit his head on a rock, and had to go to the emergency room. That was so long ago. The creek was polluted now—walking down the pathway near it, he'd once seen a dead fish spitting bright green blood, and strange fluorescent yellow rocks.

He drove past Weeks's house, yellow and flat, and past the old folks' home, where there were always two or three old women, sitting in their wheelchairs on the porch, waving.

He was the only one of his friends who lived in a trailer, and it sat on a lot between the Baptist church and a row of houses above the creek. Often he felt a twinge of embarrassment when he first saw it, coming home. But today its smallness seemed safe—as if it could only do so much harm. He threw open the thin, light door, saw his mom on the couch, drinking coffee and flipping through a magazine.

"Honey, what are you doing home?"

"I don't feel so good," he said.

He sat next to her, and let her pat his knee. He turned on the TV with the clicker, and without looking at her, handed her the medicine.

✝

THE NEXT DAY he woke up at dawn and couldn't go back to sleep, the birds were so loud. He pushed aside the curtains next to his bed and looked outside. The grass outside the trailer was long and yellow and weedy. They might live in a trailer but not like trailer trash, his dad always said. And look at that. He pulled on his jeans and went outside, got the lawn mower out of the shed, and went to work. He didn't care who he woke up. The grass had to get mowed before he went to school.

Pushing the mower at the edge of the land first, which bordered the playground behind the Baptist church, he hated Cully Holbrook, who'd do just about anything to get laid. Dex had seen him brag at the urinals. He'd seen the girls Cully had been with, pretty and ugly. Sure, Dex wanted it too, but there was a limit. He might get a girl tipsy, but he wouldn't touch her if she got drunk. And there it was—another reason it couldn't have been Willa there yesterday—she wouldn't be a drinker.

When he turned the mower around and made another path through the grass, his mom came out of the trailer in her bathrobe, rubbing her eyes, yelling.

He turned off the mower.

"Dex, what in the hell?"

"It's got to get done sometime."

"Now? You've decided to do it now? Oh, forget it, your sister's up now anyway." And she waved him away and shut the door.

He turned on the mower again and focused on the weeds, gripped the rusted handle and pushed into the yard, the frantic blade spinning beneath him, green spitting up all around.

WILLA

WILLA WOKE IN A STRANGE ROOM, dim but for the dusty beam that streamed purposefully through the curtains, carrying a message.

She sat up, felt the pinch of her open zipper, cold air on her arms and breasts, sunlight wavering on the floor next to the scrawl of her bra. "Cully?" She pulled the sheet up to her shoulders, thinking he'd be back any minute. Above the nightstand there was a small wooden fish on the wall, abstract in shape, either the Christian symbol or plain decoration, she couldn't tell. "Hey, Cully?" She did not smell like herself.

She remembered leaving school at lunch with him in his truck. He'd reached across the clutch to put his hand on her knee, his tawny face in profile, the straight, jutting nose and even chin. The engine revved at the corner, Toby Keith on the radio, a puddle of daisies in the median off the road. After that, there were just broken pieces: she'd been looking over a balcony at the ropy shadows below; someone's hand in her hair; the doll's-eye blue of the swimming pool; a plaid shirt; a boy's face, the gaze as empty as a cloud.

She hugged her knees to her chest. There was a sharp pain

between her legs that radiated into her thighs. She tried to ignore it, shifted her legs to the right.

On the nightstand, there was a photo of a woman crouching on the beach, some secret in the turn of her mouth and the angle of her eyes, waves crumpled behind her, the wet sand flat and shiny. Willa remembered now that she and Cully were supposed to go to the Lawbournes' for lunch. Was that Ben Lawbourne's mother? The woman's eyes were tiny dark squares like his, but she couldn't be sure.

She saw her own mother's pinched face. "You hardly ever make just one mistake," she always said, and that was why you had to "get right" with forgiveness.

Willa stared at the framed print that hung above the dresser, her head hollow. Across the bottom it was printed THE MUSEUM OF FINE ARTS, HOUSTON. Above that, a block of violet bled into the red space surrounding it. She prayed, *I'm just the same. Make me exactly the same.*

Outside the window she could see the telephone line and a tree. Maybe she had fainted. That was why she couldn't remember. Someone thought it was a problem with her heart or lungs and had taken off her shirt. Where was it? They'd brought her up here to lie down.

Willa saw how the violet paint in the picture had different intensities at different points in the square, parts of it worn away, so the violet and red fought against each other. Rubbing the thin circle charm on her bracelet, she knew Cully wasn't coming back, and she tried to summon a word to say to Dani, *jerk, player.*

She'd had to skip history class in order to go to lunch with him. She'd faked a note from her father because his spiked signature was easier to forge than her mother's, and the attendance clerk had barely given it a glance. That was the first thing she'd done wrong. The metallic taste in the drink came back to her.

Cully had worn jeans with a frayed hole at the knee. When they got there, he'd poured what looked like two capfuls of vodka into her glass, and though she'd never had hard liquor before, she drank it with the measure of bravado she needed to be there with him in the first place. It was a new school year, and she wasn't going to be timid. She'd said, "I don't even like you," flirting.

The delicate green plant in the corner seemed to spider up the wall. She felt that if she didn't move too quickly, if she slipped on her shirt and quietly walked the long distance down the stairs (who was down there?), she could just walk home, and it would be over. Whatever had happened somehow wouldn't be true, and she'd be back in her bedroom in her own house.

She pulled her legs over the bed, stumbled to find her clothes. The violet square was like a bright reprimand. What did it mean? She stepped into her shoes, found her bra, put it on, and looked for her shirt under the rocking chair and behind the plant. She knelt on the floor and peered under the dresser at the dusty dark. Then she just pulled the sheet off the bed and hung it around her shoulders like a cape. She walked into the hallway, which opened to a balcony overlooking the entryway. A chandelier dangled across from her like an overturned bouquet of ice chips.

Below, near the front door, a woman with red hair was watering potted plants. She turned her head, not looking up, "Someone home?"

Willa moved back so the woman couldn't see her. There was fractured light and the smell of air conditioner and soap, and then there were a few seconds of nothing. She went into the bedroom, quietly pulled the door shut, sat down in the rocking chair. She'd so wanted to impress him, wearing beneath her blouse the secret bra that she hid from her mother in the back of her dresser drawer. She studied the painting again. The violet block thrown hard against the red seemed like the blank stretch in her afternoon. "Now why is that in a museum?" her father would say. "It's just a trick on folks. A trick that makes somebody somewhere rich."

A spill of coins. Half a dirt footprint on the rug arrowing to the wall. A different one, the whole shape, pointing to the bed. Fainter ones leading to the door. On the bed, a small spot of blood smeared the bottom sheet where she'd been lying on it. Willa got up to pull the bedspread over it.

The door swung open. Willa stopped the chair from rocking back. The red-haired woman held a watering can in one hand, Willa's shirt in the other. "I thought I heard someone up here!" On the woman's chest, there were three islands of orange freckles over the low neckline of her dress.

The woman tossed the shirt onto Willa's lap. "This yours?" A spill of flowers fell on Willa's jeans. "You know where Ben is?"

Willa pulled the sheet tighter around her.

The woman's overplucked eyebrows wrinkled. Willa could see their original half-moons in the slight ghostly imprints in her forehead. "You mean to tell me you're alone?"

"Yes, ma'am."

The woman looked away, earrings jingling. "My God, there's bottles and what all down there."

She went to the window and pulled back the curtains. "I promised to keep an eye on things," the woman said. "Oh, dear

God." But the "dear" was not affectionate or sorry. "Just get dressed, okay? Then I want to call your mother."

Willa heard the digits tease and circle like a nursery rhyme, but she couldn't bring up her home phone number. Something was really wrong with her head. As she fastened the tiny buttons of her shirt, she tried to get the number straight. She picked up the phone and stared at the rows of symbols. Finally she handled the pen lying there and the pad with FRIENDSWOOD BANK imprinted at the top, and without thinking she scribbled down something familiar and handed it to the woman, who turned her back to Willa as she dialed. The numbers chirped as she punched them with her finger.

"Hello? I think I have your daughter here." Willa heard her mother's muted voice. "Yes, at Seventy-one Calling Creek Drive. I'll let her explain."

As Willa was tucking her shirt into her jeans, she noticed the small handwriting just above her hipbone, the letters cramped and dark blue. She licked her finger and rubbed her skin, but the ink wouldn't smear. *Slut.*

MRS. THOMPSON, the red-haired woman, said she'd just come to check on things as a favor while the Lawbournes were away. "I don't know what in the world to tell them. I didn't think Ben would be such a maniac as to have a party in the daytime," she said, waving her hand at the beer bottles and cans of Red Bull crowded on the kitchen counter. "My God, he's going to have to pay for this." She tilted her head. "You okay?" Willa nodded, not looking at her face. "Bet you're pretty mad at your boyfriend. Where'd he go?"

"I told him I wanted to sleep."

"Oh." It looked like Mrs. Thompson believed her. "You know, I should tell your mother how I found you, but I'm going to let you do that."

Mrs. Thompson waited now in the living room, watching television, a man's voice shouting cooking instructions, while she smoked furiously, legs crossed, swinging her foot. Willa stood at the long, thin window near the front door, watching for her mother's car. A lawn mower started up. Across the street, a sprinkler stuttered, then fountained straight up. If she didn't remember, it was almost as if she were just the same. She pictured herself naked on that bed, the pear-shaped birthmark on her flattened thigh, the dry skin.

A white pickup screeched to a stop at the corner, turned too fast, its tail gate wagging. Then her family's brown car turned the corner, the familiar dented hood slowly approaching. Willa opened the door and heard Mrs. Thompson behind her, expectant. "Your mother there now?"

"Yeah!" Willa called. "Bye!" She sprinted out and raced down the walk.

When she got into the car and slammed the door, her mother didn't look at her but into the rearview mirror, and then turned her head to look the other way through the window at the street before she carefully began to pull the car out onto the road.

Willa saw Mrs. Thompson standing on the lawn, high-heeled shoes that looked tiny beneath her plump calves, her face confused, one hand on her hip, the other hand waving.

Willa's mother waved back, but didn't smile. Her lipstick had faded, and it was hard to tell what she was thinking because the corners of her mouth weren't clear.

She didn't say anything until they reached the next corner. "Well, young lady," she started. "This sure is embarrassing." Willa knew her mother was afraid that she'd set a bad example for Jana, and it would begin all over again with her little sister one day. "Some woman I've never met calling to say my daughter's not in school."

"I went out for open lunch."

"Excuse me, but you don't have that privilege." Her mother glanced sideways at her.

"I know."

"Who drove you there?"

Willa hesitated. The thought of her mother and Cully Holbrook in the same space, even if it was only the crowded space in her head, made her sick to her stomach. She said his name, and it grated against the silence like something bulky and metal.

"Hmm." Her mother stopped at a light, looked over at Willa. "He's a senior then. What are you doing going around with a senior?"

The light turned green, and her mother stepped on the gas with a force that seemed resentful. They turned onto Sunrise Drive, past the new subdivision—large houses with turrets and windows with stained glass, the yards still a jumble of turned dirt and cement blocks. They passed the busy stripmall–gas station intersection, crossed Chigger Creek, then were on the highway toward home. Willa looked through the car window at the sky, the unknowing clouds passing slowly above her. Then they were driving next to a pasture. Two horses stood dully munching blocks of hay stacked in the grass. Another horse galloped alongside the road. She wasn't sure if it was real. Its long black mane streamed behind it, a horse escaped from history.

✝

WHEN THEY GOT to the house, Willa was relieved not to see her dad out watering the yard, or in the living room sitting with his feet up in the recliner. She ran straight up to her room, to her bed. She lay down and stared at the ceiling, a pain in her chest like a spoon scooping at her heart. Her laptop sat open on the desk, but she was afraid to check her email. Staring at the light fixture, she tried to feel nothing. For half an hour, she stared at the round gold screw in the middle of the glass.

Downstairs she heard her dad's cheerful "Hi, sweetheart" echo in the kitchen, and then the murmur of her mother's voice. His purposeful steps on the tile, then "What?" Willa knew he was loosening his blue tie, pulling it quickly from his collar.

She wished Jana were home—when there were two of them, her parents didn't watch so closely, but alone with them in the house, Willa felt like they could see through her hair and scalp to what she was thinking.

All along she'd only believed half of it (the spoon against her heart worked harder), but she stupidly hung on to the half that noticed his eyes lingering on her face, the softness in her voice like a country singer's, that time he'd made her late for class telling her how he'd got his truck out of the ditch—not the half of him that usually looked past her shoulder to some other girl or buddy of his.

She peeled down her jeans to look again at the writing on her hip. *Slut*. She tried again to wipe it off with her finger. If he'd cared about her, he would have stayed there with her. She imagined a hand against her hip bone, the green shirt or red plaid shirt. And then in her mind, a great black mud rose up like a curtain.

She slid out of bed, went into the bathroom, and locked the door. She soaped up the washcloth, rubbed it against the writing until her skin turned red. She doused a cotton ball with alcohol, then tried makeup remover and bleach, but it didn't make any difference. It looked like permanent marker, but she was afraid it might be one of those homemade tattoos, the kind people had in prison. She took a bath and lay trembling in the hot water for a long time. The red and stinging skin around the blue letters seemed to enlarge the word.

She went back to her room, not wanting to remember, but forcing herself to try. The moment that kept coming back was Cully opening a door for her, the scratch of his calloused hand at her elbow. "Here now." A beer bottle broken off at the neck, filling up with black water. When she'd walked into the house with him, four guys sat on the couch; another two stood in the kitchen, drinking beer; and outside a few lingered at the pool, throwing bottle caps into the water. Where were the girlfriends? she'd wondered, and panicked just as a tall guy with a red nose stood up from his chair to say hello. She should have left then, but Cully was holding her hand. She didn't know why she'd assumed there would be other girls there. "Let me get you a drink," said Bishop Geitner, brushing at the top of his overly short hair. "You like Red Bull?" After the drink, the time was in splinters. The faded back of his jeans as she followed Cully up the stairs. "What does she want?" Light wrinkling on the blue surface of the swimming pool. It wasn't really warm enough to swim.

Downstairs, her mother clanged pots in the kitchen. The

bedroom curtains illuminated briefly by the headlights of a passing car.

When Jana got home, they had dinner. Her dad wouldn't look at her, but told her as she sat down, his eyes on his plate, "You need to be in school when you're supposed to be in school, hear me?"

"Yes, sir," she said, passing him the rolls, a pain in her throat. She hated acting fake with him, but it seemed what he expected.

"What did she do?" Jana wore rainbow-striped knee socks, two aprons—one tied in the front, the other in the back—and a headband with two curly Martian antennas that wiggled over her head.

"That's not your concern," said their mother. "Put those aprons back in the drawer when you're through with them. They'd better be clean."

"One week," said her father. Willa already knew she'd be grounded. Eventually, Mrs. Thompson might call again to tell them what she'd seen, but she also might not, and then they wouldn't have to know anything, and then it would be over.

✝

THE NEXT MORNING she woke up, lifted her pajama top, and saw the inked block letters had faded, but she could still read the word. She couldn't make herself stand up. To have to go back to school and pretend her life was normal.

Finally, she got dressed among her familiar things, the photo of her frizzy-haired grandparents smiling by the lake, her pink iPod, the circle-faced rag doll, the ceramic cowboy boot that held pens, and downstairs, the sounds of her parents talking softly in the kitchen, the clink of cups and bowls in the sink. She had to take this familiar feeling with her out into the world and hang on to it, squeeze it into her palms and paste it to her eyes and stuff it in her ears.

When she walked to her first class, the hallway seemed impossibly the same, the long white wall painted with a billboard-sized emblem of a galloping blue mustang. Lockers slammed, a boy laughed too loudly, girls touched their perfect hair. Near the water fountain, she saw her friends conferring, Amy tugging at the hem of her minidress, Miranda with a finger hooked in her belt loop. As she got closer to them, Willa fished around in her bag for the notebook she had to return to Amy.

"I have bad news," Amy said.

Willa felt as if the ceiling were pounding gently on the top of her head.

Amy told Willa she couldn't spend the night on Saturday, because her mom was having one of her meetings then. Willa had forgotten about that plan they'd rigged so she could stay at a party until midnight instead of having to come home at ten.

"Oh," said Willa, handling her the red tablet. Soon enough, her friends would hear what had happened. "Thanks for these notes."

A flutter of blue-and-white cheerleader uniforms streamed toward them. Willa recognized Alicia, walking with another girl, and remembered Alicia's boyfriend was a friend of Ben Lawbourne's. By now, she could have heard something, but there was nothing in her face that meant she knew.

Miranda pointed to a bruise just above Willa's elbow. "What's that?"

"It's nothing. I hurt my arm." Willa held her arm behind her back and tried to think of something else to say.

"Well, ladies, I've got a test," said Amy, turning away, her purse swinging. Miranda followed. They didn't know yet, but they would soon. It was only the morning. She couldn't think about them, though—she kept her mind on the moment, vigilant at the indifferent faces passing by, the plaid shirts, the T-shirts with slogans, the sparkly headbands.

Willa went down the hall and turned in to the classroom, sat down next to the bulletin board full of construction paper triangles. Mrs. Westhauser took roll and then sat at her perch. "We need to prove that angle one is congruent to angle two." She drew an X with arrows on the four corners. "It's given that angle one and angle two are vertical angles."

Willa looked out the window at the parking lot, the neat lines of cars, a guy she didn't know walking out with an army-green backpack slung on one shoulder, the strict yellow lines in the pavement oddly pathetic, worn away by so many tires.

"Step Three. Now," Mrs. Westhauser cleared her throat. "It wouldn't be the end of the world, if you forgot this step and went directly to four, but it would be technically incorrect and sloppy. Too many of you have been forgetting steps like that, rushing on with your logic." She would now and then proclaim the beauty of triangles and well-done proofs, flinging her arm like a modern dancer. "But I still have hope that you understand the direction of the logic. It's not the end of the world." She said the last statement so faintly, Willa barely heard it. Her father said "the end of the world" like a prayer.

He'd point to the headlines and say, "See that?" Or he'd erupt from the deep cushion of his easy chair in front of the television to say, "Of course that's what happened. It's all in Scripture. After the battle, the Jews take Jerusalem. The Rapture's coming, alright—I'm not surprised one bit to see all that fighting over there."

Mrs. Westhauser assigned them a problem. Will Kent sat in a desk near the front. Willa tried to remember if he was one of Cully's friends. Pencils scribbled on workbooks, desk legs scraped against the floor, someone was coughing, and Willa heard her own loud and rapid breathing.

The round clock on the wall gave a click, clapped the minute and hour hands together. The TV monitor that hung high in the corner turned on suddenly, and Principal Johnson's stern, elderly face and bow-tied blouse filled the screen. "Students, teachers, a couple of announcements." There would be a pep rally tomorrow. Permissions slips for the field trip to NASA were due.

Willa's fingers wouldn't stop shaking when she picked up her pencil, and she had to press hard against it to keep it in her grip. She felt the soreness in her eyes, the extra muscle in her vision spasming. Red and green lights streamed at the edge of her sight line when she moved her head too quickly.

Later, in biology lab, she was dissecting an earthworm with her partner, the pink organs unfixed and shiny in the tray, when in the corner of the table, light fell in a diaphanous veil over a pair of wet-looking horns. The fixture stood there like worms twined together into antlers, while all around her, people busily wrote things down.

As she went from one class to the next in the hallway, she watched with nervous attention as peoples' faces streamed past. She looked out for Cully's loping walk and longish blond hair, the slump of his shoulders, and for his friends too. If she saw any of them and didn't have time to turn and walk in the other direction, she'd pretend to drop her purse and bend down to get it.

She passed the bulletin board that said ALUMS SERVING OUR COUNTRY, photos of the five men and women in uniforms pasted beneath, and over the head of Bobby Laker, a construction paper cross. She wanted to find Dani.

The hallway began to clear. About ten feet ahead, near the trophy case, she saw the white piping of the back of a Western shirt, that blond hair stuck up from his collar, the familiar stooped slant of Cully's tall frame. He moved around the girls next to him, lifted a book over the head of someone, and seemed to be looking at something through the glass. The black shirt finally turned around, and something hard and salty came up in her throat. It wasn't Cully, but a guy she didn't know with glasses.

In the cafeteria, Dani grabbed her hand and pulled her down beside her at the empty table. Most people were eating sandwiches and fries, but there was also a kind of stroganoff, which had the creamy acidic smell of vomit. "Sit down, quick." Her breath was hot against Willa's ear. "Okay, don't let your face move when I tell you this." This was the rumor: fifteen guys invited to lunch, Willa gone out on the balcony of the house, stripping off her clothes. "No one really believes it, and I'm telling everyone that's just crazy." Willa stared at the black lizard-skin toe of someone's cowboy boot at the next table, relieved to finally hear what they were saying. She had said to Cully, "I don't even like you," flirting, leaning back against the kitchen counter with her drink. She let him hook his finger in the belt loop of her jeans.

Dani held Willa's arm. She was tougher and louder than Willa's other friends, and if anyone could protect her, she could. "But where did they get that story?"

"Well, I was with Cully."

"Yeah. Was there some other girl there?"

"No." A flattened stray piece of paper lay among dusty footprints on the floor.

"Oh."

There were big windows on three sides of the cafeteria, but the glass was clouded and gray. "I guess I lost a few hours." She heard the forced casualness in her voice, as if it were just bad luck, like losing a jacket or a wallet.

"Shit! What do you mean *lost*?"

"I mean I can't remember. He left me there at the Lawbournes'. My mom had to come get me."

"God, she had to—What did she say?"

"You know, she was mad."

Dani's eyes veered to the side. "They said you were drunk."

"I only took a couple of sips, but I guess it was strong." Willa tried to gather in the harmless things around her. There were the plain fluorescent strips on the ceiling; there was the moving belt of dirty trays; there were the blue circular tables.

"What was it?"

"Vodka and Red Bull."

Now all of the words Dani said seemed wooden and impenetrable. "When Polly drank those, she threw up all the next day. You must be freaked. Are you still . . . you know—"

"It's like I wasn't even there."

"Look, all I care about is you. What do you want me to do?" Dani's eyes were sad. "I should start another rumor, that's what I should do."

"Don't say anything." Willa stood up. "I'll see you in the bathroom after fifth period." It was their usual meeting place.

In the last bit of locker clatter and rush before people got to their classes, she felt dizzy, and when she turned, at the periphery of her vision, strange lights flashed like signals.

In English class, Ms. Marlowe wore red. She was talking about Faulkner and the natural metaphors in "The Bear" when a student aide came to the door with a note. Willa watched Ms. Marlowe's flat, wide hips move from one side of the room to the other.

Just before class ended, Ms. Marlowe quietly called Willa over to her desk. "The guidance counselor would like to see you before sixth period. Here's a pass." Did the counselor know, or was it just that her forged note about her absence had been found out?

She passed the auditorium doorway and heard voices singing in unison. Inside, on the lighted stage, people stared up at the choir director. And there, as she turned, at the edge of her sight line, was a blurry flash of fur. She rushed down the hallway to the counselor's office.

"Hi, honey, will you have a seat?" Ms. Ryan said. "That's a pretty necklace." She had long hair that draped against her face and large, empathetic eyes.

The office light was dimmed, not fluorescent, lit by lamps and a window with a latticed blind.

"Thanks."

Ryan said, "You're on the honor roll again. Which classes do you like best?" They talked about oil painting and Emily Dickinson. Willa's hand trembled as she moved it from the arm of the chair to her leg.

Finally, Ryan clicked her tongue. "Well, I have to tell you, there was a call to the Christian hotline yesterday about an incident." The last time Willa had heard about the hotline was in the spring, when Beth Ambroy told someone she was going to drink bleach. "You know I've been at this school for years, and one thing that always makes me sit up and take notice is when a girl starts acting not like herself. It looks to me like you're headed for a good college, right? It's not like you to skip your classes." She stopped, seemed to be listening to the muffled sound of a male teacher shouting instructions in the next room. "Willa, I'm not here to judge. Do you want to talk?" Her patience was unnerving, the kind Willa remembered from a dream of a fire, someone shrugging their shoulders in the middle of the flames, saying, "What's the matter?"

"Not really." She looked away at the shelves of books, the test prep manuals and career guides. The career counselor had just given a lecture about their futures. Willa's father thought she should be a pharmacist because she got an A in chemistry, and whenever she chose "poet" as a career path on the questionnaires, the chances of making a living at it came up as something like ten thousand to one.

"Okay." Ms. Ryan looked disappointed. "You know I've seen a lot of things here—nothing would surprise me much," Willa studied her face, and wondered what she might already know. She gripped the sides of her chair, pressed down so hard that the pads of her fingers stung. On the carpeting, in the green and blue fibers, a red thread on the floor made a C.

"A lot of times I see girls who drink alcohol and lose track of themselves. And then they think whatever happened was their fault."

"I don't even like the taste of it," she said.

"So you weren't drinking, that's good." Ryan folded her hands and brought them in to the tip of her chin. "Honey, I can't help you if you won't talk." Her voice was throaty and gentle. "I don't know what happened over there, but I sure would like to help, Willa."

"I don't remember."

Ms. Ryan covered her lips with the tips of her fingers. "You don't remember leaving school with Cully Holbrook, or you don't remember what happened after?"

Willa looked away, and felt her face grow grotesque and giant, as if it took up half the room.

"Well, I'll tell you what. We may not know exactly what happened, but there was drunkenness, and when incidents like this one occur, the rumors . . ." She paused, seemed to catch herself. "I mean, well, to be safe, for your own good, we think you should go home for now, take a couple of days. How does that sound? That way, you'll have some time to think about things away from all this. And if you want to come see me, you can."

Willa couldn't focus on what she was saying. "I don't really know what you're talking about."

"Do you need some water?" Ryan stood up, nodded gently to Willa. "Let me get you some." She went out the door.

Willa pressed her fingers to her eyelids. The pressure made her see orange and red blobs, and she could suddenly smell something rotten in the trash. She opened her eyes, and a shadow slipped out of the corner. She didn't want a vision. She wanted to hang on to this room, to the flat carpet, the scratched metal desk, Ryan about to come back. Near the edge of the bookshelf, in the watery dimness, a shape emerged. She willed it back to the corner, but it kept coming, horns unfurled like waterways on maps, branching up to the ceiling in quick, silverish leaps. *"What does she want?"* The words weren't spoken exactly but flung out into the air, and she tasted the vodka again in her mouth. In a burst of dark fur, the breath went out of her, and the whole shape was gone.

Ms. Ryan came back in a rush, handed her a cup of water, and touched her shoulder in a practiced gesture of sympathy. Willa drank the water, but the vodka taste was still there. She couldn't stop shaking. It felt as if something was pressing open her heart—as if it was only the fake heart shape cut out of paper, and someone was holding it open with two hands, and anything might fall into it now.

"Willa, I'm here. I want you to know that. I'm just here."

Willa glanced at the door. It wouldn't even matter if she ran.

"Oh, honey," said Ms. Ryan. "You're really in a state, aren't you?" She clapped her hands on the desk. "Alright, then, you know what? I think why don't you just go on home now? We've called your mom."

She couldn't understand why she'd had to see that thing, why it had thrown back those words. "Why did you call her?"

"Willa," Ms. Ryan said, shaking her head. "Mothers need to know."

HAL

HAL DROVE HOME down the back road, all that land still undeveloped outside of town, where the trees and grass were bright against the black asphalt, and if you had to pull over, it might be twenty or thirty minutes before you saw another car with someone in it liable to help you. He watched the yellow lines, the flat horizon of the road. The run-down Taft house Avery handed off to him yesterday would be difficult to sell, but maybe he could find a young person who'd like the old-timeyness of the place and want to fix it up, or someone with a vision for a tanning-bed business or lawyers' offices. Maybe he wouldn't get the asking price, but he couldn't think that way now. He needed to think that odder things had happened and there were gifts of the spirit beyond his imagining.

Just over the ridge, a flock of birds stirred and flew up in the air in a flapping tent across the sky. He drove under it, thinking his chances with Lee Knowles were even better than with the sale—he was good with people, knew how to listen and main- tain eye contact, knew how to guess what someone was feeling by the way her mouth moved or by the way she touched her neck. All that time he'd spent at the cash register of his dad's hardware store had taught him to read faces. And who knew? Maybe he would get her saved too, in the end.

Hal turned into town, prosperity shining down in the sun, and drove home to his ranch house on Edgewood—modest, with clean lines and a whole acre and a half of land next to it, a four-car garage big enough for both his SUV and Cully's truck. As he walked up the brick path, he was irritated by the green hose loose in the yard—though it just meant Darlene had done some gardening—and he went inside. He was thirsty and tired, warding off a headache.

Darlene was standing in the kitchen, chopping carrots.

"Hi." He kissed her on the cheek from the back. "A good day. Even if I wasted the whole time on a couple of undeciders."

"Oh, that's a shame."

She'd bought ten orange pillows for the living room, and among her celebrity gossip magazines, they lay on the couches and chairs like giant pieces of fruit.

"I don't know why these fools can't tell when their wife is doing a number on them."

She patted his arm. "Can you?"

She was flirting, but he was too tired to flirt back. She hugged him, but he kept his body stiff. He didn't know yet what he wanted from her, but he didn't want mothering.

He opened the fridge and saw a large piece of meat waiting in a pot. He grabbed a bottle of Coke. "I'm going out to the pasture."

"Alright," she said as if to cheer him on. Darlene said it didn't do any good to worry about what you couldn't control. It was as silly as wringing your hands over the weather.

The pasture was left over from the previous homeowner,

who'd kept cows. The barn was empty now, and so was the acre of land, fenced in with barbed wire.

He set up a can with a curlicue of flowers on the label, on top of a post. Then he went into the barn and unlocked his gun from the cabinet where he kept it (Darlene wouldn't allow a gun in the house), and he stepped back away from the can about forty feet.

It was just a handgun, but it was heavy and old-fashioned, from the 1940s, he'd been told, and he liked the challenge of maneuvering it.

He cocked the gun; aimed at the frilly yellow, red, and blue design; and shot just to the right of the can, missed it.

His form wasn't good after a day of "Look at this" and "Can you see yourself living here?" Avery Taft's offer was an opportunity from God, and he didn't want to blow it; he needed to shoot the negative doodads out of his backyard. The devil was getting too damn close. He aimed again and shot the can off the fence post. Satisfied, he took a pull of Coke and trudged back to find the can, and put it back on its mark.

He'd never used a gun in any real situation, never used it to protect himself, and hated hunting, the boredom of long hours waiting around for something in the trees to move. But now that he didn't drink, shooting the gun was one thing that relaxed him. Pulling the trigger so the force backed up into his forearm, as if it were part of the gun too, the clean explosive feeling of hitting the mark, the smell of it.

He shot again, and the can had two holes, bent in on one side. When he was really on his game, he could shoot through the thin side of a playing card—he had a split jack of hearts and a split ace of spades, burn marks laced on their broken edges. He saved them in a little box up in his bedroom, along with his favorite wedding photo.

He felt hungry, but it would be at least an hour before they ate. He was about to go inside for some corn chips when a familiar dented blue truck pulled up on the street in front of the house. It belonged to Cully's friend, Trace, and Hal started walking toward the barbed-wire fence to call out that Cully wasn't there, he was still at practice, when he saw Cully pop out on the passenger side and the blue truck speed away. What was he doing here so early? Cully hobbled into the yard, his mouth slack, head hung down, his gait offbeat and off-balance in that pitiful way that Hal recognized in his bones.

"Hey!" he said, rushing to the fence.

Cully looked up at him, sheepish, his eyes lidded.

"I thought you had practice."

"Coach sent me home." Hal thought that he could smell it even from six feet—bourbon. Probably Jim Beam.

"He did, huh? Why's that? Where's your truck?"

Cully didn't answer and passed out of Hal's sight as he walked toward the front door.

Hal heard the door slam. He walked back to the barn, his head pounding, the gun heavy against his fingers. He'd promised himself not to handle the gun except when even tempered. Birds flapped out of the tree overhead, cawing in a way that sounded maniacal. Inside the barn, dim except for one clean slab of light in the corner where he stood, he unlocked the cabinet, took out the case, methodically put the gun back into the blue velvet indentations. He saw again his boy's sagging, clowning face, and felt his own blood roiling. He snapped the cover shut, placed the case on the shelf, and locked the cabinet.

He barged inside the back screen door and walked into the kitchen, where Darlene was now brushing the meat with a slick sauce. "Cully's home early, says he doesn't feel well," she said.

"Bullshit," said Hal. "He's dead drunk—can't you tell?"

She looked up at him, her blue eyes wide. "No. Is he?" She stopped brushing the meat. "You going to go talk to him?"

"Damn right."

He set his Coke on the counter. "Goddamn teenagers."

He was too angry to say anything else to her—how could she not notice? He watched her open the oven door, slide in the pan, crash the oven door shut again, his whole body filling with furious heat.

"Don't be too hard on him, Hal. And he's too old for the belt."

"Hell if he is."

"Hal!"

When Hal had fallen off track last year, Cully had been his lifeline back to the family. Even when he couldn't bear to look at Darlene, he and Cully went out for tacos in Pasadena, drove to Houston to look at the new construction. His son seemed to understand even without words why Hal had felt pushed into a corner, and he knew how to bring Hal out of his funk. But in the summer, Cully had mysteriously distanced himself, left the house most afternoons and didn't come back until late, kept his conversation to one-word answers to questions, and the space between them turned barren. Hal felt his words float up in the air like moisture in clouds, dissolving even as they hung around.

He knew part of this was just boy stuff. How many bold-faced lies had he told his own dad so he could go out drinking beer at the Ice Haus pool hall? How many close calls? There was the time he'd crashed the family car against a tree and walked away, more scared of his father's reaction than the accident itself or the gash in his stomach bleeding through his shirt. And for the whole evening his mother thought he was dead—when he walked in the house after midnight and said hello, her cup turned over, china shattering on the floor. She didn't care what he'd done to the car— he was alive. And there was nothing his dad could do to him then. Nothing at all. It hadn't been intentional, but his dad thought it was a trick, and he'd maybe never quite forgiven him for it.

He took the stairs two at a time and knocked on the door of his son's room.

"It's open," Cully said.

Hal walked in to find Cully lying on the bed, staring at the ceiling, a faint smell of vomit in the air, his shirt stained with it. On the table, the computer was on, a green light blinking against the black screen.

"Funny, you coming back early, isn't it?"

Cully turned his head, but didn't even sit up. The disrespect rankled Hal.

"You drunk?"

Cully shrugged.

"Coach Salem smelled it on you, huh?"

Cully didn't answer.

Seeing his son's head on the pillow, his dark hair mussed like that, Hal remembered the night when Cully was really little, maybe three, and his fever had spiked up to 105, his eyes rheumy and cheeks flushed. At first they'd debated, tried Tylenol and cool washcloths and said to each other, grabbing the thermometer, "What is it now?" He'd driven the boy to the hospital with Darlene in his old truck, speeding all the way, then carried him in his arms, running into the emergency room, screaming at whoever wore a white coat. They put Cully's little body on a huge gurney and a nurse stuck IVs into his fat thigh, while Hal held the tiny balled fist of his son inside his own fist, kept vigil over the tiny squinted shut eyes, and he murmured, *Please please please* until the fever finally pulled back. The doctor said Cully might have died that night, if they'd waited any longer. And now his son was taking his own life so lightly, so recklessly, and it brought back the rage he'd felt for those slow-moving night nurses, the hospital's impersonal fluorescent lights.

"You know what this means, right?"

"Yeah."

There was a small smile on Cully's face, and this made Hal want to hit him, but he kept himself in the doorway.

"I'd hate to be in your shoes, come the next practice," Hal said. "And by the way I'm taking the keys to your truck. It's still at school, isn't it?" He was hoarse.

Cully didn't say anything. Hal knew he was still drunk and might not even remember this conversation later.

"Your mother's real upset," he said, and closed the door. His own father would have beat the hell out of him with a belt. But Darlene wouldn't let him do that. He guessed it was a good thing. If he were a better dad, he would have given Cully the right line of Scripture. Something from Judges. Something to make him think.

✝

HAL SLEPT FITFULLY, a sticky film of sweat on his face and arms, the hairs on his legs catching on the sheets. A mosquito zinging from somewhere up on the ceiling kept landing in places near his neck. Still, Darlene slept soundly beside him and he put his hand on her back, her soothing breath gently rising and falling. And he worried, an endless shifting in his mind—he had a vision of sifting through a mess in his tool chest, in search of an elusive hammer.

The next morning the principal, Ida Johnson, called him at the office, and he picked up a bent paper clip, its thin metal end needling his thumb.

"Are you aware, Mr. Holbrook, what your son was up to yesterday?"

"I have a pretty good idea."

"Well, we're just getting the reports." Ida Johnson was an old gal with a bouffant hairdo and bowlegs, and she was tough in a way Hal liked and understood—she attended every game, every school play, wearing a pantsuit and horse brooch, her thin grin on her bony face. She did not suffer fools.

"There were fifteen boys, and they all missed afternoon classes. I don't know how many of them were intoxicated, but it's clear that your son was one of them. Looks like Cully fell down just walking out of the field house."

"I know. I've had a talk with him." He felt Ida Johnson's scolding was meant for him, as if she somehow knew about the time Hal got so drunk on Jack Daniel's he lay down in the middle of the street, weeping and yelling at a stray yellow dog that had followed him, until a car stopped and a man whose name and face he didn't remember took him home. Or the time he ran out of booze and went driving looking for more, when he broke out the window of his buddy Scott's house with a wrench and crawled through broken glass to find the bar.

"You know that normally we suspend a boy for this."

"As well you should." He heard the weariness in his voice.

"I've told him he won't get another chance. This is a forgiveness gift. We're suspending him, just for two weeks. It should be longer, and it's up to Coach Salem whether or not he plays. But there won't be another gift like this. I think he understands."

"Well, alright." He blew out a sigh, dropped the paper clip in the trash can.

"He's a good boy," she said. "But he's got to know he's good."

She reminded him of his uncle Earle, who'd been in the military and come back from Vietnam grinning, with flag pins for the boys and bracelets for the girls, his posture erect and his stories with morals at the end. Hal had always called him "sir."

✝

THAT NIGHT HE SAT DOWN with his son in the living room, turned off *SportsCenter* on the TV. Darlene was upstairs, rustling around in the laundry room. Outside on the street, there was an irritated honk from a Mack truck coming to that light at the intersection. Cully lay on the couch, his huge feet up on the armrest, hands folded piously on his flat T-shirted stomach. Darlene's magazines lay splayed on the coffee table. That cute young celebrity, he couldn't remember her name, her bright eyes spangled with makeup, her nose pretty as the inside of a flower. Now why would she want to do that? Just beneath her pointed chin, she held the blade of a knife to her throat.

"Son, I want you to know you don't get a lot of chances. You just got another one this week, and I think you know what I'm talking about."

He tried to sound firm and smart—but the whole time he

was talking he felt the sloppiness of his own drunken period seep through the words. Hal was ashamed to admit how many times his son must have seen him drunk. He prayed, *Help me, Jesus. Amen.*

"I know, Dad." Cully's eyes were tired and red. "I'm sorry. I won't mess up."

"You've still got a shot at a scholarship, but not if you keep up this nonsense."

"I won't. I'm going to keep steady." He made a fist in the air, but it looked weak.

Hal tossed the Bible on the couch. "Here's the good book. Don't do anything you're going to regret later. That's the problem with drinking—it's a regret machine. You sure you got your head on straight?"

Cully nodded.

"You sure about that?"

"Yeah."

There was just a thin hint of fear in his voice, a quaver, and at this, Hal inwardly rejoiced.

LEE

THAT NIGHT LEE had a long, slow dream in which Jess was a lamb, weaving among the speeding cars on Route 2351, and she had to watch her be crushed again and again, until gradually she turned into a small sun, a tiny ball of fire on the TV that bounced over the words of a song she couldn't read.

The phone rang. "Don't hang up," Jack said.

Her eyes were still unfocused, and in the dark, the bright blue curtains on the windows seemed to swell with wind, though the windows were shut and the air conditioner was on.

"Why?"

"Why'd I call?"

"Why would I do that?"

"You have before, darlin', don't you remember?"

"Oh."

She fought back the pull of sleep, sat up with the phone to her ear. For a moment, she thought she saw some kind of animal perched on the dresser, a cat that had got in through the window or something, but then she realized it was only a pile of dirty clothes. The dead blare of the air-conditioning seemed to coat the room in a fuzzy substance.

"What is it, Jack? It's the middle of the night." She wondered if he'd been drinking this time.

"I just gotta ask you, why is it that we're not together right now? Why is it that I'm not there in that bed with you?"

"You left me, remember that?"

She missed the solidness of his body more than anything, the long tapered fingers with sharp knuckles, the calluses on the palms. The leg he limped on was just slightly skinnier than the other, and he led with that leg when he moved to get on top of her, his shoulders muscled, though thinner in middle age. He smelled like smoke and deodorant, and scattered hairs pressed against her cheek when she laid her head on his chest.

"That was a long time ago. I didn't mean it."

"Yes, you did."

"Well, you were acting crazy then."

"What makes you think anything's changed?"

"Talking to you like this. I can tell."

"Maybe you're crazy now too. Ever think of that?"

"No." He sighed. "I did have this weird thing happen to me the other day. I walked into this little grocery store to buy some milk, and in the next aisle, there were these two women I didn't know. I'd never seen them before. But I just knew they were talking about me. It was a real strong feeling."

"I think you're paranoid. What did they say?"

"One said, 'He was born in Nacogdoches but he tells everyone he's from Beaumont.'"

"You do that."

"I know! And then the other one said, 'I don't know how he could leave her like that, just up and leave after everything.'"

She didn't want to say anything to this. She didn't trust it.

She looked up at the ceiling, at the mossy dark. She remembered that trip they took to Mexico, down to Oaxaca. They'd stayed in a hotel that had once been a rope factory, and at the hotel restaurant patio, they ate ceviche, looking out over huge bright pink flowers, like wadded, cheap panties, and palm trees, solemn by comparison. The owners came out and sat with them, bought them drinks, talked to them about Texas, and then they all played a game of pool in the back room. She remembered the man wore a Texas flag pin on the lapel of his elegant suit, and the woman had a cheerful gap between her two square front teeth that showed every time she laughed.

"She's in the next room, so I can't talk long." He was whispering now. She'd always loved his full-throated loudness on the phone. "But, goddamnit, tell me again why she liked that stinker, the one with the bowling-ball head and blond hair?"

"You mean Louie King."

"Yeah, that one. I could smell him all the way down the block."

For that Mexico vacation, they were truly alone for the first time in months, her body leaned toward his in the heat, their bodies shiny with sweat. They sped down the heat of that empty highway in a small car, and he reached over and squeezed her knee, cacti coming up on the horizon like giant green men holding up pistols.

"All the girls liked him. He played football. He had that handsome face."

"You thought he was good lookin'?"

"Not me. But I know what girls like at that age. He was harmless probably. Not like the other one."

"That guy. I almost kicked his teeth out and sewed them to his eyeballs."

"You're drunk."

"I am. Had a good reason to get that way." Her hand made a fist, and she pressed her nails into her palm.

"What's that, Jack?"

"I don't want to go into it. You ever see bowling-ball head around town anymore?"

"Not usually. But by chance, I did run into him the other day."

"Where?"

"Just saw him getting lunch over at Bob's—he had a suit on, didn't recognize me." So many of Jess's old friends didn't notice her anymore—they'd forgotten what she looked like, or maybe without Jess, she was invisible to them.

"Figures. Tell me, why is it that Jess had such bad taste in boys? I mean, look at me." He laughed and then snorted in his habitual way.

"You always were modest."

"I miss you."

"Where's Cindy?"

"Oh . . . she's in the next room. Snoring. You never snored. You kicked. Kicked like I was a football. Now I'm sitting here in this room, and you know what? The walls remind me of football fields."

He sounded very tired. She could hear the slur in his voice "How?"

"I can see the plays on them. Anyway, what have you been doing with yourself down there? How's that Doc?"

"He's fine."

"Still have that piece on the side?"

"I don't know. He doesn't tell me."

"Probably. You can't even recognize the wife anymore. Plastic lips. Rubber titties. I'd rather get me a blow-up doll."

"Jack."

"What? I would. So what do you do all day?"

She knew what he was asking, but she wasn't going to let him know whether or not she was seeing anyone.

"I've got some plans for a project. It's going to keep me occupied, hopefully get me past the seventh."

"For another year anyway, right?"

"Yeah."

"You're not writing those pissed-off letters again are you? Because, I tell you what, those suckers in the government, the last thing they want to hear is from a pissed-off lady."

"No, not that. I told you what I found. And now there's research that might actually go somewhere." She wouldn't go into the details because he didn't appreciate them. "I'll let you know how it goes."

"You do that." He started coughing. "Hey." He couldn't catch his breath. "I'll call again next week. If I can."

"You mean if you can get away from Cindy?"

He coughed some more and then was silent. She could hear the electronic waves on the phone like a rhythm of water. Sometimes they had these long silences between them on the phone, and it was strangely comfortable, almost as if they were back in their old living room, one of them just lying on the couch, the other sitting up in the easy chair.

"Jack."

"Yeah."

"You take care."

✝

THEY'D BEEN SITTING at home that night. Hard to believe it was another lovely, ordinary night of iced tea and television and library books. Jess ran in the house and said, "There's moving vans parked in every single driveway of South Hill Street." In the faint lines around Jess's mouth, Lee could see she was scared. This was just when she had the sore throat that wouldn't go away.

"It's all this hysteria," said Jack. "Everyone will move back eventually." They didn't know it then, but two babies had just been born on the same street, one boy with an arm that ended at the elbow and one girl who had no reproductive organs. On Cherry Street, four people had sudden liver problems, though they didn't know what was causing the pain under the rib cage and the itchiness in their hands. Other people noticed red-and-blue sores on their necks and forearms. A teenage boy on Hawk Street came down with a high fever and deep cough that would not lift. A week after Jess saw the moving vans, Lee, Jack, and Jess left their home too. They'd told themselves it was just temporary at first, just a precaution, and then little by little, they moved out all the furniture. Lee went back to their house alone one day, to pack up the last of their things, and she saw the garbage truck and the mail truck racing through the streets—only a handful of the houses weren't empty. Doors and windows were boarded up, stray cats roamed yards overgrown with bright yellow dandelions, and the emptiness felt like a recrimination

AT HOME ON SATURDAY, Lee poured the dregs of her coffee into the sink, the grounds catching on the white porcelain like stilled bugs. She ran the water, let it cool her fingers. She'd written to Cass Brown, to see if she had the name of the EPA rep who'd been coming around to see some of the old Rosemont people. Cass wrote back about how well her son had done at UT. "Now he's thinking of med school, and if he gets in, we can afford it." She didn't get to the EPA rep until the bottom of the note. "It was such a quick visit from him, but I finally found his card. Lloyd Steeburn. Here's his number." Lee would call this Steeburn as soon as she had her facts, as soon as Professor Samuels gave her the new readings. She wouldn't talk to him until she was well armed.

Someone knocked and she went to answer the door in her bare feet, her shirt untucked. It was that neighbor Hal. Flushed and grinning. Behind him, the dogwood tree sagged around the lower branches, and the grass that needed cutting was turning brown.

"Howdy," he said. There were dark patches of red, broken blood vessels at his cheekbones that made him look just bruised. "You know I heard about something at work—and I said, well, Ms. Knowles is my neighbor. I should just go on over and talk to her about it."

"You live in that gray house," she said.

"Sure do. I guess you know my wife, used to go by Miss Dobb?"

"Oh, Miss Dobb! She was my daughter's second-grade teacher."

"That's right."

She'd thrown a party for the class when the jar of marbles was full, each marble marking a "good deed," and Jess, though she'd been devoted to her, had once been punished for stealing marbles and putting them in the jar, unearned.

"I hear you have some issues with Taft Properties building over there near Banes Field. And, believe you me, I can see why you'd have them. It was a tragedy what happened to Rosemont. All those homes."

"I don't just have some issues. I used to live there."

"You know, I heard that too. I'm real sorry about that." His mouth twisted to the side, and he seemed to be waiting for her to say it was all okay.

"Say—" He paused, seemed to be testing her. "My wife and me got to talking, and we thought we'd see if maybe you'd like to go to church with us sometime. We belong over there to the Victory Temple. Lots of real friendly people."

"No, thanks," she said, smiling. "I'm a happy heathen." She grabbed the edge of the door. If he hadn't been married to Jess's old second-grade teacher, she would have closed it on him.

"Any chance you might change your mind? I sure would like to talk, if you ever got the inclination."

"No, no inclination."

"Alright then, well, the other thing is, I just want to reassure you Avery Taft has done his due diligence in getting that land tested. He sure has. The EPA came out not once but twice." She wondered which office Steeburn was from, the one in Dallas or the lab in Houston. With Professor Samuels's signature on the new readings, they might pay attention if the numbers were high enough.

"Did they? Did Taft Properties send you over here?"

The smile on Hal's face seemed to scatter, the features pulling away from one another. "No, no, no, no. I just wanted to save you some trouble. See, we're going to be selling the houses over there, and I have two thick notebooks of scientific evidence that the soil in Banes Field is now toxin free. Completely safe for human health. You can see it for yourself if you'd like to come by the office sometime?"

"I appreciate your concern, I do," she said, summoning sweetness. "But I'm looking out for some new test results. I could show you those when they're ready."

"Ms. Knowles, I don't mean to be rude." He scratched his forehead. "You really think you've got something better than the EPA?"

"You know what?" she said. "I'd like to see."

"Excuse me?" The two alcoholic red patches on his cheeks darkened into flat, dead berries.

She noticed the pen in his shirt pocket, the reasonableness of his blue shirt. "I do appreciate your trying, but you know I don't need to see your binders. That's about the size of it. Bye, now."

She closed the door. She went back into the house and emptied all the cabinets looking for aspirin. An image came to her of Jess, playing in Banes Field, kneeling in the mud, building something out of rocks with another girl. She'd come back bleeding, having scraped her knee—toxins probably getting into her even then.

On the radio now, the news was blaring about a woman who'd donated her liver to a stranger and saved his life.

✝

RUSH CAME OVER, and they sat outside on the patio, drinking wine, trees spreading a green lace against the sun. Only a few of the oak trees' leaves were starting to yellow.

"This is nice. A little breeze here." Rush sat back, took small sips from her glass.

"So, you'll come out to New Braunfels with us in November, right?"

"We'll see. Maybe."

"Tom has a lot of friends up there—some of them single."

"Can any of them dance at all?"

"I imagine."

Lee envied the way Rush tended calmness like a garden. Part of that equanimity, though, was bought—now and then she disappeared and met an old boyfriend somewhere secret, just platonically. They got drunk on margaritas and flirted, but neither of the spouses knew—and that was how she was able to give the rest of herself to the family and to surly Tom—there was an economy to her mothering of them all.

"Have you seen Sam?" Lee asked.

She shook her head, looking into the glass. "I ended it."

"Why?"

"Because I could see where it was going. Bound to go. I've got my kids. And Tom . . . he's clueless, sure. And he'll never change. I've given up on that dream. But I built this life and I just decided I'm going to live in it, you know?" She narrowed her eyes.

"You could get Tom to take you out once in a while."

"Hah. Maybe." She bit at a fingernail. "Marin's real good at art class—did I tell you? She drew this portrait of me. Line drawing. Even I have to say, it's the spitting image. But there's these creases on either side of my mouth. They made me look so depressed. I was telling her how great it was, but the whole time I was thinking, do I really look that bad?"

"You're just as beautiful as ever. Even sad."

Lee wanted Rush to have her flirtations back, or she wanted Tom to come back to seeing Rush as something other than his burden. Maybe it wasn't that bad. Rush had Bryce. She had those beautiful girls—they put their shiny-haired heads on her shoulder. They held her hand.

"Well, it's not like I couldn't get a boyfriend if I wanted to." Rush's hair blew to the side in the breeze, the skin on her chest gently wrinkled, faint red lines rivering to the middle.

"Well, that's obvious."

"You could too," she said. "Tell me, I've never understood why you don't go out and get one."

"It's just Jack."

Rush flicked her a stern look. "Yeah, you need to move on. What's the girlfriend—Susie?"

"Cindy."

"Well, he's moved on. What are you waiting around for?"

Lee shrugged.

"I think he was an ass for leaving when he did. I'll never forgive him for that."

"Oh, I wasn't all there back then either."

"Of course you weren't. You were in shock."

There was a day she'd just lain in bed, afraid to move, afraid to open her eyes, something fragile held under her hands at her chest. She could hear outside the huge flowering of the world, all full of itself, birds, wind in trees, traffic on the streets. But it was the thing under her hands that needed solidity, and she pressed against it hard, afraid it might dissolve between her fingers.

"I can't even imagine . . ." Rush lowered her eyes. "But I want you to be able to have fun again. Remember how we used to go to the Marles and drink and dance? Remember how we used to take the kids out to Galveston and ride the waves?" Over the radio, Willie Nelson's mournful crooning.

"Yeah." Pleasures like that seemed trivial to her now, but she didn't want to say that, to make it true. She noticed a pale green fungus growing in the knot of the birch tree, like small torn pieces of paper glued there.

"Well."

"Well." Lee slapped a mosquito against her thigh, drank down the rest of the wine. "Aren't we having fun now?"

HAL

HAL WALKED HOME after trying to talk sense into Lee Knowles, lay down on the couch in front of the local news on the TV, and fell fast asleep. When he woke up, he pulled the computer onto his lap, got to his email and sent this message to Avery Taft: "Hey good buddy. Made some headway with our greenie neighbor. Will report back soon I hope."

Avery called him a little later. "Did she say anything about some pictures of a container?"

"No, she sure didn't."

"Huh. Here's where I need you to keep my confidence." He coughed. "See, one of the containers where they buried the chemicals, it popped up after the hurricane."

"Is that so? Well, it seems bound to happen."

"It's nothing, a natural occurrence, but you know someone could make something of it."

"They like to do that, don't they?"

"So, right away, as soon as I heard about it, I hired all my Mexicans and their buddies to go out there and dig a hole and rebury it that night, put it back down ten feet where it couldn't hurt anyone. It was a real tricky situation. But somehow she got

out there before I got the thing buried. She has these blurry photos, but she's mouthing off about it all over town."

Hal might have underestimated her, but he'd get her to back
down, even so. "Oh, I don't think she'll be mouthing off again,
Avery. We had a good chat."

"I hope you're right, buddy. Let me know about that old
property of mine too."

A little later, Darlene came home and then Cully, sullen, as
he'd been ever since he'd been suspended. Hal had fought to
make sure the boys could still play football after the two weeks'
suspension, and Principal Johnson had agreed, just barely, at the
urging, he suspected, of Coach Salem. But still, with Cully at
home, Hal was afraid his son might be absorbing all his own
failures, and he prayed about it constantly, as he did again, that
night, in the dark of their walk-in closet, his head among the
tails of his cotton shirts, Darlene clattering downstairs in the
kitchen, Cully in his room talking secretively into his phone.

A little while ago Hal had opened a box in the attic to find his
crumpled letter jacket with the tiny football sewed onto the *F*
and trophies with tiny gold quarterbacks, one arm cocked back
to pass, the other pushed out to defend. The pose. They perched
on cheap marble squares marked with gold plaques for the years
1979, 1980. There was a tangle of blue ribbons for track and
sportsmanship, all faded now to purple. And he wouldn't let the
nostalgia grip him, quite, but the feeling was of looking at the
relics of someone who'd died. His son still had all of that glory,
the bright, athletic blue, unfaded. Why would he squander it?

He knew that stupid incident at the Lawbournes' had only
happened because Cully was drunk, because his pals were there,
because it took discipline and practice to learn to restrain a lust.

Thank God Principal Johnson didn't know the whole story—it would have been the end of the season. Cully had confessed it, that he'd had sex with a drunk girl, and then found her a little later with one of his buddies in the bed. He said no one knew except the ones who'd been upstairs. There always were and always would be girls like that, Hal told him, but it was a man's job to judge the situation. Darlene didn't know either, and he told Cully to keep it that way. "Ask God for forgiveness and move on. Do not talk to the girl again, you hear me?"

Hal prayed to bring goodness and rightness back to his family. He prayed for guidance and strength and wisdom. Hal knew he could pass his success on to Cully too, and actually, he did feel the wealth coming, like sunlight in the clouds, the way one beam would come down and seem to point itself directly at him, how, when he prayed, he felt a face above him somewhere, nodding in agreement.

✝

HAL WENT OVER to Quaker's Landing to show an old colonial. The prospective buyer was a pretty, almond-eyed blond woman with a tattoo of a bluebird on her upper arm, dainty, just at the curve of biceps. They walked up to the black wooden door with a strange pilgrim-head knocker. Taking the colonial cues too far, if you asked him.

"I like that park down the way," Ms. Lansing was saying.

He put the key in the lock, and it wouldn't turn. "The high school just made the list in *Texas Monthly*. I know a lot of the teachers myself—went to school here with some of them. And my son's there now." He wrenched the key in the other direction. "Just having a little trouble." He leaned against the door and turned the key. It moved halfway, but wouldn't click open. He moved away and jiggled the door while he turned the key, trying to make it catch, but that didn't work. "I'm sure this is the right one."

It had happened to him before, not with this house but with others. The owner got accustomed to the loose locks and the specific trick to unlocking them and forgot to tell the person showing the house.

He rang the bell again. "Maybe someone's home. Just a minute." He was smiling, thinking, *Goddamn these fuckers.*

"I like this one," she said in her kitten voice. "It's the perfect size, and I like those columns, I don't know why." He called the owners on his cell, but he got the answering machine.

"Well, let me try this one more time."

He put the key in the lock and telegraphed a sense of his will into the key, and this time, by God, it turned.

"Hooray!" said Ms. Lansing.

"Hello!" he called out. "Hello! Realtor here!" Just to be safe. He'd more than once caught people in bed, usually with their pajamas on, but still.

They walked inside, and he saw Ms. Lansing's posture wilt. On the table, plates with the dry yellow lacy remnants of eggs, a pitcher of souring milk. In the living room, kids' Legos scattered across the carpeting, a dirty doll with blue chewing gum stuck in the hair. A faint smell of diapers and diaper wipes. Standing in the mess, he felt repelled by humanity. People, wanting to fail. It was easy enough when you weren't trying.

"I guess they forgot to tidy up this morning," he said.

She averted her gaze out the window to the next-door neighbor's well-kept yard.

In the old days he would have already been planning how to get a drink in him, but instead he said a small, positive prayer to keep himself on track.

He always told Cully the same thing—God wants you to do good. "Let's see what else we've got for you today," he told Ms. Lansing. He only had to walk with his eyes straight on the path and not look away.

He was back in the office, emailing with a mortgage broker, Dennis, an annoying, self-important guy with a huge forehead, who relished his power, took hours to return emails but even longer to return phone calls. Diana, the company's administrative assistant, was out sick, and though the office was quieter, everything was taking longer to do. The water cooler stood nearly empty next to the bathroom door. He could hear only Stan at the cubicle way at the other end, clicking at his computer keyboard.

When his cell phone rang, he hoped it was Dennis, so he could finish their damn deal, but he saw Cully's name flash on the screen.

"What's up, son? I'm in the middle of work here."

"I ran out of gas."

"What do you mean you ran out of gas?"

"I just forgot I was on low, and didn't see the light, and I was driving back from the gym and got stuck."

The rectangles of fluorescent lights above him seemed to zap and intensify, a spidery headache forming in his forehead. "Dammit, Cully!"

Hal had found a hundred cigarette butts behind the house by the spigot to the garden hose. And Cully had been falling asleep regularly just after dinner on the couch in front of one of those stupid shows where the guy or the gal gets a rose. Since his suspension, it didn't seem as if Cully always showered in the morning, and his mother scolded him for the stubble on his cheeks.

"Sorry, Dad." Something in his voice sounded tremulous, just a shade.

"Where are you?"

"Out in the oil fields."

"Now what in the hell are you doing out there?" The fluorescent rectangles seemed to be clacking together, the papers strewn over his desk shuffling themselves—he'd never get it all untangled before night.

"I'm in the middle of something. Where's your mother?"

"Don't know. She's not answering." It wasn't like him to run out of gas—he treated that truck like a treasure.

"I've got a mountain of work here, Cully. It's got to get done today. Can't you call a buddy or something?"

"I could, but I think my phone's about out of juice."

This was not like his son. One of the reasons he'd trusted him with a truck in the first place was that he so lovingly and responsibly took care of it, the regular oil checks, a wash on Saturdays. And he had dozens of friends he could have called, was on that phone all the time.

"Dad? Are you coming?"

"Just sit tight. You may have to wait, but I'll get there."

He got his car keys from his suit jacket and went out to the lot.

It was so hot that his dress shirt stuck to him in sweat. What was Cully doing out there near the oil fields anyway? Hal got into his car and drove to the gas station, filled up a small gas can, and put it in the trunk. When he got back in the car, he looked at the index card on his dashboard, and remembered what Pastor Sparks had read from Scripture the other day. "There is no lack, for my God supplies all my needs." No lack.

He spotted Cully's truck parked on the shoulder at the end of the dirt road, the black oil rigs seesawing in the dry land beside them, bobbing their heads up and down. The thin smell of heat and chemicals.

Hal put the can of gasoline on the ground next to the truck's back wheel, and opened the passenger side door. Cully's face was red and covered with sweat.

"Whatever made you want to come out here?" Hal asked.

Cully looked at him blankly, then lifted the corner of a smile. "Sometimes I come out here to think."

"Think?"

Cully nodded. The pimples around his chin formed an angry purple beard, and he was still wearing his dirty gym clothes, which smelled rank.

"Think about what?"

"Stuff. A lot going on right now. Seems like it's hard to keep it all straight. Never mind. You got some gas for me?"

"Look, I know you're missing the big game with Spring," Hal said, "but you can't let the pressure get to you. You've got to practice as if you're going back tomorrow."

Cully pushed his hair, wet with sweat, away from his face and nodded. "I know. I just feel it's all bad out there, that there's not one good thing."

Cully was upset, but Hal felt manipulated, having to come to him this way. "You want to talk about it?"

Was it the girl? There was a prickling at the back of his neck. Hell, he'd seen the same thing and worse, back in the day.

"Nah. Just makes it worse."

Cully had maybe not told him everything, but he wasn't going to pry—these were teenagers, and prying only led to stony silence. "You've just got to be logical about it. Say your prayers. Tell Jesus what you're working for."

"Jesus, isn't he already supposed to know?"

"Don't bullshit me. You know that isn't the point."

Cully rubbed the tops of his thighs with his hands.

"I'm just saying you've got too much time on your hands now. Just do your schoolwork and run your laps. Don't think too much—think long, you think wrong. There's a lot of wisdom in that. You okay, son?" Hal needed to talk to that Dennis, start to move toward closing on this house.

"Yeah, I'm good." Cully nodded, his face pointed at the front windshield, as if he was determined to get out of there.

Hal wasn't sure he believed him, but the papers on his desk seemed to spread before him in phantom slips, floating around the car. "Alright, I'll get going then. We can talk again after supper."

Cully got out, opened the gas can, and poured the contents into his truck.

Hal got out after him, and walked over, put his hand on Cully's shoulder. "I'll wait to make sure it starts."

He and Darlene had spoiled him. Cully didn't know what it was to have to get himself out of a situation. Hal wondered if maybe, for Cully's sake, he shouldn't have answered his phone.

Hal got into his car and sat there with his hands on the steering wheel, smelling the bitter, vaguely plastic air. The equipment they used out here so often looked like cartoon versions of spaceships. Down the road, and off to the right, a squat blue round tub seemed to spin in the heat over the gravel, but when he stared at it, it kept still.

WILLA

WILLA HEARD THE PHONE RING, and then her mother talking hoarsely in the bedroom. "She wouldn't do that."

Beneath Willa's feet, the red, yellow, blue, and green stripes moved, just barely, as if someone were tugging at the rug. She paused, halfway down the stairs, listened hard, imagined the voice on the other end of the line.

Ever since her mother had driven her home from school, planes cruised through the clouds overhead, cars had obediently followed patterns of traffic lights, and the world had been too quiet. Even her mother—though she'd smoked one cigarette after another in the car.

Willa heard the rustle of her pacing in the bedroom. She heard her say, "No, I didn't know."

Willa plodded down the stairs, swiveled on the end of the banister to turn in the entryway, passed the living room, and went into the kitchen, where two carrots lay chopped on the cutting board, the long green leaves hanging over the side of the counter. She took a glass down from the cabinet and held it under the faucet in the sink until it overfilled with water.

There was a prayer and maybe a medical operation you could

do to get virginity back. She was trying to remember where she'd heard that. Girls resurrected themselves that way, but how could it really work? Either you were or you weren't. She could have left when she'd been offered that drink. She could have pulled her hand away from Cully's and told him to take her back to school.

When her mother came down, her face was flushed and shiny. "That was Ida Johnson," she said. "You need to tell me what all happened over at that house."

Willa closed her eyes and leaned her head back to drink down the glass of water. She remembered now another guy who'd been there, his blue sneakers, and a gravelly but high voice. And she didn't know if she remembered or had imagined someone leaning over her, asking if she was alright.

Willa turned on the faucet again, stared at the glass while she filled it. "I told you, Mom. I don't remember, I swear." Without looking, she knew what was in her mother's face—lines and lines of disappointment, chaotic scribbling.

"You have to tell me," she said, but her face said the opposite thing. She waved her arm as if to get rid of a circling fly. "Come on, get your shoes on. We have to take you to Dr. Davis." She said it as if medicine might still be able to rearrange what had happened.

As they passed the open fields and the storage warehouse, on the radio in the car, there was a warning that Bush Intercontinental's air traffic control signal had gone off the grid. She looked out the window at the clouds, wishing for the hole in them to widen and pull her up into it. If she didn't remember, how could it possibly be her fault?

✝

A LITTLE WHILE AGO, she'd read a book about the dispensa-
tion period, the ten years when people would be left behind, just
before the Rapture. The book opened with an airplane ride, babies
and children disappeared from their seats, sprung off to heaven;
one pilot was gone too, and one (who was having an affair with
the stewardess) was not taken. As they came in for the landing,
other planes were crashing all around. "You know what I'd do if I
heard the world was ending tomorrow?" said Dani, when she saw
Willa reading the book. "I'd plant a goddamn tree."

The doctor's office was in a string of buildings, each one made
up to look like an identical house with a triangle roof and an eave
over the door. Dr. Davis, who was an old friend of her mother's
(they used to play in the marching band together), wore gray
braids, and she had a low, kind voice. First Willa' s mother went
alone into the office, and Willa could hear her through the door.

"We don't want it to get out, whatever happened. Willa made
a mistake, that's clear enough. Can you just take a look at her?"

The doctor's talking went on in a muffled way.

"She's just a girl. I know. I don't want the police. You know
what they might make it out to be. You know what they'll say."

The doctor said more Willa couldn't hear. She stared at the
window's calico curtains. The tiny red flowers were meant to
seem homey, but here among the modern, plain furniture, they
seemed cheap and dishonest.

When her mother came out, she said, "Go on in, okay?"

Dr. Davis led Willa to an examining room, handed her a blue
paper gown, and gently asked her to undress.

On the wall, there was a diagram of the female anatomy cut neck to midthigh, the purple uterus a paisley at the center. Next to it, the tall *T* of the scale. Overhead, the white lights sputtered like lightning.

Dr. Davis examined Willa's body under the drape, while Willa stared at the ceiling, crossed with strips of fluorescent fixtures. She'd managed to scrub the inked letters off her skin, but now Dr. Davis would know what happened anyway. Making her voice extra gentle, the doctor warned her about the speculum, which was somehow worse than it would have been if she'd been brusque. "Now, here," she said. Against her eyelids, Willa saw dancing orange fireworks. She wanted to ask how two sips of vodka and Red Bull could make you lose your memory. She wanted to tell her how she'd trusted Cully, and then the hours flew away, but the doctor wasn't asking any questions, just seeing for herself. The orange fireworks stretched and disintegrated.

"Are you in any pain, honey?" That had gone away days ago.

"No."

"You and your mom can trust me, you know."

"I know."

"Do you want to tell me?"

Willa opened her eyes and turned her head to the wall. "There's nothing to tell. I don't remember."

"You don't know who did this?"

Willa's eyes began to ache. She started to speak, but only a crushed sound came from her throat.

"Okay, Willa," said the doctor, her smooth hands patting Willa's ankles. "You can get dressed now." She left the room, and Willa heard the doctor's soothing, professional voice, talking to her mother on the other side of the closed door.

There was a bottle on the equipment table with a wide bottom and a narrow top, and a small fracture at the top of the glass. So now her mother would know too. Below the table, near the floor, something emerged from the white, its horns short and conical, the face a lamb's. Another one. When it opened its mouth, maggots crawled around the tiny body of a dead mouse: its paws folded together, its tail hung stiffly over the tongue. The beast averted its face, and in its whimper, there was that same voice she'd heard before: "What does she want?"

Willa pulled off the gown and stepped into her jeans, buttoned her shirt, and when she looked up, the beast was gone. She came out from the examining room, saw her mother's face, terrible and red.

On the way home in the car, the sun fell in flat yellow panes on the windshield. They passed the junior high school, ornate lettering on the faded green sign. It seemed unbelievable that just three years earlier, in the seventh grade, Willa had sat in the ancient auditorium, studying scratched initials on the old wooden seats, wondering whether or not the kids who'd scratched them were grown-up now or already dead.

Her mother said, "I think you better tell me."

She wanted her mom to stop talking, but she knew now, and there was no good way for Willa to explain. "Well, I had some vodka. I didn't think it would do that to me."

"Do what to you?"

"I didn't think it would hurt me."

Her mother's hands trembled on the steering wheel. Willa had to tell her what she didn't know, or the questions could go on forever. "I can guess what probably happened." The air in the car seemed frozen, as if she'd have to hack through it to speak again. "But I don't remember it."

Her mother shook her head. "Now what will you do?" She rooted around in her purse, and Willa knew she was searching for a cigarette. She smoked secretly, away from their father, and kept extra cigarettes in the zippered pockets and pencil bags. She always said she was praying for the will to quit. "Was this Holbrook the one you talked to after church?"

"Yeah."

"Evil," she said, so upset she forgot to roll down the window. "But no one's going to care about that because we have to protect you instead of getting to him." She exhaled, and for a moment smoke clouded her face.

They passed the Kroger's, a small kingdom of cars organized by parking lights and red and green flags. "We've always looked out for you. We have. Don't you understand? No one else ever has to know. Just tell me."

Willa's eyes stung in the smoke. "I shouldn't have had that drink. It just wiped out everything."

Her mother stopped at a light. She put her hand on Willa's arm. "Alright. Alright. I believe you." She shook her head, a screen of smoke between them. "We just need to pray," she said, lifting her chin. "And pray and pray. There's a way out of this."

Willa watched the houses pass by, the bikes leaned against garage doors, the swing set with the drooping double seat, the bouquet of pink balloons tied to a front door.

✝

HER PARENTS PARTLY BLAMED DANI for what happened, even though she'd told them, Dani wasn't even there. They didn't want Willa to see her, and Dani was practically the only person she wanted to see. "I can't believe he left you. That's the thing that gets me," Dani said on the phone. "You know he had the nerve to ask me how you were. 'Well, how the hell do you think she is?' I told him. I gave him a chance to tell me his side of the story, but he said I wouldn't understand. He only got suspended for two weeks for skipping school and getting drunk. Big effing deal. Willa, I don't care, he should get more than that. They should lock that guy up. How could they not know what really happened? They really should know."

No one could help her with her brain erasing those hours, just as no one else could see the beasts—they were just there. She kept turning it around in her head, what it could have been that had made him hate her so much. He had held her and talked to her in that voice, and then he'd let that happen. "Anyway, it's all over with now," she told Dani.

"Well," said Dani, "I'm sure not ready to put it behind me. For instance, why are you the one who's not in school?"

"Look, I don't want to be there. You know that." None of Willa's other friends, Miranda or Amy—or any of the others from church—called or texted. The life she was supposed to have led had somehow slipped off without her. She missed being careless, having conversations about shoes or hair, all those things that didn't matter. He might as well have shot her or run her down with his truck.

At dinner, over pork chops and rice and greens, her father spoke to her, but with his head turned sideways toward her mother, using her as some kind of shield. Jana chattered on about a dodgeball game. She wore a tiara with pink fur along the top in her dirty-blond hair.

After dinner her mother came to her room, stood at the door

and sighed, her hair awry on one side, mascara flaked under her eyes like bits of tar. "We have to pray about this," she said. Willa knew this was what they were supposed to do—to pray for a way out of crisis, to pray for peace—but it wasn't something they often did together, and it embarrassed her, even at the dinner table if her father veered from the script. *God is great. God is good. Let us thank him for this food.* There was no script now, and to pray with her mother felt as awkward as it would have to bathe with her.

"Okay." She couldn't say no.

They knelt next to each other, hands folded, and leaned against the edge of Willa's bed. "Dear Lord, please . . ." Her mother's voice was raspy. She smelled like dish-washing soap. "Willa . . . my girl . . . she needs—" Her voice wavered, and audibly she took in a breath, as if she'd lost her balance. "We're putting our trust—" When Willa opened her eyes, her mother wept, pressing her fingertips to her eyelids. "I'm sorry, I can't. I'm so sorry." She got up from the floor and went out of the room.

WILLA'S PARENTS AND THE COUNSELOR had agreed to put her on home study, and the substitute teacher would come to the house once a week to go over the lectures and assignments. The rest of the work Willa could do at her own pace. Usually, people only went on home study if they broke their leg or if one of their parents had died, and the only person she knew who'd done it before was Tonya Harp, who'd had to have an operation on her spine. But Willa was glad not to have to go back to school, which seemed now like a building full of booby traps catching those who fall through them in little, dark closets.

Willa stared down at her hands: bony, long fingers like her mother's, each nail bitten down to a sliver of painful red skin that showed above the edge. The nails themselves looked like fragments of shrimp shells, the blue veins between her thumb and wrist forming a shape like a wilted *Y*. It seemed if she studied her hands closely enough, she might understand, but the hands themselves were inscrutable, the whorls of wrinkles at the knuckles and joints, the red callus on the third finger of her right hand.

She could feel the weight on the mattress. When she looked up, the lamb beast sat at the end of the bed. Its body was now covered with perfect almond-shaped blue eyes, and it smelled like shit. There seemed to be a radio caught in its throat, a raspy clip, "Fifty-two killed in a car bomb attack. Fifty-two killed in a car bomb attack, suicide, suicide, suicide."

LEE

SHE VISITED PROFESSOR SAMUELS at his house, over near the community college, and his wife brought them lemonade to drink in the living room, where he sat in a leather-upholstered wing-backed chair. He could speak again now, but only slowly, and sometimes the aphasia turned around the words. His hair and face were more gray than when she'd seen him before the stroke, his body slighter and crooked now in a way she couldn't exactly place. The slowness of his speech, as she watched his mouth, kept giving her the impression that he was deaf. John, the graduate student, had just sent him the new findings from her samples.

"The benzene is bad," he said. "It's probably even worse than the tests show. Also the toluene and the styrene."

His wife, short haired and minx faced, was on hand to translate. "Did you get that?"

Lee remembered the course she'd taken with him at the community college, just trying to find out for herself what had happened in Banes Field, how he lifted slightly to his toes whenever he mentioned the name of an environmental stressor, the diagrams he drew on the chalkboard using pink and green and yellow chalk. He didn't like to use the computer for his presentations, he said, because he didn't have enough to do with his hands then, and he got nervous in front of a crowd of people, so he scrawled on the board and taught with these mapped-out, messy, impromptu pictures.

"I just wish I knew how to communicate to the right people what that increase means," Lee said. "Hypotheticals don't seem to matter much around here." He was an expert, but he was not an advocate.

Professor Samuels scowled and awkwardly punched at the air. "Let it blow cake."

"What honey?" said his wife. "Say it slowly."

"Let it all blow in cake."

She took his hand, leaned in closer. Lee was aware, suddenly, of her own apartness, her aloneness in the world. He whispered in his wife's ear and then nodded.

She pulled away from him. "He said, 'Let it all blow up in his face.'"

"Sooner or later, it will," Lee said. "Someone from the EPA's been going around talking to people who lived on Crest Street. Actually, I was thinking we could call him now. We've got the documents, and if I get something confused, well, I've got you right here to back me up, don't I?"

Professor Samuels gave her a half smile, and a weak thumbs-up.

His wife stood. "You'll want to use the landline, right? I'll go get the phone."

Lee sat next to Professor Samuels, the folders of data on her lap, the cheery oranges and apples in a bowl on the table. The phone rang, and she asked for the general operator. "Lloyd Steeburn, please."

There was a pause. Professor Samuels patted her hand, then put on his eyeglasses. The operator said, "I'm sorry, but that person no longer works here."

"Oh," said Lee, defeated. "What happened to Mr. Steeburn? Is he at another office?"

"We can't give out that kind of information."

She finally spoke to someone who'd been assigned to their district, and it was a moment before she realized it was the same woman who'd appeared at the city council meeting last month, Ms. Dawson.

"Oh," said Lee, defeated. "I know you asked to see this report. We're just about to send it. What's the correct address?"

She drove back to work. The billboards suddenly erected at opposite sides of town advertised for Taft Houses, and "coming soon" Pleasant Forest, at the end of Veemer Road. One billboard, next to the Children of Paradise church, showed a beefy-faced Avery Taft, smirking, wearing a string tie, his hair slicked back as if for a special occasion, a photograph of a large house and a pool dangling next to the text. The other billboard, in a field on the way out to Alvin, read TAFT PROPERTIES—WE'LL MAKE YOU AT HOME, and the photographs of houses, each in its blurred, dreamy cloud, constellated around the words.

✝

DOC LEFT EARLY FOR THE DAY, but they had to keep the office open until 6:00. Lee looked out at the orange plastic chairs in the empty waiting room, the pebbled linoleum floor. In the beginning of Jess's illness, she'd waited in so many stark rooms like this one, rooms that clarified boredom and anxiety—stacks of magazines on the tables, vases of silk flowers, a TV. Jess's illness began with the sore throat that wouldn't go away and then more grisly nosebleeds and a fatigue that overtook her, so that Lee would find her asleep on the easy chair, asleep at the kitchen table, or curled up at the foot of her parents' bed, snoring softly on her old tattered baby blanket. They'd waited two whole hours that day before they saw the oncologist, and by the time they got into his office, Lee was nearly numb from sitting and the strain of not showing worry. Jess had chewed down her fingernails, intermittently turning the pages of fashion magazines, and she seemed to want to pretend Lee wasn't there, so Lee indulged her. When the nurse in her teddy bear–print scrubs came to call them in, Lee took Jess's hand, and she could feel her hanging back, walking slowly. The doctor was bearded, bright-eyed, a bearish man in a white coat that barely fit him. "If I could just have Jess there go with Sally." He nodded to the nurse. "I'll be in to examine her in a little while." He snapped his fingers a couple of times.

Jess got up from her chair, looked sideways at Lee, then, with a slight shrug, followed the woman down the hall.

The doctor's hands formed a small steeple in front of him on the desk. "Now," he said, "I don't want us to panic, but I have to tell you. Her counts are way down." He went on to explain the way healthy blood worked, but every time he said "platelet," Lee had an image of a machine missing its part. If only they could find the part and put it back, Jess would be fine.

"It looks something like leukemia, maybe, in the family of blood cancers."

The word *family* sounded obscene. "She has a kind of myelo-dysplastic syndrome. You may find bruises on her skin soon or tiny purple marks. And she will be mighty tired."

"How did she get this? I mean, she's just a teenage girl. It seemed like it was the flu. That's what we thought, right?"

"It presents itself that way at first a lot of the time," he said. His plump mouth pushed up and then to the side, and only then because she could tell he was uncomfortable, was Lee aware of her fear.

"It's those chemicals they found in the dirt, isn't it?"

His office was twenty miles away from Rosemont, in the heart of Houston.

"I don't believe I know what you're referring to."

"It's been in the news, our subdivision. It's right next to an old oil refinery and they just dumped all the chemicals . . ." It frustrated her that she wasn't better informed, that she couldn't explain it objectively, scientifically. "All those babies born with birth defects."

He nodded. "Well, we don't know yet. We just don't know, do we?" And then he took out a pad of paper and began writing down the tests Jess would need, the possible treatments, talking all the while in this language of *cytopenia*, *myelogenous*, and *hematopoiesis*, and the words formed a fence around him.

"What do you mean?" she kept asking him. "What does that mean?" It was as if she'd suddenly been transported to a foreign country, and had to learn the language right away in order to avert disaster. It wasn't fair, but she had to study it fast, learn the pronunciations and grammar of it, and it seemed if she could only say the words correctly, the doctor would have to let her into the country, so that if he couldn't cure Jess, she'd have the means to find the one who could.

When the doctor left her in his office while he went to examine Jess, she called Jack. "Jess is real sick. It's a blood disease, the doctor thinks."

He didn't say anything at first, but she could hear him breathing.

"You have to come get us."

By the time Jess came out of the examining room, Lee had dried her face, and drunk some water. She was relieved to see that Jess only looked tired, with purple marks pressed around her eyes, her just-brushed hair long and glossy on her shoulders. "Hey, Mom," she said, unfazed, hauling the strap of her gigantic purse over her shoulder. They waited outside the office building, and Lee made an excuse about their car not working, so she could explain why Jack was coming to get them.

Weeks later, at the hospital, in the chemotherapy room, Jess would hold Lee's hand while the poison—an alien fluorescent orange color—dripped into the port in her arm through a clear plastic tube. Jess wore earphones to listen to music, which sounded tinny and faraway as Lee tried to read or stared out the window. The doctors and nurses were always in a hurry—they wouldn't look her in the eyes but called them both by pet names. "Hon," "Sweetheart," as if Jess's cancer had made them all kin. When they got home, Jess would eat ice cream with M&M's on top, French fries. The steroids, with all the other medications, the antibiotics, the antinausea pills, made Jess gain weight. Her face turned puffy, and she cried when she could no longer button her jeans. Lee bought her all new clothes two sizes larger and reassured her the weight would come off. The doctors wanted her to eat potato chips, hamburgers, nothing with too many vitamins because it might help the cancer to grow. Jess's toenails turned black and fell off. Her skin turned to a thin, white leather, and when she scratched it, the red marks stayed there for days. All that time she sat with Jess in those rooms, Lee could practically feel her own skin stretching, phantom folds of flesh growing in Jess's direction, wanting to take the punishment away from her daughter's body.

One day Lee was vacuuming and she found a black tress lying on the floor half under the couch. At first she thought it was the horse's mane from an old stuffed animal that Jess used to play with, but then why would it be in the living room? As soon as she picked up the bunch of hair, she went to the desk, found an envelope, and sealed it inside there, thinking Jess might need it later.

She had a lot of rituals those days for keeping away catastrophe. She called the labs to follow up on every blood test, to make sure nothing was lost or confused. She read the literature the doctor gave to her in flimsy mimeographed packets, and then she followed up to research what she didn't understand at the library. She learned the language: *lymphocytes, monocytes, petechiae.* She tried to explain what she knew to Jack, but when she did, his eyes went slack with fatigue. "Now why do that to yourself? That's what we have the doctor for." Every week, she went to each of Jess's teachers to pick up her homework, and she organized visits from Jess's friends, with ice cream and movies. She bought a lap table, bright silk pillows, stuffed animals, and a new comforter for Jess's bed. Their friends and family sent hats, scarves, board games, fruit baskets, lip gloss, lotions, perfumes, quilts, a giant stuffed giraffe, and a pink dog, so many gifts they crowded Jess's room. Lee bought guidebooks to Paris, for the trip they'd all take when Jess got better. "So what do we do next?" she asked the doctor.

They'd moved away from Rosemont and into the house Jack's parents' had left him, but even then, Jack didn't think Jess's illness had been caused by Banes Field, and Lee, though she knew it, buried her certainty. She kept up the march of pills; she memorized the regimen of shots; she begged Jess to eat; she scanned the guide for TV movies Jess might watch. Rush helped when she could. Once when Rush asked Lee if she'd eaten, all the blood rushed to her head. "Who the hell cares? That won't move things forward one bit."

Rush said, "Sweetheart," and put a sandwich on Jess's nightstand. Lee hoarded all of her strength to nurse Jess, and at the time, the protestors around Banes Field seemed frazzled and distant. She saw the grainy flyers for community meetings pasted up at the grocery stores, heard reports on TV and in the paper, all so much noise as she sat in the bedroom, looking at Jess, while the sun came in at a certain slant over her face, just across the lovely curve of her cheek.

DEX

LATE TO BIOLOGY, Dex walked with Wendy, who worked as an aide in the principal's office. Construction paper helmets with glittered numbers for each of the players had been arranged in an *F* on the wall next to the giant blue mustang painted there. Some of the helmets lay smashed and wrinkled on the floor, where people stepped on them on their way to class. Wendy told him that someone had left an anonymous note in all caps addressed to Noelle, the super-Christian student council president; Principal Johnson; and "others." The note said "JUDGE NOT, LEST YOU BE JUDGED. ONLY GOD KNOWS THE TRUTH."

Later, the janitor's closet had been left open, and a cat had got in there. Dex watched the janitor go inside and look around but come out empty-handed. Waiting outside Binnie Priller's drama classroom for a conference with his Spanish teacher, Dex watched two girls practice a mock sword fight with cardboard tubes. They were wearing poofy, sequined skirts. Down the corridor, he spotted Coach Salem walking purposefully and blank faced into the principal's office, followed by the counselor, Ms. Ryan, who walked tentatively behind him in her long loose skirt. Dex wondered if there would be more punishment for Trace, Cully, and Brad, if the coach or the principal had found out what happened that day. Of course, they wouldn't want to lose Cully for the whole season, and maybe not even Brad, so they could choose, maybe, to downplay the rumors, to pretend they hadn't heard. Trace, Bishop, Cully, and Brad had only been suspended for two weeks—because, officially, the principal knew about the drinking and the truancy, and nothing else. But he'd seen Principal Johnson come out to the coach's office in the gatehouse last week, which he'd never witnessed before, and there were so many rumors about Willa at that party, even guys who'd been there didn't know what was true.

On the Wednesday when they'd all come back, Cully's eyes had a wariness to them, and he seemed hunched over. Trace and Brad walked down the halls together, cutting a swath in the crowd—a tic in Trace's strut, which seemed put on, and Brad's face so empty it seemed comically blank. Some of Dex's friends said they didn't blame them for being drunk and taking advantage—a girl was a girl was a girl. But, Dex said, "I heard she wasn't even awake." Whenever he passed one of the three in the hallway, he made it a point not to say hello.

After class, Angela and Sharon and another girl he didn't know were standing outside the gym, talking loudly, and as he got his books out of his locker, Sharon said, "This is all just a setup. Brad and Cully, these are quality guys, good guys. They don't have to force themselves on a girl." She slammed shut her locker.

Dex and Weeks were driving around, past the old Quaker church, past the intersection of competing gas stations, where one of their friend's older brothers worked, flabby and moving slackly when there was a problem with one of the pumps or when a lady wanted full service.

"You know Stewart used to work for Rue Banes," Weeks told him. "Dumped chemicals into the creek late at night, and sometimes they got on his skin or his clothes. His brother thinks it made him stupid."

"Huh," said Dex. "But maybe he was stupid to begin with."

"Yeah, it's hard to say."

They were supposed to be looking for a party over in Eagle Heights, but Weeks was looking for Heather's car at the Dairy Queen, at the laundromat parking lot, even though it was early for that.

"She's probably at home, washing her hair or doing homework, Weeks," said Dex. "What makes you think she likes you again? Oh, yeah, she asked you to dance once. Were there any other males within spitting distance?"

"Shut up."

Weeks was hurting. He hadn't been with a girl since last year when they all went to the community center for a teen night, and the girl he liked, Heather, happened to be trying to make her boyfriend jealous.

Weeks fiddled with the dial of the radio, tried to tune in the decent station. "I need a real sound system in this thing." A pop song shimmied out. "Yes!" There was a huge red zit right at the end of his nose, like something in a cartoon. "Let me ask you. You still like Willa? After all that?"

The post-work traffic passed them in the other lane, one person after another, driving, looking pissed off. "Yeah."

"I don't know." He shuddered, but Dex didn't think he really meant it.

"After all that skeeviness."

"Shut up."

"I heard something today." Weeks puckered his lips and blew out a sigh. "You know Bishop always has practically a pharmacy in his pocket. He put a roofie in her drink. Snow saw him do it. He thought the drink was for Bishop at first, that he was trying to make one of his special cocktails for himself. To make sure he got good and fucked up."

"Does Willa know that?"

Weeks threw up one hand. "Hell if I know. I'm pretty sure it's true though."

"What are you saying?"

The lights ahead seemed to stab at Dex's eyes, scramble up the scene they were driving toward.

"She was drugged, buddy."

Bishop seemed to always have Xanax, one of the drugs Dex recognized because he'd picked up the prescription for his mom. He'd never heard of him having roofies. The road rose up in a blur of red and white lights.

"Whoa," said Weeks. "Fuck." He swerved his truck into the Safeway parking lot, just avoided hitting a light pole. "Goddamn Jeep!"

"You're saying she's skeevy because Bishop Geitner drugged her, and that gave those shitheads permission," Dex said.

"Shit! Did you just see what almost happened? We nearly ate it because of that Jeep!" Weeks pounded the steering wheel, breathed slowly and loudly, a hand on his chest. After a moment, he turned to Dex. "I'm saying it's a sad thing. A real sad thing. She shouldn't have let herself get mixed up with Holbrook in the first place. But in all those texts, they don't say she was drugged."

"What texts?"

"Well, they're mostly in code. From Bishop and Brad."

They drove around for another hour, but they never saw Heather's car, and they never found the party.

It was a time when, if he could have, he'd talk to his dad. He tried calling him that night when he got home, but there was no answer, and the next morning, his mom said he'd written that he was out on a rig. Dex didn't want to be part of the lying about Willa. He knew they'd tricked her somehow, or Cully had brainwashed her into going to the Lawbournes' in the first place. And then they'd drugged her. How many people knew about that besides Weeks and him?

That afternoon, Dex drove out to Casa Texas, the place his dad had taken him solo, no Layla, the last time he'd been in town. They'd eaten tacos and his dad had let Dex sneak occasional sips from his beer bottle. The restaurant was a little way out of town on Farm Road 1, but it was worth it, for the food and the friendliness, his dad said.

Somehow, his dad had known the owner and a couple of the waitresses, and the hostess had seated them right next to the small dance hall, though the stage was empty, next to the scuffed wood floor.

"Best tacos this side of Mexico, my friend," said his dad.

The whole night they talked about the food and the mechanics of oil drills, and three times, someone came over to say hello. First, an older, chubby woman named Carlita, who held his dad's face in both of her hands and then kissed him. Then, a busboy named Juan, who wore a bow tie and an old-fashioned, slicked-back haircut, and joked with his dad in Spanish. And then the owner, Fred Holgine, slammed two shots of whiskey on the table and sat down with them for a bit. "Your dad," said Mr. Holgine, "he's my friend. You need anything? You're my friend."

Dex hadn't been back to Casa Texas since the spring, but he had a craving for tacos, and thought his dad would be amused to hear he'd gone there on his own—they'd have something to talk about on the phone for once.

He sat near the front, by the plate glass window with the *Casa* letters painted into jalapeño pepper shapes. He looked out the window at the parking lot and the small yard of modest trees. What was it his mom always said? *Don't worry about tomorrow. It always comes.*

The chicken tacos were good—served with lime and chorizo and a delicious spice he didn't know. There was a cute waitress in a short black skirt and white blouse, who set the tables behind him. Her black hair was in pigtails.

When he was almost finished, Mr. Holgine appeared at his table. "You're Mac's son, aren't you?"

"Yeah, I am. We met." Dex held out his hand, but Mr. Holgine didn't seem to notice. "How were the tacos? Good?"

"Yeah."

"This one's on me. Don't worry about it. Always remember, your dad's my friend." Bright-colored piñatas swayed from the ceiling—hot-pink horses with purple yarn manes, lime-green dogs with stupid grins. The music was cheerful and yearning. He wanted to stay there. And Mr. Holgine, standing there, smiling, seemed to want to chat, but Dex didn't know how to take him up on that.

"How's your dad doing anyway? He's out on that rig?"

"Yeah, he is. Until the fifteenth."

"He works hard, that man." Mr. Holgine scratched his forehead. "How old are you?"

"Sixteen."

"You got any interest in a job? Because one of my busboys just quit, and we can always use good people." Mr. Holgine must have seen maturity in him, or wanted to do his dad a favor by extending a hand to his son. His dad had seemed to love this man, with his neatly pressed colorful shirt, the shark tooth he wore on a chain around his neck, but Dex had other responsibilities.

"I've got my job as a trainer for the football team." He felt loyal to the Mustangs, to Friendswood, and felt he should still do his part.

"Oh, yes, of course."

Dex didn't want to seem ungrateful. "I appreciate you taking an interest."

Mr. Holgine smiled widely, clapped him on the back. "You come back, Dex. Anytime."

✝

THE NEXT DAY AFTER SCHOOL, the trailer smelled of hamburgers grilling because it was Layla's night to cook.

On the stained couch, playing cards splayed next to his mother's magazine, open to a page that said "How the Stars Lose Weight!" and "Halloween Babies."

Dex sat in front of the computer, moving the cursor through emerald woods as he searched for the evil dwarf. Layla was behind him, holding a greasy spatula.

"Mom and her were screaming, and it got real nasty," she said. "It was embarrassing. I haven't seen her that worked up in a long time."

Dex shrugged and onscreen entered a menacing meadow,

where he might be attacked from all sides. Layla's voice went on behind him. She liked to analyze a thing, look at it from a few different places, and then still keep her opinion in reserve. He was afraid she might be smarter than him, even though she was only thirteen. He was going to ignore her as long as he could.

"I mean, Mom really let her have it in front of all the other mothers. It was a costume meeting, so our uniforms look right. And Mom threw down my skirt on the floor. Don't you want to know what she said?" Layla sighed, and he felt her looking over his shoulder at the screen. "Dex!"

He concentrated on the wizards rising out of the pool, exploding with stars of color as he sent his lasers. "Kind of."

"Yes, you do."

Layla walked to the kitchenette stove, and he heard three hissing sounds. Then she was behind him again. "So this is what she said to the other mothers. She said these boys need to learn that not everything comes to them—they're not entitled. They need to stop spending so much time staring at the Internet, thinking they can have whatever they want."

Dex didn't turn around. He wondered for a second if his mother had found out somehow that he'd once, almost accidentally, visited the advertising clip on the porno site. Two girls had lifted up their T-shirts to bare their breasts, their nipples like laughing eyes.

"Anna's mother said girls are always the gatekeepers. She said girls need to remember that—to set the line at a reasonable place. And Willa was reckless to go to a house full of boys if she wasn't looking for trouble. The message she sent just by going, she said, was *I'm trouble*. Boys can't be expected to control themselves in a setting like that. When the present is right there in front of them, they're going to open it. That was when Mom flipped. It was super embarrassing. She was like, 'Men have been using that excuse for years—where have you been? My Dex knows how to control himself, no matter what *present* he's offered.'"

Sometimes when he got an erection it was like falling through the air and not being able to stop yourself, or like getting the flu.

Dex didn't turn around. He blasted the wizard, then two more enemies emerged from the pixelated woods.

"You know what I think?" she said. "That girl thought it was going to be one thing, and when she got there, it was something else. It's like those movies that start out seeming like country vacations and end up with bloody axes. It could happen to anyone."

He swung around in his seat, looked at his sister now, her brown eyes wide, her mouth twisted into a smirk, her cheerleader's T-shirt spattered with grease. "You better not trust anything any guy ever says to you, that's what I think." She was trying to look like she knew it all. "No matter what they say, always assume he wants to get in your pants." His father would have put it less crudely, given it a gallant cowboy spin, but Dex didn't know how else to express his authority on the subject.

Her smile shrank, and he realized he'd scared her. "But Cully Holbrook—he's okay, isn't he?"

He softened his voice, but kept it stern. "Doubtful," said Dex. "I don't want to say."

"You know Willa Lambert?"

He looked back at the screen, crowded now with bright haloed green trees. "Yeah, I do." He moved the keyboard to scope for the bad sidekick. The screen popped out in a green bubble because he'd been shot and the game was over.

His mother came home a little later, out of breath, her full face grim. "Dex, what do you know about this thing at the Lawbournes'? I really can't believe it—Steve Snow and Cully Holbrook? They were both there?" She slammed the door.

Dex looked down at his jeans—they were worn at the knees and stained on the thigh, he noticed, with something brown from lunch. He'd already pictured telling her that he was at the party too, how he'd explain that he had nothing to do with what happened to Willa, how he wasn't even drunk like the others, and that was something. He looked at her swollen arms tight in her thin sweater, at her small, fierce dark eyes, the extra chin cupping her original, delicate one, that face which was both beautiful and terrible to him. "I heard about it."

"There were all these boys there just sitting drinking downstairs or swimming. Why didn't they do anything to stop it? It just kills me that boys here would do that, boys I've had in my own house."

"Mom, you're yelling at the wrong people," said Layla.

Dex's mother threw her bag down on the floor, keys jangling, and plopped down on the easy chair. "I just don't like what it says about this place that something like that could go on here."

It bothered him that she couldn't let it go. "I heard most of the guys didn't even know there was a girl upstairs."

"Oh, honey, they knew," she said. "Believe me, they knew. That's what I told Ms. Louder."

"Hey, Mom? Lionel Louder was there," said Layla.

Dex's mother turned her head. "Well, that explains it. She's not going to be talking to me anytime soon."

Dex turned back to the screen, where pixilated monsters ran amok, blinking behind and above Egyptian pyramids. He turned it off. He thought his mother might ask him about where he'd been that day, but she trusted him too much, and that was a wrench in his heart.

WILLA

WILLA DID ALMOST ALL OF HER WORK for school independently in the mornings, finished by noon—she'd written ten poems in just two weeks, and she'd numbered them. That Tuesday she began her day eating yogurt in front of the computer, watching the *Looney Tunes* she'd liked as a child, and looking up random facts about Emily Dickinson: She liked white dresses. She attended Mount Holyoke Seminary, but left for mysterious reasons. After a certain age, she didn't like to greet people at the door. She had a dog for sixteen years, and when he died, she mourned him. She only attended church for a few years, and never made a formal declaration of faith. At some point, she wrote to a friend, "Home is so far away from home."

When Willa clicked on her email, she saw the headline about Iraq, and she went to the news story—the video clip of a bomb exploding in a café in a street, plastic chairs and broken glass blowing up out of the smoke, then settling. She didn't look closely at the sidewalk, but thought she saw a severed bloody foot next to a crushed Coke can. Alone today in the house with the tick of the coffeemaker and the digital chimes of the clock, the odorless smell of clean carpet and sunlight, she saw nothing out of place except a mug next to the easy chair, as if someone had been spirited up from their seat. She looked back at the computer screen, clicked on the video, and watched the explosion one more time. It gave her a strange solace.

She finished her science homework, and that was all the work she'd been assigned for the day. She made a sandwich for herself and sat at the picnic table on the back patio. After lunch was when she usually got most anxious because there were fewer things to occupy her, and the visions tended to come. Sometimes she tried to pray, but she couldn't lately—she only heard her own words come back to her, but in a nasal, mocking voice.

As she ate her sandwich, she watched the neighbor's black-and-white cat balance along the top of the wooden fence, its tail curled as if to hold it up. It took a few tentative steps, then fell, scurried down, and ran through the hole near her mother's vegetable garden. On the other side of the yard, trash lay scattered where a possum had got into the garbage can. When she finished eating, she walked through the trees to clean up the mess. Otherwise, her mother would be irritated and ask her why she hadn't bothered. She picked up a plastic bottle, and saw three strange mushrooms with broad, dotted hoods, red berets on top of them. She'd gathered up the milk carton, orange juice tube, and foil pan when she saw the pink and orange wildflowers lolling above the grass—she'd never seen them before, their orange velvet middles surrounded in a sun of pink. She looked at them for a long time.

Later in the afternoon, she was emailing with Dani, who was in the school library, supposedly doing research for her paper on the Constitution. She'd gone to see Cherry Bomb at a club called Sevens in Houston, Dani wrote. There was a singer who wore a red choker like a slit of blood and two cute guys on guitar. Willa knew she was trying to cheer her up. "Strange-trend alert: Ellen Almodóvar and Pam Riggins dressed up like pirates at school today, eye patch on one eye, full mascara and blue eye shadow on the other. Then I saw three girls I didn't know wearing the same thing. There's a rumor that they are stealing people's wallets. One girl got sent home because she wouldn't take off her eye patch, and she couldn't read the overhead screen in calculus. I gotta know, are people always this weird? And, excuse me? There are felons in my classes with me. And you're at home. What's fair about that?" Dani wrote. "I heard Ms. Carpenter call Cully 'trash' in the hallway. She actually said it to someone else, but loud enough for him to hear it. He just kept walking."

Willa glanced away from the screen, thinking what to write back. In the corner of the room emerged a shadow the size of a large dog. The wet fur appeared first, two huge paws, then eyes scattered across the body and limbs, eyes she'd seen before but couldn't place. The face was so much like her dog, Junior's, when she'd held him as the vet injected the needle—she recognized that hurt, relieved look just before he'd died. But this beast's head sprouted a tangled, mangy lion's mane, crawling with worms, and ears that flapped like skin-covered books. The voice seemed to be inside of her, as if she'd already heard it, even before the noise of it hit her eardrum. "What does she want?"

The beast defecated on the floor, and the shit ran bloody all the way under her dresser. The eyes began to look less like eyes and more like weeping sores, and she was crying. She stared beyond the beast at the chair, the wall. Finally, its shape blurred, first hovering like hundreds of colored dots and then dissolving as if the dots had been rinsed away with water. She had to find out what the beasts meant, what message they carried.

+

PASTOR SPARKS'S OFFICE was in the back of the church, next to the sanctuary, a large auditorium. The walls were filled with photographs and notes like pages of a scrapbook. There was a photograph of him preaching next to an American flag, with "The 700 Club" printed beneath it. She'd watched his televised testimony a couple of times. Standing on that TV stage, he'd looked smaller and thinner than he did at the pulpit, as if fame had shrunk him, and he paced back and forth in his brown suit, punching the air, preaching how he'd been saved. She still remembered parts of it well, how he'd grown up in a fancy, formal Presbyterian church where everyone was quiet and no one would know the Holy Spirit *if it bit them in the face*; his mother had told him he was stupid and after that he stuttered whenever he talked. *There was something in me, just mean and ugly. I couldn't shake it. Sunday morning came, and I was in a ditch of despair.* He'd almost died twice, and the bullets were still in him somewhere. *I was working the late shift. And one day, this guy comes through the door, blasting a gun.*

Willa's father had made the appointment for her. "Pastor will set you straight," he said.

His eyes shone, even in this small office light—there was a fierceness in them that had sometimes moved her during church services. "Well, Willa, what can I do for you? Why has the Lord brought you here?" He had a strange accent, a Northerner turned Texan.

She was confused because she hadn't expected to have to explain herself. "Well, my dad thought—"

"I want to know what you think." In church, she'd watched his face up close, projected large on the screen that hung over the altar, the tired, red lines wound under his skin, especially near his nose, just above his gray mustache. She'd heard him preach lots of times, had shaken his hand after the service, but had never before had a conversation with him alone.

She studied the beige carpeting, very clean, thick weave. "Something happened to me, but I don't remember it."

"You don't remember."

"No." She looked out the window. Outside, a pudgy man calmly rode a John Deere mower across the church's lawn; on either side of the vehicle spouted furious wings of grass blades.

"Wow. Now, Willa, were you drinking?"

Her parents had made the full report to him of everything they knew. But she wanted to show him that she was a good person. "I don't like the taste of it."

"Is that so?" Before he was saved: *I tell you, I held a dirty knife right against my wrist.* "Don't keep having a taste for it, thinking it's bound to be better the next time." He shook his head. "Your folks sure are worried about you," he said. "You know that? Your mother is so worried." It was the same voice he used from the pulpit, emphatic, as if he were speaking to a thousand people and not just to one. He told her about a woman he'd known back when he was young, someone who had the world at her feet, beautiful, smart, poised. He looked at Willa and said, "You've got a lot in your favor, you know that?" Then he went on to say how the girl had started to drink, and she'd started to go with one young man and another. And she ended up a "lush" without a church or a home. "She lost everything," he said. "Just chasing boys who said she was pretty."

"It's not like that. I mean. It's just . . ." She didn't know how to fix the misunderstanding. "The whole thing still doesn't seem real."

"But you know it was real, right, Willa?"

She nodded. From the hallway, there was a smell of coffee and cookies baking in the church kitchen.

"Willa, have you ever thought that might be a blessing that you lost your memory? Even in our darkest times, God wants to save us from that pain. That memory loss might just be a gift." His voice went softer and higher. "You sure you weren't drinking anything that day, Willa?"

In the trash, there was a cup with a bright, twisted cartoon face imprinted on it, smiling through the waste bin's metal bars. "I just want it not to have happened," she said.

"Of course you do. Of course you do. I tell you what, I'm sure you're not the only one either." He paused. "I'm sure there's another person who wishes none of that business ever got started. Is there anything else you'd like to tell me, Willa?" He smiled at her skeptically. It would have been a relief to tell him how Cully had put his arm around her, how he'd implied that other girls would be there soon.

"Let me ask you something, are you angry?" He seemed to shift his tongue around in his mouth. "Are you angry at Jesus for letting this happen?"

Her arms felt suddenly too bare, goose-bumped in the air-conditioning. "Because you know you had free will to go to that house, didn't you? God gives us free will because he loves us—he doesn't want us to be robots."

Fifteen years earlier, in an instant, everything had changed for Pastor Sparks. As he told the story, God streamed straight into his blood, and he ran out into the street screaming, "I'm alive! I'm alive!" Willa always remembered that. She wanted to know what he'd told Cully Holbrook, or what he'd like to say to the other two, who didn't attend their church. Did he think they were angry at Jesus too, and that's why they'd done it?

"I'm not trying to be a robot."

"Well of course you're not," he said, his voice suddenly gentle. "You just keep praying, and Jesus will tell you something. Wait for that. It always comes."

The snow globe at the edge of his desk resembled a giant, empty eye with tiny hidden things clotted at the bottom of it. It was becoming clear to her now why she was here, how adversity might have come to her for a purpose, to make her a messenger, and it suddenly seemed urgent to tell him. "Can I ask you something?" Willa said.

"You can ask me anything."

"In your sermons you're preaching that these are the end-times."

"Certainly seems that way." He nodded to a photograph of the soldiers on the wall. "See that? The troops are bringing Jesus to the Holy Land. Even some of those Arabs can still be saved. That's what the message is." Around his eyes, there was a new, open expression.

"I think I might be seeing signs—you know, of the end of days."

His upright posture sagged. "Phew. I think I need you to tell me what you mean by that."

"I think I saw the Beasts that are in Scripture. The ones before the Rapture."

He rubbed at his temples and bunched up his lips. "You saw them where?"

"A few places, in my room mostly."

"In your room. Now, Willa, don't you think if Jesus was

coming back this very minute, that he wouldn't be keeping the signs secret, just showing them to a teenage girl?"

It hadn't occurred to her that he'd accuse her of arrogance. "But Joan of Arc, right? She had visions from God when she was only twelve."

"Joan of Arc. Was she even real? Well, that's what the Catholics say, sure, but with all due respect, you know what I think, right? I don't believe in saints that way. You know why? I don't believe you have to be special to know what God wants for you. Let's be honest. Catholics don't know Jesus the way we do. We don't pray to statues, we pray to the man himself. Believe me, when the end-times are coming, we'll know. We'll all know, and it won't be any secret."

"But I did see something."

His mouth looked stricken. "Look, Willa. You just need to pray and look inside of yourself. Look inside of yourself and find out what it was that made you go to that party. What kind of life do you want, Willa? Do you want to be with Jesus or do you want to go it alone? Because I'm telling you, what it sounds to me like— it sounds to me like demons are giving you those signs, and if you'll look closely, you'll see that. Where are those demons coming from?"

Just outside the door, there was the raspy sound of the janitor sweeping in the hallway, the clunk of a bucket.

"Believe me, when the Rapture gets here, it won't come in little daydreams—there will be no mistaking it. God wants all good things for you, Willa. I believe that with all my heart. Do you believe it?"

She knew what she was supposed to say. "Yes."

"Well, then, good."

She didn't let herself cry until she got back in the car with her mother, who'd been sitting out in the parking lot, waiting. Willa could smell the cigarettes. "Did that help, sweetheart?"

God was long gone now, hidden somewhere in a cloud.

✝

AT HOME, she knelt on the floor, rested her hands on the bed, the tiny flowers on the quilt, the careful highways of stitching, the crumpled mountain of pillow. Her chest tensed up in the silence. She stared at her clenched hands in the lamplight, the faint hairs on her fingers, the wrinkles of her knuckles. She had the feeling that someone was about to break into the house, shatter the glass of the windows with a hammer. Her heart was about to stop. There was a tumor in her that would soon explode. She listened for roaring winds, for the gallop of horseshoes on concrete streets, for monstrous locusts, or a rubbery kind of stretching silence. In the dark outside, beyond her window, she sensed a swirling preparation, a kind of angelic weather.

A minute later, the room seemed very far away. She was looking in at herself through the window, at a girl sitting on the floor in her nightgown, who seemed to have always been there, body glued to the beige carpet. She was a silhouette of a girl praying, like the one she'd seen in an old-fashioned book, candle lit on the table next to where she knelt. She didn't know what to pray. She sent up a wordless thing that was like a blinking light, or the true flicker of that candle in the picture.

LEE

SHE MET WITH Councilman Atwater at the coffee shop, glass fishbowls of licorice and bubble gum arranged on the counter. The smell of coffee and *churro* doughnuts was strong, Porter Wagoner lilting over the speakers. Maisie Rodgers had put her in touch with Atwater, who was new to the city council, because he'd mentioned to her his concern over Banes Field. Lee sat at one of the tiny square tables, and he brought over two coffees in small Styrofoam cups. He put down his cup, sat, and rubbed his thighs as he looked again at the photos on the tabletop. She'd printed them in high-definition eight by ten prints, so the cracks in the container's surface were visible, the peculiar pink stains. "It sure looks concerning to me," he said, wiping his half-bald head with his hand. "And you're pretty certain they reburied it, huh?"

"Very. That's why I'm showing you these. Plus, the professor I work with found some high numbers in the soil samples I got when I took these pictures."

"It could be bad if the leakage started up all over again. But it could be years before anyone noticed, before there were any real side effects."

Maisie said he'd only been elected by default because no one ran against him. He had a degree in chemical engineering, but for some reason he worked at the public library now, which meant he wasn't one of the good old boys, even if he had been once.

"My point is," she said, "we don't even need the container to come up to show there's trouble. The soil samples I took have benzene concentrations higher than allowable toxicity levels. Have you ever looked at the cancer registry for this town?"

His demeanor was earnest, but his tentative mouth and bland face made him seem like an unfinished person. He stared at her with pale eyes. "Yeah." He pressed his lips together. "You're right. I don't know if we even need these photos, to tell you the truth. If we can just get someone at the EPA Dallas office . . . or someone at the Texas Commission on the Environment . . ." His voice trailed off.

A tall man wearing an obscenely large silver belt buckle walked up in the line at the counter behind a curly-haired boy and his mother. The man pointed to the stuffed bunny sitting on a shelf in front of a sign that said DO NOT TOUCH. "You see that?" said the man to the boy. "When I see that, I just want to touch the thing." The boy buried his face in his mother's loose, flowery blouse. All of them seemed more made of flesh than Atwater.

"Do you know, back, when was it, five years ago, what one of these EPA guys said to me? When there first started to be talk about building near Banes Field again? I said, 'Look, can you at least give me a list of all the chemicals buried at the Banes site?' And he said what they always said, 'We've tested the soil, and it's not a threat to human health.' 'Well, okay,' I said. 'What are the chemicals?' 'We don't know,' he said. 'Well, then, if you don't know,' I said, 'how can you say it's safe?' Do you know what he said? 'Because we don't know it's unsafe.'"

Atwater winced. "Sounds about right. They really don't know what all it might do. I don't even think all of those compounds have names."

"Do you know anyone over in Dallas who might listen?"

"Maybe. Honestly, it's not easy, as you know, with Texas laws. They're all set up to protect the Goliaths, not the Davids."

"Can I ask you something? What do you do over at the library?"

"I'm the head librarian. I used to work for Garbit, until I got tired of the whole nine to five. But I have enough funding. Let's just say I have enough funding to do my own research at this point." He smiled, and she saw his teeth were chipped. "I'll look at that new study. Was that with Professor Samuels?"

"Yes."

"And I'll call a couple of people." He paused, brushed his hand again over the bald part of his scalp. "I'll do what I can." He smiled again, and it did not fill her with confidence.

Back at the office, she still had a few more minutes to keep the phones manned, so she trolled the Internet for the news.

The local paper ran a story about Taft's plans for Pleasant Forest, the luxury homes he'd build, the jobs it would create, Taft's track record for successful subdivisions. At the end of the article, a sliver of a paragraph appeared. "Now that more than ten years have passed and the land is safe again, cleared by the EPA, local officials are eager to see it well used."

On the Taft Properties website, there was a photograph of the scrub grass with a bulldozer parked on it, and next to that, an animated slide show of the plans for the first three model homes.

Professor Samuels's wife had sent an email dictated by him, about the other chemicals besides benzene that they'd tested for in Banes Field. There was a 5 percent increase in toluene, and a 7 percent increase in styrene tars and vinyl chloride. It probably wasn't enough different from the other studies for anyone to care, but Lee went back to the research on priority pollutants and looked at the health effects:

Benzene causes chromosomal aberrations in humans.

Long-term exposure to vinyl chloride is linked to liver cancer, brain cancer, and some cancers of the blood.

Sometimes late at night, she trolled the sites online, asking questions of Google, as if it were a tarot reader or a Ouija board or an advice columnist. "How to stop builder who wants to build on toxic site?" The replies were enigmatic. The story of kids living in an old pesticides factory in Albania. Instructions for building a toxin-free home. The story of a realty company in Florida that built a subdivision right next to a field of buried, unexploded bombs from World War II. She scrolled from one entry to another, sleepless, reading the same information again and again. Though she might start the vigil with a string of hope, by the time she'd followed the strand, she always had the same feeling in the end. She was very, very small, just a pinpoint of energy.

The *Ecological Defense Manual* still lay on the coffee table, brown and unassuming. She picked it up, went back to reading the instructions. "The best way to disable a bulldozer is to introduce an abrasive (salt, gravel, sand) into the oil system. (1) Locate the oil filler cap, (2) remove the cap and dipstick, (3) pour the abrasive through a plastic funnel." The reasonableness made it sound as feasible as cooking or sewing, or fixing a chair. For a girl, Jack used to tell her, she was pretty good with tools. And she was reasonable. "The monkey-wrenching kit you'll need includes fabric gloves, a plastic jug or bottle, a plastic funnel, and a can of spray lubricant to remove any leftover abrasive grit on the surface." No one else had seemed this helpful lately; or at least it had been a long time anyway since she'd felt any support in her efforts. "In addition, bring a wrench, preferably one wrapped in black electrical tape to eliminate its shininess and to keep it from banging against another item in your bag."

She wondered about the author of this book, how much he or she succeeded behind the scenes, without anyone knowing. The text seemed to prepare one so carefully, down to the flashlight with the red beam, less visible in the dark, the advice to buy each piece of hardware at a different store so as not to arouse suspicion. She'd begun to trust the practical, evenhanded voice, and to read the instructions gave her solace, the way she imagined her mother, during her sober periods, had gotten relief from reading her book of inspirational sayings.

Lee could picture herself there at Banes Field with a monkey-wrenching kit, at the bulldozer maybe, if she methodically followed the careful notes, if she did the act as if the sabotage were really a repair.

✝

LATER THAT WEEK, she sat in her car at some distance from the construction site. She wanted to see what they'd built so far. The empty bulldozer held its square and serrated head at an angle to the ground, and the cement blocks of the foundation lay flat and gray in the turned red dirt. She watched three men work, carrying slabs of metal or pipes over to the foundation, one of them pounding with a hammer, the sun beating down on their yellow hard hats, their brown arms. It seemed inconceivable to her that they were actually building there again, in broad daylight.

She was parked a quarter of a mile from where her own house used to be. One of the construction workers walked closer to her car, and he leaned over and hugged a large spool of wire, then lifted it, but dropped it again. The car smelled like coffee. That same song came on the radio that she'd heard five or six times in the last day, and then, "Once we've executed Osama bin Laden, America can assume its rightful place again. Won't you donate to . . ." She looked to see if she could find the oil filter access and the fuel gauge on the side of the bulldozer (which she'd seen in diagrams), but this far away, the details were blurry.

The cowboy dangled from her rearview mirror—Jack had got it on a trip to Fort Worth: a golly-gee face with a hat way too big for his head and across his belt buckle the words COWBOY KITCHEN.

It started to rain, at first just a few drops nailing on the car roof and then a spill of them. She could barely see through the gray scrim of water. When she was little, Jess liked to play in the rain, her fat toddler stomach and skinny arms, and she'd ride her tricycle through the muddy ruts in the grass, and no matter how many times Lee called her, she wouldn't come inside.

Lee waited there while the construction workers took shelter somewhere, and the rain poured down around her. She took out some paper and a pen from the glove compartment to note the make of the bulldozer. She drew a diagram of the building site. The thunder sounded like giant rocks falling from the sky.

✝

WHEN SHE GOT HOME there was a voice-mail message from Doc giving her the next day off. He was going to a golf tournament. "I see Taft's got his permit," he said. "Guess there's not much more to be done, but you sure did try, Lee. No one can take that away." She poured herself a bourbon, and studied the manual. She took out some old toy blocks, laid them on a piece of paper, and redrew the diagram of the site where the building had begun.

On the computer, she followed the links she'd marked, and read again the stories of the Earth Liberation Front, especially the ones posted about those who'd been imprisoned, with websites pleading for support. "The prison refuses to provide a vegan diet." "Her sentence is years longer than that of another prisoner who committed armed robbery." There was the case of the half-built Seattle subdivision, burned to the ground; the note posted on one remaining brick wall read: "Built Green? Maybe Black! ELF." Whenever she saw that acronym, she imagined the activists with pointed ears and small, impish bodies. Even when they were older, they all looked like moribund, pale, vegetarian college kids, bored with their ordinary lives, looking for mischief.

There was a new appeal in the works for the woman who'd set fire to cars in Oklahoma. She'd been sentenced to twenty years. Lee clicked to her link and there was a photo of her with her young sons, sitting on a blanket in the grass, a dog roaming in the background. There was a plea to donate money to contribute to her defense. There was a plea to donate money to her family.

✝

THAT NIGHT IN HER DREAM, she was lost in a house with many beautiful rooms. Each had a small swinging door at one end, for a dog or cat, but she kept thinking that she would never be able to squeeze through it. And though it was night in her dream, the sun shone through the windows on all the gleaming furniture, and she was desperate to get out because a gas had been released somewhere—it was like a perfume mixed with rancid eggs—and it would kill her if she didn't find the way out. She heard a distant bell in another room and went toward it, and then she woke up, realized it was her cell phone ringing. When she answered the time appeared on the screen—it was 3:18 a.m.

"Listen," he said.

"Okay."

"I mean, listen. I've been thinking about what you said about the house making those weird sounds. That roof hasn't been fixed since my folks still lived there."

"Do you know what time it is?"

"You want me to come over and take a look?"

"Nah. I could always hire someone if it gets to be a problem."

"Do you ever see Rush or Char? It seems you're all alone over there."

"Sure. I see them all the time. Rush anyway. It's not as bad as all that. Actually, I've got a fine social life. But honestly, it's the first time you've had that thought?"

"It's just the first time I've said it, and I'm not drunk, either."

"Congratulations."

"Well, also." He cleared his throat, and made his voice colder.

"It also occurs to me there are some things there I'd like to come and get."

"Like what?"

"Like some of those old records I left, the ones I used to play my harmonica to."

"Oh brother." He'd made these overtures before, but they'd dissipate after a while, and he'd stop calling. Then later, if she called him, he'd act as if she were putting him out.

"I'm serious. I've been playing again. It's all coming back. I don't have any of that old music here, and besides it sounds different—even if you can get it—when it's not a record." She missed dancing with him, the way his limp syncopated the swing, and she missed the way when he kissed her good-bye, he'd grab a handful of her hair.

"You're welcome anytime," she said, but she knew he wouldn't come, and now it would take hours for her to get back to sleep.

HAL

IN THE MORNING, he told Darlene he had a stomachache, though he exaggerated. He showered, dressed, and left for his 9:00 a.m. appointment at Avery's old property on 2351. He hadn't even been inside yet, but he'd looked at the pictures online, and he knew how to bluff his way in with one of these old homes—the details, the vintage, the homey, the kind of parents who'd lived there. The "looky here" and "looky there."

He pulled up in the driveway, and realized how loud the traffic was, even though the house was set far back from the road. But the wood was painted that old green you never saw anymore, and the flat spread of its ranch-style girth felt welcoming—the house seemed honest and good-natured, like a lot of the people he used to know. A few minutes later, a blue Range Rover pulled in, and the client stepped out. He was a young guy, looked to be just a few years out of college, but he wore a suit—probably on his way to work at his new job. Not what Hal had expected.

As they shook hands and made introductions, Hal was aware of the leanness of this Bill's body and the confidence in his chin. Hal read him right away—he was all set to say no, as soon as he saw the outside of the place, but was too polite to say so before

Hal showed him anything. Still, with some skill, Hal might at least get him interested in going to a few other listings, the town house over on Groveland Street, maybe.

When they walked inside, Hal was unprepared for the cozy smell of old wood and dust. There it was again, the cheap, paneled wall in the living room, the dark green shag carpet that had probably been there since the late seventies. He remembered being there with Avery and a few others when they were teenagers. They'd come that day after school was out for the summer, and Avery's mother had given them all lemonade and chili with saltine crackers, and Avery's dad had worn glasses broken at the side and held together with tape.

"It's a fixer-upper, maybe," said Hal, sensing that this Bill was almost hopeless. "But there's a good structure, nice detail in the fixtures, the cabinets. They don't make them like that anymore."

Bill walked over to the curtainless window and looked out at the tangled weeds in the yard. Hal led him down the hallway to the bathroom, cheap white tiles flecked with gold, an old, dingy tub. Even in here, you could hear the semi trucks drone on the highway. Then he led him back through the bedrooms, wood floored, small, the walls still scuffed and discolored from where the furniture had been. "The owner would give it a paint for you, of course," said Hal, ashamed of himself, feeling like Avery's goddamn slave.

"I like it," said Bill, nodding, and Hal tried to interpret his eyes, but he couldn't. "Do you think he'll come down on the price?"

It was a trick, and Hal wouldn't be fooled. A sale could never be this easy. He either didn't have the money, or he didn't have the credit score.

"Uh, not sure about that. I can ask."

Hal led the client back through the living room, and he remembered that day again, how Avery's dad had, for some reason, just lost his job, but he'd anyway seemed so proud to have his son and his friends in his house. Acted like the only thing keeping it from being a grand mansion was its size. He'd told them all stories about Beaumont football, praised Hal for his speed on the field, gave each of them half a glass of beer. Hal led Bill into the kitchen, where the cabinets and tile looked newer than what was in the rest of the house. "New stove. New fridge." On the windows, thin red cotton curtains faded by the sun, and the linoleum floor, a blue brick pattern, was cracked just under the sink, as if something had fallen there. There was a smallness here, an evenhandedness that made Hal think of his own family. What did a single man want with it? Hal kept seeing Avery's dad's face, smiling, his blue shirt neatly pressed, still tucked into his trousers, his tooled leather belt. He'd had a reassuring laugh, and such confidence in all of them, the way he said they were all going on to great adventures, the way he'd turn to his wife and say, "Did you hear that?" She'd been tall and thin like him, with big white teeth and a genuine shy sweetness in her aproned gestures. Avery's dad was dead now from a heart attack a couple of years back, and Hal didn't know what had happened to Avery's mom—if she was alive or in a home somewhere.

This Bill was smiling, opening each kitchen cabinet and sticking his head inside. "It's real close to my work, and I like a small house, not an apartment," he said. For a moment, Hal wondered if he was a homosexual, and then dismissed the thought because he was afraid Bill would see it in his face.

Hal led him around to the back, and they looked at the yard.

They went inside the musty garage. Coming out of its dimness, Hal handed Bill his card, and walked him out to the driveway. "I have some other properties too, if you'd like to have a look."

Bill shook his head, held up the card and said, "I'll be in touch." He couldn't have meant it, but it was nice to deal with someone who had manners at least.

✝

AFTER CULLY'S FIRST GAME BACK, a catastrophic loss to Sugarland, Hal drove Cully home, so he wouldn't have to sulk on the bus. Hal could almost understand why it happened the way it did because Sugarland was deft and large with defense, and Friendswood leaned all of itself on Cully and Sid Tomes, the quarterback, so if those two fumbled, the team lost. "You've got to get your defense to bulk up, not be so afraid to hit," he told Cully as they drove down the dark highway, the lights from passing cars sweeping over Cully's red, shiny face. It was less understandable the next Friday night on the home field, when Cully fell apart like a snowman when the guy bumped him, and in the next quarter, Cully dropped an easy pass. Sitting next to him and Darlene, Wes Starkweather said, "They'll come back," but he wouldn't look in Hal's direction. By the end of the game, Hal could have sworn he saw him spit into the bleachers.

The following week, Hal was fixing up a different contract when the client Bill who'd looked at Avery's property actually did call and said, "I want to make an offer—I liked that place." Hal could hardly believe it. It was ten thousand less than Avery wanted, but when Hal called and regretfully told him the amount, Avery said, "I don't mind. I just want to get it off my hands."

"Can I ask you something?" Hal said, after he and Avery had mostly finished with the initial business of the sale.

"Yeah."

"Your mom still alive?"

"Yeah, she lives with her sister in Garland now. Why?"

"When I was over there at the house it all came back to me, how your folks used to have us over. I remember your dad and how much he liked to talk. Didn't he have a joke about a man in a croker sack suit—kind of a shaggy-dog story thing?"

"Hell, I don't know. That's all so long ago," said Avery, yawning. "That house is so *old.*"

"Yeah. But I remember this real nice day. Me, you, Ulsher, and Robbins. It might have been the first time I tasted beer. Your mom made chili and we watched a game."

Avery didn't answer, and Hal thought he heard clicking—he was probably typing on the computer keyboard. There were only some men you could talk to that way, and here he was, chatting into this rich, platinum shell. Words bouncing back to hit him.

DEX

AFTER THE GAME FRIDAY NIGHT, as he was walking out of the field house, he saw Bishop Geitner, Cully Holbrook, and a few other guys who had been there leaning against their trucks, arms folded. "Hey, Dex," Bishop called. "I got something for you." He grinned, but not in a friendly way.

He supposed he didn't have a choice but to talk to them, though he didn't want to be seen doing it.

"We've just been saying," said Bishop, "that here's the thing." So they'd been waiting for him. His face was serious, but it looked like he was holding back laughter. "That girl Willa invited herself to the house, right? Whatever she's saying now she wasn't saying the same thing before, you know?"

"What is she saying now?" The field lights and headlights daggered off all the chrome. He squinted at Bishop, wishing he could tell him and all the other guys to go fuck themselves. "Look, I don't know what the hell happened over there," said Dex, "but I do know that Willa's a nice girl."

"Oh, yeah, she's real nice, that's what we've been saying."

"That's not what you're saying."

"Look," said Louder. "So far you're not on any lists, are you?

No one's going to ask you about anything, at least not yet. You're free, you're goddamn innocent."

"But Ida's calling us in now for some reason," said Bishop, "and this is what we're telling her. If you want to go in and say something different, that's your business, but we're not saying we'll cover you."

"What the hell's that supposed to mean?"

Bishop shrugged.

"Holbrook and Trace admitted to fucking her. Now someone's saying there were three. I'm not saying that. Are you? We're saying what I said we'd say. But who's to know there wasn't three? There were a lot of guys who saw you there too. It could have been anyone."

"You're threatening me?" Dex shook his head. That was a piss-poor way of standing up for Willa, but it was the best he could do right now.

Bishop shrugged, turned his gaze over toward the parked cars.

"I left early," said Dex. "If you're gonna lie and say something else, that's your business. I've got to get home, so—see ya."

He walked away as fast as he could, all the while expecting one of them to come up behind him and throw an arm around his neck.

✝

AFTER SCHOOL, he was on his way out to the field house, lugging his backpack of homework, when he saw Dani sitting cross-legged on the cement, just outside the glass door, her wavy black hair against a pink shirt. They had been in science class together

last year, but he didn't know her well, only well enough to hear
about her acquaintance with someone at the Coastal Club in
Houston who would sometimes let her go backstage.

"Hey," he said.

She was leaning over her phone. She barely looked up. "Hey."

He sat down a few feet away from her on the cement, looked
out at the half-empty parking lot. "Why are you still here?"

"Drama Club," she said. "You?"

"Oh, football . . ."

She looked at him sideways.

"I'm a trainer."

"Oh." She nodded.

"You're friends with Willa Lambert, right?"

She lowered her phone and turned to him, lifted up her chin.
"She's my best friend. And if one more person tells me some sick
rumor about her, I'm going to kill myself."

"I know," he said. "I'm not gonna do that."

She held up her phone. "Someone's texting a line about Willa
and a stripper. I'm surprised no one actually took pictures. Thank
God."

"Does she know?"

"I'm just trying like hell to shame them into stopping. I swear
we go to school with future criminals. These dickheads are
going to end up in Huntsville."

Dex figured that she didn't know he had been at the house.

"She's a cool girl," he said. "She doesn't deserve that."

Dani threw back her head. "Nobody *deserves* that, idiot."

"I mean—"

"I know what you mean. I know you have English together."
She looked down at the phone screen. "Shit. I can't believe how

mean people are. Now they're saying she called up Bishop Geitner and asked him to come to the house. I hate this fucking place."

"She didn't do that."

"Of course she didn't." She shook her head, put her chin in her hand. "If only we weren't trapped in this idiotic place. Like if we were in Houston, someplace else, Willa and I could write songs, and I could play them and someone might even give a damn. I can't even understand half the stuff she writes, but it's cool to read."

"What do you play?"

Dani shrugged. "Nothing. A little guitar," she said. "Listen, just be nice to her. Those rapists just walked right back in here like they owned the place."

"So tell me this. Because I don't get it," he said. "Why didn't anyone call the police?"

"She doesn't remember anything. It's just their word against hers. You know that, right?"

"Huh." He started to put pieces together, things he'd over-heard in the locker room, and his defense of Willa felt even more crucial—as if it would prove something important to himself. "I'd like to hang out with her more," he said. "How long is she on home study?"

"As long as she wants to be," said Dani. "And good luck with trying to hang out with her, if her parents are around. You haven't given yourself to Jesus yet, have you?" She slapped at a mosquito on her leg. "Actually, you should probably just leave her alone. She doesn't need to have to negotiate anything with a guy. She hates all of you right now. She was telling me some crazy shit on the phone, and then her mother made her get off. They think I got her over there to the Lawbournes' somehow. But I don't even know that Lawbourne guy." She stood up, smoothing the front of her jeans. "I've gotta go."

†

In English, whenever he turned his head, he saw Willa's empty desk, scratched blond wood top, black plastic seat back. Ms. Marlowe leaned against the chalkboard, sighed, and looked out at the class with doleful eyes.

"We're about to start a unit on Existentialism."

"Uh-oh," said Ben Lawbourne.

"That's about enough of that," said Ms. Marlowe. "You'll need a partner for the main Camus project at the end."

Ms. Marlowe handed out a packet of papers that explained everything because she refused to give assignments online. As she outlined the work, marking up the board with her scribbled uneven notes, Dex felt uncomfortable in his clothes, the waistband of his jeans seemed to dig into his stomach, his socks felt tight around his ankles, his shoes suddenly too small.

At the end of class, as everyone was leaving, he went to Ms. Marlowe's desk. She pushed back her wiry gray hair, raised her unruly eyebrows. "Yes, Dex?"

He didn't care what Dani said—she didn't know for sure what Willa would want. "I was wondering, I don't know if it's true, but I heard Willa was on home study."

She pressed her lips together, and the muscles under her cheekbones seemed to twitch.

"I don't know if she'd agree," he said, "but I was thinking we could be partners on that project if that would be okay."

Her face softened. "I can't say it was my assignment," she said, "or whether or not what you say is true. But if you have a way to get in touch with her and would like to do that, then by all means." She smiled slightly. "That might be a good thing to do."

Dex noticed Ben Lawbourne then, lingering around the door, tapping the floor with the heel of his boot. "I mean, I don't know. Maybe. Whatever." His ears felt hot.

Ms. Marlowe nodded to him indifferently, the way teachers tended to, and when Dex looked up at the door again, Ben was gone.

✝

ON THURSDAY he drove to Walgreens and picked out flowers. He only had ten dollars to spend, but he found a nice bunch of assorted ones he didn't recognize except for the roses. They were wrapped in a cone of green tissue paper and tacky clear plastic, but he didn't know what to do about it. At the checkout counter, the pregnant clerk smiled and winked as she took his money.

He'd been surprised at how quickly Willa had written back, agreeing to do the project with him, willing to meet him at the Dairy Queen. Waiting for him at the red plastic table by the window, she looked prettier than he'd remembered, small curves of reflected light in the waves of her hair, her eyes large and clear and mature. She wore one of those billowy Mexican blouses with bright designs around the neck—he usually didn't like them because they made girls look like fat cushions, but on Willa, it looked okay.

"Hey," he said, laying the flowers down before her. "These are for you."

She looked up and flinched, but her second expression was friendly, one side of her mouth curled up. "Well, thanks." She took the bouquet. "You surprised me," she said. Her face looked different, the bones more prominent, the skin pale. He wanted to reassure her that the bouquet was meant for her straight out, just because he liked her.

"So, hey, I just wanted to say thanks for working on the project."

"Okay."

"I wrote down some ideas." She pushed a sheet of notebook paper toward him, her round neat handwriting like a neatly arranged ink garden. One column was marked "Life"; another was marked "Death"; and the third was marked "????"

They worked for half an hour—she had to help him understand the book first—and he bought them each an ice cream sundae, though she only ate a couple of bites of hers.

He told her he'd heard that Mr. Minkowell, who taught computers, was beating his wife, and that Mr. Ludman, the history teacher, tall and gray and dapper, had lost half a million dollars gambling in Vegas. She licked her small spoon, and he was watching her pink mouth when she frowned.

A little later, after they'd worked more, when she came back from the bathroom, her beauty rushed at him all at once, the intensity of her eyes flaming up in front of him. She smiled. "I probably shouldn't stay too much longer. My mom's coming."

He didn't know why he imagined they'd have more time. "Alright, then."

"Thanks for coming by. And thanks for the flowers." She touched a strange blue blossom that looked as if it had been dipped in paint. Another rose, yellow, was already drooping its sorry head. Now they seemed shabby and gaudy, and all wrong. A car honked in the parking lot, and she got up.

"Well, see you later," he said, and he turned and walked fast to the opposite door, the vibration under his chest saying, *Jackass. Jackass. Jackass.*

✝

AT LUNCH THE NEXT DAY, Dex ate a corn dog with mustard and those strange fried rectangles of potato slivers, a kind of food he'd only seen in a school cafeteria.

As he made his way with the crowd heading to the exit for fifth period, Bishop, Trace, and Cully were suddenly beside him. "Hey, Dex, what's up?"

"Just getting to class." He thought he might puke from the grease of the lunch.

Bishop lowered his voice and put his hand to the side of his mouth. "Was that Willa Lambert with you at the DQ yesterday?"

Dex felt a cold sensation on the back of his neck, and realized it was Trace's hand, patting him there.

"We're doing a project for English," Dex said.

"Is she your girlfriend or something?" said Bishop, suppressing a smile.

"You don't want to get yourself in the mix here, do you?" said Trace.

Cully didn't say anything, but walked along, nodding.

They were out in the hallway near the water fountain now, and Dex leaned down to get a drink. He'd hoped they'd get the message and move on, but when he turned back, they were still there, waiting for him.

"That girl's trouble, no way around it," said Bishop. "Crazy and a liar, right?"

Dex remembered how in math class a couple of years ago, it became clear that the guy couldn't multiply, though he pretended he was only making a joke. He was in that strange, quasi-frat group, the Texas Totem—they all wore matching baseball shirts on Fridays.

Dex shook his head. "I can't believe you guys." He turned his back to them and started to walk away. People stood in the halls now, watching.

Bishop grabbed the sleeve of Dex's T-shirt, put his mouth up to Dex's ear. "What the fuck? You know it's the truth."

From the other side of the hallway, Trace yelled, "Whoa!"

Dex swung around and punched Bishop on the side of his jaw. "Fuck!" Bishop held his hand there and bent over. "You prick!" Cully came at him in a bear hug, threw him against the locker, and his spine slammed against the metal. He felt a rattling in his head. Bishop was kicking his leg with the hard pointed toe of his boot, and he spit in his face. Dex rose up and pushed Cully away. He hit Bishop in the neck, heard teeth click as Bishop's head flew back. A dance of white lights, and then Vice Principal Harrison was grabbing him by the shoulders. "Alright, son, you better hold up." Mr. Harrison smelled of mouthwash, and his hair was sticking up in all directions. The security guards grabbed Cully and Bishop. Mr. Harrison screamed in his ear, "In my office!"

At first, the three of them sat in silence while Mr. Harrison glared at them from behind his desk. Dex scooted his chair away from the other two and touched the bruise on his leg where he'd been kicked. Finally, Mr. Harrison said, "Okay, gentlemen, what seems to be the issue?"

Cully slumped darkly in his chair, arms folded, and nodded to Dex. "That guy hit my friend."

Mr. Harrison puckered his lips judiciously.

"Sir, we got out of hand," said Bishop. He had a way of being overly polite with adults, fake and deferential. "But the truth is, we have a disagreement about a girl." Dex could see where Bishop was going with this, with his slick features and sober expression. But if Bishop would only mention Willa's name, it would have an effect on Harrison, make him see Dex was right. Behind Harrison's desk, there was a shelf of self-help books—*12 Qualities of Highly Effective People, The Better Than Good Life*— a wooden plaque with a gold plate the shape of Texas.

"A girl, huh?"

But Dex didn't want to bring Willa into this, to say her name and soil it again. She didn't deserve it.

"Dex, what do you have to say for yourself? If you have something to say, son, you'd better say it."

Dex stared at Mr. Harrison's pale yellow tie with the *U*s of blue horseshoes. To not reply seemed the most honorable response.

Harrison warned Cully and Bishop that they were a hairsbreadth away from another suspension. Harrison didn't know Dex had been at the party, or that he'd skipped school—because he'd had the fake note from his mom.

"Dex, you too. A hairsbreadth, you got me?"

After school, Dex went out to the field house, saw Cully run out to the field in his grimy practice clothes. He went to every practice, but he either wasn't playing or he was playing like shit—there was some satisfaction in that at least.

Dex went into Coach Salem's office, and as soon as Coach lifted his silver bristled head to him, Dex said, "I'm going to have to quit."

Salem's face always seemed to have the texture and energy of rock.

"You sure about that, son?"

"Yeah."

"Mind if I ask why?"

"I've got some pressing things to do now, and they're taking up all my time."

"Well, I'm sorry to hear that then." He nodded again. "You'll be missed." And that was good-bye.

When Dex got into his truck, as the players in blue jerseys and shoulder pads ran in a line out to the field, he tried to think how he'd break the news to his mother.

WILLA

IN THE MIDDLE OF THE NIGHT, she heard footsteps in the bushes. Through the curtain in her window, she saw grasshopper-like insects with strange long teeth shrieking all over the lawn outside, and she saw the moon, one full curve of it barely limned with red.

In the morning, white toilet paper hung in all the trees like an infinite tapeworm. Whole rolls dropped in the yard, a hundred white fingers poking up through the grass. She went downstairs and saw the shaving cream on the front porch: smeared now, but who knew what word had been there. She smeared it more with her foot and a crude paper ribbon fell across her face.

Her dad was already bent down, gathering the toilet paper in his arms. He should have been getting ready to go to work. She crouched and pulled up from the ground one of the white fingers—a plastic fork. They ruined lawn mowers, so you had to pick out every last one.

"Don't you worry about this," said her father. "Go on upstairs and get dressed."

"I should help you."

He was angry, though he was trying not to be, she could tell by the way his eyes squinted, how his smile pulled too tight across his face. "What you need to do is go put some clothes on. I'm going to take a break in a sec and get some breakfast."

He grabbed a string of toilet paper from the branch above him, and a white clump fell onto his shoulder. "I've just about had it," he said, and went inside.

Willa held a handful of dirty plastic forks. A gray car came to the corner, paused, then turned. The neighbor's bulldog, Pugsie, came to the edge of their yard and barked at her. Pugsie growled and danced around a dirty rawhide bone. Through the branches in the trees, she looked up to tug down a last stream of white.

By lunchtime, all the toilet paper and plastic forks were in fat garbage bags by the curb. A little later she heard her father mowing the lawn. He'd taken the whole day off from work, and she knew that in the afternoon he'd be restless in the living room, flicking the remote, rustling through the newspaper and complaining that the air conditioner needed repair.

SHE READ THE BOOK OF REVELATION straight through, only looking up now and then to stare at the curtains in the window, to ponder a phrase or a line. There were several beasts, not just one "beast of the Apocalypse," the way she'd sometimes heard it before. The beast she'd seen had the jigsawed body parts from different animals, and the eyes "front and back," but the beasts in Revelation also had more than one head, and a dog's face was not mentioned. She'd loved her dog, Junior, for the way he ate everything he could find—chicken bones, panty liners, Silly Putty—

and for the way he lay over her feet in the bed and barked wildly at horses and mice. She'd loved his beastliness, actually, more than anything. She didn't understand why his face had attached itself to the vision. She'd been taught that if your heart was open, you understood Scripture (because it was all there, Pastor Sparks said, clear as day). *They and the beast will hate the whore; they will devour her flesh and burn her up with fire. For God has put it into their hearts to carry out his purpose by agreeing to give their kingdom to the beast.* She understood that God was asking someone to write this all down, that marks and words would be written on bodies, that people would die. *Let anyone who has an ear listen.* She recognized what she'd heard before, many times, that God would come like a thief in the night, that there would be an Antichrist, that you had to be ready when this world was about to be destroyed. But no matter how much she tried to open her heart, she could not make sense of the whore of Babylon, or the secrets that different people would harbor and why, and she couldn't picture the four angels guarding the sky, or the scroll rolling up like a cloud, because the images as they were described kept changing. How could this be clear as day?

When her parents came home from church, they seemed to be angry with her—it was in the pinch of her mother's smile, in her father's averted eyes. "I was thinking we'd invite Miranda over for dinner next week," said her mother.

They were in the kitchen, and Willa didn't look up from rinsing off her plate.

"Willa, will you look at me when I'm talking to you?"

"Alright." Willa looked at her. "Can we do it later? I don't feel much like having company."

Like a small propped-up structure that had fallen, her mother's smile collapsed back into her face. "Come on, you need to see your friends."

Her church friends had not emailed her, or texted her, or come to her house. They were afraid of her, afraid of what they might hear, afraid of how they might have to come to her defense, and then, by association, be called sluts too. Willa even suspected that Miranda had been the one who'd called her at home the other day, said, "Is Cully your boyfriend?" and hung up.

Today Dani emailed her to say that someone had painted white over the legs of the giant blue mustang in the mural in Hall A, so it no longer ran but "sort of sat." She said she had spoken to Dex, who seemed nice and told her about the Camus project. "I wish I could see you. Maybe soon??"

She sat with her father in the living room, studying her history dates, the news blaring while he lay back in the recliner. A street with a mosque in the background, scattered scraps of cars and chairs everywhere, a man's arm sticking out from under a crushed table. Two car bombings, thirty-four dead, sixty-two injured. *With such violence Babylon the great city shall be thrown down and will be found no more.* Her father glanced at her and sighed. "Never ending, isn't it?" On the screen orange and yellow flames raged behind the glass, whipping up and waving like bright rags. Firefighters were flocking to California, to help contain the raging fires, said the newscaster. More than two thousand people had fled their homes. *Hail and fire mixed with blood. Trees and grass burned up.* Her father picked up his can of Coke and took a long sip, sighed, then set the can down again on the table beside him. "They just have to figure a way to trap it," he said. "You know, one thing they do is to sometimes get a fire going in the opposite direction."

Later, her parents sat on the patio furniture in the backyard. Her mother's face seemed a faded blur through the window, but the movements of her head suggested that she was telling Willa's father something she wanted him to do. Her parents knew more than they revealed to her and seemed to be planning some new resolution. Her father had not spoken about it to her, but had relayed through her mother the message about not going to the police because it would only be worse for her. It seemed better for him to never look at her directly again for the rest of her life than to have to tell him what she did and did not remember about that afternoon. Her dad rubbed his neck as her mother spoke, and then his hand shot out with his finger pointed, and he shook it at her mother.

That night her mother came with a box to her bedroom door in the afternoon. "Ms. Marlowe sent you something. Isn't she your English teacher?" She put it on the desk and stood slumped against the doorjamb waiting for Willa to open it. Her mother's hair hung limp, framing the sadness of her sagging cheeks. "We want you to see your church friends, but I talked to Ms. Ryan, and we can keep you on home study until the end of the school year. That's the best thing, right? I just have to fill out some forms for homeschooling, not that I'm going to do anything but make sure you do your homework. I told her that, and she said it was okay."

"Well, that's good." Willa slid off the bed and went to her desk.

"They'll keep sending out a substitute teacher every other week."

Her mother handed her a pair of scissors and Willa cut through the packing tape, folded back the box flaps and tissue paper. There was a book of poems by Emily Dickinson.

"Oh, what's that?" Her mother touched her shoulder.

"Poems. We read some of them in school."

"Oh, look at the *gold*," she said, thumbing the gilt on the cover. "But it's not like it's Scripture. They make it look like the book is holy or something." Her mom's shoulders slumped as she put the book down. "Was she a Christian writer?"

"I think so."

Her mother opened the book, and Willa wanted to take it from her because she knew she wouldn't understand and might even find the poetry blasphemous. But her mother just closed it up and put it down again. "Too deep for me, I guess. I never was able to get poetry—the symbolism and all." Willa took the book and read to herself:

Just Infinities of Nought—
As far as it could see—
So looked the face I looked upon—
So looked itself—on Me—

I offered it no Help—
Because the Cause was Mine—
The Misery a Compact
As hopeless—as divine—

Willa sat at her bedroom window, looking out. A jay pecked at a twig, its tiny black eyes bright and unseeing, and as it fluttered its wings to the next branch, revealed an otherworldly fan of blue. The tree swayed slightly, light patching through the leaves. She tried again to pray, to summon up at least a reach to what wasn't visible, but she kept thinking of her butt cheeks pressed to the corner of hard wood, the scrambled eggs roiling in her stomach, and a very faint taste of blood in her mouth. She didn't even try to say words anymore because then the prayer sounded fake and rehearsed, even demonic. She admired how the leaves on different branches fluttered at various syncopations, how the thinner branches swayed and gestured.

The meanings of the poems seemed to move as soon as she thought she'd found them. She read pages and pages of them. She fell asleep with the journal open on her bed, the pen tucked inside it, leaking onto the page.

At some point in the middle of the night, she woke up, glanced between the curtain sheers at the moon, turned off the lamp, and went to sleep. It was a sleep like a tunnel, as if she were going into the deep past, before anyone she knew had been born. In the dream, she saw face after face like fabric screens she was falling through.

She woke up in a patch of sun, eyes wincing at the light. She pushed herself up against the headboard, started to stretch. The muscles in her bare arms felt good as they lengthened, and she tightened the muscles around her knees, pointed her toes. Then she noticed it. On her forearm, there was writing. Cramped and spiked, but unmistakable. *Sense flies away from spirit. The purple ages pause.*

She rubbed at it, her heart pounding, the skin where the words were written was hairless and healed in the space where there'd once been a small scar.

Her mother opened the door and came in with an armful of laundry. Willa was still staring at her arm. She felt a strange satisfaction and relief seeing the words, as if they'd claimed her, and there was a sweet taste just under her tongue.

"Here's your fresh shirts," said her mom, laying them on the dresser. "You need a new nightgown." Her mother looked at her, straight at her arm, and didn't seem to see the writing. "You slept late. Hope you're not fighting off something."

Willa turned her arm again, held the writing face up to her mother. She still didn't see it. "Want some oatmeal, honey? Why are you holding your arm like that? Did you hurt it?"

If demons were showing her these signs, then they were demons born from her own head, and why wouldn't they also come from God? Had the visions come from some rogue part of her brain trying to escape? Because there was something inside her trying to loosen itself lately, in the poems she wrote so quickly, pressed down so hard on the page that her hand hurt. And she didn't know what the loosening meant, in the same way she didn't always know what a poem meant—or it was like a jewel that had a different shape and color depending on the angle you turned it.

Something clattered in the hallway, and just for a few seconds, she looked back into her room, and there were both of the beasts, standing side by side, Lamb and Dog, she called them now, to undermine their nastiness. Lamb's face was streaked with a substance the color of pus, and around its neck, a chain of severed ears. Dog was part lion, with a cantaloupe-sized tumor on the side of its head, and a fluorescent green powder all over its fur, eyes erupting in patches of it. "She's going in the night like a thief," said Dog.

"Go," said Lamb.

Willa turned away from them and looked down at the yard, where yellow dandelions had sprouted up in a dot-to-dot pattern she tried to trace—a boat or a rat. "They're all laughing at you," said Dog. Its voice sounded like radio static and coughing. "Saying what they got away with."

She could feel the pressure of the beasts fade when she looked out the window, but she could still hear Dog. "Maybe you could just go."

A caterpillar inched timidly across the bottom of the wire screen, and as she watched its slow progression, a breeze went through the trees, a hushing sound. She leaned into that neutral solace. She put her mind there.

HAL

WHEN PRINCIPAL JOHNSON CALLED HAL at work to say
Cully had been in a fight at school, he knew this would be the end
of football for him, though they were entering the play-offs and
Cully, at one time, had been the best wideout on the team. "We
can't have it, Mr. Holbrook."

"I understand."

"We can't have our leaders—our leaders—acting this way. He
could have walked away from it, by all accounts. He was not personally provoked."

"I understand," said Hal, and saying good-bye to her, he had
a vision again of his uncle, passing out tiny American flags on
toothpicks to him and other kids on the Fourth of July. "It's our
flag, you remember that," he said. "No matter what size it is."

Hal had planted his in a ball of play dough and kept it on his
dresser for years. And when his uncle died in old age, his widow
was presented with the life-size flag solemnly folded into a tight
triangle.

He'd have to tell Darlene about the fight, but he figured it
was easier to do by phone. "Cully's been in a fight at school. He
won't play in Texas City," and it surprised him how hard it was

to say, how much he got choked up. If only he'd had more money to give as an offering to the church, if he could only show his devotion better.

"Oh, Hal. Maybe it wasn't his fault."

"Nope, he willingly joined in. Came in to help his buddy Bishop apparently."

"Well, he was helping his friend then."

"Darlene, it was two against one. He must have had a good reason, but you can't tell Principal Johnson that."

"Well, we have to fight it now."

"I know."

He hadn't been successful with Lee Knowles—no surprise, but still he had hope. Avery told him she must have gone to Toxic Texas with something because they called him to crow about it. Hal would have to try with her again. He needed to break through his limited mind-set and imagine what God could do for him. He just needed to keep at it.

He drove over to the school and went to the field house to see Coach Salem. In his office there was a photo of a mustang running duct-taped to the cinder block wall. Coach Rowan had occupied that same office twenty-five years earlier, and Hal had always been proud to be beckoned inside it.

Coach Salem, in his silver buzz cut and blue coach's shirt, smiled at him, his teeth even and perfect. He had the tan, fit appearance of clean living—he was a Quaker like the old guard in town—no drinking or dancing for him.

Hal told him his son had done a stupid thing, but he was a smart boy, and he hoped this wouldn't impact his game. He just needed to be forgiven.

Coach Salem raised his thick, gray eyebrows and heaved a

sigh. "I've had him in the weight room all fall, to make up for the one thing. And now this."

The muscles bared under the coach's short-sleeved blue shirt were taut, though he must have been past fifty, and they felt like an affront to Hal's own lump of clay body.

"The truth is, Cully hasn't been playing great, and I think you know this—he hasn't been acting like a football player either. He hasn't respected the position. His body is here, but his heart isn't. I've been thinking maybe it's better he takes some time to sort things out, get himself together." His voice was so gravelly it sounded soft-spoken.

"Are you serious?"

"Oh, I am." He chuckled. "I've been real disappointed in him, frankly. Real disappointed." He slapped his palms on the desk, as if to dismiss Hal. "You played too, didn't you?"

"I did, class of 'eighty. Hell, he's a better player than I ever was. Coach, please."

"Well, if you played, then I'm sure you know I've got a team to think about." He narrowed his eyes. "I'm not in the touchy-feely business, Mr. Holbrook. I do football. But Cully needs something." Coach nodded, his face an austere blankness.

Hal left the field house, walked past the electric-blue lockers and the silver-flecked posters of Mustangs. Cully needed something alright. He needed the holy spirit in him. He needed righteousness. He needed faith. And then the football would come back to him.

LEE

WHEN LEE HEARD BACK from Ecological Society for Texas, there it was, the standard answer: "Thank you for sharing with us your recent soil sample readings for Banes Field. We have put the site on consideration for our watch list for the future." And she put this in the pile of other tepid replies: "We have placed this on our list of sites to watch."

She was so angry as she drove home from work, she couldn't think logically but kept saying the word to herself, "Assholes." She drove fast, the red lights on Friendswood Drive like the tips of scolding fingers, trying to warn her, and on the highway, a car pulling a horse trailer slowed in front of her. Through the window in the back, she saw the brown butt, the long, swiping tail. Horse people always acted so entitled, as if they alone were keeping Texas authentic and that's why they deserved to block the entire lane. When she tried to pass the trailer she nearly sideswiped a white car she didn't see.

She had ways of taming her anger these days that might or might not work. She tried taking a shower. She was soaping herself, thinking about her next step, when his face suddenly came to her, handsome Chris Hite, who'd just moved back to town to start a newspaper/website funded by his father (whose own newspaper had gone out of business). *Friendswood Dispatch*. That was it. She'd seen just one copy, over at the counter of the dry cleaners. And she'd run into Chris Hite at the drugstore, where they'd chatted for ten minutes or more. He'd grown beefier in the arms, fuller in the face, but his smile was still sweet, the lines of his face pleasing. "You're a sight for sore eyes," he'd said. "My God, look at you!"

She got out of the shower, dried off, pulled on her robe, and went to find his number. He had his work voice on when he answered.

"Oh, hey. Well, what can I do for you? You want to subscribe?"

"I want to do that. I also want to give you a story. And I've even got the pictures."

She told him someone needed to investigate Banes Field again. She told him what she'd seen and about the recent readings of the soil samples, and when she'd finished, he was quiet. "I can't just go at it, you know, attack Taft Properties. Not without more sources."

"Make it all about me, then. I'll give you what I've got. I've got numbers; I've got pictures. People need to see it for themselves— I know they'd care if they could just see it." She watched herself squeezing the pen in her hand as if it were a knife she could stab at something.

He sighed. "You really think there's something there, huh? Go ahead and send it along, then," he said blandly. "I'll take a look. I can't promise, but for an old friend, I'll take a look." She picked up the file from the table and dropped it, photos and papers scattering in the dust and crumbs on the floor. His indifference marked the end of a hope, the end of a certain fair-minded resolve in her,

and when she hung up and knelt to gather the documents, what
came to her was fierce and chaotic.

✝

SHE FOUND HERSELF drawn back to the *Ecological Defense
Manual*, for the fantasy of what someone might one day do to
Taft. She lay on the couch one evening, held the book up in the
lamplight, ignoring the loud music from the next-door-neighbor's
party. "When finding where to lay the blame for a corporation's
cold-hearted actions, avoid the lay managers just doing what
they're told." That might be Hal, or not. "Look for the criminal in
the corporation. His or her car can be targeted for slogans nam-
ing the crime—at his house, the office, in a parking garage. Don't
fool with the engine, which is risky, but consider slashing the
tires." Avery Taft drove a white Mercedes. She'd seen him pull
out of the parking lot at city hall. He probably had at least one
other car—a truck or a Jeep, something for hunting. What would
she write on his car? I BUILD HOUSES ON TOP OF POISON.
BUY A HOUSE FROM ME, MAKE YOUR CHILD SICK. It
seemed a cheap, childish thing to do—the slogans. People would
take his side if they saw the paint job ruined like that. She gazed
for a minute at the clutter of the coffee table, a half-drunk glass of
Coke. The couch smelled musty, and when she slapped a cushion,
dust wafted up. She'd neglected so many things—the dirty windows, email from friends, and there weren't any groceries in the
refrigerator. "Stay away from complicated disguises, which tend
to arouse suspicion, but wearing a fake beard or mustache is a
good option." (Really?) "For instructions on how to best apply
facial hair, see books like *Werner's Stage Makeup*." If she wore a

wig, maybe, she could convince herself that she was entirely someone else, someone who hadn't lost so much.

She went to the computer, and on the Internet, she studied the faces of the ones who'd been caught. The woman had long, blond frizzy hair, a rabbit face—she'd planted a bomb at a fur factory, and she'd been arrested two states away for her crime. The man looked like a balding schoolteacher, with his granny glasses and timid chin—he'd camped out in front of a forest and shot darts at the police who tried to physically remove him. Another man had a pudgy boxer's face—a mouth that curled up on the sides. He'd spray-painted over the billboards of oil companies WE KILL PEOPLE, and then he'd manufactured bombs out of milk bottles. They were all proudly ELF, and the adolescence of their anger bothered her. Their acts—no matter how justified—felt like teenage hijinks. The government called them terrorists, but they seemed too immature for that.

She clicked over the words she'd read so many times already and felt anger manifesting itself as physical pain—in the crick of her neck, the base of her spine. If she were to do it. If she were to ruin some part of the building site, the wooden frames. Her eyes ached from staring at the blue-lit words. She twisted a rubber band until it pressed the circulation from her fingertips.

When she got up from the chair, her muscles were so stiff she could barely walk. It would be a destruction of property that didn't belong to her, a kind of theft, but wasn't Taft's a crime too, and more violent than anything she wanted to do?

She went to the window and saw the partygoers out on the porch next door, a woman's body swaying to the music, a man holding up a large plastic bottle of Coke. They didn't drink, her neighbors.

It made her distrust them, though she herself liked to keep a measure of control when it came to substances. Her mom's drinking had seen to that. But there were times like now, when her rage seemed worse than alcohol: an ocean of hidden monsters and sharp, torn shipwrecks, and an unpredictable tidewater. If she were to set herself to do one of those things in the manual, she wouldn't be able to say if it was logic or rage that had moved her.

The music changed to some awful, clinging guitar, and a woman opened the back door, carrying a bunch of blue, helium balloons and a giant crepe-paper-covered baby bottle.

She went back to the computer, sat down and stared numbly at the screen. It looked homemade, this website, a crooked photo of a newspaper article, an inelegant diagram. She followed a link to an ammo site. Who were these people? She scrolled down the comments page, bright blue sentences, elliptical bursts of emotion. "Love the Super-XO." "The Winchester Western will blast away just about anything." She stopped at the user name, Overlong, in Alvin, Texas. "Easy enough to fix with a Dyna-igniter." This guy—he had to be a guy—had a few posts. "If you have trouble detonating from a safe distance, try the Extra booster detonating cord. Go see Allen at Alvin Fireworks. Trust me." The thrill of his proximity sang through the anonymous screen of Internet. She clicked the link for this Allen, and it went to a cheesy ad for a fireworks stand she'd seen just off the exit of 2351, three girls in camouflage bikinis holding rifles. "We buy BIG!! We're cheap, and we're stocked!" She hated free-form fireworks. It scared her that anyone in Texas with a face could walk into a store and buy fireworks and a gun.

She got up from the computer, went to her desk, found her tallies of the cancer rates from the local cancer registry (she got this through Doc), and saw the rate of brain tumors was still five times higher than the national average. Lee wasn't a scientist, but she was keeping track, and it could be the vinyl chloride, maybe coupled with solvents. No one wanted to hear this. She put down her notebook and walked through the kitchen out the back. The party next door had moved inside. She watched a squirrel on a branch. It made a sound like a piece of wood breaking. The moss was all over that tree now. She could see it even in the dark, a bright green strip of velvet.

SHE DROVE DOWN 2351 in the dark humidity, highway lights like perfect white fish in an aquarium, and hovering over them, the stars bright flecks of algae. Soupy, her mother would have called this weather.

She wore black socks over her shoes to disguise her footprints, black cloth gloves, and a black ski cap, though it was hot. In the trunk, there was a bag of gravel, a small can of oil, a funnel, a flashlight, a ballpoint pen, a pair of pliers, and three kinds of screwdrivers. Everything but the gravel would fit into a small canvas bag that Lee would wear over her chest. A truck was on one side, speeding up, and in the whoosh of its passing, her car shuddered.

Lee took the exit ramp and drove down the feeder road, past the dark gas station, past a stretch of woods, and turned down the dirt road. She parked the car at the edge of the woods, where it might be hidden, and she got out and walked toward the field.

The sky was a voice overhead that she couldn't understand. She felt separate from her body in a way that quickened her nerves, made her movements feel strong and deliberate. She found her way slowly by flashlight to the area of the construction site, and then she noticed the trailer Taft must have recently parked on the premises. The lights were off inside it, and there wasn't a car.

She walked up to the trailer from the back, then went around to the side to peer into the first window, seeing nothing but the flat brown shapes of furniture. The other window was curtained off. If anyone answered, she would say she'd had car trouble and needed to use the phone. She knocked, then gently turned the small handle on the door. It was light and swung open easily. She went inside and shone the regular, bright flashlight onto a card table filled with bottles of a strange blue liquid. She turned to the right and saw an open trash can filled with beer bottles. There was an orange-brown couch, a file cabinet; and when she shone her flashlight in the back room, it was empty, just a miniature sink and pantry shelf, a low table between cushioned benches. As she was coming back out, the light caught on a flat female face that startled her. A beat later, she knocked over the stand-up cardboard cutout of a girl in a bathing suit, a flat white smile, made-up eyes. At Lee's feet lay a large mesh bag full of shovels.

Back out in the dark, the humidity clung to her clothes. She walked past the foundation of one new house, near neatly stacked plumbing fixtures, and she knocked over the piles of pipes, cringed at their clattering. From where she stood, the bulldozer looked like a large, still animal. Approaching it, she felt like she should shush the thing, calm it down. She climbed up into the seat, lay on her stomach, and hung down to reach the oil filter cap. She had to feel her way to the lock. She squirted oil into the seams of the opening, unscrewed the six screws, and used the pliers to pry off the top. It took about fifteen minutes. When the spring came back from the top, it pinched her finger. She pulled out the dipstick, inserted the funnel. She maneuvered the cutoff plastic container of gravel to meet the funnel's lip and poured the gravel into the hole. It made a soft, crackling sound as it went down. She poured lubricant into the opening to spread the abrasive better. She pushed the dipstick back into the opening, twisted the lid back on. Her hands only began to shake as she pushed the screws back into their holes and she tightened them with the screwdriver. For a few seconds she thought she heard footsteps, but the plodding noise stopped. She lay there, very still, listening. Unless the directions were wrong, or she'd misread them, she'd killed the oil filter system.

Just as she jumped to the ground, she heard something like rocks dropping about ten yards away. She looked over to the trailer, but the lights were still off. She saw a shadow, maybe a dim silhouette gliding back and forth in front of the opening in the fence. But that was wrong, had to be. Anyway, she was mostly invisible. If she'd had a lookout, she could have taken her time.

She trudged through the uneven terrain. The flashlight with the red beam only gave her the dimmest sense of the ground ahead.

Ten yards farther, she spotted a giant roll of copper wire, gleaming. People broke into houses just to steal wire like that, and she guessed whoever usually stayed in the trailer was supposed to keep an eye on it. It seemed to be calling to her suddenly, as if the universe did not want it left there, but without help, she couldn't take it. And she remembered the manual said, "The prudent monkey-wrencher never acts spontaneously. His every move is planned ahead of time."

To find her car, she had to walk farther than she remembered down the dirt road, and just when she thought she'd lost it, there it was: next to a little pine tree. Driving home, on the nearly empty highway, her body light, she looked out at the passing headlights, turned past the vacant, darkened gas station, and something pressed against her heart, as if to remind her who she was.

✝

LEE SAT IN THE MORNING HEAT of the window, drinking her coffee. She looked for some sign—in the paper, online—that the bulldozer had actually been disabled, that she'd disrupted Taft's construction, but all the local news was about Thanksgiving, soup kitchens serving turkey to the poor, what Texas looked like during the time of the pilgrims, a corn festival at the Alamo. Maybe they didn't even know the bulldozer had been sabotaged— it had to have been sent in to the shop by now. She wanted to go back to make sure she'd done it right, but that would be stupid.

At the grocery store, in the aisle lined by soda bottles, exposed under those lights, she ran into Jack's old friend Wesley, now the chief of police. She might have swerved her cart and walked away from him, but if he'd seen her, that would seem odd. She thought if someone had spotted her car that night at Banes Field, she might still dispel doubts about herself with aggressive friendliness, by swaying the conversation back to him.

"Hey there, you still playing the sax?"

His eyes looked puffy, pasty in their folds, as if he hadn't slept, and he didn't seem to recognize her at first. "Sure am?" And then he knew her again.

"Still out at that place in Houston?"

"First Saturday every month."

"I'll have to get out there sometime," she said.

He nodded and seemed to be searching her face. "Hardly seems worth it, surely not just to see me play—I stand in the back."

"I've been meaning to, but I don't make it to Houston much."

"The traffic." She felt him looking at her chin, her nose, her eyes.

"You alright these days?"

Maybe her voice had betrayed her, or the way she held her arm against her chest. "Oh, yeah. Right as rain." She pushed her cart toward the green bottles and cereal box faces in the aisle ahead.

She drove home, and as soon as she stepped out of her car, an SUV pulled in behind her, and her neighbor Hal stepped out of it with a rueful, pious smile. As he came toward her in his blue suit, the polyester weave of it caught a sheen.

"Howdy," he said. "This'll just take a minute. You've got a minute, don't you?" She didn't like his tone.

The manual said, "Keep calm and practice a blank face."

"I know what you've been up to." He was smiling, shaking his head. "Oh, don't think I'm not paying attention."

She smiled, but there was a war drum in her chest. They stood in the shade, and she folded her arms, glanced up at the brown, curling leaves.

"It's just not going to do you any good," he said. "So I'm advising you to just hold up right there."

"Do you always go around with orders like that?"

The Zindlers next door stood over by their mailbox with cups of coffee, Myrna talking behind her cupped hand, and her floppy-haired husband nodding. They would favor Hal's side, but it might actually be satisfying to be caught, to defend what she'd done.

"Oh, I think you know what I'm talking about. All that tinkering with soil samples. It's not going to make a bit of difference. Not a bit. And it's trespassing too, you know that. You can do whatever study you want, but if it's not sanctioned, it's not legit. From now on, no one's getting away with setting foot on that property—it belongs to Avery Taft."

"I'm sorry. I'm confused. What's your part here?"

Hal rubbed his cheek. "Well, that's easy. A little while ago Taft asked me to partner with him." He turned his head to the side. "I want to see those homes sell. People need jobs around here."

"Thanks for the warning," she said.

"Taft's building is going ahead. It's approved. It's good for everyone. You know that, don't you?" He cleared his throat. "Hell, I've even talked with your boss when we were out golfing the other day—he agrees wholeheartedly."

Either this was a lie, or Doc had been out drinking beer, trying too hard to be gracious. She'd have to ask.

"Well, you've stated your opinion there. Thank you," she said. "Very helpful."

"You know I admire your conviction, and all the work you've done on behalf of the community." He held up his index finger. "Just hear me out. What we do need people to be in an uproar about is that Robertson Park. Do you know that if we don't get a spending approval for that park, we'll lose a good part of that acreage? That park is the center of our city, one of the only places these days where our kids can go and just play."

"I'm sure there's others who've got that about covered."

"Don't sell yourself short. I'd be glad to coordinate something for you."

"No, thanks."

He squeezed his eyes shut and grimaced. "Now, you're a reasonable lady. I know you are. Do you really believe all this effort's going to come to more than a hill of beans?" He lifted his hand, then dropped it again. "Well, alright then. So we understand each other?"

"We sure do," she said, turning to her door. She left him standing there on the driveway, and she went inside her house, lay down on Jess's bed, and closed her eyes.

DEX

WHEN THE RAIN CAME AGAIN, and just three months after the hurricane, it flooded under the trailer so it looked like a rectangular boat floating on top of a hill, and the vegetable garden drowned; and because it was another of his mother's fantasies that they would all eat those string beans and tomatoes, he knew she'd ask him to replant them.

The storm pounded the roof like some misbegotten broken engine rattle, and he couldn't sleep those two nights, afraid as he watched the water rising. He hated his dad then, and there was nothing to do but watch rain in the window. His mom had to be everything; she had to take up so much space to make up for his absence; she had to be larger than was healthy for her. Those days as they waited by the TV, to see if they'd need to leave, a dampness in the couch, a leak dripping onto the stove top, his mother had seemed strangely calm and buoyant, teasing Dex and Layla that they'd all have to get aboard a boat, that she had two kids and two cats and that was enough for their little ark. She seemed supernaturally confident that they would be okay.

It turned out the trailer was perched on high enough ground, and the rain had stopped just before the water would have soaked the rug on the floor. He'd heard that the game room of the Baptist church next door had filled up with water and someone would have to gut it.

Now that the streets were dry again, he looked out the window and noticed that some drunk had knocked over and crumpled the stop sign on the corner, and he knew his mother would be on the phone yelling about it for days. She seemed too big for their home lately, kept bursting through all the careful, invisible walls he'd built around himself. He went to the Xbox to put on *War*, so he could stare at the soldiers running away from him before he exploded their tank, and he could go far into that rectangular tunnel of battle, and when he hit a convoy in the distance twice, he felt elated and proud, as if he'd just defended his family.

Then she came in the door, breaking through it even though she'd only opened it, hadn't even slammed the cheap, light thing, as she so often did.

"You didn't tell me, goddamnit! Dexter William . . ." Her face was tight and young looking. "You lied to me. Where's your sister? I don't want her to hear this."

"She's out. Mom, I didn't lie."

"You sure as hell did. You know how I had to hear you were at that party? From Wanda Betts."

"I felt bad."

"Well, I sure as hell would hope you'd feel bad. You'd better swear to me right now you didn't touch her." His mom had no idea he'd been going out to see Willa, but he didn't think telling her now would help.

She threw her bag on the couch, and coins and makeup spilled out on the floor.

"I didn't know she was there until it was too late to help."

She shook her head and walked to the kitchen area, slammed open a cabinet. "First, you nearly get suspended for fighting and now this. I can only imagine what your dad would have to say." The walls of the trailer were squeezing in to make a smaller tunnel, a smaller life, as his dad and the rest of the world grew larger, louder, forgetting about them. "I'm ashamed of you," she said. "You know how much I hate that?"

He felt a pressure on the top of his head and against his shoulders.

"God, Mom," he said. "I'm sixteen years old."

"Goddamn right," she said. "You've got to do better than that."

✝

AFTER HE DROPPED OFF WEEKS, he didn't want to go home yet, and he didn't know where to go. On an impulse, he turned down Farm Road 1 toward Casa Texas. They'd still be serving even though it was late.

The parking lot was crowded and when he got inside, the restaurant was darker than he remembered, and there was a sweet, chlorine smell, and then the smell of spices. Carlita stood at the hostess stand in a hot-pink, billowy dress.

"How many?" she said. She didn't remember him.

The tables were filled, and in the back, he heard the loud music, could just make out a few couples dancing.

"Oh, I'm not here to eat. I wondered if I could see Mr. Holgine?"

Her chubby face was shiny and exasperated, her pink lips painted to match her dress. "What about?"

"He offered me a job a while back."

She shook her head no just barely and said, "He's real busy tonight, but let me see if we can find him."

She turned and shouted something at a waiter in tight pants and asked Dex to wait in one of the wooden chairs lined up along the entranceway.

He waited for half an hour, watching the people, the handsy couples, the families with the screaming little kids, the women in heels and low-cut dresses, laughing at one another's jokes. He started to get hungry from the smell of tortillas, and when he saw the clock over the margarita machine, he realized how late it was.

He went back up to the hostess station. "Did Mr. Holgine say he would see me?"

"We've got a full house, see?" She pressed her body back to let a few customers walk past her.

"He's a friend of my dad's." He didn't want to leave before he had that job.

"Oh, alright." She blew a strand of hair out of her face. "Let me go check the kitchen."

A few minutes later, Mr. Holgine came back, looking for him. He wasn't smiling as he always had in the past. "What's this about, son?"

"I'm Dex, Mac's son. You offered me a job a while back?"

His small, dark eyes swept to the left, then to the right. "Yes, my friend! How is he?" He clapped a hand on Dex's shoulder.

"He's good. Out on a rig again now."

"You'll work hard like him, won't you?"

"I sure will."

Dex watched Mr. Holgine's sharp nose and long chin, and tensed himself for the warnings and details. "Be here tomorrow at five," Holgine said.

"That's it?"

"See you." Holgine waved, smiled, and turned to rush back to the candlelit dimness of the dining room.

Dex drove home, wind picking up garbage along the shoulder, spinning pale plastic bags and silver cans into the dark. He'd replace his excuse for lateness with his victory about the job, and then she couldn't be mad.

✟

WHEN HE TOLD HIS DAD about Casa Texas, he seemed to want to keep Dex on the phone. "Oh yeah? Well, what do you know? Did you meet Marquis yet? Marquis's a character. Ask him to tell you about Merides."

"I just met Mr. Holgine, but he was too busy to talk."

"Huh. Well, Fred Holgine will take care of you. He's a good man. Tell you what, if you can save a thousand dollars, I'll put the rest toward a new truck. And next time, you, me, and your sister will go out to dinner there. Get us some fajitas."

Dex's mom didn't like it that he'd "quit the team," and warned that if his grades dropped even by one letter, he'd have to stop working. She didn't say it, but Dex had the sense that it rankled her, him working for one of his dad's old friends.

✟

AS SOON AS HE STARTED WORK, he picked up the skills, mostly being invisible. He watched the people eating at the tables, waiting for them to put down a fork, to push away a plate, and then he was there to take it from the table into the kitchen, where he stood over the trash, cleaned the plate, and then, steam coming up into his face, he fit the dish into the prong of the dishwasher, while the old, skinny dishwasher with stringy, pockmarked arms talked about the rodeo he'd signed up for. "Man, I'm quitting this hog hole," he'd say every night. Later in Dex's shift, he helped the waitresses refill the salsa jars, the salt and pepper shakers. He wiped down the tables. Each waitress was supposed to give him 10 percent, but there was a mean one with sharp cheekbones and wizened, narrow eyes, who only gave him five bucks, saying, "Sorry, just didn't make quota." Still, it was good money for him, fifty or sixty a night.

As he was leaving, when the dining was slowing down and there was just one waitress left on call, the dance hall in the back would start to fill up, and he'd catch glimpses of slow-dancing couples with their bodies pressed together, a hand cupping an ass or a woman showing her breast from the open side of a sleeveless shirt. Or he'd see them two-stepping, drunker seeming, stomping and stumbling. He could remember watching his parents dance the two-step just once—at a wedding. And he'd been surprised to see his dad's big body so graceful that night, the swivel of his shoulders, the nimbleness of his booted feet, his mom smiling at his lead, her skirt swirling as they turned together, and how their footsteps mirrored each other's.

Later that week, he stayed on to watch the dancing from a dark table, where miraculously, someone had left a full bottle of beer, and when he was sure no one was looking, he took sips from it. There was a band that night on stage—a guitar player and a lanky singer, a drummer, and a fiddler with a goatee, whose wild, tangled gray hair whipped around as he brought the fiddle to the crook of his neck.

Dex liked being among these people who had nothing to do with high school, as if he'd been allowed for a night to visit the future, to live in a twenty-year-old's body. It made him feel superior. He wanted to take whatever this was and have it at the ready the next time Cully or Bishop or Trace gave him shit. Here he was learning what it meant to be a certain kind of man, the kind who could handle himself, who could talk to women he didn't know.

The singer called out, "Alright, y'all," and started playing a catchy song Dex almost knew but didn't—a woman cheating, a man abandoned, but the tune wouldn't let sadness get in the way of its swing. The sharp heel of the singer's boot tapped along.

"You know how to do it?" said the mean waitress, whose name he'd just learned was Pammy.

"Do what?"

She nodded to the people dancing. "That."

He shrugged. "Not really."

She pulled him up by his arm. "Dance with me. I'll teach you."

He kind of hated her for all these weeks of her bossing him, then shorting him on tips, but for now he stood taller than her, and smiling, she taught him to shuffle his feet, to lead, and if he didn't look at her face, worn-out skin and triangular bones, he could pretend she was someone else. He liked the steady sway of her hand in his, how the rough waltz took him back in time to some older country music, before TV, before computers, before his parents were even born.

HE'D BEEN RIGHT about the garden. His mom sent him to the nursery for more seeds and chicken wire, told him to save what he could of the plants. He dug in the mulch, sweating through his white T-shirt. His mother was on the phone about the fallen stop sign—through the window, he could hear her talking loudly, as he eyed the intersection and waited for one car to crash into another.

He dug small holes with the spade and planted the carrot seeds. They didn't have the garden when his dad had still lived with them, but it pleased his mom so much to see a vegetable grow—when the sprouts came out, she grinned at them as if no one else in the world had ever planted a seed and these were miracles given just to her. "Look at that little radish." He imagined his dad had fallen for a girl who danced at a bar, or a girl in a mask of eye makeup who promised to give him everything. Dex didn't know. But his dad had fallen, and now he lived with a woman his own age with sticklike blond hair (in the one picture Dex saw), though his dad wouldn't say her name, and Dex's mom lived with him and Layla, and that was it.

He pounded in new stakes with a hammer around the plot of the garden. He'd not appreciated the way those guys talked to him, even before what they'd done to Willa. They'd goaded him; they'd used stupid, whinnying voices. They'd let him know he wasn't worth their time. There was damage he might do to their cars in the middle of the night—a key scraped against the door or a windshield broken, so they'd notice and not be able to do a damn thing about it. He knew where each of them lived. If the means were not ones that his mother would have been proud of, then so be it. He imagined that if she found out, she would not be too terribly disappointed.

He wrapped the chicken wire over the stakes, nailed it secure, the delicate leaves just coming up like green hair against the black dirt.

He went back to turn the mulch a bit, pull out the weeds, and as he stabbed the spade into the dirt, he remembered how good it had felt to have Bishop's neck against his fist, and then he thought about Cully's pathetic excuses, and then, at the intersection, he heard the metal crunch of two cars colliding, and one horn started to blare.

WILLA

RUNNING, WILLA GLIDED OVER THE WORLD, rushed forward to the rhythms of her breath, the pound of her feet. In Robertson Park, the trees' green mosaic slid beside her, the path twisting through the grass, past the playground, past the old Brown house museum, past the tennis court, the gazebo, a street of houses, and then she ran the circuit again.

On her third lap, through a gap in the trees, she saw Cully. He was washing his truck in a driveway. She was afraid he'd turn around and see her if she kept running. Still trying to catch her breath, she stood behind a tree. He lived over near the junior high, not so close to the park. Why was he washing his truck at someone else's house?

He wore an orange baseball hat that bobbed up and down as he walked around the side of the truck, spraying the hose at its shiny red bed. Then he tossed down the garden hose, lay halfway across the hood with a rag to polish the metal, one sneakered foot lifted off the ground. She didn't see his face clearly again, but he jumped back to both feet, and he went around to the back of the truck with that distinct rolling rhythm of his walk.

Out from behind a pine tree in front of her, something shimmered in the dimness, and she saw the antlers, thick and gold. When she blinked, the vision stuttered, and the thing had seven identical heads as if they'd been digitally multiplied. The legs and feet were a lion's, peaked green scales on the body, and it was the same face of her old dog, Junior, repeated seven times, though the mouth snarled in a way her dog never had. *You are dead.* The words came into her head as if she'd said them herself, or someone had said them to her. *You are dead.* She couldn't see Cully anymore—the beast blocked out the sight of him, a tangled mass of white beetles at the edge of one claw. She felt her breaths go shallow and rapid, and looked around for help.

There were the low-hanging black *U*s of the swings, the rusty rails of the monkey bars, the dull metal slide. In the other direction, the vacant tennis court with the crisp net, a squirrel standing on the clay, holding up its paws as if it carried a purse. She smelled something like horse manure and a burning electrical wire, and then she saw the clotted gray smoke coming up from a golden urn. From the nostrils of one head, a faint hum of a hymn she used to sing at her grandmother's church: "*Somewhere in outer space, God has prepared a place, for all those who trust him and obey. The countdown's getting closer every day.*" Another head opened its mouth, and in the back of it, she saw the film: a body in an old white T-shirt and boxers, flames raked across the chest until the form trembled away in a spasm. The beast closed its mouth. A sour taste came up from her throat. She took two steps back, walking away.

All at once, she heard the whisper and honk of traffic behind her again on the road. The vision dissolved beyond the pine tree, and she saw Cully pivot around his truck and go into the house.

She heard the door close. She bent to tighten the laces on her sneakers, stood up, and took off running.

When she got home in her room and shut the door, in the shadow by the bed, she saw the scaly, scabbed tail, and then all of those heads, which seemed to be watching her. *You are dead. You're not even alive.* She couldn't feel her hands or feet. One of the heads opened its mouth. Lying on the orange tongue was a small, dead baby squirrel, its tiny heart exposed and pink.

✝

HER MOTHER DIDN'T TRY to pray with her anymore, and she didn't try to find out more details, and her father had never referred to what had happened at all. They were embarrassed, and they loved her, and they just wanted to ride it out, and what else was there to do, really? Willa's father had begun to drink his coffee in the backyard, standing up among the trees, while her mother washed the dishes and cleaned up after dinner alone.

But a change had worked itself within her—the extra eye muscle, the lines of poetry that appeared on her skin some mornings—but more than that, there was a pain in her that was hardening, barely held back and concealed, like a gun held against her flesh.

Later that night, she was at the family computer while her parents sat with their backs to her, watching the news. She heard the voice of the newscaster, a suicide bomb killed twenty-one in Baghdad, a five-year-old girl had been taken from her bed, and then the anxious, martial tune before a commercial. *Ba-bum-bum.* "Drixel Upholstery Cleaner will pick up anything." She was careful to open emails only when they weren't looking. There was an email from Dani, saying, "Please consider telling the police. I will help you. Read this article." The link went to a site with plain, military-style letters: "One out of every five American women has been the victim of an attempted or a completed rape in her lifetime." She read the line quickly, then clicked it away. And then the next email opened so quickly she hadn't even glanced at the sender. In the dark screen, the beast was there, fluttering in 3-D, the eyes like flashing lights. In green capital letters, the word *REPENT*, and in the background, bombs going off in Iraq, soldiers' bodies blown apart, guns ratcheting out of tanks. She closed the screen, deleted the message from txcklopy@inet.com.

She turned around and saw the tops of her parents' heads above the headrests, the buzz of her father's graying hair, the shiny crown of her mother's brunette. "Don't forget, tomorrow, we have that church dinner," her mother said. Willa got up from the chair and went to the back window and stared out at the darkness. It stared back.

HAL

Hal LINGERED IN THE LIVING ROOM, waiting for dinner,
restless. Darlene had sprayed green apple room scent all around
the couch, and Hal went to the window, just to get some air.
Across the street, he saw Lee Knowles in her yard, tending to
flowers on a bush. She had a shapely figure beneath the bulky
men's shirt and work pants—her breasts high and firm, her legs
slender and long—and though she never did much to help it, she
had a pretty face. For that, he somehow hated her more.

So many people he knew were out of work. There was Larry
Mivens, with three young kids to raise, a house the bank was
about to foreclose on—there was Binx Dooley, laid off from the
oil refinery and promised his job back only when business picked
up. He had a mother with cancer, who lived with him and his
wife. Lee Knowles might as well have been storing up jobs in her
attic, just hiding them from people—because whatever Taft did,
it would bring back jobs. Hal watched her, fussing with that bush,
chopping at a branch. Truly it was the unhappy people in the
world who caused so much misery for others.

He wished he could make her afraid, but she seemed impervious. A demon sprung out of grief had got into her, manned her up, and now there was only so much he could do.

Later that night, as he helped Darlene with the dishes, she said, "How'd it go with the neighbor?"

"Oh, she listened alright." He pictured Lee's face, the way her full mouth turned down in doubt.

"She going to stop bothering Taft? Really?"

"She said she was sorry for the trouble she'd caused, that she'd only wanted people to be a little more cautious, but she certainly didn't want to stand in the way. She knows what it would mean to people to have that subdivision—I talked to her all about that. What it would mean, those jobs."

"What did you say? How'd you work your magic?"

"I said I appreciated all she'd done for us so far."

"Well, that was thinking. Flattery." She shook her head. "I guess it pretty much always works."

"I think she just misplaced her love, you know, that's all. I've been reading about that in this book from Pastor Sparks."

Darlene pulled a plate shaped like a ladybug from the soapsuds, laid it on the counter for him to dry. Why did she buy so many dishes that looked like children's toys? Even Cully wasn't a kid anymore. "Hal, I wanted to give you a chance to catch your breath first. But your mom had an accident today. They gave her the wrong medication and she threw up in the common room. They were real apologetic, but still. She hasn't been eating since then."

"Those skunks. What do I pay them for?"

"It happens sometimes. I think generally they do a good job. At least they told us about it."

"Assholes."

"Hal."

"Okay, I'll go visit. Soon as I can." He remembered his mother's crumpled, wilted face, how she held her stomach like a sack.

"I'm bringing her some soup tomorrow," Darlene said, "and I'm going to tell her then that you're coming."

"I will. I do want to see her." It was the right thing to say, and he wanted to say the words anyway, to make them true, but instead, the lie burned in his mouth.

✟

THERE WAS A NEW PLAQUE on the wall of Avery Taft's office that said I'M NO BELIEVER, BUT DON'T WRITE THAT ON MY TOMBSTONE. Hal tried to pretend he hadn't read it, as he waited for the good word, for the ray of sunshine from Avery. Hal had just told him about his visit to Lee Knowles, how he'd told her that even her new studies would certainly not hold up to the EPA's, how Avery would keep binders of evidence available to the public in his model homes, in case there was any question.

"I may have changed my mind about that," said Avery, smiling, "but go on."

"It's a good idea. If they're thick enough, no one will want to read them anyway." Sunlight suddenly streamed through the window. Hal was on a roll. "And, I tell you, the lady listened, and I think she felt a little embarrassed at herself really. I think she might leave you alone for a while now, sir. And, really, what can she do anyway?"

Avery shrugged. "Now I've got Councilman Atwater after me. Apparently, he found some minuscule increase in benzene, he claims. He's got this gal at the Texas Commission on the Environment on the case."

"Really?"

Atwater was the kind of man Hal was accustomed to pity, short in stature, thinning hair, an earnest smile with too many vulnerable teeth. He wore blue shirts and red ties and navy slacks. He was the kind of work geek who actually wanted the picnics, the birthday parties, who looked forward to this fellowship because he had no other. It was hard to believe he'd be capable of much.

"Avery, I'll talk to him too, if you like." God was helping him. After he walked away from Lee's house, back to his own, who knew what had happened beyond the curtains, inside of her soul?

Surely he'd been telling Avery the truth, though now Avery seemed to be studying him, weighing his trust. "And I've got another problem now too. Someone's fooling with the equipment. Probably just kids, and I've got my friend José there most nights on the lookout in the trailer. Except Saturday when he goes to the Chinga Club to flirt with the ladies. Hey, do you think Cully might be interested in taking over that night? Make a little extra cash? Nothing's going to happen. But just having someone there makes a difference to my peace of mind."

Hal felt slighted only for a moment. Cully was meant to play football, for greater things than odd-job security. Then, staring at the wood of Avery's desk, Hal turned the idea around. Or God did it for him. Cully needed something to fill up the absence of playing ball, and this offer came with a rock-solid connection, a boon he might later call on.

"Well, I'll sure ask him." He nearly felt a cord tightening his connection to Taft, as he sat there, more confident in that leather seat, blessings coming down from every angle of the room. "I sure will."

"Have him come see me then, and we'll set it all up," said Avery.

"Alright, then."

"Let me see what I can do." Hal stood up, and it felt good to be the one ending the visit. Avery had been lucky, but Hal might be blessed. He'd been praying well every morning at the breakfasts at church, he'd been keeping his thoughts clean, his liver sober—and as he bounded down the stairs toward the ornate door with the Mexican filigree, he could feel it coming to him, all that money, all that light.

LEE

WHEN LEE FIRST GOT THE LETTER in the mail, even though it was certified, she didn't read it because she thought it was a bill. She put it on the phone table and continued to cook her baked chicken. She ate dinner, drank a bourbon, listened to a record that Jack had liked of old-time country, the crooners with their high warbly voices, the silliness of the lyrics. "*Oh, Lord I made a mountain out of you.*" He'd said he liked it because they didn't take their feelings so seriously, they just made them into songs.

After she finished her bourbon, she poured another, looked out the back window at the dusk, where the neighbor was packing away the cushions on her patio furniture, and Lee wondered if it was supposed to rain again. She watched a little bit of the news, the fighting in Afghanistan, the photograph of the turbaned terrorist subject, and then, abruptly, young girls wearing blue eye shadow and cowboy hats, high-kicking across a stage. Finally, she forced herself to open the envelope. It was printed on thick stationery, the letterhead of some lawyer.

This is to advise you that Avery Taft, of Taft Properties, charges that you committed fraud when you submitted false photographs of his property to *The Friendswood Dispatch*. This is an order to cease and desist with all communication having to do with properties belonging to Avery Taft. Unless you agree to comply . . .

She couldn't afford a lawsuit. If it were anyone else, she'd think the threat was toothless, but Taft was litigious—he'd sued one of his daughter's teachers, and his wife's cosmetic business partner. Taft's brother-in-law was a lawyer, she'd heard, so he got a deal on representation.

She felt tired, as if the flu had suddenly come over her. She folded up the letter, put it back in the envelope, and laid it on top of her electric bill. She could not spend the anniversary as she had before, first hysterical on bourbon, then catatonic. She always did whatever she could not to be locked inside the fact of her daughter's death, and the days still crept nearer, closing in. And she didn't yet have a plan.

+

THE NEXT MORNING, she woke up to birdsong. She waited a few hours, vacuumed the floors, and because it had not rained after all, watered her plants. Finally, when it was after ten o'clock, she called Jack. She wanted to tell him about Avery Taft's threat.

"I was thinking the other day," he said, "about how Jess liked those ring pops. Remember? Like big little girl rings that she wore, but made with candy? Turned her mouth purple? Genius, whoever invented those."

It was risky and against everything in the manual, but if she told him, he'd understand that she was taking action, that her grief had a new shape.

"I broke into the old Banes site again, where that Taft is building."

"You've got to be kidding me."

She couldn't tell if he was angry or amused. "No, I'm sure not. I messed up his bulldozer."

"You what?"

"You heard me. I learned all about how to do it. It's going to cost them, and they'll lose at least three days of work."

"Lee, do you know what they're liable to do to you?"

"Me? A lady? Hell, they're after me for the pictures I sent to the paper. Taft got his lawyer to threaten me. No one's going to suspect the other thing. I only wish there was some way to find out if it worked."

"Don't do anything stupid."

"I bet you never thought I was capable of mechanics at that level."

He sighed. "Jesus, Lee."

That day when he'd left her, he was packing his things in suitcases, and within her everything froze except this tiny, hot ball of hope that she'd been protecting. As small as a marble or a penny. He said, "I just can't abide being with someone who's so far away, even when I'm in the same room with them." He locked up one of the suitcases. "Goddamn, I've got my own sorrow. And I have to go it alone?" She'd sat in that chair and watched him as if he were someone on TV, someone she couldn't ask for anything.

"You know why I did it," she said now.

"Of course I do, but that doesn't mean I don't think it's dumb. You'd better not tell another soul, hear me?" She heard in his voice that he was afraid for her.

"Promise me you'll stop it," he said. "Hell, you need to get out more. Or something. You need to let go of this thing."

She said it, not meaning it. "Okay." But then she did mean it. "I will." The relief streamed through her, as if she'd been swimming away from a shipwreck for a long time and had now come to the end, washed up on shore. Okay, she was done.

✝

IN THE FOLLOWING DAYS, she took care of tasks she'd been ignoring. She scrubbed all the floors on her hands and knees until she had bruises, she dusted the baseboards with a torn old towel. She threw out threadbare or stained linens, cracked saucers, a clock that she would never get fixed. She hid most of the research documents in the black file cabinet, lugged boxes of correspondence up to the attic.

When she was finished, Jess's old room—the desk bare except for a lamp; the rippled rag rug emptied of her piles of papers; the bed made—looked ready for a guest.

✝

RUSH THREW A CHRISTMAS PARTY one night, and Lee went. Tom was playing classic rock on the stereo, and he'd built a bonfire in the back, where he and his buddies kept vigil over the keg. A ball of mistletoe dangled above the sliding glass door, and the tree in the living room was strung with silver tinsel and red and white lights. The house smelled of peppermint and vodka.

Lee waved to Esmeralda, homecoming queen of the class and still darkly beautiful, who, with a huge, guilty smile, poured herself a glass of eggnog at the bar. Lee stood near a table set with guacamole and chips on a Mexican platter, and a big man in a short-sleeved button-down shirt walked up to her. "Rush said I should introduce myself. The name's David."

He had an appealing, bearded face, and the dark facial hair underlined his kind, green eyes.

"I met Tom over at my shop. I sell boats over in Galveston, but Rush says you like to dance."

"I used to anyway."

"Why used to?"

"Well, there just stopped being opportunities, I guess."

He nodded and smiled, as if he'd just noticed something he liked in her face. "What do you think the chances are for dancing here?" A large birthmark—the shape of a walnut—flashed from the back of his hand.

"Not great. Tom likes to keep the bar area clear for the serious drinkers." There wasn't any reason why she shouldn't like him, why she shouldn't flirt a little, and she couldn't quite identify her lack of interest. She wasn't dead yet, as Rush liked to say.

"Oh well."

David sipped at his drink, leaned against the kitchen cabinets.

He smiled at her sideways. "I like to dance." There might be something good in him. But his beefiness and beard reminded her of one of Jack's old buddies at the beach, and then that made her wonder if Jack would come back to see her after all.

Mavis Leman joined them, and it seemed she would flirt, with her blond-streaked hair, her large breasts pressed into a white blouse. She taught the seventh grade and told a story about the man wearing a bathrobe, who'd tried to lure one of her students into his house. "He told her he was sick, that he needed someone to come in and call the hospital. He was sick, alright." Her round, blue eyes and tan, plump features moved so quickly as she spoke, it was hard to listen. "I looked up his address when she told me where he lived. He's a registered sex offender. Do you believe that? Lives near all these kids. When the girl refused to go inside, the man ordered fifty magazines in the girl's mother's name, and months later, when she got the bills, her mother tracked him down. He just wanted to get caught at something, I swear." David leaned toward Mavis, asking more questions, and Lee went to the other side of the room to look for Rush.

There was throaty-voiced Olivia. "Lee!" Tall, pale faced, black hair—she had a voice that creaked pleasantly like wood.

"I moved back from Austin!" She came over to Lee, and she smelled of almonds. She had a kind of practical happiness in her, a Catholic kind—Lee remembered her saying her rosary one night in high school, after they'd snuck into a dive bar and lied about their ages.

"Welcome back." Lee wanted to be cheerful for her, for the sake of old times, but she was already straining her smile, already feeling her shoulders slump forward. "Where are you living?"

"For now, back at my folks." Her mouth pulled down on the side. Olivia's older sister had died suddenly last year, when, just after she ran to her car in the rain, a blood clot got to her lung. Lee had helped arrange the photos for the wake—Olivia's sister's curly dark hair and toothy smile; the baby pictures; the snapshots with ill-chosen boyfriends. Lee had written down the names of people who sent flower arrangements to the family, and she'd sat with Olivia and her friends at the funeral, had wept. People saw Lee as one acquainted with grief, someone who had special knowledge—she needed to take her part. "How are they doing?"

"My dad lost all this weight, and my mom doesn't joke around anymore. Will they ever be the same? I don't know." Then she changed the subject, told a funny story about getting up on a chair to grab the sugar and falling on her butt—described the black and blue cellulite on the backs of her thighs.

A woman in a silver minidress swayed to the music, her giraffe-like husband with his tiny head, leaning down to hear her talk. Beyond the sliding glass doors, around the bonfire in the back, Tom and other men hunched over their plastic cups of beer. One of them smoked a cigar.

Lee saw Char over by the glass door with her daughter, Willa, taller and skinnier than Lee remembered, heavy black eye makeup that made her appear by turns angry and Cleopatra beautiful. She wore jeans and a silk old-fashioned blouse, and there was Char in her Christmas sweater, red with a green cat woven just under her chest.

Lee and Char had been good friends after all, years ago— they'd written one another notes on paper they folded into tri-angles and swans; they'd lain around for hours in each other's bedrooms, gossiping. What had happened to the friendship was nothing but years, really, and Lee saying no to invitations to church. Lee went over to her, held up her drink. "Merry Christmas!" Lee leaned to hug Char, but her shoulders went stiff.

"Well, hi there, Lee. Honey, you know Lee." She nudged her daughter, whose wide, smooth face seemed to awaken.

"I hear you've been quite busy again over there at city hall."

"I was. Done with all that now."

Char studied her, as if waiting for Lee to deny it. "Goodness. Well, what have you been doing with yourself, then?"

Lee shrugged. "Working out in the yard."

Olivia was there then, pulling Char away, to introduce her to someone involved with the school, and Willa turned toward the picture window and sipped at her drink. She looked alone standing there, the only kid at the party.

Lee called to her, "Hey, why don't we go sit on the couch."

The girl looked relieved.

They were next to the Christmas tree, bells ringing in the music coming over the speakers, small gold snowmen delicately swaying on the branches whenever someone passed. "Now tell me, you're a junior now, is that right?"

"No, a sophomore."

Lee wondered if Char had ever told her daughters about Jess. She had to navigate this territory carefully, not wanting to weep or frighten the girl, not wanting to draw attention.

"Is Ms. Marlowe still teaching tenth-grade English?"

Willa lifted her face and nodded energetically. "She just sent me a book of poems by Emily Dickinson."

But Lee also didn't want to begrudge Jess, who'd had a whole life after all, who'd once held down the center of everything. "Oh, she was a good teacher, I remember. My daughter liked her." Ms. Marlowe had sent a condolence card after Jess died that quoted Shakespeare and said in loopy handwriting at the bottom, *She was a gem. I will miss her.*

Willa turned her head away, hair swinging, and that signaled that Willa did know.

"I'm writing a paper on Dickinson now."

She said she was doing it on her own, and Lee could see the intensity of her feeling for the homework, maybe because she didn't have to worry about what the other kids thought of her ideas.

"She was a recluse and wore white dresses all the time— every single day. Then after she died, her little sister discovered a box with all the poems tied up in packets, thousands of them. Dickinson had been sending them all along to this man, this former minister, and he kept saying they were good, but not really poems, and in the end, he changed them up and published them." The girl seemed desperate to talk.

"Unbelievable."

"It makes me sad for her, but also not."

"I know what you mean. She must have got something from it. Storing it all up like that. She must have known they were worth something."

"I think so." In her wide-eyed intensity, the way she pulled in her bottom lip, there was something Lee recognized. A flash of Jess, then gone.

"What else do you like?"

Willa shrugged. "Hanging out with my best friend, I guess." She had an awkward beauty, falsely bold in the eyes, mouth shy and small in a way that made youth spill from her. Lee had almost forgotten what it was like to talk to a teenager, to feel the neediness.

Willa reached for her drink, and Lee noticed a dark red rash on her forearm—like an amulet just above her wrist. "You okay there?"

Willa covered her forearm with her hand.

"Listen, I work at a dermatologist's office. You should get that checked out."

Willa's lip trembled. "I know what it is. I just need to keep face lotion on it. I was writing too much there."

Lee nodded, not wanting to make the girl squirm. Writing phone numbers? Did kids still do that?

"In my sleep."

"Huh. Interesting."

Willa adjusted herself in her seat, then flung out her hand. "In regular life, I like to write poetry too."

What was it about teenage girls and poetry? Practically all of them wrote it, and it was mostly bad, but at least they tried to make something out of their cyclones of feeling, tried to tame it instead of letting it blow them away.

"Well, what do you write in your sleep? How do you even do that?"

She shook her head and shyly smiled. She probably thought she'd said too much. Lee wanted to prolong the time away from the other adults, to catch that radiant expression again that felt so familiar. The girl had something. Willa talked about Ms Marlowe's new husband, how everyone knew he'd made a lot of money on stocks and he'd donated money for a garden. She went on talking, and in her eyes, she looked hurt—the pupils seemed slightly cracked, the whites bloodshot.

Lee caught another echo of Jess, this time in Willa's voice. "I don't know. I guess I'm just weird that way." She sat up straight, pulled her hair over one shoulder, and gulped her drink. Lee tried to form a reply, to ignore the longing for her own girl.

Then Char was at the couch with them, tugging on the bottom

of her sweater. "What have you two been up to?" Over by the keg, a man was singing "White Christmas" in a campy voice, and the smell of the bonfire blew through the sliding glass door.

"Willa's telling me all about poetry."

Char screwed up her face as if she hadn't understood. "Oh, yeah. She's into that English, alright." Then her white teeth glared up in her smile. "Willa, come meet Mr. Mitchell over here." She crooked her finger, winked at Lee. "Thanks for taking care of her."

Olivia came to the couch with a bourbon for Lee, lowered her voice. "You know it's real sad what happened to Char's daughter. I'm surprised in a way that she brought her here. I guess because there's no other kids around. It was nice of you to take an interest."

"What?"

"You didn't hear? It's real sad. She drank too much at a party a while back. You know these boys, they were all over her. I guess she's not pregnant, but Char won't talk about it."

"My God. What did they do to her?"

Olivia shrugged, rolled her eyes. "I don't know exactly. Enough. It was bad. These kids shouldn't drink."

"She's just a girl."

"Not much parents can do now, I guess," Olivia said, swallowing the last of her clear cocktail. "You know it doesn't change. It's one of the tragedies of life. High school doesn't change." Olivia touched the necklace at her throat, and looked behind her at the rest of the party.

Lee stood up from the couch, with her gaze at the level of a blank-faced, silver-winged angel. Her stomach turned. She remembered how protective Jack had been, how he'd made fun of every guy who tried to date his daughter—ruthlessly imitating them, pointing out their most obvious physical flaw. If something like that had happened to Jess, if she had been raped, it would have destroyed him.

Over at the door, Char and Willa stood with Rush, saying good-bye, Char's face puffy and tired looking, her hand on Willa's back. Willa stood slumped over, arms folded at her breasts as if she were cold. Suddenly Lee didn't resent all of Char's churchgoing and prayers—ruse or not. Lee only wished for them to have whatever solace in the world there was.

UNTIL CHRISTMAS PASSED, she kept herself occupied, sending presents to her nieces and nephews. She wrote cards to all the relatives back in Beaumont she never saw anymore. She served a holiday dinner in the soup kitchen at the Quaker church. She watched the Christmas specials on TV—it was all an indulgence she'd used to share with Jess—Jack only had so much use for the holidays. And the busyness, the forced cheer of it, gave back to her a small part of maternal duty.

She spent Christmas with her brother and his family in Texas City, glad to be around people who'd once known Jess. This was how most people grieved, she thought, sitting at the fire with Jonathan and his two boys. If she'd felt no pain at moments like this, then it would have been as if Jess had never been there at all, but the pain was virile and energetic—it kept Jess close to her tonight at the dinner table and next to the fragrant tree. When she said to Jonathan, "I'm done with protesting. I'm retired," she was happy to find that she meant it.

"I never liked it," he said. "I gotta be honest. I didn't like the way it took you over. But I always thought you were probably right."

"It's not enough. I've gone through almost all of my money. And now they want to sue me. I'm just tired, I think."

"Well, aren't we all?" he said. "I hear that." His cheeks were red and puffy from drink, sentimental and hangdog in the way their father's had been. "That's why it's so good to have you here. To just take some time, you know? The boys haven't seen you since the summer." Sleeping in the same house as her brother again, seeing Jess's eyes in his eyes and seeing the echo of Jess's nose in the noses of her nephews, she was almost able to feel her daughter's presence, just sitting still there at the table. Until they went to bed, she stayed up and taught her nephews how to play poker, and they'd played for hours, and she'd tried to remember all the strategies Jack had taught her, tried to be wise and shrewd for them, as they ate cookies and one of them held a candy cane in his mouth like a pipe.

DEX

DEX AND WILLA MET at the McDonald's. The guy with the small oval-shaped head sat where he always sat, in the window, with a plate of fries and three or four Bibles spread on the table before him. He furiously scribbled into a spiral notebook.

"My mom went to high school with him," said Willa, nodding. She leaned in close and whispered. "He had a brain tumor ten years ago, and after the operation, this is what he does all day, writes sermons that no one will hear. She said he was the salutatorian of their class, that he used to work as an engineer before."

Dex wanted Willa to know that he'd been defending her. He remembered Bishop's pointed nose and tiny eyes, and wished he'd made him bleed more. "At least he's still alive. That DJ my mom liked to listen to on the radio—she was hilarious—she just died from a brain tumor."

"It scares me, the idea of a ball of something bad inside your brain."

"Well, I guess they're pretty rare."

"I don't know? My mom knows someone else who died from a tumor. She was the valedictorian of her class. Sometimes if I get a headache, I feel around on my head for lumps." She laughed.

"I just try not to think about those kinds of things. If my head hurts, I take an Advil."

She genuinely seemed happy to see him, and he felt guilty about this—as if some part of him felt he finally had the advantage.

On the table someone had left a *Friendswood Dispatch*, and Willa picked it up, opened the pages, and started reading the headlines about the Mustangs in a mock-serious voice, which made him laugh. "MUSTANG MANIA! THE MUSTANGS MUST HAVE IT!!" He hadn't known before that she could be so funny. She wouldn't care that he'd been a trainer, that he'd felt this responsibility to football, even if he couldn't play.

She held up the cover page for him, two murky photos of the Banes site, and a headline that said "TAFT PROPERTIES STILL TO BUILD?" In the gray-blue photographs, there seemed to be a giant rectangular box pushed out of the ground. Willa read the article in her normal voice, and she seemed curious, so he tried to act interested too. The photos supposedly showed that the toxins buried a decade ago had come up from the ground, proving that the site was not safe for building homes nearby. But the reporter went on, "No evidence of the emerged tank was there after the sighting was reported in September, according to Mayor Wallen."

"That's my mom's old friend," said Willa, pointing to a name. "I just saw her the other day at a party. My parents think she's lost it. But there must be something up with that field." An agency said they would investigate the pictures, and send someone out to the site for monitoring, and then he lost interest until he came to this part: "'All I've got is my reputation,' said Avery Taft. 'It means a great deal to me. And when someone accuses me of being careless with plans, careless with human health, well, that makes me upset. All the hallelujah is just false chemistry.'"

"Well, it's definitely the warehouse on the Banes site in the picture. I went mudding over there once."

She seemed impressed by this. "Was that fun?"

"Kind of." He wanted to reassure her. "I don't know—that container—even if it is what she says it is—looks pretty small to me."

They drank their milk shakes, and he finally told her about the fight with Cully and Bishop, but not what had been said. "I don't know what happened but I kind of went crazy on them."

She was looking down, picking at the blue polish on her nails, and he realized how stupid he'd been to mention their names, to try to impress her just because he'd thrown a punch. "Hey, do you want to go for a walk or something?"

"No, my friend's about to pick me up. Do you know Dani?"

"Oh yeah, sure."

She tapped her fingers on the table as if she were playing keys on a keyboard. "I'm not supposed to see her, so we had to make a plan."

"Oh." He wanted more time with her. "Hey, maybe we could do this again. Get a bite to eat sometime."

"Yeah, maybe." Her eyes whisked away from him. It didn't seem possible, but she was more beautiful to him now, even under the harsh lights, which exaggerated the dark circles under her eyes and the black makeup. She looked sad and vaguely foreign and more original than the other girls he knew, but only he would be able to see this.

"I should go outside." She gathered her books.

"I'll wait with you."

The car was a beat-up black sedan, the kind almost no one drove anymore. Dani didn't look at him, but Willa touched his shoulder when she said good-bye.

✝

Dex began to get back at Pammy by occasionally lifting a few dollars from the top of a tip pile left on one of her tables. It made her arrogance more bearable, especially on the nights when he worked for her alone. He gave a third of his money to his mom, even though she didn't ask for it.

Once or twice a week, he'd stay late, knowing his mom wouldn't like him hanging out at the Casa Texas dance hall if she knew about it, but he'd come to need those nights, and he even convinced Weeks to join him a few times. Mostly they sat and watched the women, their glittered eyelids and glossy lips; their long, shiny hair; and the curve of breasts, big and small, under snug shirts. Dex liked their tight jeans, the muscles of bare shoulders just where the tank top strap hit. Weeks was impressed whenever one of the ladies asked Dex to dance, and it happened more often than not with the regulars because he could two-step, and they knew he wouldn't make a move on them either. Weeks never got asked. He just sat back in his chair with his arms folded "watching the ladies."

Dex had become acquainted with a few of them, who, in between songs, liked to give him advice. "Never tell a girl she looks skinny or fat—always say she's just right." "Girls like questions. Remember that. Ask your date a lot of questions about herself." "Girls like a man in a proper shirt." Sometimes he thought of Willa when they said these things, and sometimes he didn't, but he liked these women, with their fragrant hair and smooth faces. He liked feeling his hand on a taut waist. He felt protective of them, even though they were older than him; and once or twice, he'd saved a woman from a drunk who seemed to be bothering her, just by asking her to dance. He'd watch the relief come over her face, and enjoyed the man's scowl as they left him at a table with his lonely drink.

One night Mr. Holgine walked up to Dex and handed him a hundred dollars. "Here's your bonus. I see how hard you work." Holgine always left by ten p.m., but he must have heard about Dex staying late sometimes. "I talked to your dad the other day and bragged on you."

"Thanks."

"But see here—I want you to tell me if you see any stealing around here, alright? Or any slacking off? That would be real helpful."

Dex didn't want to be paid for spying, but he didn't want to offend Mr. Holgine either, so he nodded and said, "Yes, sir."

His mother was still mad at him, but it helped when one night he took her and Layla to Casa Texas for dinner, and Mr. Holgine personally brought them extra fish tacos to taste and margaritas for his mom. "Dex is driving, right?" He winked.

"I see why you like working here," his mom said, her face flushed. "The people are real nice."

He wanted to bring Willa there, to show himself to her in that atmosphere, introduce her around, maybe they could even dance.

HAL

HAL HAD BEEN UP LATE, half watching a game on TV in the dark, among shadows of furniture and upholstered pillows. The game ended, the Cowboys lost, and he opened his laptop to check email. There it was. "Wanted to let you know Cully's doing a fine job, José said. Not a brick out of place. Avery."

"Goddamnit." Hal slammed his computer shut, and the shadows around him just sat there. In the bedroom, Darlene would be snoring softly, wearing the flannel nightgown that reminded him of his mother. His head felt too heavy to hold up, his shoulders sore and fatigued. He pictured himself taking off his pants and getting into bed next to Darlene, and had a strong feeling he was not going to get the exclusive listing from Avery Taft. He'd had his chance, and he'd failed somehow.

Cully should have been working an internship, doing something for his future, and instead Avery had him doing toady work, work whose danger Hal had played down to Darlene because he'd been so desperate to have a line back to Avery.

He felt his face burning in the dark. He felt the smallness of his house around him, the cheapness of its furnishings.

He had to fight against this defeatism. Attitude was everything. He'd given a hundred dollars to the Victory Temple last week, but it wasn't enough. He wanted to give more. *Bring ye all the tithes into the storehouse, that there may be meat in mine house, and prove me now herewith, saith the Lord of hosts, if I will not open you the windows of heaven, and pour you out a blessing, that there shall not be room enough to receive it.*

There had to be an answer to this. He was a good man. He loved his wife and son. If he prayed, if he was patient, there had to be an answer. He lay there all night, waiting, stared out the window at the streetlight's metal hook and luminous tent.

The next night, around eleven, Avery called to say copper wire had been stolen. Two bolts had gone missing, plus some copper-plated pipes that had been locked up in one of the homes, and Hal began to worry about Cully out there in that trailer all alone. Plus, if Darlene found out the half of it, she would be furious.

He told her where he was going, her curves hidden beneath a thick white shirt, her eyes red from watching TV, but he lied about the reason, said he was just going out there to keep Cully company for a couple of hours.

"It must be boring," she said, "just sitting out there. I hope he's at least using the time to get some homework done." She was talking from the side of her mouth, as she did more and more lately for some reason, as if it was too much trouble for her to turn her face to him.

"God willing," he said, hiding his worry with a smile and wink. He was almost too good at hiding things from her now.

"Bye, hon," she said, snuggling down into the couch pillows, some woman on the TV cooing about diamonds.

Hal called to tell Cully he was coming, and Cully said he'd leave the gate open for him.

When he got to the site, he parked next to the sign that said NO TRESPASSING: TAFT PROPERTIES. He took a flashlight from the kit in his car, and used it to find the gate in the hurricane fence, which Cully had left slightly ajar. He wiggled the beam over the empty territory ahead. As he walked through the dirt and weeds, the beam caught on a gray rabbit, hopping through the long grass, and its frenetic aliveness startled him. He could just see the glare from the TV dribbling through the trailer's window. As soon as he got there, he opened the screen door, knocked, and yelled, "Hey, it's your dad!"

As he walked in, Cully stood up, his plaid shirt untucked, his face slack, and his hair all mussed, though it was only eleven. There was a book open on the table, an empty glass, and a crumpled bag of potato chips. Hal didn't want to think about what Cully might have been doing, but he certainly didn't look ready to catch anyone at anything. Hal had expected to find him at attention, his posture straight, eyes alert.

"You alright, man?"

"Yeah!" Cully said, rubbing his eyes. "I guess it's just been quiet out here—you know, nothing happens. Once in a while I go outside and stare at the dark, listen for cars."

"You've got a big responsibility here."

"Yes, sir."

He told Cully what Avery had said about someone stealing copper wire and pipes. "Yeah, Dad, he told me, but I don't know—if José didn't see anything, I don't see how I'm supposed to."

"Look, the way he's paying you, I think you do whatever Avery says, right? You'd better keep your head up. Where do you sit? Over here by the window?" Hal got up and went to the cushioned bench next to the spot that looked out in the direction of the buildings. "You can see the warehouse pretty well, I guess."

"Depends on the night."

"But you'd see a car coming along, wouldn't you? Avery should light it all better. I'll ask him about that." But even as Hal said it, he knew he probably wouldn't. It had to be just some kids that had stolen the wire—a one-time thing.

"And you go on rounds?"

"Two or three times a night."

"Well, I'm going to sit up here with you. At least for tonight. Give us a chance to catch up at least, right?"

Hal looked at Cully, his muscled shoulders, that face, young and plump, the mouth always angled, but he had the sense that his son's sleepy-eyed passiveness might actually be fear.

He'd been ignoring it all this time—that Cully just wanted to make amends—but Hal blamed himself that the thing with the girl had ever happened. He hadn't set a good enough example. He had never said to Cully directly, "Look, you need to honor a woman's body." He had never said, "Protect the weak." He had never talked to him about how he'd tamed his own lusts. It hadn't been easy.

Cully turned on the TV, and they watched the end of a basketball game. The frantic push to the net, and one black guy's long arm octopusing upward. Hal much preferred the slow, magisterial span of football—but he let himself go with the frantic back-and-forth, got fascinated by a freakishly tall white guy who barely had to move once he got under the basket.

"Dad," Cully said.

"Yeah."

"I'm really okay out here by myself. I can handle it."

"Oh, I just wanted to talk, to tell you the truth."

Cully sighed. He was so far away, with his legs up on the chair, denim fading at the muscles, his hair too long over the ears and all awry—Cully was drifting even farther now. What was in that cheap wood cabinet over the sink—not groceries? Tools, he guessed, flashlights. He rubbed the skin just under the top button of his shirt, an itch there. And just then, he made a bargain with God: *I'll make it right with Cully, and you can please swing the blessings my way—get Avery to set things in order.*

"I want you to forget about that thing that happened, son." He wanted to win his boy back, to feel his own benevolent authority again. "Get it out of your mind and stay as far away from that sort of thing as you can. Stay the hell away, you hear me?" He was surprised at the violence in his voice and saw his hand fisted on the table, the wedding ring glinting in the one light. "God gave us sin so we can know his mercy. And you know his mercy, boy, you got me?"

Cully gave him a salute.

LEE

SHE'D BEEN NAPPING when the knocking at the door woke her, and with her mouth tasting like salt water, her hair in her face, she propelled herself to the door. There was Atwater, his face flushed and birdlike, shiny with sweat.

He held out some papers. "I found out some things. You'll want to know."

She felt almost too tired to stand and hold the door open, a lethargy in her limbs, and a phrase from Avery Taft's letter repeated itself: *Cease and desist* . . . She invited Atwater inside anyway, and poured them each a glass of iced tea. They sat at the kitchen table.

"I think I told you I had a little money put aside for research. And here's what I've got: you know, Garbit gave Rue Banes a lot of the oil remains that she used for refining—that was true. They offered to help her with the technical side of disposing of the leftover chemicals after refining, what to do with all the stuff she couldn't use, and then they didn't. They just didn't. But they knew even then that the oil solvents were bad. I have that right here." He tapped at the stack of papers.

She wanted to be drawn in, but it was too late. "Of course

they did. How could they not? To tell the truth, I don't know how much energy I've got left for this anymore."

"The new benzene levels are actually through the roof. Even worse than the ones you found. But that's not even what I came to tell you. I found some new combinations of oil solvents. Let me give you an example. Have you ever mixed cleaning products? Like Ajax and bleach? It makes this whole other gas. Worse than either one. Well, same thing here. There's likely a lot of other chemical combinations down there, you know. The agencies don't like this because there's no science. There's no way to keep everything stable and just have one variable. Data doesn't work too well when everything is changing all at once."

He gazed at her with a childish earnestness, as if he expected her to shout about this with him. He reminded her of the ones who believed in a Jesus about to come—he still believed a lot of people were bound to care. She sighed. "What do you mean by all this, really? You know it's old news to me."

"I may have found a combination in Banes Field that, in high enough concentrations, will harm people pretty fast. It's not that high now, in the soil I tested—but who knows? There might be very high concentrations somewhere else around that property. One shovel in the wrong place."

Okay, he had a point, but she resisted it, felt so tired, a headache coming on. She was impatient suddenly for him to leave.

"You know better than anyone that those chemicals may be buried, but that doesn't mean they don't migrate," he said. "That doesn't mean they don't get pushed up when it rains." He was right. She felt a hammering on the inside of her forehead.

"Well, you have to do something about it, Councilman."

"I can't. That's why I'm telling you."

"What good will that do? What the hell have I done that's made any difference? Aren't you the one who was elected to handle this sort of thing?"

He fiddled with his glass on the table, turned it with his thumb. "I've got an agreement with Garbit. Anything I say, I've got a multimillion-dollar corporation coming after me. I signed my life away."

So that was why he worked at the library now: he'd done something wrong at some point—they had something on him. And it was urgent, what needed to be done, even without these new findings, but she'd lost her ability to think about it anymore, to make any plans. "What do you want me to do?"

"Petition. Get the city to pay for the right kind of incinerator—one that will burn this stuff safely. They want to build houses, so get them to buy the incinerator. That's the only way to eradicate the compounds."

She didn't fool herself. The blank, bland faces at the last city council meeting had not been moved. Instead, it seemed she herself might go blank. A hot sweat gathered under her arms. She was done. Anyway, Taft Properties would try to stop anything else she might do.

"We have to find someone else," she said. "I've got a legal situation of my own, to tell you the truth."

He pushed the papers toward her, with their crazy, dangerous numbers.

"But will you just look at this?"

"Avery Taft threatened to sue me."

He sighed, forked his fingers into his hair.

"I'm retired," she said. "I can't do it. Why don't you try the EPA? Get them to do their job."

"I already reported it to them. Took a chance on that one, but I figured they'd protect me."

"What did they say?"

"They said they would investigate."

"So why can't they?"

"Avery Taft is already building. They've approved the land for use. They don't want to admit they made a mistake." Atwater's shoulders hunched around his skinny frame. "I never wanted to get into any funny business. I wanted just a clean straight shot. That's how I live. You know, this isn't for me." He sat back in the chair, and the wood creaked. "Will you think about it at least?"

"I'm always thinking about it. It doesn't help."

✝

SHE WENT TO THE REFRIGERATOR for a lemon, and she noticed the calendar. The number seven in the square seemed to stand up and bend as it foundered in her vision, darker than the other numbers, set against emptier white space, sacred and obscene. She went to the wall and flipped up the calendar page to March, covering the photograph of a dew-dropped yellow rose. She looked at the square day with the seven there, a Friday this year. It was always hardest as the day of the anniversary marched closer, and she dreaded how she'd have to mark it, usually lying on the couch with a bottle—staring at the walls or at the TV until the day was obliterated. Last year she'd killed her laptop when she spilled whiskey all over the keyboard and woke up to acrid smoke leaking thinly from the hidden battery.

She'd just finished eating a sandwich by the window, watching between the curtains, the small gray birds hopping in the grass like leaden rocks with eyes and legs and wings, and above them, the white blossoms already beginning to explode from the branches on the tree, and then Jack called. He hardly ever called when it was daylight.

"Listen."

"I'm listening."

"I got cancer," he said, "of the lung."

The cold of the air conditioner pressed against her cheek. "How do you know?"

"Went to the doctor. Cindy cried her ass off when he said it, so I'm pretty sure he meant it. He wasn't just running off at the mouth."

"You should get another opinion."

"I did. He's it."

A sound like ten old metal fans came on in the silence between them. "Well, I can't have you dying on me," she said.

"I might not be able to help it." Beside her, the curtains seemed to have turned from fabric into wood. She thought of the snakes of chemical sludge, how she'd first seen them, had known even then that they could crawl inside her life and coil up there. "Listen, I want to say some things to you," he said.

She couldn't keep talking. "Not now, okay?" The ceiling seemed to be steadily lowering itself. An opaqueness in the windows. "Later? You need to let yourself get better first." She had to get off the phone.

He sighed. "Alright then."

She hung up. His "alright" echoed, small, in her ear.

She stood up at the window, looking at bark and green, and she paced through the living room to the front door, opened it, wanted to go somewhere. There was the dogwood tree, the white flowers shivering in the breeze. There wasn't anyplace to go. There wasn't anyplace in the world she could go.

A half an hour later, she called him back. "Okay, tell me what he said."

He had a tumor in the right lung. Chemotherapy for eight weeks, followed by radiation. Three rounds.

"You'll get through it," she said. "Is Cindy being good to you?"

"She baked me a pie." The scratch and lilt of his voice. If she could see his face, see that it still had color.

"You need me to come up there and do something? Will you let me know?"

She looked at the dirty pot on the stove and felt a crick in her throat. The worn tile floor beneath her had been his family's, walked on by his father and mother and him for decades.

"Sure will. Doctor sat down and told me all these stories today—people recovering at wild odds, people going on to run marathons. That'll be me, running to the finish line in little tight shorts." He chuckled.

"Well, how do you feel today?"

"I feel good really. I ate brisket and then I drank a beer and walked about a mile. It felt good."

"You do know how to enjoy yourself. That can't hurt."

He might still recover. They might still talk like this.

"This councilman just came to me with more terrifying stuff about Banes Field."

"You've got to quit that."

"I want to quit, I do. I'm tired. It's just, if something else happens, how can I not be responsible?"

"Lee, we couldn't have known. No one knew what in the hell might happen."

"Except Rue Banes."

"Not even her. How could she have? And then still gone on with it? Hiring all those teenagers?"

One of them, a grown man now, prophesied the Armageddon in the Safeway parking lot. Of the others she knew about (there had been several), one was dead from a car accident, and there was Stewart, who pumped gas, his face eager and worn. "But you couldn't have known and all the pan-banging you've done doesn't change that. I mean—"

"Next month is the day again," she said.

"Goddamnit. I saw that. Look," he said. "Cindy's calling me. I'll call back soon."

She went outside in the backyard and stood among the trees, so much taller now than they'd been when they first arrived at that old house, and made a new room for their sick daughter. But the yard had not changed. She wouldn't let it, with its pines and the large, pink stone in the middle, the metal bench painted gray. It had always calmed her to look out at the bird feeder dangling, the burnished texture of bark, the sameness. But now it agitated her.

She would help him as best she could. She'd done this before. Jack might be tired and nauseous, but there were remedies for it, little tricks she'd known about when she'd gone to the treatments with Jess. When she was looking for the pamphlets on managing chemo, she lost her eyeglasses.

She went to the phone station, paperback books shelved above, a notepad stuck to the wall below, phone books pillared neatly on the desk. No files. They weren't in the file cabinet either, and in the dimness, her vision seemed foggier than ever. She checked the table under the coat rack in the entryway. Back in the kitchen, she opened the refrigerator to get the pitcher of cold water and in the widening fan of white light, something fell to her feet. She bent to pick up the case—her glasses. Then, in the jumbled drawer beneath the kitchen counter, she finally found the documents from the Samuels research that she'd been meaning to file away, along with the cancer file, and the *Getting Through Chemotherapy* pamphlet. She checked to see if she could find the last email from the Texas Green League guy, to tell him he could keep her on the Listserve, but she was essentially done, and she opened something from an address she at first thought she recognized: Burns@scn.com:

THE MAN CHRIST JESUS ARRIVES IN HARTLING, TEXAS IN MARCH. THE WORLD IS TALKING ABOUT THE ARRIVAL OF THE MAN CHRIST JESUS ON MARCH 7; COME AND MEET THE MAN MAKING NEWS HEADLINES IN EACH COUNTRY HE VISITS AND LISTEN TO HIS MESSAGE WHICH CONFIRMS HIM AS THE SECOND COMING OF CHRIST. FIND OUT MORE ABOUT DR. DIEGO EMMANUEL DE JESUS THE INCARNATION OF GOD IN MAN, AND SEE WHY HIS FOLLOWERS ALREADY KNOW IT IS THE YEAR OF THE SECOND COMING.

Below this, there was a fluorescent painting of Jesus in a white robe, cut to show bronzed muscles. Where was Hartling, Texas, anyway? This handsome, pissed-off Jesus looked strong and nimble, and he was coming on the right day, the seventh. If she wasn't going to cause trouble anymore, maybe he would.

✝

THE NEXT DAY she met Rush at the diner off the highway. They sat at a table next to a photograph of Minnie Pearl in her hat with the price tag dangling. Years ago, Lee had groaned at all those jokes her mother had watched on the black-and-white TV. And Minnie Pearl's smile looked manically efficient, exactly the same. She'd told Rush the news about Jack quickly, in a hurry to get it out, and Rush was quiet for a minute. "I'll be thinking of him then, hoping," she said, but now they were talking about her daughters, about Sam, who'd been calling her again, despite her rejections. Then Rush said, "Tom wants to see about reserving one of those houses in Pleasant Forest for us. We need more room."

Lee watched Rush's face for laughter or a blink that would call her bluff. "There's no way you're serious."

"The prices are good. We want to put in a pool."

"You know why the prices are good. That's no bargain. You told Tom what I found, right? The benzene rates? The container of toxins just popping up like nothing? And there's more now too. Councilman Atwater found something really dangerous, if he's right."

Rush smoothed her hair. "You know I love you." The waitress whisked by them. There was a tattoo on her arm of a dove diving into a rainbow. "You know I believe you found those things. But, look, by this time, isn't all the land around here polluted? I mean, what isn't? We've got oil fields right next door to us." She tapped the spoon at her saucer.

"It's not the same, and you know it." It was Tom bullying Rush into this, had to be. "I can't let you do this to your kids."

"Well, I am fighting it. I don't particularly like the look of it over there off Veemer Road anyway. But I guess Avery Taft offered him a pretty good deal. Former classmate and all."

The cup of coffee in front of Lee suddenly smelled acidic. "I can't believe you. Really?"

"I didn't want to say anything, and nothing's for sure, but I didn't want you to find out another way."

"Jack has cancer."

"You told me that, sweetie. As soon as you got here. I'm so sorry."

"It started at Rosemont. That's why he's got it."

"But didn't he smoke? I don't mean to be cruel." A table of old men next to them burst into laughter, and one of them held up a crumpled cowboy hat. Another held up an unlit cigar. "But y'all haven't lived in Rosemont for ten years."

"You know that doesn't mean it didn't start there, with that first exposure."

Rush turned and started rummaging in her purse.

"I think I'm feeling dizzy," Lee said. The old men looked over at her with rheumy eyes, the one with a Moses beard was nodding, as if he agreed with her, but he couldn't have heard what she'd said.

"Oh, don't be like that," said Rush, pulling out a tissue to blow her nose. "Look, Avery's offering because he feels guilty. I didn't tell you, but we had a thing. It was short-lived, but it was a thing."

"You're not serious."

"It was before he started building over there, and we just started having lunch, and, you know, nothing really happened but it sort of did. I couldn't help it—it was a bad time for me, and he was real charming."

"Are you kidding me? He doesn't feel guilty. He wants you nearby. He wants you to owe him something."

"Oh, he doesn't mean anything. It's over between us. It's just that no one's been that nice to me for a long time. But really, nothing much happened there."

"You keep saying that." The floor felt insubstantial as she got up from the table. "You've got to listen to me."

The Moses beard whistled through his teeth—and she thought she heard him say as she left the diner, "Isn't it a shame?"

She drove down the road and passed Taft's giant face again on the billboard. She gave him the finger. How could Rush have stood it, even for a minute? Driving past the gray blocks of strip mall, the long fields of weedy grass and hurricane fence, Lee tried to picture her own failure, and couldn't, and she focused on the shreds of clouds in the sky ahead, like ripped-apart bandages.

At the bank, the lady in line behind her with her squashed nose and pig eyes would not leave her alone. "Do you know Jesus as your savior? I just have to ask because you look a mite unhappy."

"I'm not interested," said Lee, the way she hung up on telemarketers.

"Well then, you must not know him because he's interesting alright. Jesus is real interesting. Did you know he came to save you from your sins?"

God, she hated the ignorant arrogance of them, their promises of immortality, and there were more now in town than ever, as if someone had bussed them in. She thought of the fluorescent, hunky Jesus supposedly about to arrive in Hartling, Texas. At least he looked like an outlaw, someone who wouldn't abide excuses.

She turned to the woman. "I think what I believe is private. Try someone else." She felt her eyes tearing up, her hands clenched. *Jack is sick.* And the line wasn't moving, so the woman went on. "Yes, he did. He sure did. Jesus wants you to be happy, to wipe that frown off your face."

Lee turned her back, but the woman kept on talking. *Jack is sick.* The banker finally lifted his head from his desk, and it was her turn.

IV

WILLA

HER FATHER WORKED LATE almost every night, leaving Willa, Jana, and their mother alone for dinner. Jana clowned, but no matter how silly her costumes, their mother wouldn't laugh, and Willa couldn't make herself pretend to. Willa sensed that the rift between her parents had to do with her, but she didn't know exactly why, and she was afraid to ask her mother about it. Once, her mother came into the kitchen while Willa was cleaning up and said, "Your father's only willing to wait so long before you come back to church. You're going to have to face it, one way or another, sometime soon, honey." Her mother's chin had a sudden wooden appearance, puppet lines along either side of her mouth.

"No, not yet." There were crumbs on the kitchen table, a huge black fly landed on the center seam in the wood. "Can you ask Dad to give me more time?"

"I'll ask." Her mother nodded. "That boy will get his punishment, I know that. It's coming, if it hasn't already."

As Willa got undressed for bed, she looked at her body in the mirror, the pale shadows under her breasts, curved against her hip bones, and cupped next to her clavicles big and small commas of shadows. Her face and body were bonier now, but she didn't mind it. In the length of the mirror, for the first time in months, she could see she was not ugly, that her breasts were still full and small, her hips narrow and studded with a single small mole on the right, her shoulders square and even. In the mirror behind her, there was a skittering movement. She pulled her nightgown on over her head, and sat down at her desk.

Dog tapped its heads together until she couldn't think, and two of its heads shoved their faces over either side of her desk, so she couldn't look at her notebook. "Why are you here?"

Lamb stood on the forked tail of Dog.

"Often it's good to be washed in a blowing wind," said Dog.

"You look sad," said Lamb. "The Lord is writing himself through you." The words appearing on her arm were hers, but also from somewhere else—she was a vessel for them—and though they belonged to her, they had not exacted any conscious effort—they might be gifts. But it was possible they'd been foretold.

Later, she woke up in the dark to find Lamb alone, lit up at the foot of her bed, its voice whining and revolving like a siren. "What does she want? I know what she wants. What does she want?"

✝

THE DOORBELL RANG, and Willa opened the door to sunlight and Dani, in torn jeans. "Hey, are you alone? I borrowed a golf cart from my cousin."

"Yeah, I've got three hours before my mom gets home."

"Then, come on, Nilla Wafer, let's go." It was February, but not too cold out, and Willa went to grab a sweatshirt.

The grass was long and weedy, the sand traps filled with rocks and old leaves. The Blue Creek Manor golf course had been out of use for years, and the golf cart paths were overgrown, the hills eroded and unevenly spaced in the land that stretched emptily behind the houses. They drove past a woman wearing a pink bathrobe in her backyard garden, surveying her plants, holding a shovel aimed at the ground. Around the curve was a girl hanging laundry on a clothesline.

"You don't see that much anymore," said Dani, tapping a cigarette on the steering wheel. "It's kind of pretty, the white sheet blowing like that."

They drove down the old paths, a cheerful, thin motorized hum as the cart lifted them over the hills, the cement cracked and half-covered with weeds like long hair, the greens dotted with dandelions.

They talked about Mrs. Grand, who'd suddenly started yelling to her students that she wanted them all to suffer for their art, and when one of them said they didn't have any ideas, she said, "Well then go home and set your hand on fire."

Dani pulled into the parking lot of the 7-Eleven. "Got a surprise for you."

Before she could say anything more, Willa spotted Dex, thin and sheepish, leaning against the bed of his truck. He'd been sweet to work with her on the Camus project and bring flowers, though his shy attentions mostly embarrassed her.

"He wanted to see you, and I told him I'd take you," Dani whispered. "You're not mad, are you?"

She knew he liked her, and felt flattered and wary about it because she didn't feel that way about him.

"No. Not mad." He was wearing a jean jacket and a black T-shirt that said COWBOY, and the black made his eyes look bluer. She couldn't tell yet if she was glad or not to see him.

Dani sped up the cart and stopped short. "Hop in."

Dex sat in the back behind Willa, and the golf cart hummed through the parking lot, onto the grass behind the duplexes, and a little farther on, over cracked cement and an old golf cart path. Dex said he had a test tomorrow in earth science.

"I hate that class," said Dani. "Or maybe I just hate Ms. Shranken."

"I know. The way she always asks you if you'd rather drive an electric car or a nice Range Rover."

Willa noticed the jagged top of a can littered in the grass, a greasy-looking white rubber glove. "They should clean up around here at least. That's pathetic."

"Can you believe the golf course used to be exclusive?" said Dani. "You actually had to pay? And look at the country club now. Real exclusive."

It was a frequent subject at dinner between Willa's parents. The owners had closed it down because they wanted to build houses on the land instead, but the homeowners' association protested it, so they just let the golf course grow weedy, let the country club go abandoned, waiting for the authorities to change their minds.

"The freaks hang out there sometimes," said Dex. "And the Texas Totem."

Dani looked vaguely to her right, as if deciding whether or not to turn down that path. "Should we check it out?" She stepped on the gas pedal. They went up and down an incline, turned, and the cart careened down a hill. The lightness Willa felt as they went down was as if she'd thrown off something heavy.

They drove over the path that wound past what used to be a putting green and was now just grass and trees. The brick walls of the country club were spray-painted with graffiti—BUSTER SUCKS BIG ONES; I LOVE BRIAN AND WILLY—a maze of neon pink, winding up to a tree.

"Want to go in?" said Dex. "I hear it's pretty weird. Too creepy?"

"No, let's do it," Dani said, leading the way through the space where a glass door had once been.

In the room to the right, where there used to be a golf shop, old golf balls lay on the dirty floor like unnatural eggs, fluorescent pink and green and blue golf tees scattered in a way that reminded her of pick-up sticks. The shell of a cash register stood on a square pedestal, a few plastic coat hangers scattered beneath it.

Then her eye caught on a stained, flowered blanket bunched in one of the corners. Somebody slept here. They picked their way over broken glass and empty beer cans. They looked inside the door to the left. "That used to be the snack bar, I think," said Willa.

Crippled chairs and folded-up tables were pushed to the walls, and in the center of the room, an old black garbage bag that looked full, the sun streaming through the windows over cigarette stubs and more golf balls strewn on the floor. "Looks like someone's been partying."

They walked out the back door and down the rocky hill. "It kind of smelled in there," said Dex. He pointed to the fence in the back. "Let's go check out the pool."

He climbed over the fence easily and then held out his hand to help her over it, then Dani. The pool had been drained, and the bright blue surface was flecked with weeds and old leaves.

It was like a pure sculpture of sky, nearly the same color, its stunning emptiness useless in a way that made you look at it more closely. They sat at the edge of the deep end, dangled their legs. Across from them, on a wooden bench, someone had spray-painted a row of fluorescent orange lines like little fires. Just beyond, the sun and tree shade dappled the green of the old tennis courts.

"I know it's weird to say, but it's kind of peaceful here." Dani shook out her hair and swung her feet, as if to take in some luxury.

"They left the ladders," said Willa. "We could climb down there. But it might not seem as nice." At the bottom of the chlorine-blue cement, circling one of the drains, a broken strand of red beads and a jade fragment of glass.

"You heard about the painted-over mustang, right?" said Dex. With his loose T-shirt and hairless face, he seemed too skinny and shy to let him get any closer.

"Yeah." Sometimes, in the way he waited for her to speak, in the way his eyes searched her face, she suspected he was confusing pity with a crush.

"Hey, can you give us a minute?" Dani said to Dex. "No offense." She winked. "Just girl talk."

He stood up. "Sure thing." He walked over to the other side of the pool, crept out on the diving board, pulling his legs and butt along to the end of it.

"So, I've been thinking about everything," said Dani.

"About what?"

Dani sucked on the end of her cigarette, sighed out the smoke. "You know." She paused. "You have to go to the police. I think I can figure out how to hypnotize you so you can remember."

In the red spray-painted side of the pool, she could make out the letters *J* and *M*. Bird poop slung like paint over the exclamation point. "They won't believe me. I waited too long."

"You could still make a report. At least. Look, who knows? Who might be next? I've been reading up on this, and you could hurt yourself forever if you don't tell someone. You know it happens a lot. It happens more than you think."

Willa had overheard her parents talking about it the other night, how Trace's mother was dead from breast cancer, and his father wouldn't apologize for him exactly but told her parents he was sorry for "what had befallen everyone." They'd agreed together, some of the adults, not to report it, noting that Brad's parents were mired in bankruptcy and divorce, and surely that had something to do with it, surely he'd influenced the others. Her dad had checked it out with someone he knew. To tell the police what she remembered would only make her have to feel it all over again, and what evidence was there? She was afraid the beasts would multiply, show up inside her shoes or hovering over people's heads. "I can't think about that," Willa said. "It's too hard for me."

Dani pointed to Willa's wrist. "What's this? You ran out of paper?" Dani held Willa's forearm and read the words that had just appeared that morning. *Our unfurnished eyes wait.* "Is that a tattoo?"

Willa pulled away. "You can see that?" She'd thought they were visible only to her, that others could see just the rash.

"What the hell does that mean?"

"It's just a line from a poem. I wrote it down so I wouldn't forget." Every few days she woke up with new words scrawled on her forearm or wrist, something she'd made up, or remembered. She'd only just admitted it out loud to Lee Knowles at the Christmas party—sometimes the reason for it seemed logical—she must have been writing in the night, the way some people walked in their sleep.

Willa looked over and saw Dex leaning back on his hands, kicking his legs, his head turned away toward the abandoned, netless tennis courts.

"My parents wouldn't let me get a tattoo anyway. Maybe someday I'll get one."

"It hurts like a motherf—" said Dani, pulling up her leg to examine the orange and yellow flower on her ankle. "Even this little one, I almost cried. And I thought the guy who did it was going to try to kiss me because he gave me such a discount." She was smoking a lot now, bringing the cigarette to her mouth as soon as she exhaled. "Okay, you can come back now!" Dani shouted over to Dex. She pushed the packet of American Spirits toward Willa. "Want one?"

Willa was afraid her mother would smell it on her. "Nah."

The sun prickled in her eyes. Over by the old tennis courts, sharp triangles danced on their corners, and the heat fell hard on her bare arms. Dex told them he'd started work as a busboy at Casa Texas, as he'd quit being the trainer for the football team. "I just realized I hate too many of those bastards." He exchanged a glance with Dani that Willa couldn't read.

Dani punched the end of her cigarette into the concrete lip of the pool. "Look, Willa—we have your back. We want you to make those shitheads pay."

Willa felt something squeezing just next to her heart. It wasn't her heart, but just next to it.

"I have to tell you something," Dex said, poking a stick at the small blue cup at the lip of the pool, where there was a tiny dead brown frog floating. He didn't look up, but kept tapping at the cup. "I was there that day at the Lawbournes'. I swear I didn't know what they were doing . . ."

She began to shiver—a sensation of ice on her neck and under her arms. She started to get up, but Dani grabbed her hand, so she stood awkwardly there above them, looking down at the glossy tops of their heads.

Dex didn't turn, but spoke into the pool. "I thought you were there with Cully, so I didn't say anything."

Dani looked up at her and squeezed her hand. "Dex could go with you to the police. He remembers things."

"They put something in your drink," he said. "I mean, I heard at the end what they were doing, but I didn't believe it, and then I left. I feel like shit about that. But they put something in your drink. Bishop Geitner had it planned all along. He wanted to prove something."

Willa's heart seemed pulled by a string in the direction of the road; she took her hand away from Dani's, and she started walking.

Dani and Dex got up and followed her. She climbed over the fence, went around the side of the country club where the wall crumbled into a disconnected toilet, past the bushes with red berries and a broken water meter. When she got to the front, the tree branches looked low and drooping, and in the grass she saw a yellow plastic bug-eyed cat, its face smeared with dirt.

Dex ran up behind her. "It's been killing me to know all this stuff."

She couldn't look at him.

"Honey," said Dani, "I want you to see your way out of this."

She wished they'd be quiet.

"I'm going home," Willa said.

"Listen," said Dex. "You want to know how much I fucking hate them?" She was crying now, but there was a pressure still in her forehead that wouldn't release. "Last night, I slashed Trace's tires. I went to his house and cut them with a knife, and I broke the windshield. And I drove to Brad's house, and I did the same thing to his shitty car, but keyed it along the side. He ran out but he didn't catch me." Beside her now, he pushed his shoulders back and clenched his teeth. "I didn't fucking care. Let them catch me." He bent to pick up a bottle from the street, threw it down again in a rage, shards of glass flying up beside him.

He bent to pick up another bottle at the curb, and she kept walking.

It's not going to change anything, she was thinking, winding past the Summers' house on St. Abbans. She could barely see where she was going. Behind her, she heard glass shatter again on the street.

The road seemed to flick up and fall down again beneath her.

"FUCK FUCK FUCK," Dani screamed. Willa turned. Dex sprawled near the jagged pieces of glass. He started to get up and cradled his bleeding elbow in his hand, the bright red seeping through. She couldn't help it. She turned away again and kept walking.

LEE

LEE HAD BEEN DEEP in a dream of bluebonnets and lilacs, moving and proliferating like accelerated film time, over garbage heaps, spilled gasoline, tossed-out celebrity magazines. Because she wasn't responsible for the growing, it had made her feel almost unbearably happy. And it ran on without her, even as she woke up to the phone ringing.

"Hey, beautiful."

It took her a few seconds to recognize his voice. "What the hell, Jack? It's three in the morning."

"Is it? I've lost track."

"Where are you?"

"I'm just driving around—it calms me down these days. And the best thing is, in the middle of the night, there's no traffic."

"What does Cindy think of all this?"

"Oh, I don't think she has any idea."

"Surely she notices you're not in bed."

"Nope. She takes these pills now. Sometimes with a little wine—and she's out. Dead to the world."

A car horn blared in the background.

"What do you want to talk about?"

"I haven't been able to say it, but I think you know, right? They told me three years, but I don't think they ever really know." She felt a fire jump in her chest. "Well." He could still have decades to go. He could still get better.

"Remember that day she rode the neighbor's horse? I about killed you when you told me about it, but then you used your womanly wiles, and she was good on it anyway."

"I didn't want her to be held back by your fears."

"I know. I still won't get on one after the things I've seen, but it was strange how it was fine, in the end, watching her. Like something outside me was protecting her." There were shapes in the dark witnessing this, leaning forward. "I'm glad she got to do that. She loved riding that horse, didn't she?"

Lee squeezed her eyes shut for a moment. "She did."

"I want to see you. I want you to come up here."

"You're driving around drinking beer, aren't you?"

"Does it really matter? There's no one but me out on these roads. Hell, it used to be legal anyway."

"God, I hope there's no one out. Will you at least pull over for a little while?"

"Alright." He sighed. A minute later, it was quieter. "Here I am." Those days after the funeral, in the house, Lee walked helplessly from room to room, with nothing to do with herself. The doctor had given her pills to calm her. Every time she opened a door and Jess was not there, Lee would have a vision of her tossing a drape of hair over her shoulder, or the way her eyes lowered while she listened to music, how she talked with her hands when she was upset, as if holding out what she said as an offering.

"Jack?" He seemed so drunk he might not be able to hear.

There was a way Jess smiled when he played the harmonica, as if she didn't know whether to laugh at him or just enjoy it. "Jack?"

"Good night, then," he said.

He hung up. She tried to call him back but he didn't answer. She thought about calling the police to ask them to go check on him, but she didn't want him to get arrested for a DUI on top of everything else—she finally decided he was probably telling her the truth—he was sleeping it off right there on the side of the road. That would be just like him.

Back at work, the phone rang almost immediately. A woman wanting to make an appointment for a mole check, and then a man called because he was losing his hair. "For no reason!" he shouted into the phone. "No reason at all!" Lee had to hold the earpiece away from her head. She looked up at the note pinned to the bulletin board: "Order cotton swabs." Over the past few weeks, she had been glad for the distraction of faces printed with anxiety, irritation, or boredom, for the job of soothing. Just then, Char and Willa walked into the waiting room, and she was surprised, because she hadn't noticed *Lambert* on the books. Char just waved at her as she left, leaving Willa to tell Lee she had a 4:15 appointment. "He's running a little late, I'm afraid," said Lee.

"That's okay," said Willa. She went to a chair and took out a book.

It turned out that Sue, the nurse, had to leave early. "I want to get out of here at a decent hour," she said to Lee. "Will you take the last appointments back to the rooms?"

"Sure." Lee picked up the phone and talked to a drug rep and made an appointment for Doc to meet with him. She called an insurance company to ask why they hadn't covered a lab test.

At 5:15, Willa was the last patient, and Lee led her back to the examining room. Willa hitched herself up on the paper-covered table and rolled up her sleeve. "My mom wants the doctor to look at this." She held out the inside of her forearm, which was raw and dark red, with dry flaking skin along the edges. It looked almost as if it had been burned.

"Oh dear." Lee studied the mark. She wrote "laceration or rash?" in the chart. "I'm sorry he's late, Willa."

"The thing is," she started. "I mean, that's okay—I know I told you a while back at that Christmas party? I've been writing there on my arm in my sleep—I think. But my mom doesn't know that. I mean sometimes I sort of remember the words I wrote and sometimes I'm surprised."

"You're scrubbing it off?" said Lee.

"Yeah."

"I understand." With everything that had happened to Willa, Char could only address the rash. Of course. Because you could rub a cream on it, clean it up.

"I don't want her to know about the writing." Willa sat with an expectant look, her young complexion perfect and pale under the harsh fluorescent lights, only a tiny red dot on one cheek, more visible because of the surrounding perfection. Her legs in dark jeans wrinkled the white paper on the examining table. How many times had Lee sat like this with Jess in a doctor's office? The huge silence, and the tiny, bright room. The chrome and glass sterile instruments lined up on the counter nearby. Lee found herself staring at the girl's graceful small hands, the red chipped fingernail polish. "What could it be?" asked Willa. "I mean, did I do this to myself?"

"We'll have to let the doctor take a look. It might be a simple allergic reaction, you know. Something with the ink. Or the soap you use?"

"Maybe. I've been getting headaches and stomachaches too. Might also be from the allergy."

Lee had laid warm washcloths on Jess's forehead for the pain. She'd rubbed ice on the soles of Jess's burning feet, wanting to exchange her own body for her daughter's. There should have been a way to do that. All that technology and they couldn't substitute a mother's body for her child's—it seemed ludicrous. One time the pain was so bad Jess asked her to lie down beside her in bed so she could squeeze Lee's arm. Jess's grip had been so tense that it left a bruise.

"Is it really that awful looking?" asked Willa.

Lee realized she'd been biting down on her lip. "No, sweetheart. Probably he just needs to give you a prescription." Willa's face seemed to absorb all of the light in the room, air conditioner humming in the silence. She wanted to be kind to the girl beyond what would have been reasonable. She wanted to mother her. Doc's sneakers squeaked down the hallway, and then he breezed in with his white coat and string tie, whistling. "Hello, there, ladies."

THAT NIGHT, as she went about making dinner, she kept thinking about Willa, how so little had been done for her, how curious it was that she'd been writing on herself, recording maybe what no one would say. And it was worrisome that she had the headaches with the rash. How many brain tumors had she recorded in Jess's high school class alone? Three. But then again, Lee imagined cancer everywhere now, even in those who were perfectly healthy.

As she chopped the zucchini, her anger stoked up again. The girl had not been protected. She had not been heard. As she rummaged in the back of the cabinet for the cheese grater, she came upon an old dish and pulled it out, sticky and covered in dust. It would need to be washed. It was a plate that Jess had painted decades ago, a funneling storm of colors beneath the glaze that had once been meant to be, what? a house? a tree? Holding the dish, she felt more tenderness than anger, and as she stared down at the swirling blues and purples, she thought of Char in all this, how she hated mess.

Back in high school, she kept in her car a container for candy and a small box for emergencies that contained tissues, aspirin, Windex. She'd hated not being able to explain why her parents split, worried about the gossip, and Char had finally told her friends: "Some people just don't match." It had been a good enough lie when they were girls, to cover up her mom's affair. But what happened to Char's girl—there was no way to order it or to hide it.

Lee ate dinner, listening to talk radio, and as she was cleaning up, washing the dishes, the heavy garlic press slipped out of her soapy hand and fell into the water, and she heard it crash on the plate. She fished around in the water, and the sharp edge cut her finger. Stunned, she held up the broken, jagged piece of ceramic as a small stream of blood dripped down her soapy hand. The piece was blue-black, ugly, and she pressed against it, weeping, not because of the cut, but for the pain inflicted upon them all. She couldn't let go of it.

✝

SHE DROVE PAST THE STRIP MALL made up of fake wood houses, past the Texas Rug Company and the Children of God church built in an old Kmart, and it seemed to her she'd been timid all this time, that her talking and complaining, even her one small act of sabotage, all of it had done nothing. Of course it hadn't made a difference. She passed the fireworks stand in Alvin. There was a neon sign of a busty woman, kicking up her legs, and next to it, a sign that said RED DAHLIA, SHOT PALM, AERIAL BARGE. How much could her best friend, Rush, have been listening? She didn't know how Rush could stand five minutes with Avery Taft, the perfect smarminess of his manner, the way he wore his jeans with a crease down the middle of each leg, the way he squinted his eyes so no one could see what he was thinking. It made Lee wonder how well she really knew Rush, how well she even knew herself.

She pulled over on the gravel shoulder, parked, put a scarf over her hair, tied it in the back, and put on her white plastic sunglasses, though it was cloudy. She'd read that you could get almost anything here—that the guy who owned the place had a delusion that he was some kind of soldier. She'd entered a movie and become the character she wanted to follow.

A small explosive, maybe, a baby one. She knew men who'd used some equivalent of dynamite to clear out an old shed or a patch of trees.

The stand was a crude wooden overhang with slanted tables full of neatly stacked tubes and boxes. A young guy with a buzz cut in a tie-dyed T-shirt with the sleeves ripped off stood behind the goods next to a metal box.

"Are you Allen?" she asked.

He pointed with his thumb at the shed nearby. "He's over in there."

She'd walked over the pink gravel and into the film, where she'd be the actress, speak lines that had come to her as if she'd heard them before in a dream.

When she got to the shed in the back, there was a deep groove down the middle of the door. It looked like someone had tried to break through it with a metal pole, but hadn't quite. After she knocked, she heard him say, "Just a sec," but it took a few minutes for him to open the door.

"Are you Allen?" she said. "Someone from the Ammo Chat sent me."

"Ammo Chat?" he said, as if he'd never heard the name.

"Yeah. I've got a proposition."

He wore a yellow bandana on his head, a dingy white T-shirt. "Come on in." She was surprised at his friendliness. When he smiled at her, she saw that his top two teeth pointed toward each other in a V.

"I heard I could get more here than just what you got out on the for-sale tables."

"Someone on Ammo Chat said that?"

"Yeah."

"You might do better at the gun and ammo place down the road. You got ID and everything, right?"

She looked down at her scuffed-up boots. He was trying to see how much money he could get from her. "Not really." There was a handmade contraption for holding a beer that hung from the ceiling, a reclining chair attached by wires to some kind of mechanical instrument in a gray box.

"Well, then, that is a problem." He turned to walk toward a table where there was a huge aquarium. It was filled with large, fluorescent pink rocks and strewn with dirty pieces of chicken or pork, and she could just see the sharp end of a reptilian tail in the corner, where the thing had burrowed itself.

"I need to blow up a shed in the back. We're making room for a pool. Can you help me out with that?"

He appeared to be about her age, with gray, wiry hair to his shoulders and a fat, boyish face. "Well, normally, you'd need a permit for that. There are folks you can hire, you know . . . who know what they're doing."

"I've looked into that," she said. "But it's so expensive. Isn't there something else we could do? I kind of wanted to do it myself, surprise my husband, to tell you the truth. He says he won't build a pool because it'll be so costly just getting rid of the shed. I'd like to show him, you know? Just have him come home, and it be gone." Against a corner wall, a pile of neatly folded dirty rags, and on another table, vials of bright blue liquid aligned next to a large plastic bucket.

"These aren't toys. You could hurt yourself."

"Really, are they any worse than those cherry ultrabombs y'all sell?"

"Maybe you could send your husband over, and I could show him."

On her way to the shed, she'd glimpsed a battered-looking ATM over next to the stand. "I've got five hundred," she said. The reptilian tail curled up.

Allen sighed and shook his head. "You sure you want to do this?" He scratched at his chest, and she could see the mat of hair beneath his thin T-shirt, a big purple scar there like a misshapen watch.

"How much will that ATM machine let me take out?" She knew it was weak not to bargain, but she didn't care.

He shrugged. "I don't have anything for you." She went out of the shed to the machine. She had to submit five different requests in order to get three hundred more dollars. She was surprised she could get that much.

When she came back and held out the money, he was friendlier. "What's your name?" he said, tilting his head.

"Debbie."

"Will you take off your glasses? I want to see your eyes, you got such a pretty smile."

She wiggled her glasses up and down as she backed away from him.

"You really want to do this?"

"Yes."

"Give me half of that money, and I'll tell you how. But you got to get your husband to help. Go look up how to do it on the Internet. Try AmmoArm dot com. The plastic one. You either have it all at home or you can get it. Follow the directions to the letter. The temperatures have to be exact."

She handed him the bills. "You really won't sell me one?"

"Really. I don't have anything, and if I did, you know these days, that could get me in a lot of trouble. I mean, you're not an

Arab or anything, and I don't think you're a crackpot, but still. I've got to protect my business."

He wouldn't have cared about his business if she'd been a man. "Alright then?" He led her out back, behind a ten-foot-tall cement barricade that went along the highway. It was loud because of the traffic, and he had to shout at her, even though he stood just a few feet away. "Awesome! Pack your fuse at six yards. I can sell you that part." He handed her a tennis ball–sized spool of thick cord. "You should smile more. You've got a nice one."

He rubbed at the side of his neck, and she noticed grease or dirt in the wrinkles there. "Just plan it out," he said. "And get ready to run."

DEX

ALL DAY AT SCHOOL, his elbow bandaged, he'd been rehearsing what he'd say to them, even writing down an occasional word on one of his notebooks: *PILLS, LOUD MUSIC, UPSTAIRS.* After school, as soon as the bell rang, before he could change his mind, he got into his truck and drove to the station. He parked in the back, afraid his mother or one of her friends might see his truck there and worry.

The entrance area was messy and busy, a lady at a desk on the phone, policemen walking in and out, signing papers, ignoring him standing there. Finally, the lady at the desk asked him what he wanted. "I want to report something," he said.

She clicked her tongue. "You're going to have to give me more than that, son."

"Okay. I know about a crime against a girl." He couldn't say the word, especially not to this lady, with her broad nose and her dull green eyes. "Can I please talk to an officer?"

She softened slightly, raked her fingers into her long black hair, and picked up the phone to talk to someone named Rob. Dex pushed his hands deep into his jeans pockets, felt for the change and folded bills in there. She hung up the phone. "Okay, let me take you back."

She led him into a large, loud room, where a radio blared and men shouted over it. Short partitions separated the desks. At the back, there was another door, and this was where she was taking him. The placard outside it said ROB GRACIA. She opened the door for him and said, "There you go."

The man sitting there motioned him inside. He had brown skin, a blocky frame, his hair so neat it looked almost fake. "What can I do for you? You said you witnessed a crime? What kind of crime?" His voice was kinder than Dex imagined it would be.

Dex doubted that he himself had used the proper words. He thought of Willa's face, felt Bishop's cheek against his knuckles. His smirk pasted there right up until the last minute.

"So a girl I know was at a party. This guy put a pill in her drink." A bulletin board behind Mr. Gracia was covered with xeroxed notices, handwritten notes, and two grim mug shots of a man and a woman. Dex's eye fell to a note that said "Call Dave" in red marker.

"Where was this party?" He pulled out a pen and legal pad.

"Lawbournes, Seventy-one Calling Creek."

"Who was this guy with the pills?"

"Bishop Geitner."

Mr. Gracia nodded, but his face didn't show any emotion, and this made Dex more nervous. He'd expected somehow to be encouraged, to be guided along in his narration, and he saw how that was all wrong. Mr. Gracia seemed not to care whether he told him the whole story or not.

"How do you know this?"

"I was there. There were a lot of guys there, and everyone at the school knows about it, pretty much, but the girl didn't report it. Willa Lambert." He wanted to see more reaction in the guy's face, for God's sake, but he seemed to be willing it to stay still. He seemed more like a paper pusher than someone who would carry a gun.

"How do you know her?"

"She's my friend."

"Girlfriend?"

"No."

There was a snapshot of lightning pinned to the bulletin board, and a yellow ribbon that said THIRD. Dex felt more and more wrong in that space the more he talked, but something pushed him along, some force of motion that had been gathering, the way speed gathered in the pedals of his bike.

"How many people were there?"

"I don't know. Fifteen?"

He would have thought Mr. Gracia might be shocked by this, but his face was passive, and he scratched his nose. "And where were the parents?"

"I don't know."

"Were you drinking?"

"I had half a beer." Mr. Gracia raised an eyebrow, but didn't look up from his pad.

"What about the others?"

"Bourbon, beer, Red Bull."

Dex said he wished he'd come earlier, but he hadn't known what to do. As much as he disliked Cully, it might not have been his fault—Willa had probably liked him, and it was Bishop who put the pill in her drink. Maybe Cully hadn't known? But Bishop, Trace, and Brad—they'd planned it.

He finished saying what he knew, and the awfulness of it still physically pained him, burned his stomach.

"Okay, now, my question for you, Dex, is why hasn't the girl come forward?"

"She's ashamed."

"Her parents know?"

"I think so."

Mr. Gracia nodded. "So, there's not much that we can do on our end if the girl doesn't report it herself."

"She doesn't remember it."

Mr. Gracia sighed and shook his head. "What was she doing over there?"

"She didn't know. She didn't know what they were..." He thought of his mother's chubby, disappointed face, and Layla, with her blue pom-poms. He thought of Diana, that woman he'd danced with the other night, who'd wept on his shirt and wouldn't say why. Willa, he realized, would probably never be his girlfriend.

"Okay, then," Dex said, wanting to be done, afraid to say more.

"You kids." Mr. Gracia pinched the end of his nose, pulled at it, then shook his head. "You don't even know what you're doing half the time, do you?"

A man opened the door. He was shaking his index finger at Mr. Gracia, and said loudly, "I have one word for you: Dannon!"

Mr. Gracia looked up and grinned, held up his open hand. "Told you so, brother!" It was some kind of victory. After the man closed the door again, Mr. Gracia's smile faded. "Alright then. Dex, are we finished here?"

HAL

AVERY TAFT'S OFFICE was hot and airless, and through the window, the sky looked pewter, solid as a plate. "Well, that's funny," Avery said, "because I heard again from the lady at the EPA—Atwater and your neighbor are at it again apparently, sending over new soil readings."

Hal's nose and forehead started to ache. "Well, I sure am surprised to hear that. I must have sat with Lee for an hour in her living room."

"I'm going to see what more my lawyer can do now, I guess."

Hal couldn't let it go. His heart quivered like a goddamn bird's, singing *prosperity, prosperity*. "I was glad to be of help with the sale. I sure would like a chance to work with you again."

"There's not much I can give right now, except to my lawyer. At this point." There was an unfamiliar grit of aggression in his voice. "I never promised you a thing," Avery said. "Did I?"

"No, you sure didn't. I grant you that." The room went dark for a second, then flashed back to the hard, white lights.

On the drive home, Hal felt fat and tired, passing a slow-moving metallic green car driven by a gnome in a green hat, and he sped up to meet the bridge ahead, where the trees hung over the creek. Goddamn Avery Taft. Hal was mostly annoyed that he hadn't known from the beginning that he wouldn't get the exclusive, pissed that he hadn't got right enough with God to deserve it, pissed that Taft had beat him yet again, though Taft had been puny and hapless on the football field, and Hal had been the good one, the really good one, and none of that mattered anymore, though it should have, because what had made him good he still had inside of him. He knew it. Darlene knew it. God knew it. But Avery Taft didn't, that bastard, and he'd cut him off.

Now Cully seemed to feel he had something to prove by going to that trailer every Saturday night. Well, alright. But he was still his father.

He passed the old fig plant, the construction crowding up the highway over near Bayside, and he saw a picture of a girl on a vodka billboard that looked like her, so he couldn't stop thinking of Justine, the twenty-five-year-old administrative assistant they'd had at the office a couple of years before. She hadn't been exactly beautiful, but there was an assuredness in the way she moved, a grace in her fingers when she wrote something down or handed him a check, that brought to mind visions of her touching him. There was something around her mouth too, that resembled Darlene, but Darlene in a younger, thinner state, a reality apart from her kitchen gear and nail polish smells. He had a hard time not blushing when he was around Justine because, in his mind, he'd done all kinds of things to her, and she to him, daydreams he had to hide, but he felt them glowing through his face when he looked at her, as if his skin had turned to a TV screen showing it all to her as porn.

He tried to concentrate on his hatred and resentment of Avery, but all he could think about was Justine. Where was she now? Did she still want his advice on selling property? She had gone off to Plano to work for one of her father's friends, as he recalled. He thought he had her cell phone number somewhere. It seemed that her smooth skin could calm him, make him feel the possibility again. He could imagine a whole new life with her if he closed one eye.

He said a prayer. *I've got the devil in me. Help me here, Lord. Where has your prosperity gone? Why am I so misbegotten? Why have you not held up your end of the bargain?* His son out for the season, his wife annoying him, his business in shambles. He looked up through the windshield at the clouds, clotted and dull, listless up there near heaven.

Then there was Dawn splashing into his mind soon after, naked in a blue pool. Recently he'd been so ashamed to think of her, so sorry for Darlene, but now, as he drove in his car with the coffee stain on the seat, the crack in the plastic dashboard, as the trees streaked past, he felt as if he'd deserved that affair, every minute of his hands on her skin, every time she let him come inside of her. And hadn't he returned to Darlene, loving her even more?

When he was driving down near the boat sheds, he called Darlene on his cell. "There's a possum tearing up the backyard," she yelled. "You need to come take care of it."

"Sweetheart."

There was no getting away from her—she was in one of her hopping rages, when her voice went flat and shrill like a tiny metal train track. "You get on home. There's glass and plastic all over the place, and I hate those things—he bared his teeth, Hal. He's liable to bite me."

He started driving home to her on 2351, but the car seemed to take over without him, as if it were a live thing, a mechanical

horse with its own will and purpose, and it took the exit headed
to Pasadena. If he was going to drink again, he was going to do
it spectacularly.

He ended up at the Ranch House Bar, a place he'd frequented
in years past. It was an old-fashioned cowpoke place with a neon
sign the shape of a lasso, a gold thread of lights circling the rope
around the "Ranch House" letters, and plate glass windows
behind which the dark bar hid a jukebox with lights shaped like
strawberries. When he walked in, he recognized the bartender,
whose name was Sid, though his sideburns were long now, and
his gray hair had an old-fashioned curled lock in the front.

"Hey, there." Sid's small blue eyes reflected nothing.

"Remember me?"

"I can't say I do, but welcome back." Behind him, the rows of
bottles like jewels with labels.

"Give me a bourbon."

"Yes, sir," he said, swinging around to grab a bottle.

To Hal's left was an enormous woman with black hairs on
her chin, and to his right a dapper young man in a purple snap
shirt with sunburned cheeks. He was talking to a skinny old guy
with a chin that spooned under his face. "I can't believe you don't
remember me, Sid," said Hal, trying to get a smile out of him.

"Sorry, y'all come in here pretty frequently, it seems like."

The fat lady snorted into her drink.

"I guess so. I guess so," said Hal, pulling the glass toward
him. The flashing lights and darkness were either a kind of paradise or a kind of oblivion. He still had time to be afraid of it, to
push away his drink and walk out of there. Sure, God wants the
best for us, Pastor Sparks was always saying, but he gave us free
will. We are not automatons. He tried to think of a prayer, but

his mind went blank and fuzzy—just like the television when
cable went out.

The first sip tasted hard and metallic and fortifying in a way
even as it hurt his throat. "Well, I did that," he called out to Sid.
"I might as well keep going."

George Jones crooned on the jukebox. An older couple wearing matching polyester Western suits was dancing the two-step
in front of it.

Sid plunged glasses into the sink behind the bar, his forearms disappearing, and the fat lady said, "One more, Bubba."

"You see," said the young guy beside him. "She always understood me. That was what was so great about her. I never had to
explain."

The boy's candor struck him like a hammer, and he thought of
Dawn. That was why he'd loved her. That was why she'd been so
hard to give up. She'd understood him in a way Darlene never had.

"She would just look at me, and she knew when I needed her,
knew when to take off her clothes." His lips were slack and wet,
but the light in his eyes spilled into Hal. He finished his drink
and took out his cell phone and went out to the little cement
walkway to call her. Maybe she'd even talk him out of having
another whiskey. Because she always understood what he was
going through. She'd know what to say to get him back. He
stood on the cement with his legs a little apart to steady himself.
Traffic whizzed by on the road, a quick cacophony of rap music
out an open window as he listened to the phone ringing.

"Hello?" Her sweet, low-pitched voice.

"It's me."

He heard something in the background, a small motor.
"What do you want?"

"I just want to talk, baby."

"Okay, talk."

"This real bad thing happened with Cully." He told her everything, the behemoths crushing his son out on the field, the Indian-given exclusive at Taft Properties, the cigarettes out by the lawn hose, and even Cully's confession about the girl and how he'd counseled Cully not to tell anyone.

"Are you a monster? Hal, I don't talk to you for a year and a half, and you're calling me to tell me this? My God, do you hear yourself? Did you ever, ever think about that little girl?" Cars sped past, the wind and exhaust of them in his face.

"She's hardly little." He went back to how he pictured her, brassiere straps sliding out from her tank top, that black and blue stuff all over her eyes as if she'd been prettily hit—and wondered idly why he'd never bothered to look up her face in the church directory.

"She's a person, Hal, a girl person. That must be hard for you to imagine."

"Sweetheart."

"Goddamn you."

Her cursing stung him. She had never cursed at him before. "I called you, a 'girl person,' because I thought you would understand what I'm going through here. I'm at a bar. A bar on this woeful highway." A semi truck hurtled in his direction, horn blaring, but he was far away, well on the road's shoulder, gum wrappers and an old condom mixed in with the gravel around his feet.

She hung up.

He looked at the pale sky, the smell of car exhaust everywhere, the rectangular grays of the Houston skyline in the distance. He'd reached the end, and God wasn't there.

WILLA

WILLA SPENT SO MUCH TIME in her room, she almost didn't
see it anymore—the furniture, the arrangement of three windows, her figurines on the shelf—all blacked out by familiarity.
Dog had started losing his fur, at first just in mangy patches, and
then nearly all of it, so the pink skin was bare and wrinkled, and
he looked like a large piglet. One of Dog's faces was Junior's face
again, watching her, the eyes red and turned down, full of pity
and pain. All the other eyes on Dog's body overflowed with water,
leaking into the few spots of black fur, which stood up in pointed
tufts. Dog had made it clear, not unkindly, that she should die.
The question was how? She saw herself crossing the street, hit in
the shoulder by a speeding delivery truck, spun up and around,
hitting her head on the concrete. She imagined falling into the
creek with an injured arm, drowning while the rain poured
down overhead. She might contract a flu that wouldn't leave her,
a high fever and sepsis, so that her organs shut down one by one,
every last one of the doctor's attempts to save her, failing.

   She'd heard her parents talking that night about how Lee
Knowles's daughter had died, just six months after her diagnosis.
They'd thought at first it was just a bad sore throat. She'd died

when she was only sixteen, the age Willa would be in June. When you got cancer, she'd heard, your complexion got very clear and white, no more acne, no more scars, just pure, luminous skin, and then it started to look transparent, as if its purpose was to let people see through it to your soul. What scared Willa was the way people lost their hair—it made their faces look so bare and vulnerable, no matter their age, like babies. Jess had lost all of her long dark curls, and she'd had to go around like those other people Willa had seen, wearing their helmets of baldness. Any worry about being pretty would have seemed a long way off to her then, across an ocean, across a continent. What must it have been like for her to know she only had so much time, to have to pretend that she was getting better when everyone knew she was not, and to feel, as close as the pillow beneath her head and the just-washed sheets against her bare legs, that she was going to die? She imagined Jess, alone in her room, eating ice cream and listening to music, reading notes from her friends who missed her at school. She would chew the bits of chocolate in the ice cream, try to focus on some gift her mother had given her a long time ago—a stuffed animal with button eyes. The toy could take her far back into the past, and maybe that distance she covered in memory could comfort her, because if she couldn't move forward in time, she could always move backward.

Willa tried to interpret the Dickinson poem.

On every shoulder that she met—
Then both her Hands of Haze
Put up—to hide her parting Grace
From our unfitted eyes.
My loss, by sickness—Was it Loss?

She was trying to write her analysis of the poem when she first heard her dad come home and the TV downstairs switched on.

Or that Ethereal Gain
One earns by measuring the Grave—
Then—measuring the Sun—

Jana ran into her room, wearing a rainbow-striped T-shirt and a purple satin tutu. "Where's my brush? I know you took it!"

"I did not take your brush."

"Yes, you did." Jana lifted the pillow off Willa's bed and looked under it. She had a wild horn cowlick on her forehead. Jana went to the dresser, scanned her hand over the surface. "You always take my things."

"I do not."

Outside, there was the crunching sound of a car's tires over stones in the driveway. "Who's that?" Jana said, running to the window. "Wow! It's the police. Are we in trouble?"

Willa went to the window behind her, and saw a man and a woman in uniform get out of the squad car. "Their lights aren't on." Willa felt a violent sadness fall from her chest to her stomach, a heavier gravity. The doorbell rang.

Jana ran downstairs. She would want to watch the action, whatever it was. Willa decided to stay upstairs until they made her come down.

"What does she want?" said Lamb, in that creepy voice he didn't always use.

"The stars will rain like hail," said Dog.

A minute later, her mother knocked softly at her door. "Willa, honey, you need to come down. We're all in the living room. I've sent Jana to her bedroom." She paused. "You come on down when you're ready."

Willa looked at herself in the mirror, at the yellow smudges beneath her eyes, the blank roundness of her cheeks, the faint red marks around her nostrils. She smoothed her hair, pressed the pads of her fingers against her cheekbones until she felt their familiar shape. She did not look like herself.

When she came downstairs, she saw her parents in the bright green living room, her father gripping the arms of his easy chair, sitting very straight, her mother holding her hands in a little cage in front of her. The police, in their dark uniforms, sat awkwardly across from them.

"Come on in," said the woman officer, rubbing at her black pants. "We just need to talk a little bit. Would that be okay?"

Her father's knuckles looked huge against the armrests, his face smaller somehow, drawn up. "The question is whether we make a report."

"It's awkward," said the policeman. "My name is Robert Gracia, by the way." His smile was gapped, with very white square teeth against his brown skin. "But someone filed a report. They said they were at a party where someone put a pill into your drink, and that's a crime."

"If you decide to tell us what you remember," said the woman gently, "we can go forward."

Willa sat down on the couch next to her mother, but kept her eyes on the policeman's large face. "We don't want this out," said her father. "It's not fair to her and it's not fair to us."

Her poor dad. He didn't know how many people already knew. Willa heard her voice like she was listening to someone speak on the radio. "I don't remember it, but it wasn't my fault, I can tell you that. I was just supposed to go out to lunch with a friend."

The man took out a pad of paper. "Who was that?"

Willa glanced at her mother, and her mother nodded. "Cully."

The man wrote something down. "Cully who?"

"Stop talking to them," said her father. "They can't help us. That's all you have to say. Any more than that's not going to do us any good."

"Actually, we can try—" said the woman.

"Really? That's interesting," he said. "Because you know what will happen to this family if you try? Our daughter will be dragged through it again, and in the end, it will just be her word against theirs. What's the try in that?"

"Mr. Lambert, if your daughter was the victim of a crime—" said the man.

"She told you already she doesn't remember—tell me what good that will do her?" He was moving his chin in a strange way, as if it wasn't quite connected to his face.

Her mother's face was very red, her teeth clenched. "We just want to protect our girl. That's what we want."

Willa felt a strange pain in her knees, as if they'd been twisted in order to pull them up from her bones. She should never have been so vain as to believe Cully Holbrook liked her. It seemed inconceivable now that it had ever mattered. "I'm sorry," she said. "I'm really sorry."

The female officer looked at her with wide, frightened eyes. "You didn't do anything wrong, Willa."

The policeman looked panicked, and half stood from his seat. "Well, without a report there's not much more we can do. I just want y'all to understand that."

"I'll go back upstairs," said Willa, in the same disjointed voice she'd used before.

"Has she seen a counselor?" she heard the woman officer say.

"Yes, she's seen the pastor of our church," said Willa's mother. "It's really helped."

"Is there anything else you want to report?" said the man. "Just understand. We have to follow up. It's our obligation. We have to make you . . ."

And Willa closed the door to her room, so that all she could hear were muffled noises. When the police finally left, it was just beginning to get dark. When her dad came up to call her to dinner, she told him she wasn't hungry, and he left her alone to the star-patterned quilt, the book splayed open on the pillow.

Lamb said, "What does she want? We know." His head had grown huge and tubular, much too large for his tiny, frail body, and the legs kept collapsing beneath it.

Dog said, "Your name will be written in the scroll of Time."

"Your name will be written in the scroll of Time," said the other, cruel head, grunting, and then the five others repeated the words, out of sync and loud against her ears, until it finally stopped.

She sat by her window, looking outside most of the evening, watching the occasional car pull up to the stop sign at the corner, watching the late-night speed walkers and the lone motorcyclist. Around ten, she saw the man who lived across the street come out to his yard and turn off the sprinklers, gather up the balls left in the grass, and hook the lawn chair under his arm as he made his way back to the porch. After she heard her parents go to bed, she saw smoke rise in the distance over the rooftops of houses. It seemed like a signal from everyone she knew who was already dead, her dad's parents; her great-uncle; Lee Knowles's daughter, Jess. The smoke billowed and thinned to a gray screen as it rose up toward the moon. What the dead were telling her she didn't know.

LEE

SHE FOUND THE WEBSITE without any trouble, and the recipes were surprisingly easy to locate. "This thread is purely for informational use. Do not do anything illegal with this information." The instructions were mixed in with videos of teenage boys making smoke bombs and advertisements for *The Anarchist Cookbook*. She settled on the recipe posted by Jolly Jim because it seemed precise and the ingredients were easy to get. "An explosion is a sudden, violent change of potential energy to work"—it was a gunpowder that had sat latent inside her all these years—"which transfers to its surroundings in the form of a rapidly moving rise in pressure called a shock wave. The shock wave can cause substantial danger." The chemicals pushed against one another of necessity. She imagined the war on a microscopic level, and it seemed fitting that one could use these orderly, measured substances to protest a chaos of them.

It was hard to believe she would do it, hard to see that when she poured the plastic bottles of nail polish remover into the glass jar, it would actually amount to anything with any power at all beyond removing chipped red lacquer from someone's fingertips, and she watched herself pour a brown jug of hydrogen peroxide with fascination, the pungent liquid filling the bowl. She cleared out the freezer, threw out the package of meat, ice cube trays, plastic bags of frozen fruit and broccoli, and she put the glass jar in the center, alone. She waited the prescribed one hour.

She had to relieve the pressure. There was no other way. It occurred to her that this may have been exactly as those men felt, boarding the airplanes with their box cutters, a buildup of stymied energy within them that could only be relieved by action. She felt reasonable and reassured, though, in her measurements, in following directions for something she didn't know how to do. When her mother had been too drunk to cook dinner, Lee had taught herself to cook this way, blindly obeying the words on the page. Sometimes it worked out, and sometimes the dish ended up bland or burned, her mother passed out on the couch, snoring, so Lee had to eat it alone. But the litany was there, written down: do this, do that.

She took the concoction out of the freezer, added it to the swimming pool chemical, followed the instructions to stir, wait. After the glass jar spent two more hours in the freezer, she was told she'd find a kind of white powder on the bottom. She'd imagined it would look like ground seashells or teeth. But when, holding her breath, she opened the freezer door and looked, there was only maybe a quarter of a teaspoon of something like salt at the bottom of the glass. She realized she didn't know what she was supposed to do with it.

That afternoon she went back to the fireworks stand in Alvin, wore her sunglasses and a scarf over her hair. She went straight past the skinny salesman by the stacked display, and back to the shed.

She knocked, heard laughter beyond the door, and then Allen swung it open.

"Hey, there," she said. "I could use some more help."

"Come in then, I guess," he said.

On the table behind him sat a woman with very tight, short orange curls, grinning and eating scrambled eggs from a plate with her fingers. There were marks all up and down her bare legs and arms, small scabs. Lee had obviously interrupted something, and the woman scowled, pulled her plate closer to her hip.

Lee told Allen what had happened with her failed attempt, and it was a moment before she noticed the iguana, nosing around his ankles, its scales uneven in places as if they'd been scraped off and had grown back in a crooked pattern.

Allen started laughing, and then the woman did too. "What shit are you really trying to get rid of, lady? Did he screw someone else? Is that what happened? What are you *really* after?"

"They all do at some point." The woman chewed on the eggs. "You just have to get over it. Or not."

He stepped closer, flicked at her sunglasses. "What you got going on back there?"

There was no other way. She'd have to just take the humiliation and answer this guy. "I just want to scare him, I guess."

"Huh," Allen said, folding his arms. "Is that it?"

She held out two one-hundred-dollar bills, and he took them from her, pushed them into the front pocket of his jeans. "Alright, then. Go back to the website. That recipe you tried is nearly impossible to get right. Do the one with wax. Make sure you get a meat thermometer. And be patient."

He kicked at the iguana, and it scurried into an open cabinet at the back of the room. "Make a long fuse. I'll get you one. You sure you just want to scare him?"

Lee nodded.

"Well, make sure he's not in the vicinity then, or you might scare him to death."

The woman held her stomach and cackled.

Lee wanted to tell Allen she would never hurt anyone, but as he picked up a beer bottle from the table and started drinking from it, she realized he didn't care. He just didn't want to be arrested himself.

She gave him two hundred more dollars.

"Tell me how to do it, walk me through it."

The woman's eyes went wide. "Hell, I'll tell her if you won't."

He took the money and called back to the woman, "You don't know fuck." He turned to Lee. "Come on, let's get you some special fuse."

She followed him out to the fireworks stand, and he pointed to a box that said FUSE—EX—BOLDER. He went through the instructions with her, his demeanor suddenly serious and teacherly, as he nodded, drew a diagram of what the bomb should look like. He touched her arm. "Hey, you don't look like a woman a man would cheat on, you know." The ends of his fingers were stained with something black.

She picked up the box. "Thanks." She walked again past the clerk selling fireworks beneath the shelter, and got into her car.

HAL

FIVE TIMES, he drove out to the Ranch House Bar and drank as much as he thought he could get away with and still drive home. Darlene thought he was working late. He had a trick with lemons and hot sauce followed by licorice that hid the smell.

He'd argued for a while now that Cully should quit his work for Taft—to have his own son serving that liar. But Darlene felt differently—she'd recently become friendly with Taft's wife and wanted her beauty secrets and still thought Avery a potential benefactor to them all—it surprised him that she didn't worry about Cully out there at the site all alone. But he couldn't go traipsing down that path, because he'd landed Cully the job, and Hal wasn't going to lie to her—he wasn't worried about any physical danger so much as he was worried about his son's soul. He hadn't done enough for Cully's soul. He'd made a bargain with God, but hadn't held up his side of the deal.

Hal took Cully out to dinner at Casa Texas, over in Pasadena, because he remembered the tacos were good, he liked the ambiance, and while Darlene was at church for her Pilates class, he wanted to have a talk with Cully, man-to-man.

Cully startled a bit when Hal ordered the margarita, but Hal winked and said, "Don't tell your mother. I got this."

Cully shrugged, tapped his feet under the table, staring at the menu.

After they'd ordered, Hal said, "How's the work, son?" He took the brilliant, first tangy sip of margarita.

"It's fine," Cully said, nodding. "That guy, José, who trained me. He's a good guy. He comes by sometimes at the beginning of my shift. He's got all these stories from fighting in the desert. He said the heat's nothing like Texas heat, that it practically melts your eyeballs."

"I don't envy them, over there. He just get back?"

"No, he was in the Gulf War. He's older than you, I think."

Hal saw an opportunity. "Well, if you'd like to quit, don't feel obligated to stay on my account."

"I'm not a quitter." Cully's mouth set itself in the habit of Darlene.

"That's not what I meant. I meant that we can find you a better job if you decide this one isn't for you." There was a smell of roasting jalapeños, an acrobatic Mexican polka on the speakers.

"I just said I like the work."

The riotousness of the music seemed to undermine Hal. "Oh, alright. I just want you to set your sights high." He raised up his hands. "Keep your eye steady on a goal, and you keep your head out of trouble, know what I mean?"

"So, Dad, I don't know, but José told me some messed-up stuff about something he found out there on the field."

Hal chuckled. "Now, do I have to tell you not to believe everything you hear?"

"No, seriously. He was digging something up for Avery, planing the field because there was a slope there, and he came upon this black stuff in the dirt. He said it smelled like rotten cheese and had a strange consistency. Totally fucked up his shovel. So he put it in a jar, covered it, and went to show Avery."

Hal drank his margarita, felt a trembling fire rising up in him that he needed to drown.

"Avery told him to bury it deep, cover up the hole, and never mention it again or he'd be canned."

"Well, you know, Cully, it's hardly news. There's stuff like that all over town. There are oil fields just off I-45. There's a refinery in Alvin. Been there for years. I don't see the point in getting all worked up about it."

"I don't think this was ordinary oil."

"Why's that?"

"Because he got a rash all over that arm. Really red and it peeled. It was gross. And when he went home that night he couldn't breathe."

"Well, he's breathing now, ain't he?"

"Yeah, I guess."

"See that?"

"But now his asthma came back, and he blames it on the stuff he found. He's worried. He said he's going to quit as soon as he can find another job."

"If you don't want to work out there, I'd be glad to help you make a graceful exit. In fact, I'd prefer it."

"I'm not leaving until José does."

"So that's what you want." Hal really wasn't worried about whatever this stuff was that José found—just because he'd seen it didn't mean it had anything to do with the asthma—he could easily just have asthma. He'd known others to be paranoid about their symptoms, who blamed them on their polluted surroundings, as if the ground itself had it in for them. And now Hal was too drunk to care if his son was planning to fuck over Avery Taft. In fact, he might prefer it.

Then the food came, and they were both so hungry, they ate for a few minutes in silence.

"To tell you the truth," Cully said, "I'd like to find work with an architect firm. You know, design nice houses like the mansions in Memorial."

"Huh. None of those firms around here that I know of . . ." Cully's confession baffled him. "Is it seeing Taft's houses come up over there?"

Cully scowled. "I just always liked seeing how things get put together."

"Well, you'd go to UT for that?"

"Sure thing." They would have that at least, the same college, *Hook 'em Horns*. Orange T-shirts with silhouettes of honorable steer heads.

"Fine." When they finished eating, a boy started to clear the table, and Hal felt he'd seen him somewhere before.

"Hey." The boy glared at Cully, and Hal felt a flash of protectiveness.

Cully winced and made a *pah* sound. "You work here?"

The boy didn't answer, keeping his head to the table, gathered their utensils and plates and carried them away to a noisy kitchen door with a square window of white light.

"That's Dex."

"He's the one?" said Hal. The boy was thin and narrow shouldered, and Hal couldn't believe Cully had let himself fight him, two against one, to beat. "Now that's the kind of coincidence

God puts right in front of you, just so you can do something about it. It's time, Cully, for you to ask that guy to forgive you."

"Dad!"

Hal raised his hand and ordered a third margarita. They were so tasty, like a candy he remembered getting at the convenience store as a kid, but better. Forgiveness was exactly what Cully needed. "I swear it, son. We are not leaving this joint until you apologize to Dex for fighting him and ask him to forgive you."

Hal sat back, and Cully folded his arms and pursed his lips. "Really, Dad? Really, you're going to do this tonight?"

Dex moved around another table, piling dirty plates on a tray, wiping the crumbs with a rag. As he worked, his mouth made a small, tight-lipped grimace. He reminded Hal of a friend's little brother, who, back in the day, had followed the older ones around, regaling them with details about the Alamo, the line drawn in the dirt, the Mexicans outnumbering the Texans five to one.

Hal felt shiny, as if the tip of God's finger had come right down and polished his face and Cully's face with a fateful gold leaf. This was exactly what his son needed. Of course. And he'd be willing to wait. Cully took out a pen and began doodling on the paper tablecloth. Hal finished his drink and ordered a shot of tequila. The bright crepe paper scallops on the wall began to jigger, and the stained glass lamps overhead swayed to the music that had just started up in the back room.

"Alright then, son, I'll pay the check, and we'll just wait on you while listening to that music. Dex isn't going anywhere either. He's at work."

The band was good. He'd forgotten how much he liked live music—the guitars following the swiveling path, the piano fast and banging. A dark-haired woman sang with a long, pretty face he wanted to get closer to, her voice as twisting and spell-like as smoke, her narrow hips kicking out so her belt buckle flashed in the light. Behind her a Buddha of a piano player, grinning, and a boy banging on the drums with his ecstatic face lifted to the ceiling. Hal and Cully found seats on the metal folding chairs against the wall, and a few people started to dance.

"I'm not going to do it, Dad. You know why? It will embarrass him, and it'll sure embarrass me."

"You will," said Hal. He tapped his foot to the music, and the waitress brought him another shot, and then the world got blurrier and brighter, as if he were looking through water splashing against a mirror.

At some point, he left Cully, got up to go back to the bar, and he got angry talking to the businessman next to him who said he had a good scheme he'd tell Hal about as soon as he could trust him.

"Don't I look like a good man?" Hal said. "Jesus saved me two years ago. He saved me and then he gave me a sign tonight if only my son would listen to it, and here I am getting lit in a dark bar. I got a wife prettier than roses, a football star son—I mean, and I got a good job, a great occupation, if only I could believe in it. I can't seem to believe hard enough. I do believe, but it doesn't seem to make a profit. That's the thing. I pray and I pray and I pray, but I can't goddamn believe enough. But don't you say I'm not trustworthy. I'm loyal, no matter what."

He was back in the dance hall, holding a dark-haired woman, country waltzing as he had in his youth. "You know. You don't know," he told her, and it seemed a good idea to nibble at her neck, when something pinched his arm and yanked it. "Excuse me, sir." It was the skinny guy, Dex, wild-eyed and smooth-faced, whose head suddenly seemed huge. "The lady doesn't want to dance, okay?"

Hal couldn't quite get his footing, and his boots spluttered beneath him as he began to protest and look to her to help him, but when he turned around again, the woman had disappeared into the darkness, mobile with dancers and lights, and he was standing over Cully, whose hand covered his face. Dex shouted out over the music, "Sorry, but you're going to have to leave."

"I know that," said Cully, uncovering his face. And finally he apologized to the skinny one. "Sorry about all this." The darkness shimmied with shadows, but at the word "sorry" a light high-beamed from the ceiling. Good. He'd done good.

Hal put his arm around Cully. "See that?" Hal let himself be dragged out, past the dark tables with the chairs stacked on top of them, past the margarita machine's shiny chrome.

On the way home, Cully's apology seemed to hang on the silvery glisten above the road, but then Hal felt dull again within himself, unredeemed, and the lanes kept multiplying from two to three, and the road twisted and buckled like a piece of taffy, each billboard about to smack the front of his car. He squeezed shut his eyes and drank half of a Coke from a can very fast, and that settled things down for a bit, until at some point in his journey, his head cleared, and a big white billboard rose up from the side of the road, black block letters as large as cows standing up to shout at him: HAL. God had singled him out, and he couldn't even keep the road straight. He looked over to say something to Cully, and caught his breath in relief, because it was his son at the wheel, not him. He'd been saved. Again.

LEE

SHE WOKE UP ON FRIDAY, got out of bed, and went to the window, where she looked down at her street, at the neighbor's station wagon, its windshield strung with fallen Spanish moss, and the green yard bisected by the winding stone path. She made herself a cup of coffee and sat out in the yard, listening to Patsy Cline, that full, double-sided voice, the words sorrowful, but matter-of-fact, her neighbor Mike Bergen over in his yard, sweeping leaves off the black bed of the trampoline.

She remembered the time Jess had found Lee's old aqua prom dress and put it on. She was still little then, and the loose satin crumpled against her tiny frame, as she walked around the house saying, "I'm the mother queen," and when she got to the top story, she opened one of the windows and shouted it out toward Banes Field. "I am a queen!" And Lee let her scream for ten minutes before she felt she had to say, "Hush, you're bothering the neighbors."

Later, in her kitchen, she poured a gallon of bleach into a pot over the potassium chloride and turned on the stove, her nose stinging from the sharp odor. After a few moments, she held the tong of the hydrometer in the liquid and watched the red light move to "full charge." She put the pot in the refrigerator, so that the crystals would form, and she sat in front of the TV, not really watching the news footage passing over empty fields, a politician's simian face, then the camera cut to a woman in a sequined minidress with the face of a panther.

When the alarm clock went off, she opened the refrigerator and saw that the crystals had formed at the bottom, small white teeth, glinting unevenly. She used a spoon to scoop the Vaseline from two large tubs into another glass pot. Then she dropped the shavings of old candles into the goo, and melted the two together. When the Vaseline and wax had cooled, she added the gasoline and kneaded the mess with the crystals. She pushed the substance, slimy and white, into two empty plastic boxes.

"Place in a cool, dry place," the instructions said. She put the two small waxy packets near the cooler in the garage, knowing she wouldn't be able to relax as long as they were there. What was she doing?

Her thoughts stuttered and grated on her, wheels on a track that somehow couldn't get traction in the right direction. She was doing what she had to do. All night, she drank water, paced in front of the windows, rehearsed. The gloves, the socks over the shoes, the way through the gate, the string of fuse to the wax rectangles. The instructions scattered in her head, then rearranged themselves, and she had to pick up each one again and hold it. At some point, she heard a bang in the garage, but then, the house was still there, everything was still there, and when she went out the door to look at them, the wax packets sat there calmly. They probably wouldn't even work. It seemed too easy that she could make these things and they would work the way they were supposed to. After all these years, why should they?

CULLY

CULLY LAY in the curtained bed in the tiny back room of the trailer, on top of a worn musty blanket, knees drawn up, phone pressed to his ear. "I wish I could go, but I have this shit job," he told Brad, who wanted him to go to some dive bar with him in Alvin where they didn't card.

"Can't you blow it off? What are you, the security guard? It's not like anything's going to happen if you leave."

José had warned him off guys like Brad, who tried to use meanness as a masquerade for manliness. José had called earlier from his rented U-Haul truck to say good-bye to him, his terrible hacking cough like a motor trying to start in his throat. "Now, you stay away from the crazies," he said. He was on his way to a job in El Paso.

"Alright, then, Cully son, I'll get Lawbourne to go with me. You have fun out there with your dirt." Brad hung up.

He was trying to escape without their noticing, but Cully didn't want to hang out with Brad and Bishop anymore. In the trailer, he could drink beer all night if he wanted to. He could watch TV and eat potato chips and get paid for it. He'd got bored by Brad's bullying; and the time he'd taken one of the pills

Bishop offered, he'd felt like his head had lifted off his body, spinning like a pumpkin, somewhere apart from him. It wasn't anything personal really. But with them, there would be more accidental fuckups like the one with Willa Lambert, which still clawed at him, the way her face looked when she'd passed out in that bed. He still had no idea what exactly Bishop put in her drink. And there was no one to tell that to.

Cully went to the miniature kitchen, which he got a kick out of—the tiny stove, a refrigerator the size of a doghouse. He made himself a turkey sandwich on whole wheat and put on his music. It was a CD he'd found at a garage sale, and he'd never heard of the band, but he'd liked the cover art, a gun growing out of a skull. *"My prophecy is spelled in bones, / The world breaks apart, and blades make it whole."*

His dad wanted him to pray more, but fuck that, he didn't get from prayer whatever his dad did. He wished he did. He wished there were a remedy for the damp pain he got in the pit of his stomach ever since that day with Willa. He'd been so drunk he'd blacked out, and his consciousness had only flickered on again when he was already fucking Willa, who was asleep, and he'd pulled out right away, his dick wilting in the open air. He'd had sex with two other girls previously, but they'd been willing, very willing. He hadn't needed to trick Willa and hadn't intended to; he hadn't even been quite sure how he'd got there (only later Bishop told him how, powered by whiskey, he'd lured her upstairs to watch TV, how he had his hands all over her on the way up the stairs, but Cully didn't remember any of it, and as Bishop retold the story, it felt eerily as if he had been a puppet master, moving people along for his entertainment).

He'd thought at first that if he could only work hard enough, he'd start playing football the way he used to. If he pushed it, ran enough miles, maybe carried the ball everywhere, he'd stop feeling bad. But the blackness had infected his game. And now he didn't give a shit about football.

Somehow, it killed him that she slept with her mouth open, her long black eyelashes pressed to her cheek. *"Your pain calls birth an affliction, and the number is marked on your brow."*

The sandwich was salty and satisfying. He took a Lone Star beer out of the minifridge and sat at the long, sliding window, looking out. There was a sight line from just outside the trailer all the way to the warehouse on this side. On the other, he could barely make out the skeletal outlines of the houses. He didn't care anymore about doing a good job, either, keeping watch. Once Avery had come over to the trailer on a Saturday night and brought Cully a plateful of brisket and pickles. "Thought you might be hungry." He was grinning and strutting as he approached the trailer. He ate with Cully at the miniature table and rubbed his chin. "Don't ever take it for granted, what you have, son. You just don't know when it could be gone. Don't ever think it'll be yours forever."

Goddamn easy things to say when you were richer than God. Cully didn't feel like drawing him out, letting the man give him more of his fake wise advice, like a Texan Yoda. "Yes, sir."

"You work hard for things and then you might get them, but you don't ever take it for granted. That's my secret, if you want to know." Avery winked. "Look at what happened back in September with the hurricane. Those people who lost their homes."

But if they'd appreciated their homes, they'd still have lost them in the end, so what did it matter? "Yes, sir," Cully said.

Avery's face was serious, but there was bluster in his mouth, as if he might burst out laughing any minute. "I knew there was something real smart in you and now you've confirmed it." He stood up. "You're a good man," he said, and he slapped Cully on the back as he left. As if that sealed it. The guy was an asshole.

Nothing ever happened out there, but Avery Taft believed someone had sabotaged the bulldozer months ago, and Cully had been there when Avery ripped José a new one. "Under your watch!" Avery shook his finger at this man—easily fifteen years his senior and more honorable than Avery ever would be. A veteran. A man who told stories that held lessons, a man who stopped by every Saturday night to give Cully one of his wife's cinnamon cakes and some coffee. Avery had walked away in his tight jeans and his too perfect shiny boots. He always held his head back and snorted before he spoke, and he held his eyes either in narrow, suspicious slits or in lazy, heavy-lidded boredom. Cully had tried to tell his mom about it once, started in on his imitation of Avery's drawl, but she waved her arm at him and said, "Hold it right there, mister. You respect people. That man gave you a job. He may be your father's partner one day." It was sick, it was so obvious that Avery believed he knew better than anyone else—and that was why Cully stole the copper wire and pipes from him.

After the bulldozer incident, one night when José brought the cinnamon cake and coffee, Cully mentioned that it would be easy enough to "lose" one of the spools, and José said, shaking his head, laughing, "No, man. Some guy tried to get me to do that a couple years back. Has a warehouse in Texas City—sourcing from all these constructions sites."

"I'm not kidding," Cully said.

"Yes, you are. You're a good kid."

"The way he talks to you? Don't you deserve something for putting up with it?"

"No, no. Not my way."

"You're too honest, that's why."

The cinnamon cake was still hot, moist in his mouth. José wore a battered sailor's cap, pulled it low over his eyes. There was a jagged pink scar on his cheek that made him look like a badass, though he wasn't at all.

José clicked his tongue. "But I didn't say I wouldn't tell you where the warehouse was."

The place was over in Texas City next to a way station. Cully drove the wire and pipes over in his truck and sold it to a guy with a red Mohawk in a dirty corduroy jacket. He'd smelled for some reason, like bananas. The guy gave him a stack of strangely crumpled hundred-dollar bills that didn't seem real but were. Though José protested, Cully gave him half.

Cully turned on the TV and watched a little bit of a preseason baseball game. Soon it would be time to go on his rounds. He watched the white ball arc against the green, the left fielder moving back to the fence, catching it in the pocket of his glove. The fans were stomping in the bleachers. A man had painted his face green and wore an alligator-jaw hat.

He finished his beer, turned off the TV, took his flashlight, and went out. The land seemed more like country in the dark, not as gnarly as it looked in daylight. They'd have to do landscaping to make it look livable, even decent. He walked over the rutted dirt, headed toward the warehouse, with its single overhead light, crickets humming in and out. He slapped a mosquito off his arm.

The moon was a crescent tonight, hanging like a hook. He'd picked up the CD at a neighbor's garage sale for twenty-five cents, the plastic cover all scratched and smudged, and he'd listened to this: *What is evil but good pained by its own hunger*

and thirst? Truth finds bread even in the desert, even in desert."
He'd known better than to take Willa to the Lawbournes' house.
He'd known by the way she looked at him that she hadn't done
much before with any other guy, and he'd liked that, her perfect
trusting face, how its look made him feel a power over her—as if
he were fire or a gun. After it all happened, he wanted to apologize, but he didn't know how—she was different, smeared, blurrier. And anyway, it would have always already happened to her.
One of those things.

He circled the building site, made his way up to the slope
toward the hurricane fence. José always liked to go around this
way, by the gully. He was almost back to the trailer when he saw,
way off, near the first shell of house, a ghostly funnel of light,
which went out as soon as he saw it. He heard, maybe, branches
breaking, and started to walk in that direction.

LEE

IT WAS JUST AFTER MIDNIGHT when she left the house, a square of blue light across the street two houses down; a car coming back late pulled into a driveway at the corner; and she stepped behind the trees, the heavy canvas bag strapped to her shoulder. She felt elongated in her spine, and full of nerves, as if more of them were growing just under her skin.

At this hour, the traffic was light. A semi truck lumbered and groaned, passing in the next lane, and the speed of it shook the frame of her car, the bright headlights briefly lit up the interior, then darkened. Ahead, the gray and looming overpass looked nearly ancient, monumental, its plain thick arch over the flat landscape. She concentrated on the highway lights until she turned off at the exit.

At the gravel road, she parked at a tilt in a shallow ditch. An accident or sabotage. Let people wonder. In her black ski mask, black shirt, black pants, black socks over her flat shoes, she was a moving part of darkness. Her steps made crunching sounds on the gravel, the taste of old coffee in her mouth, and the wool tight against her face.

When she came to the entrance in the fence, she saw it was

locked more tightly than usual, and there wasn't even wiggle room for her frame. She'd have to climb it. She leveraged her foot up on the locked chain and pulled herself up, clutching the crowned wires. At the top she pushed her leg over, felt the metal prongs scrape against her torso and chest, swung herself over and let go, landing with a loud thump that rang painfully in the soles of her feet. Through the eyeholes in the mask, she felt the hot breeze.

She headed in the direction of the trailer she'd seen the last time, past the large trees and toward the warehouse, though she could barely see the outlines in the dark. She wouldn't hurt anyone. She didn't have that in her. The trailer seemed far enough away from the skeletons of houses, but still. She walked toward it, and didn't see any lights.

When she got to the trailer, she walked around its perimeter, dry grass shushing around her sock-covered shoes. She knocked on the door. She knocked again and yelled, "Hello in there!"

The sound of her voice seemed to turn around and yell back at her. No one there.

The darkness softened, turned felted and warm, all the ugliness hidden under the bowl of star-flecked sky, the slopes of trees in the distance. This was just where Jess had ridden that black horse, that day Jack was afraid and Jess had shown off for the neighbors, so agile and capable.

She could still turn and go back. She could try again to let this all go, to let people take their chances, as they seemed to want to do. But something like breath hovered around her, a new coolness that had not been there earlier. The day Jess died, as Lee pressed ice against the soles of her daughter's feet, she'd felt Jess's body shrink away from her, Jess's face turned to the pillow, as she murmured in her sleep. Watching her, Lee felt the part of her daughter that wasn't flesh, what was beyond Jess's tiny, wasted legs and her altered, bony face—this invisibleness more real and alive than anything else. She'd even reached out her hand to it. Now that same cool pressure came up, insistent against the wool of her mask.

Using her red-beamed flashlight occasionally to find her footing, Lee navigated in the dark to the house skeletons, just over the ridge. She stopped near a lone tree, propped her canvas bag at her feet, wiped the sweat from her neck. Ahead of her, she could just make out the spine of the bulldozer, the etched outlines of the house frames.

She picked up her bag and kept walking, her vision on these targets. Nothing moved in them. They just enlarged themselves, became more detailed so she could make out the cage of boards, the cement floor, the giant coil of copper wire. She made her way to the first shell. The house would have been huge, the framework for ten or eleven rooms set into the outline of it, the sketch of it in wood. Just under the rectangle frame for the front door, she reverently arranged the waxy square, whispered under her breath, "Do it right." She stood to run the fuse through the thick bush until she stood five yards away at the end of it, holding the cord like a leash, then setting it down against an angle of old branches. She walked through a small clearing to the other house frame, taller, narrower, a head of wood eaving the top. She skimmed along the edge of the foundation to a spot with a stubborn impression in the cement, cradled the waxy square there, on the side closest to the other house. She strung the fuse through dry dirt, lit the end, and went to light the other fuse. Maybe the fuses were too long, and one or the other wouldn't work. She waited until the last string was confidently burning, then turned and ran far, almost to the trees. She crouched near a wild-leaved plant.

She tasted the wool in her mouth, the sweat under her mask. She stared out at the dark, where the frames were no longer visible. The leaves rubbed against her pants, smelling like turpentine. Something small and alive moved in the grass nearby, a bird, maybe, or a rabbit. From all around came the few sounds in the silence, the far-off whoosh of traffic, the rustle of leaves and weeds in the breeze, a bird or a bat flapping wings overhead. There were black bursts of cancer inside Jack's lungs. She pictured them in the dark. When she listened for a second, she could hear the gallop of blood in her veins, the wrinkle of her shirt sleeves. She carried Jess with her everywhere, even here, worked to keep her alive by staying alive herself, heart thumping now under her bra, stars blinking just under her skin. All of Jess's faces, her gestures, things she'd said, still alive inside of her. The dark space loomed between her and the house frames. She could just make out or imagine the tiny lights of the burning fuses.

Then the ground fell up to the air, and she crashed onto her back. She quickly sat up again, saw pieces of wood and rocks fountained over the flames. Golden hair unfurled into the sky. Quills of smoke pushed up confettied debris, then faded to fainter and fainter exploded gray feathers. She didn't know how long it took to settle.

Wood planks lay in giant bonfires, but the sky was still black, unflinched. There was a metallic smell in the smoke. The wing flap in her chest was sinking fast now, something dead in her. The large eave of the second house fell from the top of the pile.

She crept back to survey the damage, so she would know what they would find in the morning, and when she got close, the flickering light caught on a face in the grass. She wasn't sure. A paleness, a shape. She walked closer, shone her red beam down on the body of a young man, his mouth in a grimace. He had wide, muscled shoulders, and his arm was bleeding through his plaid shirt, but he started to stand up, leaning on the other arm, his face so bloody she couldn't see his eyes. "I'm okay," he said. "I'm okay." He was in shock. A roll of copper wire lay overturned next to him, gleaming in the shrub.

Somehow she remembered the questions she should ask. "What day is it?"

He stared at her. She was still wearing her mask, and she felt the nakedness of her eyes. "Saturday." He slurred his *s*.

"How many fingers am I holding up?" She made a peace sign. The flames might spread toward them.

"Two."

"What is your name?"

"Cully Holbrook."

Through the fires all around, out of the past, the name crept back to her. It couldn't be. There had to be a million of them.

"You aren't Hal's son?"

He rubbed at his bleeding face. "You know him?"

The boy's eyes rolled back in his head, then returned. He could have died. He might still. "Don't try to move."

He was already standing up, stumbling. She went to grab his arms so he'd lean on her, and this way, he could walk. They made their way slowly, chased by the heat in the air. "I'm okay," he kept saying, his face covered in blood.

He was moving, stumbling, but she was relieved that he could walk if he leaned on her. She walked with his weight on her.

After what seemed like a long time, they got to the fence. He said, "Here." He took out keys, and handed them to her, and she unlocked the gate. Somehow she got him to her car, though he was taller than she was, and heavy, and still in shock. She wondered if he would even remember her voice or what he'd seen other than her mask.

She started the engine and drove quietly and quickly down the back road. What felt like a hard packet of salt pounded outside of her chest.

The boy sat with his head resting against the window in the car, and blood ran down the side of his face from a cut at his temple. "Don't go to sleep," she told him, afraid he might go into a coma. "Stay awake." As she turned the car, his head knocked against the window. "Stay awake. Stay awake." She started singing the song her dad had sung on longer car trips to keep himself from drifting off.

The night highway was nearly empty, which seemed unbelievably kind, given the shakiness of her driving. She could barely see the lines or read the signs. She took the Pearland exit and went down a road of strip malls toward the hospital. She would say they'd been in an accident. She would say they'd witnessed an explosion. None of that mattered really. He was breathing heavily, but the blood was mostly on his face and his arm. She didn't see any bone, though he held his arm at an impossible angle, twisted away from him, as if to pull it off. She hoped there wasn't some secret injury from the impact—something ruptured or torn.

She nearly hit a car passing in the wrong lane, and the honking roused him. "Huh?"

She took off her mask, her face cool and light, and the mobility of her chin felt strange. "I'll get you to the emergency room soon. Just a few more minutes. Can you talk?"

"Yeah."

"Can you see?"

"Kind of." He slumped farther down in his seat, and she thought she heard him crying.

"I'm sorry," she said. "I'm so sorry."

"It's my fault," he said. "God! I saw this coming. This is my fucking punishment!"

"What are you saying?" She just wanted to keep him awake.

The hospital, unstately and brown, was easy to miss, but she spotted the lit red sign for the ER, and swerved the car into the turnaround. She had not been back since Jess's last high fever, two weeks before she'd died.

She parked, pulled the socks off her shoes, got out, and opened the passenger side door to help him.

When he stood up, she saw the deep gashes under his eye as he looked at her for the first time. He nodded as he began to walk, surprisingly stately as he headed for the door. She followed, and he turned to her. "I got it." He flicked his hand at her shoulder. "You can go."

"I need to make sure you're alright."

He seemed too weak and stunned to protest. She helped him inside the violently white room, accompanied him to the desk and signed him in. "He's been in an accident. He needs to be seen," she said.

The woman at the desk was unsurprised, frowsy haired, in floral scrubs. Her large, pale eyes were heavily made-up, black insect wings blinking slowly. "I guess bring him on over here, and let's have a look."

Lee started to go with him through the swinging doors to the back, and he shook her off. "I said I got it!"

"I need to make sure."

"No, lady. You don't get it." His eyes widened, and they were clear in the midst of all the dried blood. "Just get out of here. I don't want you here with me. It was supposed to happen like this."

The lights seemed hot, and a drunk was snoring loudly on one of the waiting room chairs. "I mean it!" Just as the door swung open, he shoved her away. "I fucking hated him too. I'm alright." He turned away from her, said to the short and moon-faced nurse, "Where do I go?"

Lee walked past the desk, past the wan, hollow-cheeked mother who hovered over her crying toddler boy, smoothing his sweaty hair, past the purple-faced drunk who sat staring at the road sign in his lap. She walked out the glass door and got into her waiting car.

She drove by habit down 2351, the road unrelenting, black and straight, and she hardly noticed where she was until she came to Main Street. The sobs were caught in her throat and wouldn't escape. She'd done what she had to do, and now there was nothing but to wait for what was to come.

She passed easily through the empty intersection, past the Kroger parking lot, dark except for its sign like a cereal box logo, past the store with a neon sign the shape of a cowboy boot, past the bank, where the black letters on lit-up white said GO MUS-TANGS! Though football season was long over, there were silhou-ettes of blue horses on stakes planted in the yards of businesses and homes. She counted five before she came to the Quaker church, two more when she passed the library, five more as she passed the junior high school, and as she rounded the corner where the tiny, white flimsy house stood, she saw the horse's blue, galloping legs, frozen in wood, and felt she was running along with it.

At home, she called the hospital, pretending to be Cully's

aunt, and asked how he was. He hadn't been admitted, and when she called again at 5:00 a.m., he still was not a patient, and she guessed that meant he'd gone home. Okay. That was it.

The past ten years had been speeding to this point in time, to the tenuous assembly of bombs to the shattering of wood and cement, to the flames, the dread, and the angry, injured, bloody face of the boy. He would tell his father and mother what happened, and then what? She poured a glass of bourbon and drank it, sitting on the floor by her bed. Even here, in the dark, things seemed to be moving that she couldn't see. Outside the house, so much she could not control. Her body trembled. She'd held on for so long, but she could no longer bear Jess's death. Back in Banes Field, in the grass and the flames, it had broken her apart, and she knew now that she'd wanted it to break her.

HAL

HAL MOWED THE LAWN; he showed a house on Pine Hurst to a young couple; he watched TV with Darlene; he didn't drink. He'd felt that something needed to be said for days, but he didn't know what to say or to whom. Then the call came from the hospital. When he and Darlene met Cully in the emergency room, his son's face all cut up, blood on his shirt, his sprained arm in a sling, Hal put his arms around him and said he was sorry. That was the message God had been trying to get out of him.

The boy seemed still dazed, but he told them everything, propped up on pillows in the small bed where they kept him until they finished the tests. Cully had heard something, seen the explosion while on his rounds, and it had knocked him out for a while. He'd seen a group of men leaving the site, running to the hurricane fence with backpacks, three or four men wearing hoods and caps. Somehow he'd got himself to the road and a woman picked him up and drove him to the hospital.

"She just left you there?" Darlene said, her arm around his shoulder. "My God, she didn't even call us?"

Cully shrugged, smiled a little. "I told her I'd called you already. She could see I was basically okay."

"Well, thank God she found you." Darlene wiped at the blood on his shirt.

Hal felt his voice turn thick in his throat. "I'm sorry I even sent you there to Avery."

"Dad, I'm okay."

"Well, you're certainly not going back," Darlene said.

"No, I don't guess I will," Cully said. "Do you think they'll let me out of here yet?"

On the way home, in the car, they heard a late round of sirens, and saw the smoke rising from the direction of Banes Field, a shimmering gray screen unscrolling upward. There would be hell to pay for someone.

Cully had been too much in shock to talk about the lady who had picked him up on the side of the road. She'd waited to see if he was okay before she left, but unbelievably, she left the hospital without calling anyone. She was on a nightshift, he'd said, she'd had to go. What kind of woman was that? Surely not a mother. Still, if she hadn't found Cully he might have lain there, bleeding, for hours. Hal didn't like to think of it.

✝

THE NEXT DAY, there was a rotten, burned smell in the air, even as far away as Hal's house. Avery called. "I'm not saying Cully knew who did it."

"Hold on right there." Hal suddenly had all this extra saliva in his mouth, and he spit into his coffee cup.

"I'd just like to talk to him, hear what he might have seen." Avery said he didn't get how anyone could sleep through that racket, and Hal said, "He didn't. He was on his rounds like he was supposed to be. And then he was knocked out."

Avery wasn't even logical. It made Hal want to kill him.

"Well, alright," said Avery. "I don't want to place any blame on the boy, for sure. But the inspectors might need to ask Cully some questions."

"Well, I've had about enough of that," Hal said. "He told you last night. He saw three or four of them running away—he told you. It was the middle of the night, goddamnit. He's a seventeen-year-old boy," said Hal, and he hung up.

He hadn't spoken to Avery again since, though Avery had called several times. He let Cully give reports to the police, and the inspectors would just have to look at those. Hal was done with Avery, and now that the gases had come up from the soil, Hal didn't want to sell homes over there anyway. The smell alone closer to the building site was implacable, bitter and cheesy, and the truth was Avery was in deep trouble. Just yesterday, *The Friendswood Dispatch* ran a story heavy on quotes from José, who, once he was away and safe at his new bank job, went straight to whoever would listen with his story—he'd seen black tars and pools of green brackish oil near the construction—it had given him breathing problems. "I reported everything to Avery Taft, and he said those were all normal things at a building site. He told me to just take a day off and get better." José said he'd been asked to hire a crew to bury a huge plastic box—they were told it was debris from Rosemont—but later, he'd learned, it was really a container of poisonous chemicals. José had written a log; he had photographs. For a while, Avery was going to have a hard time selling anything. Maybe even the houses on the clean land. Hal almost felt sorry for him, and he'd included him in his prayers.

✦

HAL INTENDED TO BE CONTRITE and sober from here on out. He stirred the chili powder into the steaming pot of tomato sauce, meat, and whole beans. He'd been forgiven. Lately, Darlene watched him warily, as if he might collapse, and Cully stuck nearby, washing his truck watching the game on TV, though there was a new sharpness in him that Hal supposed had to do with maturing. He spooned up a bit of the chili and tasted it. It needed salt and more onions, and he'd need to let it simmer for a few hours before it was really good.

He went to the chopping board, took the half onion and their best knife, and went at it. He put a piece of bread in his mouth to keep his eyes from watering, but he felt the sting in his nose. Cully was changed since his injuries, more homebound, more liable to make conversation, and thank God he'd just had some cuts that needed stitches, a sprained arm, and a mild concussion.

The onions were tiny, clear and pale now, and he swiped them into his palm and dropped them into the pot, wiped his fragrant hand on the dishrag. After he'd scared the hell out of himself that night at Casa Texas, after he'd lost himself in drink, right there in front of Cully, he'd slept on the couch in the living room, Darlene not wanting him in their bed. He'd woken up the next morning and prayed. He couldn't ask for prosperity because he didn't deserve it. But he asked for one more chance. Just one more chance. And he asked to believe. He'd been sitting near the window with his hands clasped and his eyes closed, and into the

prayer, he heard kids outside playing tag—"Get me! Get me!"—
and the jetting stream of a sprinkler. He opened his eyes, and
outside the window, the tree swayed, a squirrel hopped down a
branch, its tail a fat gray brush; and he looked at the creature's flat
eyes, and the squirrel looked back at him, both of them alike:
creatures. Over the salty fatigue and feverishness of his hangover,
he'd felt uncovered and boundless, and (unbelievably) good. He
hadn't had a drink since that moment.

✝

THE DAY AFTER THE EXPLOSIONS, the students at San Amaro
College nearby started to get rashes, and some of them had
coughs and went to the emergency room. Hal was pretty sure it
was a few of them who'd set off the bombs, but it didn't seem to
matter anymore. The college would have to be shut down for at
least a month, and the college president had called for an inves-
tigation into Taft Properties, to find out when and if Avery Taft
had known that the land he was building on still contained dangerous oil residues.

'Ihe story had made the local Houston TV news. People
who'd once lived in Rosemont came out of the woodwork and
stepped up to be interviewed. "My husband died of bladder cancer a year after we moved away." "My wife has struggled with
liver problems for these past ten years, and it started when we
lived over there." "I had a baby, and she died." Some people worried that Taft's building so close to Rosemont tainted the Friendswood housing stock too—though Banes Field was way over at
the edge of town. But that worry would all blow over in a few
months, Hal knew.

Lee Knowles was curiously silent and absent from the reporting, and he wondered about that. Darlene asked him if he thought she might have had anything to do with the bombs, and he considered it for a moment, picturing her stern, blue-eyed face. "No. She's a lady. She had a lot of fire in her, maybe, but I don't see her buying ammunition."

"She could have hired those guys Cully saw."

"Yeah, but she seemed pretty beaten down the last time I talked to her. And, believe you me, Avery would have sent his police dogs over there—if they had any inkling, we'd know by now. But I'll tell you what, the way she liked to go on about things, I would have thought she'd be telling everyone, 'I told you so' by now," said Hal.

"If she had anything to do with hurting my boy—" Darlene shook her head.

"Look, it's over now." Hal put his arm around her.

Her voice was small and choked against his armpit. "He could have died."

"But he didn't." Hal patted her back. "We're all still here."

✝

THE HOME WAS NICER than he remembered, wooden pillars, wide shutters. It was an authentic old Texas country house, and they hadn't changed it to look different on the outside, even if the inside contained those small dormlike rooms with chrome railings everywhere. The railings bothered him. As if they predicted that someone was always about to fall.

She was wearing a blue dress, her hair made neat for them into a bun at the back. She didn't look frowsy and loose faced like the women who sat around her in the visiting area, and she was one of the only ones not in a wheelchair.

"Hal," she said, holding her hand up to him. "And my grandson." Hal hugged her, and then Cully hugged her. They sat across from her on worn upholstered chairs. It seemed the droop on the side of her face was slightly righting itself.

"I've missed you so much," she said. "Oh, I've got Scrabble here and the knitting club, and once in a while some professor comes over and tries to teach us something. I've learned all about the planets and the history of Texas, for sure. I can tell you all about it, Jim Bowie, Sam Houston. It's like they want me to get my college degree now, in the old folks' home, so I can finally make something of myself!"

"Grandma, all that learnin'!" Cully rubbed at the knees of his jeans, hooked his feet behind the legs of his chair. Hal loved his son. He could not have come here without him. Why not? Why was it so hard for him to come here for an hour or two and sit with his own mother?

"We brought you something." Cully reached into the bag and pulled out the daisies they'd bought.

"Oh, aren't those lovely!" she said.

A woman in a wheelchair nearby moaned, rocking back and forth, clutching her belly. "It hurts so much. It hurts so much where the baby's coming!" Another woman patted the moaning woman on the back. "It's okay, dear. It's okay."

"It hurts!" The woman in the wheelchair moaned again. "Oh, God, it hurts!" She bent over her belly. The other old woman comforted her again. "That was a long time ago, sweetie. How many did you have?"

There was a gleam on his mother's face, softening her wrinkles, her blue eyes bright. "It's sad the way Maureen keeps feeling it. She can't seem to forget the childbirth and remember the children."

A Mexican nurse sat at a table by the bookcase, eyeing everyone as if they were about to steal something (what would they steal and where could they go?).

"Well, I keep myself busy here, and I don't want you to worry, but I miss y'all. I just want to lay these ol' eyes on your beautiful faces."

Cully's face was all marked up, especially the gashes on the right side by his eye, indented in three finger-shaped wounds. That morning, Hal watched Darlene rub Vaseline over the scabs. They would probably scar, but he realized his mother's cataracts were so bad now she likely couldn't see them.

Hal took her hand, and this seemed to appease her.

She told a lot of jokes. Hal never remembered his mother telling jokes before. There was the story about the one-breasted woman, and the dirty joke with the preacher. Maybe she'd always had this salty side, and he was just now noticing it. "How's my football player?" she said.

"Alright, I guess." Cully shifted in his seat. "The end of the season didn't go so well."

"Well, that's football," she said. "Hal, how's that business of yours?"

He'd always lied to his mother, felt the need to rise to her hopes for him, to do as much as he could to please her, even from afar. She leaned toward him now. He had not had a drink in more than two weeks, and last night's lovemaking reunion with Darlene had opened something in him, unlocked new hope. He felt the stinging in his eyes as he spoke, "Well, now, not so great.

I haven't had a decent sale in a few months. I'm afraid I never will again, to tell you the truth."

"Oh, honey," she said. "You've got plenty of time to figure all that out." She rubbed his hand gently, in a way he'd been accustomed to as a boy. "Your father didn't know what he was really good at until he was fifty," she said, "and look how much he loved his life at the end."

Hal remembered his dad angry, furious when he couldn't finally pay the bills for inventory at the hardware store, when the insurance didn't cover all that he'd lost in that flood, indignant when he'd had to take that job at the nursery. And he'd gone around then, defiantly stubbled, in shirts with worn collars and holes in the elbows.

"He told me, you know, 'I wouldn't have been inspired to start over, wouldn't have even considered it, were it not for my kids.'"

Cully smiled, and the big round scab on his right cheek lifted.

"Oh, he was pretty low after the store flooded. We didn't have any money. He didn't know what to do. Remember, he was about to declare bankruptcy and take a job selling pool equipment if he could get it, when Hodel's brother offered him a job at the nursery. He thought his boys would like it better if he were planting things—he thought you all would learn something. And then, what do you know, he ended up loving it so much himself."

Hal was in his senior year of high school when all that happened, so involved with football he barely remembered anything else, though an image came to him, as his mother spoke, of his dad coming home, pants smudged with dirt, and Hal had been embarrassed for him.

"He never made the same money again, but we got by," said his mother.

Cully squinted, tilted his head. "Huh." Hal couldn't read him, hadn't been able to read him all year. His son might drift away from him just like he'd drifted away from his own dad. But still, there he was for now, in his denim shirt, hair all combed, kindly making conversation.

"But wasn't it hard?" said Hal. "My God, you struggled."

She shook her head. "It wasn't that bad. He was nice in those years."

At the window, the Mexican nurse opened the thick, orange curtains. He was unaware at first that he was actually crying— had perceived the tears as perspiration or flecks of moisture flung off the air conditioner in the window. He was afraid to look at Cully, and wiped with the back of his hands at his eyes.

"I remember Granddad then," said Cully. "He used to take me to look at the fig trees."

"You remember that?" Hal's mother said. "You were only about five."

All this past month before the accident, Hal had felt forsaken, but had wanted not to give in to despair like some homeless person. Hal patted his son's muscled arm. "Well, what about that? I'm surprised you can remember it." He would take it all seriously again. He would learn patience, and teach it to Cully. Every day he'd tend to things, and he'd watch these seeds, these fruits, these branches grow.

LEE

LEE SAT ARRANGING in an album the old snapshots of Jess
which until now she'd kept in a crumpled box. Gradually, she
moved the photographs from one side of the desk to the other. For
some reason only the blurry ones, the shots with her eyes closed,
or departing a room, showing just the back of her dark head,
allowed Lee to see her again in a rush, snapped back a memory to
her in a way that made Jess seem both alive and dead at the same
time, lost somewhere in the universe of the camera eye.

All afternoon, drinking water and then red wine, she searched
the newspaper and the Listserves that crowed about the explosions, and she fought off the idea of going to Jess's grave. Lee
hadn't known how flammable that soil would be, had no idea the
fires would burn all night, that the local college kids would get
sick. She looked out for a mention of her name, or the line that
might lead someone to her. She'd spoken to Atwater and Mayor
Wallen. She'd spoken to Chris Hite. She said the same thing to all
of them. She was sorry to hear the boy had been hurt, glad that
Taft would have to stop for now. She had no idea who those men
were who'd been spotted running away, but of course, there were

more people than they knew still angry about what happened at Rosemont and wanting it not to happen again.

Rush called and left messages. "Well, now they're going to do something about it, aren't they? Tom says he's glad he didn't put any money into one of those houses. Call me." "I'm worried about you. We have to talk. Call me." Rush had allowed Taft to touch her, she'd found him funny or flattering, liked the way he went on about her beautiful face, or something. She must have harbored other mysteries too. And what would she say, if she knew what Lee had done? Lee loved her anyway.

She read about a family that had already bought one of the new homes in Pleasant Forest, but were now planning to sue Taft Properties for damages and for fraud, then she heard her neighbors' car doors slamming as they arrived home from work, heard the circling laughter of kids outside on their bikes. She put on her boots and got in the car.

The Quaker church kept its great, gray brick silence, the vast graveyard behind it. Usually it was too painful to look at Jess's stone, the fixed stillness, the inadequacy of the inscription. Since she'd died, her spirit had been unfurled into a world that needed saving, *Jessica Knowles, beloved daughter, 1982–1998.* Lee walked along the gravel path, stepped over the low rock-formed fence. The air smelled of moisture and cut stems, the gravestones like blind thumbs pushed up from the earth. Some of them were mossed over and blackened, so many Browns, so many Turners and McPhersons, and there, the stone for Jack's great-uncle Edwards.

Jess's grave was at the outermost edge, near the fence. Lee didn't remember choosing the marker. Probably Jack had, or she'd done it while she'd been taking the Xanax the doctor had prescribed, those days she'd lost altogether—hours and hours of hushed voices and fatigue like an atmosphere of steel. Jess's gravestone was simple, arch shaped, a gloss on the front, but not on the sides or the back. The marigolds they'd planted there years ago were gone now, and a few dandelions had sprung up here at the edge, where they didn't mow as often, and a big red wildflower, nodding on its stem.

In the oak tree overhead, a bird warbled a testy question, the same sound again and again. Other times when she'd stood there, she'd forgotten where she was. She'd been flown back in time to the funeral, to the blight of coffin lowered into the ground, to the perfectly carved rectangle of dirt. She'd watched that, allowed the large dream like pink bouquets to assemble in the funeral home, allowed the slim girls to stand around in their black dresses, cheap material catching sheens of light, allowed the stiff-shouldered men to cough, allowed the rose to lie over the wood.

Now she leaned toward the ground, something unfinished there. She could have killed that boy. All the news of burning oil residues, the phone calls, Taft's profession that he'd known nothing, all of it came down to the way that boy had been looking at her, bloody and incredulous. The other day she'd seen him from a distance, outside in the driveway, his face still in bandages, and she imagined the gauze could just barely contain his rage. She still didn't know why he'd protected her.

A ladybug crept along the curved side of the gravestone, slow and implacable. A stream of last, pale light fell on a bush of garish flowers. Her daughter was not here. She tried to focus on what was: the smell of just-cut grass, the darkened glass of the windows in the church, four misplaced bluebonnets.

She walked back to the parking lot, got into her car, and

started to pull out. Just ahead, the slim figure of a girl walked along the curb, dark haired and graceful, holding her hair back from the breeze. Lee gently pressed the gas pedal, and as she got closer, she knew who it was.

She let the window down and called, "Hey, Willa? You need me to drive you somewhere?"

The girl turned. Her eyes were swollen, her cheeks raw. "Yeah." She nodded. "That would be good."

She went around the front of the car, and Lee saw through the windshield, the gait half tripping as if the shoes she wore were too heavy. Willa got in the car, slammed shut the door.

"Where can I take you?"

Willa shrugged. "Over to Robertson Park? I want to read for a while and I can walk home from there."

"Where have you been?"

"Just out for a walk."

"You okay?"

"I'm fine," Willa said, a thread of contempt in her voice. That boy Cully had said the same thing.

"Well, put on your seat belt," said Lee.

Willa sighed and fumbled for the latch. Watching the road ahead, Lee heard the metal click.

"How's that rash on your arm?"

"It's almost gone. I just found something written there again this morning." The girl was upset. Anyone could see that.

"What did you write?"

"I don't remember writing it, that's the thing." Lee glanced over, and Willa looked stricken, staring down at her thin pale arm, rubbing it with her hand.

"I hope you don't have another allergic reaction."

"Well at least I've got the medicine now."

Lee watched the red stoplight, the light glaring off the shiny sedan ahead of her, the bumper sticker that said ARE YOU PREGNANT? WE CAN HELP. Here was the daughter of her friend Char, who'd once been as dear to her as anything, and the girl was wanting.

"So what did you write?"

"The street of the city was pure gold."

"What's the city?"

"I don't know."

Lee hoped to God the girl had friends, that she wasn't as alone as she seemed right now, in her dirty sneakers, her tattered jeans.

"Maybe you should think about writing more when you're awake."

Willa smiled slightly. "You can let me out over there." She pointed to the pavilion near the entrance of the park.

Lee turned into the drive and stopped the car.

Willa dug into her pocket, pulled out a wrinkled paper, and gave it to Lee. "I know you know what happened to me. You don't have to pretend for my sake."

Lee unfolded the paper, saw the sinister, naive block handwriting: I AM SORRY FOR WHAT HAPPENED. I WAS DRUNK. BUT I COULD HAVE STOPPED IT. YOU DIDN'T EVEN KNOW YOU WERE THERE. YOU DIDN'T EVEN KNOW WHAT WAS HAPPENING.

Lee reached over and took Willa's hand. "Yeah, I know. I'm sorry. I also know it wasn't your fault." The girl was holding her here. Lee could hear her breathing. "Who wrote this?"

"It came in the mail today. I'm pretty sure it's from Cully Holbrook."

The scene outside the windshield seemed to fall away. Lee remembered the boy's face at the hospital, his blue eyes finally visible, staring through the blood. "Oh, God." She'd wondered why he'd called it a punishment. He'd been in shock, but he must have seen her as some kind of messenger. "But how do you know it's from him?"

"Because he's the only one of them I'd believe. He didn't know they'd put a pill in my drink. He wouldn't have let them."

The girl was holding her here. The girl needed her. Willa took the note back, and she smoothed it flat on the car seat.

"Well," said Lee. He wouldn't let her stay with him at the hospital. He'd wanted her gone.

Willa picked up her big, loose purse from the floor. "You're not supposed to hate people, are you? Can you tell me this: did God get you through it, what happened to you? Prayer?" She said it bitterly.

Lee pressed her hands flat against the steering wheel, looked out at the park's green. "That depends on what you mean. I guess it's a kind of believing beyond belief, I mean, beyond the facts."

"God, you mean."

"Well, I don't blame God. I don't think I know who He is. I don't know if anybody does."

"But, then, how can you do *anything*?"

It took a second for Lee to realize the girl wanted to fight with her. "I just do."

Willa clenched her mouth and wound the leather strap of her purse around her wrist.

"Because there's no other way. My daughter's not any more

alive if I'm gone. I have to stay and remember her. Listen to me—"
she said. Outside the car windows all around them, the magnolia
trees held up white blossoms like lanterns, but the words wouldn't
come. She looked down into her lap, and it felt like she might be
able to grasp them in her hands, but the words weren't there.

Willa moved closer, and Lee hugged her. She smelled of
lemon and chalk. She was not her own daughter, but Lee owed
her something. They all did.

DEX

DEX WAS FINISHING UP his shift at Casa Texas, pouring salt into the salt shakers, pepper into the pepper shakers, and screwing on the metal tops. He rushed because this was his least favorite part of the job, and when Pammy walked past him, he said over his shoulder, "Don't forget me. My tip jar's over there." He nodded to a shelf just at the end of the bar.

"I never forget you, honey," she said. "What are you talking about?"

"You sure did yesterday." She treated everyone this way, but now Dex understood how to work it, how to talk to her. It was almost as if she enjoyed this part.

"You mean to say I have to pay you for yesterday too?"

"Yeah," he said. It used to bother him that he had to ask, but now he didn't even care.

He put in an order for tamales and burritos to bring home to his mom and Layla, and he sat at the bar, drinking a ginger ale, waiting for the bell to ring in the kitchen that signaled the food was ready to go.

Next to him sat a man with long, gray hair, the color of dull metal pipes. He had a face like a friendly crocodile's, long bumpy chin, a wide, uneven smile that slashed the bottom of his face from the top. Last night, before he'd begun his set, he'd said, "You can't help who you fall in love with. That's for sure. It's either a disaster bad as a hurricane or it's home. But you've got nothing to do with it, that's the problem."

On the bar, the shot glasses lined up next to his beer. Dex wondered how he'd be able to play.

"You got a good job here?" the man said, bringing the whiskey to his lips.

"Yeah, I like it alright."

"You do good in school?"

"I do okay."

The man lifted his shot glass to him in a toast. "Well, keep to your studies, son. Keep to your studies."

Then the bell rang, and Dex got up to go back to the kitchen. The man turned on his stool and unlatched his guitar. As Dex was leaving, he was meditatively tuning it, plaintive, pure single notes.

At work, when Dex stayed to watch the band, he tried to think of women as shapes in the dark, as beautiful, kind vessels, but then he always ended up talking to one or another and he'd fall for a voice, or a comment about the idiocy of men. He'd seen Willa on the street outside the grocery store the other day, her graceful arm swinging a small paper sack. Then he looked up at the sky, clouds gathering like huge gray beards, an airplane inching overhead, and he let the longing for her go up into the blue.

At home his mother was reading the newspaper at the table, her hair flat, her makeup scrubbed away.

"I brought you some food. Have you had dinner?"

"Not really. Thanks, sweetheart," she said, and she looked at him again in the way he'd sought out ever since he'd been a boy. She'd told him weeks ago, "I'm glad you went to the police." Even if there'd been no discernable difference made to the pattern of things, he'd said what needed to be said.

He made a plate of food for her, and he made a plate for himself, but she seemed to want to read rather than talk. "I can't believe all this stuff about Avery Taft. Class-action lawsuit coming his way for sure. That man knew what was in the ground, but just went on building anyway. Tried to hide it. Can you imagine . . ." Her voice trailed off.

The smell had lingered for a few days after the Banes Field explosions, and he'd heard Cully had been scraped up pretty bad. A bitter sulfur taste, he'd thought, was caught in his throat during that whole week, but then it went away, and by now, Dex was sick of hearing about it.

"It looks like now they might dig up the field and incinerate what's there. They'd have to evacuate that side of town for that, but I guess that's the safe way to do it."

"Huh." Whatever they decided, it would take months. There wasn't anything he or his mom could do about it; the mayor and the city would make all those calls. "We're far enough away, right?"

"That's what they say," she said. "We could probably stay put or not. I'll be glad when this business is over."

"Yeah." He didn't want to talk anymore.

It was a tranquil night, a time when Dex was usually at work, and he'd missed being able to be out in the warm air, with the cricket sounds and dark. "I'm going to sit outside."

"Okay."

He took his food out the door and sat on the cinder block

steps that led up to the trailer. The tamales were lukewarm, but maybe even more delicious that way. His dad had said something about a certain spice, what was it? A rare one mostly found in Mexico. He couldn't remember the name of it.

He heard water running in the kitchen sink inside, a clanking of dishes. The food was warm in his belly, and the street and grass seemed lacquered with moonlight. He sat back to look up at the black sky. The Milky Way wheeled overhead, a neatly arranged arch beyond the leafy trees, all the other stars holed up in the night, not telling yet what they knew.

WILLA

SHE RAN THROUGH the foot-high grass of the old golf course, skimming along the woods, each tree as she passed it a puff of green. She was done with sitting still in her room. She felt speed back in her leg muscles, paced her stride, so she wouldn't stop too soon, felt her breath opening up in her chest. She passed the ruined bricks at the front of the old country club, the triangular roof protecting the graffiti and absent door that led into the darkness. She passed a white-latticed gazebo and a large garage, full of golf carts with dirty, bright canopies, and she headed out into the long green of the seventh hole, where the outlines of sand traps still fell off to the side.

The sunlight was low, white and crystalline over the houses. Her face was hot and salty, her hair wet with sweat, and she stopped for a moment near a tree to get her bearings. She bent to catch her breath, bowing her head, resting her hands on her knees.

When she looked up again, there, from the lowest branch, the voices like a loud breeze. Dog. Lamb. "He shall strike the earth with the rod of his mouth, and with the breath of his lips he shall kill the wicked." Where had Lee Knowles's strength come from? She had suffered so much, and she still stood upright, able to say words to Willa that meant she wasn't a slut or stupid or a piece of skin-covered meat. But of course, the beasts already knew these things. On her right forearm, she'd written *Measure the sun*. She held up this forearm against the beasts.

She gazed through their shapes to the oak tree, saw how it would grow, how the leaves would bud and spread into green hands, the branches rivered into the air. She took a step back, touched her forehead, and felt a warm sting like a sunburn. A gray rabbit hopped through the dandelions, and wings flapped in the branches above her. When she looked back at the beasts, the wind had erased them.

She went on to run another mile. Rounding the corner of her street, she saw her dad outside with the topiary clippers as he worked on the hedge, which he liked to keep square, though it grew round. She stopped running at the driveway, and walked up, pinched at her sweaty shirt to pull it away from her torso.

He stood up from his work. "How far'd you go?"

"I don't know," she said. "Three miles?"

He looked her in the face as she came toward him, and he was quiet, suppressing a smile. "Good work." He saluted her. "Better make it four next time," he joked. He leaned forward again to snap the clippers, and as she passed, he handed her a branch with a very small, blue flower. "It ain't much," he said. "But it's what I've got."

She went inside the house, ran up to the bathroom, took off her damp T-shirt and shorts, and laid them to dry on top of the hamper. Getting into the shower, she let her hands graze the tops of her thighs, which were tight again, the soles of her feet sore and tough against the cool porcelain. She lifted her face to the spray of hot water, soaped her hollowed belly, the swell of her breasts, and ran the washcloth over the words on her forearm, the skin still faintly pink and raw. She'd been taught to take a quick shower, not to hog the bathroom, but today she let herself stand under the water for a long time.

While she was getting dressed, Jana was singing along to a pop song in the other room, probably holding her hairbrush like a microphone, waving her arm overhead and swaying her hips. She was so loud sometimes you could hear her from the other side of the house, but she had a strong, low-pitched voice. Lately, when Willa heard her sister singing, her mother clanking pots in the kitchen, her father's voice calling out to the neighbors, she hoped that the beasts would leave her soon, and she could hang on to the things in front of her again.

She went down into the living room where her mother lay with her feet up on the couch, reading for Bible class. It was summer, and Willa would have no home study for three months. The days were longer, and she and Dani would drive out to the beach at Galveston, and her mother would become preoccupied by the tomatoes she grew, and Jana would practice her gymnastics in the backyard.

Her mother closed the Bible and sat up. "Why don't you help me set the table? We'll eat on the patio."

Willa took a handful of forks from the drawer and followed her mother outside. As they smoothed the bright white cloth on the table, the blue-tinted air was cooling down. "Now tell me again this thing you're supposed to do with Dani tomorrow night?"

"It's a concert at a place called Sevens."

"In Houston." Her mother set down a bowl and sighed.

"Yeah." Willa's stomach tightened. They might take even this away from her. She was still afraid that in their worry, her parents might take away her whole life.

Her mother walked back toward the screen door, and her voice wafted through the dimness, "You'll be home by twelve-thirty."

✝

ON THE WAY TO HOUSTON in Dani's car, they rode with the windows down and sang along to the radio. All of time seemed to stretch ahead of them on the road, the white lines ticking like seconds, on and on. A strip mall on the right, woods coming up on the left, the sky huge and blue and empty. She wanted to get out and feel that blue above her, like a door always opening.

They parked off Montrose Boulevard near the Texas Tattoo Parlour. At Sevens, there were sixes and nines and threes stenciled in paint along the side wall, and glittering plastic sevens hung from the ceiling. The show itself was a disappointment, three ragged guys onstage who seemed too high to sing. Willa and Dani left early and went walking along the streets downtown, stacked lights of skyscrapers in the distance. They walked past a coffeehouse, filled with faces, weary or cheerful or bored. Cars whizzed past, cartoonishly loud, blowing a hot wind against them. No one recognized her here; no one knew where the Lawbourne house even was. On this sidewalk, her anonymity felt magic.

"Are you hungry?" said Dani. "Let's get some food. Let's head over to the Disco Kroger's."

In the aisles, they saw the girls in glittery tops and teetering heels, the guys in T-shirts with gelled hair, the music blaring at this hour, because, Dani said, the management wanted to lure in the young people. A girl was actually dancing over by the pharmacy. They bought sandwiches, and Dani used her fake ID to get them a bottle of red wine, and they went back through the parking lot and out to the curb to sit on the hood of Dani's car. Across the street, there was an old house with a porch where some people congregated, smoking, sitting on the rails, talking seriously over the music.

Willa wasn't afraid anymore of red wine. She took a few sips and listened to the song trilling loud from the speakers in the upstairs windows. The woman's voice seemed to start on a tiny thread and then flew up around them like a hundred kites. Willa felt the music go through her at one point like an airy sleeve, and within her, the shape of something ugly turned inside out.

Dani struck a match on her jeans to light her cigarette. "I met a girl who lives there," said Dani, bringing the cigarette to her lips. "She goes to Rice."

"That's where I want to go," said Willa. She'd just decided in that moment. There was a woman sitting on the porch steps, with black hair that looked like she'd cut it herself, and a guy playing a bass, just quietly holding up the neck, plucking the strings, though no one could hear it over the stereo. She pictured herself on that porch; she saw herself older and new.

After they finished eating, they lay down on the warm hood and watched the passing cars.

"You look different tonight," said Dani.

"My hair is up."

"No, I mean your face. For so long you looked, I don't know, kind of wiped away. Now you've come back."

A white convertible passed by, the women wearing silk scarves that trailed behind them, and an old rickety truck followed, the bed filled up with old chairs, clattering. Beyond the streetlights, just above the skyline, a faultless darkness seemed to flow from the world's center. A motel sign at the end of the street lit up its blue neon letters, but she could just see the edge of it, which said STAY.

LEE

SHE STOPPED JUST ONCE on the way to Denison, at a Stuckey's to use the bathroom and buy the praline candy that Jack used to love. She lingered in the souvenirs aisle. When they used to stop on their long car trips, the three of them would browse those cluttered shelves. There was a cowboy doll with rope legs, a longhorn steer with a lamp glued to his forehead, shot glasses picturing the shape of Texas centered on a yellow rose. Lee preferred the old-fashioned souvenirs—the bronze lasso, the small replica of the Alamo. In front of the shoe-sized fort, tiny men with guns and knives. She bought that one for Jack.

On the highway, she drove past the billboard with the scolding faces of newscasters, three in a row like the fates, past the sign for the FRIENDLIEST TOWN IN THE WORLD, and past the telephone poles racing beside her. She was listening to an old-time country radio station, Hank Williams's jokey, yodeled songs.

Before she left, she'd waited for weeks for the phone call, for the police to show up at her door. Wesley White had come to her house in his squad car a few days after the explosion. He was nearly apologetic for having to ask her where she was that night, and then, relieved, when she told him she'd been home, sending out emails, and then he was eager to ask her questions about what she knew about Taft. But she hadn't assumed that was the end of it. She thought they'd have come for her by now—that the boy would have relented under questions and told them the truth—but somehow the urgency of what to do with Banes Field seemed to have dulled the will to find anyone to blame besides Avery Taft. In the days since that night, even seeing her old Rosemont neighbors on the news (Michelle Smalls grinned at the camera, Maisie Rodgers pointed a finger down at the ground), Lee had not felt much triumph. That all seemed beyond her now. Cully (and this was a mystery in him that she wondered about) had stuck to his story, insisted he'd seen a group of men scatter right after the explosions. He even mentioned a baseball cap, the hood of a sweatshirt.

Lee drove past a sign that said CAN YOU HEAR HIM? GOD IS TELLING YOU SOMETHING, and beyond it, a billboard with a picture of a young Latina smiling slyly with a cigarette in her hand. She passed a long field of slow cows with unseeing, pale heads, and then a train sped beside the highway, the bright rectangles shuddering past. For now, she had this day and the next, and maybe all of them. She checked the dashboard. In forty miles, she would be there.

She turned into the subdivision with the green rectangular sign PINE GLEN, and drove in circles through three cul-de-sacs before she found his street, situated on the edge of things, an open lot in the back of it filled with the trees, the house made of white stone with a large gold star pressed into the brick by the front door. It had been ten years since she had seen him, and she was skinnier now, more drawn in the face, a lot more tired. She stood at the door, hands shaking, her heart running around in her chest.

When he opened the door, the first thing she noticed was his head—all his hair gone except a silvery feather over his right temple. His eyebrows were gone too. He wiped his hand over his tan baldness and grinned.

"Get in here," he said, and kissed her. His breath smelled like dirt, but she liked it.

He led her through the living room, and into the TV room behind it, where he sat down on a threadbare orange couch.

"I brought you some things." She put the paper bag and box on the ground and took out the candy, the boxed souvenir, the record player and records.

With his long ears and thin cheeks, Jack looked like a handsome alien. She gave him the candy first, and from his expression, he liked the sight of the gold box, the muscles of his forehead moving where his eyebrows would have been if he still had them.

"Good to see you, babe. I look old, don't I?" He opened the box of candy, took a bite, and chewing, put the piece back into its wrapper.

She saw how tired he was. "And then I brought you the record player and these old things. Where can I plug it in?"

"Oh, somewhere around here."

She set up the record player on a card table with a green leathery top that was pushed against the wall. She knelt down and found the outlet behind the table leg, inserted the plug, stood up, put on the record, and then went to sit next to him.

"Old Ernest Tubb," he said, settling back into the cushions. He patted his chest and lowered his eyes. "Eight more weeks of treatment," he said. "I guess I can't eat a thing except candy."

"I brought you a miniature Alamo," she said.

He studied the picture on the box. "Remember the Alamo,

huh? Keep up the fight." One by one, he took out the pieces, the fort that was also a sanctuary, the tiny figures. His finger traced the arched line of the roof, and he shook his head, smiling. "She had one of these, didn't she?" A faint pink streamed into his cheeks. "That trip we took to the hill country and then over to San Antonio." He rearranged the small, metal figures, took more from the box and set them on the table. "Are you thirsty?" He got up and started to head for the door. "Let me get you some water."

She might have him with her only for a short while. They didn't have any plans. "Come over here," she said. "Come back."

✝

SATURDAY MORNING, light waving through the curtains into the kitchen, where they'd set up the souvenirs from their trip, the Alamo fort carved out of cheap wood, the metal figures of Jim Bowie and Sam Houston and their men. The brass horse. The barn dyed red, with its tiny cows with suede hides. The Mexican adobe village.

Jack had taken Jess, six years old, out on her bike with the training wheels earlier, and their faces were still flushed and shiny. Now Jess sat between them, moving the pieces from one side of the table to the other with her fat fingers, setting up a city, talking for the soldiers, talking for the cows. "Do you like the city I made?" They were all a family. They were all going to have a party.

Years later, when Jess learned the story of the battle for the Alamo mission, the standoff, the cannonball fire, Bowie's collapse, and the line Travis drew in the dirt to separate out the traitors, she recited the story again to whoever would listen. Each time she told it, it was as if it were new. She used the Alamo model for her history project, and kept it safe on her dresser. All that year, she loved setting the wooden pieces in their places, then taking the scene apart.

The new Alamo sat on the table now in the window light, the tiny flag the size of a Band-Aid, the rough arches and mock-stone walls painted in detail, the little men with their rifles and knives drawn up to strike. There was a pioneer woman too, in a long skirt, with one arm reached up in the air, the other wrapped around the shoulder of her child.

ACKNOWLEDGMENTS

First, I want to thank my agent, PJ Mark, and my editor, Sarah McGrath. I'd also like to thank Meagan Brown, Sarah Stein, and everyone else at Riverhead Books who helped bring this book to publication.

Early in my conception of this novel, I was inspired by reading Barbara Rossing's *The Rapture Exposed*, and I'm indebted to Mark Schwehn for recommending it to me. For conversations that helped me find my way to the story, I'm grateful to all of my old friends in Friendswood, especially Diane Benson, Denise Hearn, and Dannielle Thomas, and also to my East Coast friends, Walter Cummins, Ariel Levy, Meredith Rollins, Darcey Steinke, Karen Wunsch, and Stephanie Paulsell.

For their careful, generous readings of this novel in its many incarnations over the years, I owe immeasurable gratitude to: Jennifer Werner, Minna Proctor, Dannielle Thomas (again), Martha McPhee, Elizabeth Mitchell, Natalie Standiford, Jena Salon, Thomas E. Kennedy, Ira Silverberg, Robert Polito, Craig Marks, and Rita Signorelli Pappas. For space, food, country music, and endless edits, a huge thanks to the Masonville Collective, Rebecca Chace, David Grand, and Ken Buhler.

I'm grateful to Fairleigh Dickinson University for providing released time and in other ways supporting this project, and I'm thankful to all of my students, particularly Gloria Beth Amodeo, who assisted me early on with research, and Warren Denney. I'm also especially indebted to the amazing students and faculty in the MFA program.

For their support and inspiration, thanks to my parents, Peter and Kelly, and to my siblings, Tim, Krista, and Matt. And most of all, thanks to my son, Porter.

René Steinke is the author of the critically acclaimed novels *The Fires* and *Holy Skirts*, which was a finalist for the 2005 National Book Award. She is the director of the MFA program in creative writing at Fairleigh Dickinson University. Steinke lives in Brooklyn.